The S

MW01129653

By K.T. Munson

ISBN 978-1548357504

Cover art by Asahi Art
Copyedited by Tanya Egan Gibson

Dedication

For Harmony.

A rose by any other name wouldn't be as sweet.

Other Books by K.T. Munson

1001 Islands

Frost Burn (Coauthored)

North & South

Unfathomable Chance

Zendar: A Tale of Blood and Sand

The Gate Trilogy

The Gate Guardian's Daughter (prequel)

Chapter 1: Lyreane

ϕ

*T*he screams were matched only by the roar of hollow flames and burning wood. The rest of the world had come to take its revenge on the Shadow Clan. Even the shadows could not save them. The fire cast its light against the blood that soaked the ground of the planet Lyreane. From one end of the planet to the other, every Lyreani who could hold a sword had joined to stomp every man, woman, and child under prejudicial boots. They had ridden through their planet like a deadly wave, hunting the Shadow Clan to extinction.

Up high in the mountains, the members of the Black Council, the elders of the Shadow Clan, stood overlooking the chaos from the top of their sacred temple. Though their eyes were dulled to the violence they witnessed, their hearts were still filled with the promise of retribution. Their cities were long gone and now their people with them. They had been hunted men; now they were defeated men. In the darkness of the night, vengeance filled their old hearts.

Plans and plots for how to exact their retaliation began as vague echoes of whispered words, until one rose up in a storm among them. All of their thoughts turned to this word and this word alone—Croatoan. It scratched at the inside of their skulls until it became a carving upon their bones as they watched the last of their people burn and their screams died into deafening silence.

Gathering around the circle as one, they chanted as one, and the word "Croatoan" seared deeper, beyond all physical reaches of their being. They enacted an old curse, one their ancestors had feared and never used—a curse to take the souls of many and bind them into one. They feared it because they could not direct the curse's choice; any of their blood could become the savior. The risk seemed less now that the elders believed themselves the last of their kind. They chanted until the early light painted the black sky with colors that made the ground come to life with the rusty shade of old blood of their fallen people.

By the last of the light of the twin moons, the souls of their dead gathered together. The dawn was filled with the chaos of their screams as they were pulled, like veils upon a strong wind, into the top tower of the temple where the Black Council waited. In response, the wind became

1

enraged and bombarded the elders around the circle, causing their robes to pull thin against their skin, but the elders would not be easily dissuaded from their task. Lifting their arms, they called out the final incantation in the lost language of their ancestors, and then silence fell.

Shaped like an arrow, the searing white incorporeal souls of the dead shot around the room in an erratic dance. The men looked on in anticipation. Suddenly, the pale mass rocketed out the top of the tower, shattering stone in a deafening explosion and opening the ceiling up to the sky before it arced down toward their lost village. With debris still raining down, they hurried as well as old men can hurry to the edge of the temple and looked down upon the carnage once more. When nothing stirred below, they thought their last hope had just ended in failure. Had the members of the Black Council been able to cry, tears and blood would have mingled together on their faces as they scratched at their cheeks in desperation. Instead there was only blood.

Slowly, they walked down the sacred steps to the world below, where the crackling of the fires was the only sound left. When the hidden mountain stone door was turned aside and the first light of dawn stretched her fingers across the sky, they emerged. At the edge of their town, the smell of death loomed like forgotten rotting fruit. Silence and smoke met their hopes with an unforgiving weight.

The first man fell to his knees, his words an indistinguishable whisper. Another fell, his words matching the first. One by one they knelt until all twelve were on their knees save one. Only the crumpled bodies of the dead remained to meet their desperate cries; their enemy had fled this cursed place, and few who had joined the Wild Hunt were willing to admit the misery they had wrought.

The one man still standing closed his eyes and listened with every fiber of hope and desperation. He believed that their ancestors and their dead would not lead them astray. Then he heard it, a stifled crying.

For a moment he thought it was the trick of the wind or perhaps his own hope turned to imagination. But when another member rose and leaned forward, listening, he knew in his heart that it was a true sound.

In a flurry of black cloaks, they hurried past the village and into the woods toward the source of the sound. On the ground lay a woman with a babe in her lap, partially swaddled in the woman's shawl. Her arms were loose and lifeless; her eyes were open and glossy. Blood gathered between her breasts from a sword wound, and her skirts were soaked in blood. The newborn, still slick with blood, squirmed and whimpered.

2

When the man stepped forward, the child went quiet and turned its head, seeming to hear his footsteps, but its eyes remained closed. He bent down and picked him up, noticing as the shawl fell away that it was a boy, and held him. The infant kicked a little at the sudden cold but kept its eyes closed.

Everyone on the planets knew that the horrors of the Netherworld waited for baby killers. This child had been spared by their enemy because it was new to this world, and the Black Council's curse had found its way to him. He pushed the cloth back. Using his thumb to wipe the bloody membrane from the infant's chubby shoulder, he saw the infinity mark; the child was the chosen. He was their savior.

The man looked down at the woman then, admiring her determination to save her child. She would be the first they would bury and give final rites.

He spun toward the others. Holding the child up in both hands, he declared, "The undying!"

Chapter 2: Lyreane
50 years later

———————————— φ ————————————

*G*uards patrolled the walls and the ground, their lanterns casting shadows that danced with every step. Ki's lithe body moved in the darkness of the courtyard as though it was a part of him. Many fools were scared of the dark and what it held, refusing to allow it to become a part of them. Then again, though, perhaps those fools were right to fear the dark. He was, after all, a part of it.

The high towers of Valhaul, principal palace of the great continent Hibarr, had spires that looked like hardened mushroom tops. Slipping into the darkness against the palace wall, he held perfectly still as a group of men walked by. As they were talking, the light shone off Ki's eyes an instant. He closed them quickly so he could meld fully with the dark.

"I feel as though the night is watching me, Fadi," the first man said, glancing around nervously. Ki opened his eyes into narrow slits. He could see the sweat on the man's brow and bald head.

"You've been reading those horror stories to your children again, and now it has gotten to you," Fadi replied heartily, his round belly shaking as he clapped the other man on the back.

The thinner man shuddered, raising the lantern as he peered into the darkness in front of him. "I tell them those stories, and I swear they sleep better than I do."

"Children these days," Fadi said, shaking his head. "In my day those stories meant something…"

Fadi's voice trailed off as they walked away. Ki faced the wall. He put his hands up and started crawling up the side like a spider. His fingers felt the soft, worn groves of the wall's face as he scaled it. It was a long climb with only one window at the very top of the tower. The spires rose up all throughout the dark castle like someone had thrust mighty spears into the ground so that the tips pointed to the heavens. Ki's only way in was from the bottom up.

It had taken him months of hard training to figure out how to scale a wall of such height. Luckily this was an old castle, made of stone, and it had been weathered with time. During his practice on less guarded towers,

4

he had fallen more times than he could count, but in the end he had figured out the secrets. If he fell now, though, he would not survive.

The further he ascended, the more the wind began to press against him, but he had accounted for that. His cloak blended perfectly with the black tower rocks. Unless someone was looking for him, he knew he could not be seen. This was one of his final tests and he would not fail. Even death could not stop him. His mentors had trained him for this and he would not allow himself anything but success. Reaching the tower's window, he crawled over the side and gracefully dropped into the room in a low crouch.

Ki's eyes scanned the darkness for any movement as sweat slid down his neck. Aside from the door on the other side of the room and a few fine furnishings, it was relatively empty. He could see the sleeping figure that remained unmoving in a luxurious bed. He pulled a dagger from his belt. It looked like a vengeful tooth in the moonlight.

The young woman in the bed breathed softly as he approached. Her hair was blond and her face young. She looked about fifteen. He lowered the dagger toward her and, with one quick, clean slice, held up a fist full of her long blond hair before he shoved it into the sack on his hip.

Blond hair was rare in Lyreane, and coveted. It was said those with it were blessed by the light. Since most Lyreanis served the Sun God, it was good for a kingdom to have at least one Blessed One to bring good fortune.

Ki stood for a moment over the woman the ruling king had taken and held prisoner to bring his kingdom good fortune, then scurried over the edge of the window before she had the chance to awaken. As he dropped out of sight, he could hear the rustle of bedding. He hesitated before beginning his descent, finding himself curious about a blessed one. Pulling himself up again, he could see the Blessed One already sitting up in bed. Her face held the edges of sleep and fear. She wasn't paying attention to the window, so he continued to watch, his interest piqued. She frantically regarded the door, pulling the blankets up close against her chest. Apparently his elders were right about the Blessed Ones also being cursed ones. They were the lovers of kings or, more accurately, the bearers of the King's children, which is why many of the blessed ones were hidden by families until they were discovered or betrayed.

Most of Lyreane had adopted the rule that women couldn't marry before their fifteenth year. Yet given the history of the kingdom, this girl was likely already being bedded by the fat king with an insatiable appetite.

Ki severely hoped that once his training was done he would have the visions that would allow him to exact revenge for this innocent soul.

When her head started to turn toward him, he slipped all the way over the side and started his descent. His movements became more careful as the wind pushed him harder. Though the climb had been complicated, it had been child's play in comparison to returning to the ground safely, as he still needed to escape unseen. Time seemed to pass slower. Despite his needing to hurry, he had to be more careful here, for as night turned to twilight, the early mists would wet the stone and the dawn would not hide him.

Ki sighed when he could see the ground. He glanced to the sky. Daybreak was coming. With careful precision, he dropped into a crouch. The jump had been no more than double his height, but the grass was flattened where he had landed. Taking a final assessment of the area to be sure there were no guards, he hurried across to the adjacent wall and around the corner.

He was a prowling fox, careful and alert, his eyes scanning everything. The courtyard in the receding night would be tricky. He ducked into a small alcove and waited until a group of guards passed as they changed shift. The torch light cast shadows by the tips of his toes, and he remained as still as death without daring to take a breath. When the light was beyond him, he turned and walked in time with the group of men, staying a few paces behind them, until he could see the corner of the front gate.

He dashed across the courtyard on agile legs, but when he reached the final arch he stopped, startled to find the gate closed. Glancing up, he saw a patrolman looking over the outer wall. The archways led to various places throughout the castle and its grounds. When the guard turned, Ki rushed away from the gate toward a wide archway to his left that led into a garden.

A good planner always had a secondary escape route. He hurried along towards the servants' quarters, where there were fewer guards on patrol. He crawled over an ornate gate in the garden and came to a sewer grate. With a sharp pull, he jerked the bars free. He slipped into the sewer, ignoring the overpowering stench, and pulled the grate back into its original position.

Ki took a moment to smile at his accomplishment. He had added a hardening agent on the cut edges to make the metal refit perfectly. The slight slices did little to reveal themselves. There were similar access points, mostly sewers, to castles throughout Hibarr. Valhaul, the last of his tasks, had proven to be the most challenging.

He trudged through the increasingly disgusting water until he reached a point right before it emptied out on the cliffs and into the sea water below. Emerging from the filth, he stepped across the rushing drainage waters and onto an adjoining sheer rock face. Happy to be free of the stink of waste, he started making his way across the cliffs that continued up to the city's outer wall. His foot slipped, but he was able to catch a handhold above him. With a grunt, his body hit a jagged section as his fingers scraped painfully against the unforgiving cliffs. He thrust his legs down, pushing up on a lower foot hold, and carefully regained his footing. Ignoring the pain in his fingers and the soreness of his rib, he began working his way along the slick rocks. He could feel the cold spray of sea water against his back and into his hair as it splashed on the cliff face.

Before long he began to shiver, but he tried to ignore his body's demands for warmth. The elders believed he could not die, but as yet, he had not put that theory to the test. One of his first tasks had been to win a bar brawl without killing the man and take some of his blood on a white handkerchief without it being seen. It was amongst his belongings now, though he had nearly lost that fight. He'd almost found out that day if he was truly undying. That was nearly a year ago, and now, with the harvest moon's approach, the end of his journey was near.

Above him he could see the end of the wall of the city. With painstakingly slow precision, he continued his way across the rock face but also began to pull himself up. The dampness of the stone hampered his progress as the light of day streaked orange across the sky. The purple of the night was fading, and so was his cover.

When the ships' crews in the harbor would scurry to start the day, there was a good chance they would see the lone man on the cliff face. He began to move faster, trying to reach a point where he could see the top of the cliff bent inward. His arms and legs moved as one along the rocky face, finding the rhythm of seasoned use.

He felt relief as he pulled himself over the lip of the cliff and landed in a familiar grassy area, but there was no time to rest yet. His legs strained as he hurried along the open ground toward the tree line several hundred feet away. Reaching the edge, he paused and looked back towards the sea. The very top of the spires of Valhaul were tipped in gold from the morning light, so bright was the sun and its golden wings as they soared across the horizon.

Begrudgingly putting his back to the glorious daylight, Ki headed into the woods toward his waiting mount, a Kemshi, which meant spirit animal. To Ki's knowledge his Kemshi was the only one that existed in Lyreane. They had come over from another planet, having once been a gift to the Black Council when they had been Guardians of the Gate. Now, that task had fallen to other men with other ambitions. Only the memories and the Kemshi remained.

The Kemshi, a tiger, waited for him in a tree, his long tail swinging back and forth as he lazed about on a branch high above. He looked as though he had been there all night, but Ki knew better. The tiger was most active at night, and he had already likely gotten breakfast and returned to wait for Ki. This tree had been their meeting place in case it took Ki longer to complete his task or he'd been forced to use his secondary exit. The Kemshi turned his yellow eyes on him, which sharply contrasted with the deep purple of his face. The black stripes made it appear as though the night had fallen across his fur.

"Any trouble?" Ki asked, but the Kemshi just laid its head back down.

Ki dug around in a nearby bush until he pulled his sack from the brambles. He tried to control his excitement. It was not wise to count his fish before he had eaten them, as the world was an unpredictable place. He glanced up at his companion. The Kemshi watched, waiting for a word of command.

"Kemshi," he said with a straight face, "Come."

The feline stretched with a heavy yawn before jumping in a fluid motion to the ground. His long thin tail was curled and ready and his eyes watchful as he came to stand beside Ki. With a quick scratch behind the Kemshi's ear, Ki mounted.

"Home," Ki commanded. "Take us home."

The Kemshi turned and rushed through the forest back towards the cliffs and the sea. The sound of crashing waves grew closer, and his fists curled in the Kemshi's fur. This part always worried him, the passing. When they reached the cliff, Ki held his breath and they plunged over the side, falling for a few seconds as the water rushed up to greet them.

Chapter 3: Hystera

——————————— ϕ ———————————

"**O**ur shadows have given us no sign," an elder pointed out from the high council of the southern tribe.

The domed hut in which they were meeting had been crafted from large boughs forming the great hall. It looked like someone had taken a bowl and flipped it on its head. All the council members from the various animal clans of the south were gathered for the first time in nearly a year. Jinq Rekis's panther, Hibrius, lay at his sandaled feet, reminding Jinq he had at least one ally in the room.

"Yet these deaths continue," Jinq reminded them. His wrinkled face held the patience of a thousand lifetimes.

Much like souls, the shadows of some of their people could wander the world on another plane of existence. They were incorporeal, like spirits, but without a consciousness of their own. When the shadows rejoined with their host, they could bring back memories of their time away, stored like imprints upon their form. Jinq Rekis had sent his shadow out, but it had returned with nothing. That worried him more than if it had come back with something. There were very few things powerful enough to hide from a Keeper's shadow, and something that powerful did not bode well for his people.

"You are our tribe's Keeper," the elder from the Panther Clan said to Jinq, leaning forward, which highlighted the spots along his hairline. "You cannot go if there is a danger. It is not your purpose."

All people of Hystera had distinctive dots around their hairline, small and many, like a cheetah's. Jinq stared at the marks along the elder's hairline. They were faded with age, much like his own. Jinq glanced around at these old people and their ancient ways, a bunch of wrinkly fleabags who had forgotten their original purpose. They had been created to protect their people, but many members of the house clans had become selfish. Jinq was not an elder. He was the Southern Tribe's Keeper. He belonged to none of the animal clans and all of them. He was sacred and was their connection to the planet Hystera. There were only ever four keepers upon the planet at any time, usually two in the north and two in the south. Jinq's counterpart, Yira, was twenty years older than him and bedridden, so the duty had fallen to him.

Every species type had an elder, but birds and cats were never ones to agree. Birds tormented the felines as they flew, while the cats waited and hunted. Being of the feline clan meant that he disliked most of the bird clans on principle, but he had to remind himself to remain neutral. Jinq could see an old windbag to his right, Hindi of the Crow Clan, nodding his head in agreement with the elder's statement. Hindi was his greatest opponent.

Despite their reluctance to agree with him, Jinq knew he would be able to argue his case. Of the four Keepers, he was the youngest at only fifty-three winters. Soon Yira would pass on and her initiate would be the youngest, but that had not happened yet. He would be the best suited to take this journey to investigate the deaths on their north border.

"My knowledge will be vital to discovering what has happened," Jinq reminded them as he stroked his gray beard. "Already there are fifteen reported deaths. How many more must there be before I am given leave to go?"

Hindi turned to one of the other men and whispered something. The two came away nodding, and Jinq grimaced. There had always been a strong link between the Crow Clan and the Snake Clan. Crows were the harbingers of death, and snakes were the symbol of rebirth. It was no surprise they felt a kinship, but there was nothing to be trusted about a creature that slithered.

"We should send someone else," Mortiki of the Snake Clan offered. "Someone closer. We have heard of an unexpected death in the north, but reports are still coming in. These are dangerous times."

Jinq had expected this. "I'll take an assistant."

"You shall go, but take a young member of one of warrior groups to act as an assistant," Hindi conceded. He had a cunning matched only by his sharp and cruel ego. "I have someone in mind."

Jinq sat quietly as he considered his options. Regrettably, most of his clan was aligned with other feline clans. If he selected one of them, Hindi would say they already had a feline and another would offer no additional protection. He would have to think of a way around this to ensure that one of Hindi's cronies didn't come along.

Hipasha of the Owl Clan leaned into the firelight and lit the end of a very long pipe. Jinq's eyes narrowed as she puffed the embers on the end to life. Her short hair was perfectly straight and cut to her chin. When she leaned forward, wisps of her hair deepened the lines on her face. With a smile, he decided to beat Hindi at his own game by choosing the most neutral of their members from a clan known to be so honorable that they could not be bought and so wise that they kept mostly to themselves. They were not the strongest, but Jinq would get someone he could perhaps trust and rely on.

"I would not want to play favorites," Jinq said, and Hindi's eyes grew wide. "A child of the Owl Clan will serve on this mission as an aid."

Hipasha of the Owl Clan had remained mostly obscured in the shadows even as she had lit her pipe, but she bent forward at the mention of her name. Her eyes were sharp as she met his with an unwavering wisdom. Age had given this woman a quiet and solemn demeanor. Most of the Clans viewed men and women equally, but it was rare a woman took interest in making decisions amongst the clans. There were many more female scholars and soldiers than female clan leaders.

"My goddaughter has recently completed her training in the warrior's ring," Hipasha said in an even voice. "She shall accompany you."

"An honorable choice," Jinq answered carefully, though he wondered what use a child of not yet sixteen could be to him. "Her name?" he asked.

Hipasha smiled, her black inked lips curled back in the firelight while the rest of her face was in the shadows. She answered with a single word as smoke from the pipe coiled around her: "Kerrigan."

Chapter 4: Lyreane

φ

Ki **emerged from** a lake not far from the mountain he had called home for most of his life. He shook his head and let the water bead down his face. Pushing his black hair back, he glanced around, enjoying the familiar sight of the purple-tinted trees and soft yellow leaves that shimmered in the fading light. Though he didn't know the exact time, from the setting sun he knew night was quickly approaching.

Across-world travel was possible for his Kemshi; it was the tiger's gift. Water was a conduit through which the tiger traversed, and he could bring Ki with him. Ki had traveled across Lyreane in a mere moment. This was the reason Ki had chosen to take the tiger along when he'd left on his yearlong mission. The tiger provided convenient travel.

Ki hopped off the feline's back as it swam to shore. His tiger was an excellent swimmer and, of the four breeds of tigers, the Wata was the kind best adapted for riding. When the lake became shallow, he stood and pulled his coat off to let the sun's rays hit him in the fading evening. He was lucky it was fall now, the trees only just starting to shed their leaves. Were it winter, he could have frozen to death. His home was northern enough on the continent of Artium that winters were harsh—and even worse on the mountain he called home.

Ki walked out of the water, the Kemshi beside him, dripping the whole way. When the tiger shook the droplets from his great hide, Ki put a hand up to avoid the spray. "Hey now!" he cried out.

The tiger gave him an amused glance. Ki shook his head as they made their way toward their destination. He could all but hear the tiger explaining that given that Ki was already wet, a little more wouldn't matter. Tigers were such prideful and arrogant beings, but Ki had to admit there was cause for their egotistical behavior. They were fast, deadly, and clever—a dangerous combination,

When they approached a clearing, Ki slowed and skirted around the edge of it, looking toward the forgotten village that had once been their home. Though there was nothing left of it above ground, Ki always imagined how it had once been. He imagined wooden homes with smoke billowing from stone fireplaces and thatched roofs. Whatever had been there had long since been reclaimed by nature. Only the well remained.

A group of wanderers, with their covered wagons and rough attires, were setting up camp. Ki watched them for a spell, shivering slightly from the cold, as the final fingers of daylight faded. He wondered if they knew about the death and destruction that had happened here. Did they know that blood was soaked deep into the soil and that the bodies and bones of his people were under their feet?

As darkness rose above the horizon and he was certain the campfires of the wanderers could not reach far enough to give him away, he continued toward the mountain to the hidden passageway. As he hurried across the clearing, he heard a branch snap to his right. He turned to see a wide-eyed young girl with her hair separated by ribbons over each shoulder staring at him. When she saw the Kemshi, her mouth fell open. Tigers were not native to Lyreane.

He put a finger to his lips, hoping the fear of what the massive beast could do as well as the sight of a stranger dressed all in black would earn her silence. She nodded her head. When he reached the other side of the clearing, he glanced back and found that she was still watching him. Even if she told her family, they would likely not believe her.

Ki turned and hurried toward the entrance of his home. Though the noises of the nomads faded into the quiet forest, they still seemed too close for his liking. He reached into a damp pocket within his robes and pulled out a coin, pressing it into the side of the mountain. Rock shuddered, and he stepped back as a slab of stone swung toward him and the small entrance appeared.

The Kemshi entered first, bounding up the steps until the darkness swallowed him whole. When Ki pulled the coin out of the slot, the door started to close. He slipped in as the door slammed shut on the outside world.

He was home.

Ki hurried up the stairs. The Kemshi was waiting at the top. In the light of the lantern hanging from the ceiling, Ki could see his impatience. Their yearlong quest had not been easy, and he wanted to be cleaned properly. Despite himself, Ki craved companionship as surely as a proper bath with soap. Though he wished he could speak to the spirit animal, he hadn't the ability.

He stepped into the atrium, where a circle of hunchbacked old men waited. The Kemshi sat, his hunter eyes trained on them all, though with familiarity rather than ill intent. The men were solemn, apprehensive, as he reached to the sack on his hip.

"Welcome home, my son," said the youngest of them, one of the few who still stood tall and proud. He was named only Ra.

"I come home successful," Ki said, dropping to one knee and holding up the waterproof sack. "All tasks are completed."

"Then it is time," Ra whispered, taking the sack. "Rise and come bathe in the blood moon, so that your quest can be revealed."

Ki was full of anticipation. Decades of training and his year-long journey had led to this moment. He followed through the entrance and down a long pathway to a second atrium whose circumference was filled with more doors. This unusual set up was their strongest defense. Intruders would have to know which set of doors to take before finding their home. If they choose wrongly, they would be led into traps or left to starve within the belly of the mountain.

They finally entered rocky area where a circle was cut out of the ceiling of their home. The moon cast upon them a reddish light. Ki shrugged off his heavy leather coat. It pooled at his feet as he continued to undress under the harvest moon. Around him, his family each held one item from his trials, from a bloody handkerchief to an ornate coin.

When he pulled his shirt off and it dropped to the ground, each of his elders reached up—only Ra was the same height as him—to touch the infinity mark on his back as they walked by for good luck. He undid the sash that held up his pants and left them discarded. He took careful steps toward the center of the circle, his feet cold against the unforgiving rock and the chill of the evening. The edge of the blood moon cast a shadow on the far edge of the runic circle on the floor. He went to the middle and waited for the moon's light to fill the circumference. The Black Council began chanting while the moonlight crept along the floor. The sound filled him as the moon approached, a shadow of the sun, the stealer of light.

Ki put his fingers out as the edge of the moonlight reached him. The strange red glow made his fingers look as though they were drenched in blood. He watched as it crept along his hand and up his arm. It wasn't long before he was completely washed in the light. In that moment, the tributes were raised, an old spell was recited around him, and the spirits within him awoke.

He gasped in astonishment as a vision passed over him—faces he had never seen before flashing before his eyes. It was like flipping through still images in a book. The chanting fell to the background as his arms

14

went out. He fell forward on his knees, his breathing ragged, as he braced his arm against the ground.

After a moment, the visions passed and he heard shuffling of clothing as the light from the blood moon touched the edge of their robes. Lo's voice emerged from the background noise of their chants. "What did you see?"

Resting back on his heels, Ki looked up at the moonlight as it shifted by him. "I saw what must be done."

"What is that, my son?" Ra asked, his back as rigid as their beliefs.

The eyes of the men around him glittered with twisted enthusiasm. He hardly noticed them, though, as faces still danced behind his vision. They knew the words he would speak; why else would they have trained him to kill?

"Souls," he whispered before shifting his eyes over to Ra. "Forty-two tainted souls I must release."

Chapter 5: Tym Resh

φ

*C*ommander **Xavier** Ode stood overlooking the children in his charge with heavily lidded eyes. In Xavier's opinion, children always made the best warriors. Their kingdom may have been mostly conquered, but these children would become assassins who would give his king the victory they needed to keep their last foothold.

One very skinny boy grappled with a larger one; his nose was bloodied, but he hardly seemed to notice. There was a fire in that one. Turning, Xavier walked down the stairs leisurely, but it was a measured pace. It was good for the children to see him, especially the boys.

Many of them had been street rats, nothing more than homeless beggars and whores. Children with broken spirits died, but it was the tough ones that survived. The ones sparring now, who had survived harsh winters and hot summers, were the strongest.

Rounding the corner at the bottom of the stairs, he stood by a column while he continued to watch them. Blood spattered the floor, feet and hands were blistered, but their bellies were full.

The young boy, the fiery one, was able to connect his elbow with the larger boy's throat, causing the larger boy to gag and stumble back. Then he jumped up and slammed the bottoms of both of his feet into the big boy's chest, forcing him from the ring and flat onto his back.

Everyone turned to look at the fallen boy, but Xavier's eyes stayed transfixed on the victor, who pushed himself up and turned to make sure the fight was truly finished. Standing with his fists tight at his sides, he looked down at the fallen, his jaw tight and his resolve sound.

"Well done," Trainer Tryden said with a proud smile. "Go clean up."

Xavier waved a gloved hand to the trainer, a man with long brown hair and a flat face. Trainer Tryden walked toward them, passing the other children, who were still training. Xavier watched the victor, whose walk was nimble and sure, until he was gone from the room.

"Yes Commander?" Trainer Tryden asked. It occurred to Xavier that he didn't remember Tryden's first name.

"They seem to be improving," he said, glancing around. "Our eastern border is being pushed back. How much longer?"

"They have only been trained for a year, mostly in swords and knives," he said with an uncommitted shrug. "Their hand-to-hand combat is improving, but I'll need more time."

"We are running out of it," Xavier informed him. "Train the girls to carry knives in different places, and get them ready to be sold to whorehouses. They are to kill the generals that pay for their services and then return. Get the boys ready for a raid attack on the western border."

"The western border?" Trainer Tryden asked, surprised.

"All of our defenses have moved to the east. They will not expect any attacks in the west," Xavier said, slightly annoyed, as he fixed the gloves on his hands.

Trainer Tryden nodded. "It will be done."

"See to it," Xavier said, walking down the hall. Many of the children hit harder when he walked by. His presence gave them encouragement, as he was their greatest warrior. It was his blood that gave him power and his presence that won battles. Everyone knew that he was the reason their kingdom had its foothold.

As Xavier rounded the corner, he barely caught sight of the flashing blade before it entered his throat. His hand went instinctively for his sword, but someone else's hand pressed it back down. He tried to call out, but the blade prevented it. The only sound he could make was a disturbing gurgling sound as he fell to his knees. Blood dripped over his lips and splattered onto the ground as he pulled the dagger out of him. The blade clattered on the ground as he collapsed. His fingers groped his slick neck to stem the flow of blood as the edge of his world went black.

Xavier cursed their enemies until he saw the dark hair and the black eyes. It was like looking at a demon. He tried to pull his gloves off to take his killer's soul with him, but couldn't. He watched in horror as his killer took care to precisely aim a second long thin blade into his chest. Xavier jerked at the sudden penetration of his heart, and then his body went still.

"Your soul is free now," a whisper said as Commander Xavier Ode drowned in his own blood.

Chapter 6: Netherworld

φ

*T*he reddish-hued landscape seemed to watch Ki as he moved along the path, uneven cobblestones beneath his feet and decaying shells of a city on both sides of the road. He pretended not to notice the eyes he could feel following his every move, though he knew what watched him in the collapsing buildings. The droning red light of the Netherworld's sky cast shadows within the ruins, their details edged in varying shades of red. Paying heed to the architecture, he discerned his location by the constructs—broken and battered mirrors of real buildings upon the planet's surface that housed mortals, not monsters.

Rubble suddenly gave way behind him, forcing him to turn. At the edge of the light, a long sharp tendril-like leg peeked from the shadows of the ruins for a moment but quickly retracted back into the darkness.

From their mechanical clicking from all sides of the road, Ki knew they were Weavers. Though he was safe for now because they didn't like the light, Ki was grateful it wouldn't be long before he left their territory. The only thing he feared more than the Weavers was the coming unforgiving darkness that was night in the Netherworld.

All his life he had been told he couldn't die, but he didn't wish to put that to the test. He noticed the ruins of what appeared to be a great round building that looked like a corpse from which ravens had picked the eyes—holes gaping where windows used to be. He stepped carefully as he walked down a short hill, the stones more uneven there. In the dull red light, the rocks looked like shiny jewels. He picked up a rock and held it up into the red light. It shimmered, and he felt a strange and dark power pulse against his palm.

Setting it back down, he remembered what the elders had told him about the Nether. It existed off the pieces of souls left behind from items people touched—the ground on which they walked, the beds in which they slept, and everything in between. Every step every person and thing made upon the ground caused the ash to fall and the rocks to form. When a significant event occurred—lots of souls in terror, or in joy—a mark was left in the Netherworld.

The Weavers, spider-like creatures, could feed on those that wandered into the Nether, but their main diet consisted of the stains of the souls that died in terror and produced the dark rocks. Those who could see and speak with spirits, Seers, could sometimes hear a Weaver's clicking metal legs before a disaster. They were a promise of what was to come. If planet-dwellers were going to die in a horrible way, Weavers weren't far off, waiting to feed on the terror that would bleed through. If enough souls were lost and died in agony, the Weavers would gather the stones by the hundreds, gorging themselves on the marks the violence left. The only thing more frightening for a Seer to catch a glimpse of on the battlefield than a Weaver was a Soul Collector, a being that knew when death was imminent and took souls of the dead back to the Netherworld.

He paused outside of an old country schoolhouse, one of the few places where the grass could almost pass as green. Very few creatures of the Netherworld trespassed upon this sanctuary because innocents lived here. A flowering tree stood tall in testament to the children and their beautiful imaginings. Ki used it often as a point to cross over from the Netherworld into one of the planets.

Ki pushed open the schoolhouse gate, listening to it creak as he headed toward the building. Gnomes wearing harsh expressions danced around while beautiful butterflies with knife-sharp wings tried to dance away from them and slice at the rainbow of flowers. Pausing to watch the hushed battle, Ki wondered at the gnarly gnomes doing good while the shimmering blue butterflies were destructive. That was the Nether—never what it seemed.

The strange little cottage-sized building would have seemed to him a derelict house if he hadn't known better. Were it not for the presence of color, someone else would have passed it by. The Black Council had brought him here many times to teach him how to use the naturally occurring gates. Having once been the Guardians of the Gate, they knew its secrets and its weaknesses. He knocked on the door and entered without waiting for a reply.

"Back again?" the old orc asked, peering over his spectacles as he sat by the fire. "It has been nearly a year."

The orc had tufts of hair on his head and strange bumps across his tawny skin. He was short, a whole head shorter than Ki, with thick limbs. Ki felt sweat bead on his brow, but the orc looked content in the stuffy house.

"I've been busy," Ki said. "Your normal fee."

Ki took a large coin from his pouch and flipped it toward him. The orc caught it in one hand, three thick fingers curled around the metal, before putting it between his teeth. He had been a builder once—that much Ki had gotten out of him—but otherwise orcs were pretty difficult to converse with. Apparently the old builder had created something great and powerful, but his creation had ended up being his people's downfall. Once the machine had been built, the king to whom the orcs had sold it decided that he couldn't risk their selling it to anyone else. So he killed them all…all but this one.

"Have you found him?" he asked. Ki glanced at the orc's right arm—a sharpened blade that he put across his lap. The blade was decorated along its spine with gold.

"No, the Black King has been gone for a long time," Ki reminded him. "He was banished and died in exile."

"The Black King cannot be killed," the old orc said, turning back to the fire. "He is scattered. He will return."

"As you say," Ki said, walking down the hallway.

Ki pushed open a side door. Outside, under an awning, lay rotted benches with flowers growing in clusters around them. Wood didn't last, but ideas did. He glanced over his shoulder toward the old orc. It was sad that he was all alone. He tried to push the thought aside before he could dwell on it.

Had all orcs had such green skin and ugly complexions? They were a strange race that the world had all but forgotten. Ki had never been willing to risk losing access to the gateway by broaching the subject. The old orc at the end of the hall was likely the last of his kind, having hidden in the Netherworld waiting to exact his revenge on a dead man. Time moved differently in the Nether, so it was impossible to tell how long he had been here.

Ki stepped into the room and let the door close. He began to write on the outside of the door, focusing on the face in his mind as the chalk scraped against the door. His old scribblings were gone. When the symbols were complete, he rested his hand in the middle of the symbols, closed his eyes, and concentrated as he whispered the spell. When he opened his eyes, the chalk glowed with a slight yellow light.

Pushing the door open, he stepped through into a street in Ashlad instead of appearing back in the hallway of the school in the Nether. Closing the doorway quickly, he got his bearings. He was now in a fine school, larger than the cottages they had in Lyreane, with young people walking around. Ki headed toward the metal fence as they streamed out of the front doors to head home.

One youth moved slower than the others, and Ki picked him out immediately. The woman in Ashlad had been hard to find and would be dealt with next, but he had put this boy at the bottom of his list on purpose because of all forty-two, as he was only a child. Regardless of age, Ki knew the faces in the visions must be saved. He had put it off long enough—age should be irrelevant to a savior.

Ki followed the boy, who had a scar on his forehead and walked at a leisurely pace. He didn't seem in a hurry to return home like the other children. These Ashladians wore smart clothes; it was so different from his home. Ashlad was a place of science, advancement, and egotists. He preferred the Nether sometimes to these other worlds.

The boy paused when a black and purple butterfly flew by his nose and then watched it go without much of a reaction. His target was unexpressive and withdrawn for one so young. For some reason, Ki sensed he'd taken a life. When he entered the brick house, Ki hurried down the edge of the street out of sight. Jumping onto the thick brick wall, he crouched down as he ran along it before sneaking in through the window. The mother's room was empty when he dropped into it. Today was the last day of the school week, and the child's mother always went to the market on this day. It would be at least half an hour before she returned.

The room was the same as he had last seen it. He heard the soft footfalls of the boy as he came up the stairs. Pulling his daggers from their sheath on his waist, he waited behind the door. The boy walked past his room and down the hall. Ki pressed his back tightly against the wall. After a moment, when all was silent, he crept out. Preparing to push the door open to the study, he noticed his hand was shaking. He frowned as he gazed at it. Taking a few steps back into the safety of the adjacent room, which belonged to the boy, he pressed his back against the wall again behind the door.

Ki couldn't bring himself to release him. His heart was not content with what he had to do. With a frown, he leaned his head back. If he couldn't kill the boy, he'd do the next best thing—take the boy to the Nether and leave him in a safe place, where Weavers and Shadows couldn't go. The boy had time to remake himself, to mend his stained soul, while the others he needed to save did not.

He knew of a cave in Tym Resh that was the resting place of a priestess who had sacrificed herself to save her people. In the cave were strange translucent rocks that were gelatinous and could heal wounds when the person slept within the walls. Ki had done that very thing himself. Nothing could get him there, and any injury he sustained had been mended while he slept. At first it had unnerved him to sleep in something that could get up his nose, but the contents had not suffocated him. It was his secret place. Even the Black Council didn't know about it. Once Ki's task was done, he'd release the boy back into the world—with a warning and a promise.

He took out a small cloth and a vial from his sack. After dumping the vial on the cloth, he purposely dropped the vial, making it shatter on the ground. After a moment, he heard running feet. When the boy pushed the door open and burst into the room, Ki covered his nose and mouth with the rag. He struggled for a moment, but soon went still.

Ki set him carefully on the ground before closing the door and pulling out the chalk. If he had to, he could rectify his actions later, but for now the boy must have been a mistake. Why else would his hands shake? The others Ki had taken out had been killers, murderers, and monsters, but not this boy. He glanced down at the child and wondered what he could have possibly done to have put a sin on his soul.

Chapter 7: Ashlad

φ

*T*he sea of faces floated below her as she walked the short distance across the stage. The large lecture hall had been set up to accommodate fine dining and even finer decorations. There was something beautiful about the old building and its hundreds-of-years-old architecture. A circular mouthpiece the size of a dessert plate sat atop a thin metal stand that was hooked into a sound projection system at the base of the stage.

"Welcome," Dr. Elisabeth Avery said into the device with a smile, her voice resonating through the room. "It is my distinct pleasure to be invited to open this year's gathering of the greatest minds in science. We are here to introduce our newest innovations and share our advancements in all fields on the scientific frontier. My focus on ectoplasm research has been very successful, but I believe the best way to highlight this is by showing you rather than telling you."

A few chuckled in the audience as she tried to hide the nervous shake in her hands. She admonished herself silently. She was a scientist who could perform complex procedures, after all, but she couldn't handle a room full of people. Life really did have its ironies.

Beside her was a simple suit made of thick fabric and metal—a deflated containment suit. It was airtight with bronze details. The most noticeable part was a clear circular part for the helmet at the top of it that looked like a cage. The metal strips at the seams had rivets to help keep their shape, but the dark blue fabric was mostly bendable and sat on the stage in a pile next to her. Many people strained their necks to get a look at it.

"May I present A.J. Dennett," Elisabeth said, holding an arm out.

There was an awkward pause, which was quickly filled with whispers. Elisabeth licked her lips nervously, wishing she had thought to bring a glass of water onto stage. She put on a fake smile and glared down at the suit. Any second, A.J.'s neutrino-based mass would fill the space.

"A.J.!" she snapped through clenched teeth.

Like magic, the suit began to fill with a strange white and sparkly substance until it was completely inflated. Elisabeth had always loved the way A.J.'s incorporeal form looked when he moved around. Without something to contain him, he would eventually return to what he was—stardust.

"My apologies, Miss Avery. I dozed off waiting for this to begin," A.J. said, expressing his sympathies like a well-aged gentleman in the same accent that Elisabeth possessed. As they'd worked together for months on end, his voice had become as familiar to her as any in Ashlad. "I hope I haven't caused any distress."

"It is quite all right," Elisabeth said, finally lowering her arm. "I believe it still had the desired effect."

Half the audience was slack jawed. Many held their spectacles up to their eyes, but most were leaning forward to get a better look. Her work in ectoplasm research in the field of Fringe Sciences really should have been called "How to Trap Stardust That is Conscious," but that didn't sound quite as distinguished. If Elisabeth had learned anything in her career, it was that most of the people in the room simply valued distinguished-sounding titles.

"Good evening," A.J. said, slapping his arms to his sides as he bowed. "Miss Avery has turned what should have ended a life into a life with which I can give back."

Elisabeth could still remember the first time she'd heard about the haunted house. Never had she imagined this moment would come to pass—that after searching dozens of haunted houses, she'd find one with a real spirit and build him a body. If it weren't for Elisabeth's unique, inherited ability, A.J. might still have been there.

Someone started clapping and then others joined in, their faces filled with wonder. It was difficult not to let her feeling of victory over them appear on her face. For most of her career, her peers had all thought her unworthy of their attention. Now they would pay closer attention.

"Thank you," Elisabeth said with a little bow of her head. "Please come to my presentation on Fringe Sciences tomorrow and learn about this process. Any questions can be answered then. For tonight, please enjoy the evening."

When Elisabeth left the stage, A.J. followed her, his steps heavy because she had weighed the suit down to allow for ease of walking. When she sat down, he stood next to her, still waving to the audience. She glanced up at the swirling stardust though the helmet, hoping A.J.'s face would form. It did every once in a while, which always reminded her that he had been a person once and gave her a strange sense of comfort.

"Thank you, Dr. Avery, for that astounding introduction to our convention," the moderator said. He continued to introduce additional distinguished members, but Elisabeth stopped listening. She glanced up at A.J. again and wondered if her choice to put him on display had been a mistake. He was a sentient being who had accidently become what he was. Elisabeth was still new to the field of ectoplasm and had primarily focused on building a vessel for him to live in. Yet the laws of their world were specific about what had rights. They did not extend to spirits.

"Elisabeth?" said her protector and friend, Milo, leaning over to touch her arm, "You look troubled. It was an excellent introduction."

"Thank you, Milo," Elisabeth said softly with a forced smile. Her conscience was suddenly at war over her hurried decision to show her success with A.J., but the damage had been already done. It was kind of Milo to reassure her, even if he was wrong about what was troubling her.

When the moderator finished, Elisabeth stood, and she and Milo headed for the door with A.J. bringing up the tail. She'd nearly made it when Dr. Nive Harrid and Professor Jacob Greenly cut her off by standing in her path, wearing smug looks. They were older men with outspoken beliefs about anyone who wasn't like them—which constantly extended to Elisabeth.

"It is a miracle what you've done with the Fringe Science field," Dr. Harrid said with a half-smile. "And it only took you a few years."

"Despite your disadvantages, you have overcome everyone's expectations," Professor Greenly said with an equally coy half-smile.

"Disadvantage?" Elisabeth said before she could catch herself.

"Why, being half demon, of course," Professor Greenly clarified.

Milo took a step forward. Being a lesser demon, he could do damage, but that wasn't how Elisabeth solved things. Elisabeth's jaw clenched as she raised a hand to stop Milo, and she put on a smile that could melt facial tissue from bones. "I could not have advanced the technology I presented today without my gifts. By that token, it is an advantage. Now if you'll excuse me, I have an early morning planned."

She swept around them before they could reply. On this day, she would not let their words dissuade her. It didn't matter that it was early and that her leaving would be seen as cowardice—there were too many people too close to her. Elisabeth could remember when other children were afraid of her growing up, some even to the point of throwing rocks. Private tutors had kept her well enough away from them. But it hadn't kept them from hurling curses at her on the streets. She sometimes thought that children were the cruelest beings because the words they spoke were embedded deeply in truth. In some cases, this carried into adulthood.

"Elisabeth," Milo called, getting her attention. "You're walking too quickly."

Elisabeth stopped and turned back to find A.J. struggling to keep up and Milo bridging the gap between them. She blinked, realizing she had far outpaced them, like she always did when she was alone. She glanced down at her fingers and found they had been madly drumming against her leg. Her thoughts had consumed her, and she had forgotten about her companions.

"I'm sorry, A.J.," Elisabeth said unsteadily as she straightened her back. "I forget myself." She sighed.

"That is quite all right, Miss Avery." His voice rang clear as he drew closer.

"Don't let words bother you," Milo said softly.

"Thanks," she replied, but his words gave her little comfort. "Can you get my father on the line?"

He nodded as A.J caught up to them and they resumed at A.J.'s pace. The hallways were mostly empty because everyone was at the reception dinner. When they reached the base of the large staircase that led up to the guest rooms, Milo handed her the telecommunication disk.

"Elsa! How is my brilliant daughter?" His voice boomed his pet name for her over the communication piece.

"Papa," she said as she felt the tension go out of her shoulders, "I am well. I just wanted to let you know that I'm done for the night and that A.J. is doing well."

"And the presentation?"

She smiled, but when she glanced up as they rounded the corner on the landing of the stairs, the smile turned into a scream. A man dressed all in black suddenly slammed both knees into Milo's chest, sending him crashing back against the stone banister. She dropped the communication device, and it skidded across the floor.

"Elsa? Elisabeth?" Malthael called out frantically. "Are you all right?"

She looked toward the device and opened her mouth to answer, but saw a long thin blade leveled at her. Her eyes went wide as she looked up at the man holding it. She could hear her papa yelling her name and demanding to know what was going on. Her hands started to shake—partly from fear and partly from her loss of control.

"Unhand her!" A.J. said, lifting his arms to attack.

The man turned and punctured the suit in one swift jab, causing it to deflate. A.J. gasped and tried to stop the leak with his ill-equipped hands. Elisabeth made it to two steps away from him before the blade was pointed back at her. She froze. Her hands were out by her sides, twisting in slightly circular motions. The man in black brought a boot down and crushed the communication device, silencing her papa.

"Miss Avery!" A.J. said as he filtered out of the suit.

"Go back to your other suit, A.J.," Elisabeth said as she continued the motions. "I'll be fine."

The man made of stardust and gelatinous goo spilled over the side of the banister and down through the floor to his other containment suit. A glob of ectoplasm was all that remained. She knew he could make it to the suit, which wasn't far off in storage, before he started to dissipate. She glanced at Milo and realized that the man threatening her life wasn't there for him or A.J. He was there for her.

"What do you want? My father is rich," Elisabeth said, narrowing her eyes.

She had to buy time—the demon dogs would come for her. She kept moving her hands in small circular motions, reaching into the spirit lines and calling them to her. He stayed silent and continued to stare at her with his impossibly dark grey eyes. Moments passed, and her chest rose and fell; she felt grateful that it still could.

He put the double thin blades away. Reaching behind him, he pulled a long sword from his back. She glanced hopefully at Milo, but he gave no indication of consciousness. Elisabeth calmed herself when she felt the demon dogs near. She took a step back. The man tipped his head to the side and took a few measured and lithe steps forward, bringing the blade down.

Like slivers of white, her guardians rose from the ground. An instant before the man's weapon struck home, the Netherhounds appeared. The deadly bladed tips of their ribbon-like elastic tails shot out and blocked the man's attack. He stumbled back, caught unawares by their sudden appearance. Unlike A.J., who was something everyone could see, her guardians were half spirits that only she and those like her could see until they materialized. They stood on two hind legs with their heads down, so she could see their strange curly ears and sets of ram-like horns on each side of their heads.

Her attacker reacted to their second strike and narrowly dodged away from the lethal blades. Nathan, the guardian on her right, took hold of the sword with his tail and yanked it free, while Duke, the guardian with the chipped horn, attacked again with his deadly tail. The man flipped backwards, out of harm's reach, and pulled out his twin blades from a sheath strapped to his lower back. He landed on his feet in a crouch and immediately lunged toward them again, but his blades went right through her body and slammed into the banister behind her without doing any harm.

Touching the dog demons had allowed her to transform into her spirit form. Since Elisabeth was only half Soul Collector, she needed help to travel the spirit lines, which her guardians did with ease. She watched the man in black, with his piercing dark eyes, as she faded into the floor, and then she was quickly far away from him.

"There you are," Malthael said, putting his arm around her shoulder in a rare show of affection.

His hair was pulled back in a cord at the base of his head in an old monk style, and all that was left of his black horns were broken spikes. They had been torn asunder when he had refused his last assignment—her assassination. Those who had ordered it had felt it wouldn't be wise to have a half-bred Soul Collector among the living because she would feel too many emotions. It would simpler to kill her, they'd believed, when she was an infant. Accidents were bound to happen when creatures like her were let loose upon the planets unchecked.

"It was terrible," Elisabeth said, her hands shaking from the adrenaline. "I had to leave Milo."

He took her long slender hand in his own black ones. "Milo is a demon and isn't easily killed," he reminded her. "What happened?"

"I think a man in black was there to kill me," she said, putting an unsteady hand to her throat. "If Duke and Nathan hadn't come when they did, I don't know what that man would have done."

She glanced around the greater under-hall, her eyes falling on the gate as she took in the all-encompassing hunter green of the room. The mass of their house was greater than that of many castles. Her adoptive father's wealth came from Malthael's bartering passage through the Netherworld or to other planets. Elisabeth's gaze shifted to the twin demon dogs, who had faded back into spirits. She knew Nathan and Duke would be checking the perimeter. There were benefits, like the Netherhounds, to Malthael's being a former high-ranking demon. Her papa was the Guardian of the Gate, and being in close proximity to the interplanetary gate allowed him to age slowly. Despite that, Elisabeth could see the lines on his black-and-gold-flecked face that had become more pronounced in his worrying over her safety. Since she did not benefit from the gate as much as her adoptive father did, Elisabeth wondered when she would begin to show her thirty years.

"Do not think of what could have been, my dear," he said, interrupting her thoughts as he led her through the green marbled hall to the great stairs. "Simply tell me what he said."

"Nothing." She let out a heavy sigh. "He didn't utter a single word."

"I fear this is not over," Malthael responded, his voice heavy as well. "We don't know what drives him. This man may hunt you until he is dead or has what he wants."

Elisabeth shuddered. "I feared as much as well." She had thought it possible that he was hunting her because of what she was. It was not the first time someone had tried to kill her. She just didn't know who the puppet master was this time or who had put a bounty on her head. Some wanted her blood, others wanted to control her, and some wanted her to bear their children. Being half of something so terrifying meant she was both feared and coveted, depending on who was coming for her.

Her hands still shook slightly as she and Malthael left the chilled stony area and entered their living quarters. The house itself was a maze and if attacked it would initiate defensive protocols. It would lead the person seeking the gate to every room but the one that had the exit. Her papa released her to push the stone doorway back, and it swung free. When they were on the other side, he pulled the mounted candlestick and the door swung closed again, and she turned into the comfort of her father's study.

They crossed the study to another exit into the hall. Elisabeth looked up and down it at the old tapestries. Malthael followed just behind without saying anything. He was always quiet when he was worried. She slowed as she approached one tapestry that looked almost three dimensional, as the tablet in the weaves seemed to shift with her movements. She had loved this one as a child because it seemed like magic.

"Will I be safe here?" she asked, stopping in front of it without looking at him.

"I don't know." That was Malthael, always a person of truth. "We don't know enough about him or his motivations. We don't know what he wants."

"Perhaps it is time we spoke to one of your contacts and acquired something," Elisabeth said, her voice low, knowing Malthael would understand what she meant.

"You don't like anything from the Nether," he reminded her.

She glanced at him. "I don't like the idea of dying either," she responded, her voice forlorn. "Nathan and Duke cannot protect me unless I call them, and I can't always calm myself enough to do so."

"Do not let the fear of death change you," Malthael told her. "We are all dying, and we cannot control when we take our final breath. We can, however, control how we live."

"Says the demon who has lived many lifetimes," Elisabeth said, smiling at him. Before he'd torn his horns from his head, he had lived many more lifetimes than a mere mortal would have.

"Your point is made." He smiled back at her. "But so is mine."

"I will not speak of my death again," Elisabeth agreed, nodding before continuing down the hall.

"You may consider defending yourself," Malthael mentioned, and she stopped dead in her tracks.

She turned back, her eyebrows furrowed and her voice angry. "You told me one soul…that if I took even one soul by force, that would be it. Now you tell me to use my powers to defend myself when I cannot deliver his soul and am, therefore, damning myself? It only takes one. How many times have you told me this?"

"You are right," Malthael responded. "A lapse in judgment. I do not wish to see any harm befall you."

"You are a contradiction, Papa," Elisabeth said with a little half smile. "In one breath you worry for my safety, and in another you warn me of my impending doom."

"It is the best that a reformed demon trying to be a father can do." Malthael sighed heavily. "I do not know how you planet dwellers manage."

"As well as you have," she responded, patting him on the arm. "Perhaps it is time you taught me how to get to the Netherworld."

"I fear it is more dangerous than this man hunting you," Malthael responded contemplatively. "I shall connect with my contacts in the Netherworld. Perhaps they can track his movements and give us warning of when he might try again."

Elisabeth looked at her papa then. He had glasses perched on the edge of his nose and wrinkles around his eyes. His age was starting to show. His hair was mostly black and tightly wound, but there were some grey strands in the band of hair at the base of his skull. There were lines all over his face that had not been there when she was a child. She was terrified of the man in black, and Malthael wanted her prepared for the worst, but she knew he had no intention of leaving her unprotected. There had been many attempts on her life. She comforted herself in the possibility that that was why she'd been momentarily rattled when he'd first appeared. Once her adrenaline had settled and her hands stopped shaking, logic and reason had returned. This man was not any more terrifying than what the Netherworld had thrown at her.

"I'll stay within the house limits, and I'll be careful," Elisabeth said, hoping it would help ease his burdened heart. "I'll take care of my work from here."

"Yes you will, missy!" Tiss, a snake demon, slithered into the room. "You scared me half to death."

Tiss pulled her into a hug as her lower half coiled in anxiety. She was crying and carrying on about how Elisabeth could have died. Elisabeth gave Malthael a look over Tiss's shoulder that asked, *You told her?*

Malthael shrugged and looked away. Tiss had heard him calling Elisabeth's name when she'd first been attacked. What else had he been supposed to do?

"There, there," Elisabeth said, comforting her.

When the communication device in Malthael's vest pocket began to vibrate, he'd never been more relieved. "I'll tell you if I hear anything."

Chapter 8: Hystera

———————————— φ ————————————

*J*inq and his spirit animal, Hibrius, watched the young girl as she moved through a series of stances that were part of a meditative exercise. A basis for hand-to-hand combat, it was a series of strikes and maneuvers that Kerrigan managed flawlessly. It made Jinq's old bones ache. The exercise was primarily about achieving balance, both physically and emotionally. His gaze flicked up to her spirit animal, which was perched on a tree in the temple's courtyard. It was rare for a saw-whet owl to choose a partner at such a young age.

The girl hadn't even finished growing, but already she had a spirit animal. They would be bound forever in life and in death. It was the way of their world, and yet she couldn't have lived more than thirteen or fourteen winters. Some clans, like his, connected with their spirit animals when they were children, but members of the owl clan usually didn't until they were older, at least seventeen winters.

The owl's body was mostly brown and white, and it had little wings. Its oversized head was half absorbed by its body, making it appear almost perfectly round. It watched Kerrigan with golden eyes under hooded lids, apparently falling asleep. She finished the movements and settled into a final pose. Sweat clung to her brown hair and tan face. The peppered marks around her hairline were a deep black.

The owl family was well known for their fighters, and apparently this girl was one of the best. It was no doubt the reason that Hipasha had suggested her goddaughter would make an excellent companion. Jinq knew young Kerrigan should have excelled and been accepted into a profession, but she was going to struggle because her mother had killed herself. Suicide was considered the greatest sin amongst their people, the act not even allowed to regain honor.

When she gathered her things, the owl swooped down and landed on her shoulder. She patted him on the head before hurrying up the steps, giving Jinq only a passing glance but tensing when she saw him.

"Kerrigan of the Owl Clan," he called, turning toward her.

She hesitated as though she still wanted to run, but finally faced him. He could tell from her weary eyes and tense stature that she was used to verbal abuse. It was not uncommon for children of a suicide to be treated like pariahs, particularly by their peers. Without even a father to support her, Kerrigan could not have had an easy time of it. She seemed ready to flee and fight all at once.

"Who are you?" she demanded as her owl tilted its head to the side.

"I am Jinq of the Panther Clan," he said and watched as her tension subsided.

"Keeper." She tipped her head in respect. "My godmother told me you would be seeking me out." She shifted the bag on her shoulder. "I can be ready to leave directly. There is only the matter of provisions."

"Good," Jinq responded, watching her body language for any worrisome signs. "Tell me, Kerrigan, do you know what our mission is?"

She shifted and swallowed heavily. "We are seeing why there is a sudden string of suicides in a village on the northern edge of the southern border. I'm to be your assistant."

In Hystera only certain people were allowed to know about the gates. He was a Keeper of their people, especially attuned to the planet and, therefore, to the gate. It was like a tear in the planet. Yet the general citizens of the world did not know about the gates or the other worlds, including Kerrigan.

"Do you know why Hipasha choose you?" Jinq asked, a little uncertain himself but attuned to how the Owl Clan operated.

Frowning a little, she diverted her eyes. "Because of what my mother did." Jinq could sense her shame.

"Very likely," Jinq said, comforted by her display of emotions and attempt to control them. "Let us depart now."

"Now?" Kerrigan asked, hurrying to catch up.

"No time like the present," he replied, looking to the sky as they walked down the great steps that lead from the temple.

"We don't have any supplies!" she protested, and her owl's talons tightened as she bound down the steps.

"We have Mara," Jinq replied calmly.

"What is a Mara?" Kerrigan asked after a moment's pause.

"That," Jinq said, gesturing toward a large elephant with a pack on its back, "is Mara."

"Whoa," Kerrigan said, her mouth slack jawed as she stopped to stare.

Jinq smiled as he reached the bottom of the steps and continued toward the gate. Mara was drinking from a large ceramic pot filled with water. She filled her trunk, then raised it to her mouth. She glanced over at them as they approached, and Jinq patted her on the side as his panther rubbed up against her leg. She patted Hibrius on the head with her trunk before returning to her water.

"Where is her spirit partner?" Kerrigan asked, glancing around.

"Mara is alone," Jinq said, patting the elephant's side. "She bonded with a young girl in a village further north who died before they could complete the bonding ceremony. She has been alone longer than I have been alive."

"That is so sad," Kerrigan said, reaching out and stroking Mara's hind leg. "I do not know what I would do without Cav." Her owl cooed and rubbed against Kerrigan's face.

The elephant glanced back as she put her trunk to her mouth again before returning to finish the jar. Jinq could see Kerrigan studying Mara with furrowed eyebrows. Kerrigan may have been attacked because of what her mother did, but she still had compassion. It had not turned her bitter, a good sign. Jinq would need more than just a warrior and helper; he'd need a secondary investigator.

"Fortunately, it happens rarely," he informed her. "It is hard to find purpose without a partner, so Mara stays busy helping others. That is why it is easier for the bonded to die together; once a bond is made, it cannot be unmade."

Kerrigan's owl made a sad little noise, likely reflecting her spirit partner's emotions. It was part of the bond, the ability to sense their partner's emotions. Jinq's panther, Hibrius, turned to look at her and her little owl. The owl made a funny little noise before trying to crawl up on top of her head.

"Hey!" Kerrigan called as the little owl began making noises. "Cav, stop!"

"Hibrius," Jinq said, shaking his head, but carefully kept his lips straight as the owl continued making noises.

"What are they doing?" Kerrigan asked as she finally got hold of Cav and held him with both hands. He was all feathers, and he looked annoyed. The bird made another noise at the panther before the feline responded in kind. He roared just loud enough to quiet the little bird and stop a few people in the area. It had been some time since Hibrius had allowed himself to get into a pissing match.

"They are establishing who the dominant party is," Jinq explained as Mara finished her intake and started to turn toward the gate.

"Oh," Kerrigan said, looking down at her little bird in surprise, "but why?"

"They are male," he replied with a small shrug. "Dominance is important to them."

Kerrigan seemed to contemplate that before nodding. She whispered something to Cav, who squeaked at her before she set him back on her shoulder. The owl quieted down but he continued to stare at Hibrius with the same wide-eyed, perturbed expression of agitation. They walked through the gate and down through the great city, where the lush plants grew tall and blocked out the hot sun. Here in the heart of the south, people and their spirit animals of every kind moved through their day. When they left the city, they would have to travel to the northern tip of their domain before entering the sandy wasteland that divided the north and the south. Spots of lush paradise existed in the desert, and one of them was their destination: a little village on the upper outskirts called Himota. Jinq only hoped he could discover what was happening there and stop it from continuing.

Chapter 9: Ashlad

φ

Ki stood at the gate and looked at the great house set far back from the outer wall. The gate was made of decorative black wrought iron, massive and effective at keeping him out. The stone wall was two feet thick and towered over him. A gate and high fortification wouldn't normally be a problem for him, but this place had another defense system. There was magical protection around the entire property, keeping her safely far away from him. He glanced at the keyhole and frowned.

Frustrated, he slipped into the dark corner where the metal gate met stone. A few people passed him on the thoroughfare, but Ki was well hidden in the shadows and went unnoticed. Not even the oil street lamps could penetrate the darkness around him. It wasn't long before the two spirit creatures guarding the girl appeared. Ki frowned again and watched them check the perimeter. An Ashladian man with a bowl-shaped hat walked by, talking so loudly with a woman that it caught the attention of the two beasts. For a moment, Ki thought he, too, would be discovered. After a moment of trepidation, though, they vanished.

Relaxing against the wall, he remembered her blue eyes. Her hair was a faded blond, and she had a regal face. It was easy to say she was nice to look at, perhaps even beautiful by this world's standard. Yet it had been her eyes that had thrown him. Every man and woman he had killed had been evil and had needed saving. They all had darkness in their hearts and had committed enough sins for his Sin Eater to take their souls. Despite his having seen her face among the others, though, this woman had an unexpected air of innocence about her.

Deciding on his next course of action, he hurried to the abandoned building he used to get to Ashlad, an old theatre house with a long spiraling staircase at the entrance and a stage. He walked down the aisle between the old crimson chairs, the building empty except for faded memories and the lingering smell of musk. The stage door at the back had the chalk still on it. The runes always lasted about five hours before fading.

36

Placing his hand on the door, he thought of a place in the Netherworld. He concentrated until the chalk glowed and his destination sat on the other side. Unlike the gates, this method of travel could only connect him to the Netherworld or take him from the Nether to one of the planets, but that required the right place. In the Netherworld it needed to be a sanctuary, but on the planets it needed to be a place of historical importance. He glanced around at the empty theatre, wondering what great stories had once been told in the now-hollow place. At least a century of stories must have existed there for a bridge to the Netherworld to have been created. Ki stepped out onto the charred ground. Behind him in a ruined building drenched in the red light of the Netherworld, Weavers chattered. Ki was too close to them and their territory. Red dust was unsettled with every step he made toward the black lake. Beyond the black lake was a great hill that had steps leading up to a keyhole-shaped building.

The mounds of slime and moss-covered stones were arranged in a spiral with waterfalls spewing black liquid into a pond with a low roar. Tall columns the size of a three-story house rose up around him in a circle. He stared only long enough to get his bearing before making his way around the structure. Shorter pillars swung away from the pond and up to the house like progressively taller stepping stones.

Ki took each step with care. This was the home of the Keymaster, Riku, an infamous high demon. Unlike his brethren, who were indentured servants to a master, Riku was a loner who had only one love: making keys. It was said that he was so obsessed with his craft that even his weapons were shaped like them. If anyone could help him find a key to breach the protected house, it was Riku.

Walking up to the house was treacherous, as the stone steps were slick with the same gunk as the mounds surrounding the place. The rest of the footholds had a strange grey moss growing on them that looked eerie in the red light. He knocked on the door and waited. After a moment it opened, and Ki, with a hand on the hilt of one blade, stepped inside.

Riku sat behind a desk in long black robes that were not ideal for hand-to-hand combat. He had deeply tan skin and long black hair pulled back into a loose braid. His eyes were turned up slightly, just like the small horns coming out of his head. His horns were black and so dark they seemed to pull in the light around them. His tail swished, and although Ki couldn't see them, he knew Riku had wings on his back.

"A lost mouse," he said, standing. Riku towered over Ki by more than two feet. "What do you want?"

"A key," he answered. "I need a key to a specific gate in Ashlad."

"Ashlad?" Riku said, moving toward him. "What gate in Ashlad?"

"The Guardian of the Gate's residence," Ki answered.

Riku stopped. His eyes narrowed as he muttered. "Malthael."

"You know the Guardian?" Ki asked, surprised. Most demons didn't bother with mortals—even if this one had once been a demon himself.

"He's a former demon with a debt to pay," Riku said, tapping his long poisonous nails on the countertop. "I have that key, but the barrier stops demons from leaving once they have entered."

"I am not a demon," Ki said. "And what debt does he owe?"

Riku seemed to regard him a moment. "He borrowed a key once and never paid the due," the demon said as his nails curled the black paint off the desktop. "The key should have, therefore, been forfeited, but it was never returned to me."

"If you give me a key, I'll retrieve what is yours," he offered, hoping the demon would accept.

"What need do you have of such a key?" Riku asked, narrowing his eyes.

"My mission is my own," he responded truthfully. It was better not to tell a demon your plans, as information was frequently traded with the living for a cost.

Riku regarded him for a moment with his head tipped to the side before he opened a cabinet and took out a key. He also pulled out a piece of parchment. Ki tried not to cringe; in the Netherworld, paper was made from all kinds of skin—from animal, to planet dweller, to demon.

"Your deal is struck," the demon said with a half-smile. "Find the key and return them both when your mission is complete."

Ki held the key up. The neck was shaped like a screaming woman, and Ki recognized it as a skeleton key. Glancing down at the skin-parchment, he examined the drawing of the other key he was to look for. It had multiple spokes leading to the center, which held a single, perfect white gem. Riku rolled out a small parchment and held up a fountain pen. "Do we have a deal?" he asked with a sickeningly charming grin.

"How do I find the other key?" Ki asked.

"The screaming lady will lead the way," Riku responded, tipping the top of the pen toward him. "My keys are drawn to each other when in a certain proximity."

Ki tucked both items away before taking the fountain pen. He signed a simple "K" before handing the pen back. With a sweep of Riku's hand, the pen and parchment vanished. Deals could only be struck on the skin of the damned. Riku's wolfish smile remained as Ki nodded and left.

When the door closed behind him and he was standing in the red light again, he reached into his pocket. The screaming woman seemed awfully familiar. He held it up to the light until her mouth was filled with the red gleam. He was one step closer to finishing his list of forty-two, to saving them all.

Chapter 10: Ashlad

φ

*E*lisabeth absentmindedly pushed her dinner around her plate. She had been on house arrest since the attempt on her life. Malthael had sent out feelers into the Netherworld in hopes of discovering who her pursuer was and what he wanted. She finally set down her fork and brought her hands up, and clasping one on top of the other while she thought. Milo had contacted them and was well, but she worried they would not always be so lucky. She had never taken a life. Only twice in her life had she pulled a soul from a body, and she'd put them right back in before any permanent damage had been done.

The first time had been when she was child. She'd been betrayed by a boy she'd thought was a friend, which had awoken her ability. Thankfully, Malthael had helped her replace the soul before the boy died. The second time, when she was teenager, had been an accident. Elisabeth worried it would happen again, though, if her assassin came for her. She feared her papa was right—that the man would not stop until he completed his mission or he died. She leaned her face against her hands as she thought about it. Would she actually be able to do it? Could she take a life to save her own?

"Are you that worried?" Malthael's voice pulled her from her thoughts. He walked across the room and took the chair at the great table to her right.

"Being unsure of the future makes one worry."

"When you get that look on your face, you remind me of your mother," Malthael said with a half-smile. "She often worried for your future. Remember that Serena had the fortitude to stand eye to eye with a demon and demand your right to live."

"At the expense of her own life," Elisabeth reminded him.

"Yes, her kind was not meant to give birth to something from the Netherworld," Malthael admitted. He frequently spoke truth with no regard for emotions. He opened the paper to begin reading in the news section, ending the discussion.

She had known the truth for quite some time. Malthael had not kept any detail from her, from her father's false name, Darien Shields, to her parents' one night together, which had resulted in her conception. Elisabeth had been named after Serena's sister, Lizbeth, who had died in an accident when they were children. Malthael didn't know what kind of accident, and Elisabeth had always wondered what her life would be would be like if her aunt had lived. Elisabeth knew everything that Malthael knew about her birth parents, yet sometimes she wished she didn't know. That way she could pretend her father had loved her mother and that they had shared a special moment together.

With a sigh, she pulled herself from her thoughts and stood. Malthael looked up from his paper. His all-knowing eyes told her he understand exactly what she was thinking. She glanced at the front of the page and saw a strange disappearance of bees had begun on their largest continent, Mauven.

"I'm tired," she said, coming around to pat him on the shoulder. "I'm going to bed."

He took her wrist. "Nathan and Duke have found nothing but will continue to protect you while you sleep."

"I know," she responded before kissing him on the forehead. "Goodnight."

Making her way from the dining room down the long hall, she walked up the second set of stairs to the sleeping area. At the far back of the house was her bedroom, where the sun came in and warmed it in the morning. The room was done entirely in deep purple fabrics and green upholstered furniture. The walls were a soft cream. The adjoining bathroom was teal with a beautiful painting of a ship in a storm on one wall.

Elisabeth started to untie the bow at her throat as she closed the door. She unbuttoned her waistcoat before shrugged it off and setting it on the back of her settee. She undid the buttons down the front of her dress and the fasteners at her hip. Pulling herself free of her thick skirts, she let them slide off her hips and pool on the floor, leaving only her white petticoats. She began pulling at the ribbons to dress for bed. When she turned, she gasped. A sword was leveled at her throat.

The man still wore a mask over his nose and mouth, and she raised her hands slowly. Fear clenched her gut and locked her limbs in place. She feared death as much as losing control and killing him. Instead of possibly condemning her soul, she needed to concentrate and summon Nathan and Duke again.

"Stay back," she said, her hands shaking.

She tilted her head as the blade pressed against her throat. To her shock, the metal suddenly dissolved into dust. Carefully reaching over, she pinched the substance between her fingers and realized it was in fact ash. Her attacker was just as surprised as she was.

"What are you?" he asked, his voice was deep and accented. He dropped the sword's hilt and took a step towards her.

She stepped back and held up a hand to stop him. She shook her head. "Please, stay back," she pleaded.

He reached out and rested his fingertips on her hand without hesitation. She gasped, expecting the worst to happen, but nothing did. Bewildered, she let her other half out and tried to collect his soul. Yet again naught came of her efforts.

"What are *you*?" she asked, mirroring his question.

Chapter 11: Hystera

φ

*T*he great plains of Hystera stretched out before them like a sea of dancing short blond hair. Miles of long dry grass, as far as the eye could see, spread out toward the Dunes of Hinar—the great divider of the north and the south. Hibrius and Cav had soon gotten over their mutual dislike in order to hide from the sun. They both remained in the shadow of Mara, Cav sleeping on Hibrius's back. Sometime Hibrius would even walk directly under her great mass for even more protection from the heat. In the evening a great tent was set up that was large enough to shield Mara, and all the party members slept in a single space to conserve heat, since night was colder the further they ventured toward the desert. Once they reached the desert, all the heat that existed during the day would be lost in the evening to the open sky. Jinq was relieved they didn't have to go much further north, where the dry plains ended and the sand began.

Kerrigan had turned out to be a curious but reserved girl. Although Jinq had to admit he did appreciate having someone along to help with the campsite, he was pleased to find she seemed to enjoy the silence as much as he did. The conversations they'd had so far had been short, and they'd been few and far between. Kerrigan didn't seem comfortable talking about herself, and he doubted she'd like to hear the stories of an old man. Thus, the nights were mostly filled with the sounds of the insects of the grasslands and the crackling of a fire.

Jinq raised his head, which was covered by a wrap to protect it from the sun, and squinted against the horizon. He could just make out the fringes of green in the distance. It had been a long walk, but two weeks of constant moving had resulted in their making good time. Jinq knew time was of the essence and was thankful for Mara, who had been invaluable to their mission. Soon they would discover the cause of the rash of suicides in his village.

"There is our destination." Jinq shielded his eyes and pointed.

Kerrigan gazed across the sea of faded yellow grass and turned to him with muted excitement. "How far would you say that is away?"

"A few more hours and we will be at our destination," Jinq answered, and a general sigh seemed to take place among his companions at their journey nearly being done. He realized he'd set a grueling pace despite the summer heat and had to stifle an amused smile.

Cav woke up from his nap and ruffled his feathers as he looked around. When nothing seemed to happen and no reason presented itself for him to be on alert, he settled back down to riding upon Hibrius's back. They continued on with their deliberate steps—heavy and dragging.

As they drew closer to the splash of color among the beige landscape, something felt wrong. It felt like a ripple of dread being sent out, and with every step they were getting closer to its source. Hystera was infected, and this was the wound. Normally there was a peacefulness, a harmony, on their planet, but something was disrupting its perfect melody. Jinq felt his old bones grow heavy, but he did his best to ignore it as they grew closer. He could feel the strange shift in the symphony of the world become stronger with every step—he knew that Hystera was plagued, but he did not yet know the disease. Beneath his feet, Hystera seemed to beg him to stop, and it nearly brought him to his knees.

Patches of sand melded with the tall grass, but further ahead the vegetation was speckled with emerald patches. The arid air added to the feeling of dread, and Jinq felt lightheaded. Suddenly Mara stopped at the very edge of Himota, her complete halt causing Hibrius and Cav to suddenly be in the sun. They blinked back at the elephant as the blinding light shone down on them.

"What is it?" Kerrigan asked, reaching up and touching the elephant's side.

Mara started backing up and shaking her head. She trumpeted, and an unhappy sound rumbled in her throat. That rumble usually meant danger, yet Jinq saw none. He pulled the staff from his waistband and moved toward the tree line.

"What is wrong with her?" Kerrigan asked.

"Mara feels what I feel," Jinq whispered as his eyes swept from left to right. "Something is wrong."

Abruptly, a scream pierced the air. Jinq held a hand out as Hibrius recoiled from the sound and Cav began hopping nervously along the panther's back. Kerrigan's eyes were suddenly as wide as Mara's.

"What is that feeling?" she asked, her voice tight with fear.

"Stay here and keep them safe," Jinq commanded, and Kerrigan nodded as she swallowed hard. "Hibrius, with me."

Hibrius struggled forward as though he was fighting an invisible flood before pushing his head into Jinq's hand. Cav jumped from Hibrius's back and dove right into Kerrigan's chest, making small distressed sounds as she held him. Mara made a sad little trumpeting noise before putting the tip of her trunk on Kerrigan's shoulder. Eventually, the ache and wave of darkness dissipated after their physical contact; spirit companions were always strongest when they were together. Two intertwined souls working in concert could overcome almost anything.

Jinq pushed forward into the tree line, although the brush resisted his entry. He would have preferred a path but didn't have time to find one. After a minute or two, he could hear people calling out in distress. It wasn't long until the two of them reached an open dirt clearing. In the middle of the field, a group of people were gathered around the only tree in the open space. It stood tall and nearly barren amongst its lush counterparts.

He continued forward as the people yelled, seeming to call to someone. They were all looking up, so Jinq did too. Two women and a man were up in the tree. The man put his arms out at his side and jumped before Jinq had time to react. Appalled, he turned away a little as the body hit the ground. It was nauseating to see such a terrible sin being committed and not be able to pray.

Forcing himself to look back, he realized the two women hadn't jumped yet. He hurried across the field, moving as quickly as he could without breaking the connection with Hibrius, which allowed him to move with some ease. The pressure filled his nostrils and he was having a hard time breathing. How could these people stand around something so dark without their spirit animals? As he approached, he noticed they didn't seem to be affected like he was. Dread clawed at the back of his brain, but he pushed it down.

"Please come down," one of the women called. "I beg of you to stop. Please, sister."

"I want to fly," the woman said, putting her arms out as she fell forward from the massive tree.

The crowd moved back as the woman plummeted to her death. There was a sickening crunching noise, and a halo of blood begin to form around her head. He grimaced at the smile on her face before turning his attention to the final woman in the tree. Many more were calling for her to get down.

"Please don't, Marta!"

"Silence!" he yelled, pushing people aside.

"Who are you?" someone demanded, but he ignored him.

"Tell me, Marta," Jinq called, as the young woman spread out her arms. "Why do you want to fly?"

She stopped and looked down at him, her arms falling limply to her sides. She seemed to look at him and see through him. In a way, her eyes were not her own. Jinq swallowed heavily in fear, although the young woman could do nothing to him in her current position. Then her face spread into a sickeningly sweet smile, and she thrust her arms out at her sides again.

"I want to be free before he comes!" she shouted into the sky.

Before he could ask anything else, she leaned forward and fell head first.

Jinq turned away and only heard the crunch and snap as her neck broke. Struggling to turn his eyes to her again, his heart grieved that her body looked like a discarded doll, bent and broken. To his revulsion, the three all had the same smile, even in death. Jinq glanced around at the grim suspicious faces of the people of Himota.

"I am of the Southern Council," he informed them. "I am here on a mission to see what is causing these deaths. I request to see Councilmen Robert."

His words were met with silence. Jinq could feel the overwhelming darkness fading. Whatever had compelled these people to kill themselves was tied to the wave of gloom. He glanced around at the solemn faces of the crowd until a man finally stepped forward.

"That is Councilman Robert and his family," he informed him and indicated the bodies on the ground.

Chapter 12: Ashlad

——————————————— φ ———————————————

althael put the newspaper down with a heavy sigh as he watched Elisabeth leave. He truly did not understand how these planet-dwellers survived parenthood. He stood without touching his dinner, though he knew his cook would hiss at him later, as he walked over to the liquor cabinet. He'd saved their cook's life long ago from a higher demon, though, so eventually she'd forgive him. She always did.

Once the glass was full, he returned to his seat. Glancing at his daughter again, he mentally compiled how much he had kept from Elisabeth for her own safety. The less she knew about the Netherworld and the Divine Court, the better. He'd spent most of his life in service of a member of the Divine Court, and he would not go back. It had been a different life, and he had been a different demon then, but now he was reformed.

Even just sitting there reminiscing about the Netherworld pulled Malthael mentally back to Morhaven and his home within the Netherworld. The Netherworld had always been a topsy-turvy place, but it had its own set of order. Chaos had been reined in and balanced by the inner circle, the Divine Court, but they had grown lax over the years. Malthael had told Elisabeth the harsh and brutal truth of her birth to make her turn away from the Nether and its allure. Of anyone, a former demon would best understand the temptation of the Netherworld, but he knew, too, that it would end poorly.

"Come along, my dear," Tiss said. Malthael looked up, surprised. He'd been so caught up in his thoughts that he hadn't noticed Tiss enter.

"Good night, Papa." Elisabeth kissed his forehead as she walked by.

Tiss frowned at his untouched plate, her beautiful mortal-looking face untarnished by the grimace. Her silky dark brown hair was gathered in a fancy bun, similar to what he would see in Oran. She was dressed in a beautiful robe, and Malthael wondered if her vanity would ever wane. Malthael wisely returned to his plate as she slithered by, deciding a compliment to her would solve nothing.

The great knocker clunked thrice, filling the hall with a deep echo that rumbled through the halls. Hearing a creaking noise, Malthael looked up over his spectacles toward the entryway. His short butler, Gog, zipped across the hall. He was part dwarf and part Hysteri—the dots along his hairline a dead giveaway—who had accidently stumbled into the Nether and had somehow made his way through their gate. The dwarf spoke rarely, a trait Malthael valued, so he'd taken him on as his personal butler.

He rushed along the floor. Something about the house and the proximity to the gate made him move swiftly. Malthael smiled as he leaned back in his chair and waited. It was not often they had visitors, and he doubted the assassin would be so bold. When the door opened, he recognized the voice immediately. Malthael stood as Gog brought in the one regular visitor they did have. He was a tall, thin male with a long willowy face and a mouth that constantly frowned. His fingers were freakishly long, and he wore a long dark grey robe that was embroidered with gold decorations. The vestment dropped down to his thighs and had two twining roses, one black and one white, sewn into the edges. It was the emblem of Nauberon Det Mor, King of Morhaven and protector of the Netherworld.

Malthael's frown deepened. The Det Mor family meant trouble. The Divine Court lived within Morhaven, the pearl of the Netherworld, and oversaw all the worlds' chaos with a careful eye. Nauberon was their king. The rest of the Divine Court believed the threat was dead and gone, but the King and his kin did not believe the chaos and darkness that threatened them was truly depleted. When something threatened the peace, they would send their great warrior, Arawn, the Lord of the Hunt. Malthael could still remember his black antlers, though it had been many a year since the last time Arawn had been seen among the planets. Not since the last Great Hunt.

"Zod," Malthael said with a bow of his head in respect, "what brings you from the Dusky Woods?"

"You've gotten fat," he answered with a little frown. Plumpness was not considered attractive in the Netherworld. His eyes scanned the table, and he pointed at a pile of biscuits. "Are those wise?"

"Age will do that to you," Malthael responded with an uncaring shrug. "I know you did not come here to tell me to lay off the biscuits. So why *are* you here?"

"Your request for information on this assassin has gotten the attention of the Det Mor Clan, and they are not pleased with this *thing*," he said, his inflections growing distasteful near the end. "It has been using the Netherworld as a go-between so it can kill sinners."

"Why are you calling this man a thing?" Malthael asked, and he worried. Even the snobbish Det Mor did not call demons "things," so whatever this assassin was must be worse.

"It may have the form of a man, but it carries many souls," Zod replied, revulsion in his voice. His fingers intertwined as his natural frown turned down further. "A creature such as it becomes a *thing*. We would dispatch Arawn, but those souls are fused, and we believe it has many lives."

"You're saying he is immortal?" Malthael asked, leaning forward, his hand on the table.

"I am saying *it* is very hard to kill," Zod said with a frown. "We are searching for a way around these souls. So that we can kill it and restore balance."

"Do you have any of his recent movements?" Malthael asked, hoping to know where he was going.

"It spoke with Riku before returning to this world," Zod said with a wave of his hand. "I was here speaking with our contact when the news arrived."

"Riku? The Keymaster?" Malthael demanded as he stepped around the table, his chest suddenly tight.

"Indeed," Zod answered, giving him a strange look. "Why is that of concern to you?"

Malthael didn't answer. Instead, he started to run. "Elisabeth!" he yelled.

His heavy footfalls shook the ground and the marble flooring threatened to crack under his strength, but he didn't care what happened to such things. The flooring could be replaced; Elisabeth could not. He'd thought he would have more time to protect her, more time to prepare. This assassin, with all its souls, had wasted no time at all.

He reached the bottom of the stairs and again called, "Elisabeth!" as he ran up toward her room. He burst through the door and stopped short when he saw them. Elisabeth had a hand on the assassin's chest. While his face was mostly covered, he had nothing in his hands, which gave Malthael some measure of relief. The pair reacted slowly to Malthael's sudden appearance, turning their heads as though they were in a trance.

"Get away from her!" Malthael roared as he reached into the dimension where the Netherworld existed and pulled out his demonic sword. There were not many items demons could pull from the Nether. A full demon could usually do more, but he was no longer whole. He could only pull his sword because it was bound to him—a remnant of what he once was.

The long blade burned bright with Netherfire, and he charged without hesitation. The man stepped back from her and ducked to evade Malthael's attack. He immediately sliced the air towards the assassin again, but the man moved gracefully to the side and out of harm's way. Frustration drove him forward, and he pushed the masked man back, yet despite the skill of every swing, the man continually outmaneuvered him.

Malthael stopped mid-swing and pushed the blade down, catching the very edge of the assassin's thigh. Fire burned along the cut, but he didn't cry out or stop. Instead, the assassin leaped up onto the windowsill before dropping out of sight. Malthael was half out of the window, intending to go after him, when Elisabeth's voice finally registered.

"Stop!" she yelled, tugging on his arm, which was nearly the size of her waist. "Malthael, stop!"

"Why?" Malthael roared. "He is trying to kill you."

"He tried." She pointed to a sword handle that lay forgotten on the floor. "And he failed."

Chapter 13: Tym Resh

————————————— φ —————————————

*C*lara Reid swept out the shop before the sun rose. She wiped the back of her hand across her forehead and looked into the fog. It was strange to have fog in Loveday this time of the year. Perhaps it was one of those strange weather days she was hearing about.

She set the broom down and turned back into the shop as the baker stepped out. Fretrik Brok was a tall man, large but not excessively so. In fact, the "too thin" people were mocked in Loveday. Many people called Clara too boyish to be pretty as well, because of her slight size. Yet Clara didn't care much about that; she was young, only seventeen, and had tons of time to grow. What bothered her was when people made fun of the dark red birthmark on her cheek.

"Brown sugar batch is bad," Fretrik said with a frown and walked over, dropping the sack on the countertop. "I need it to finish the streusel. Go and get some."

"Aye, sir," she said with her backwoods-twang accent, but Fretrik didn't wait for her response. He was already back to making his goods.

Clara lifted the stiff sugar and put it into a bright red wagon for easy transport to and from the grocer's. Accustomed to such treatment, she went around the corner and pulled out a book. Leafing through the pages until she found the receipt that corresponded to the sugar, she realized they'd only bought the sugar two days earlier. She shoved the receipt into her pocket and squeezed the bag, which felt like it held rocks. The grocer must have lied about its age or exposure to moisture. Sugar never really went bad after all, but no one wanted to bake with sugar that hard. She pulled on a dull purple shawl before going out the front door.

The first light of day spread across the sky, but the fog had yet to give. Clara took hold of the small wagon's handle and headed toward the grocer's store. Humming to herself as she walked, she pulled the apple from her pocket. She took a bite and let the juices fill her senses, savoring the taste. Before she'd gotten the bakery employment, she'd only been able to afford an apple a week. Now she could eat an apple every morning, so long as they were in season and in stock—a more comfortable life to be sure.

Something shrilled in the distance, making her stop. Clara glanced around the fog, her eyes straining. The morning mist was thicker than she ever remembered it being, and it only seemed to be getting worse. She swallowed the apple, but it no longer had the same effect. Frowning, she continued on, but hurried, her feet moving twice as quickly.

When she heard a soft whistle, Clara stopped again. She smiled. She'd heard that sound before—it was a flock of birds. Feeling silly for getting worked up over blackbirds or sparrows, she told herself it was probably just a startled bird that had made the earlier piercing noise. She waited in anticipation to see them fly overhead. When she finally saw them coming toward her, as full and thick as a storm cloud, she took a step back in surprise. She had never seen that many before!

The wheels on her wagon squeaked slightly, and suddenly the birds changed direction at the sound, flying directly toward her. Clara dropped the wagon handle as the small tan and black birds with red eyes swooped down, swarming her completely. She screamed as they pecked at her, each sharp beak taking a small chunk of her skin. She heard someone call her name in the distance.

"Help me!" she screamed.

She stumbled blindly toward the person calling her name, unable to see anything but tan feathers and flashes of red eyes. Their wings whistled as they tore at her clothes and flesh. Clara tried to run, but there were a hundred or more of them. She tried desperately to pull free, but they were everywhere, working together.

The innkeeper appeared by her. She could see him trying to push them off her with a broom. "Try to run!" he bellowed.

The birds let out a terrible shriek together, as if they were one creature, and turned toward the innkeeper instead. She covered her ears as they rushed past her so quickly that she tumbled onto her backside. The man fell back as she scrambled to the other side of the street. She could hear other voices now and could see the birds starting to lift the innkeeper up into the air. He struggled against them, but they would not be deterred.

"Help! Someone help!" Clara screamed.

When she realized everyone around was lost in the increasingly dense fog and couldn't help, Clara stood and rushed toward the innkeeper. She tried to push the birds off, but they began to attack her again. One poked at her eye, and she staggered, tumbling on her back with a hand to her wounded eye. She could hear the man yelling as he tried to swat the creatures away. Then the birds' wings whistled, the man's scream was cut short, and all went silent.

Clara shook and her breath shuddered in and out of her chest as blood snaked down from her many injuries. When she tried to stand, she barely found her feet. Taking an unsteady step forward as the sun lit the edge of the valley and the fog began to dissipate, she squinted through fog. Slowly, people around her became more visible, but she did not see the man who had rescued her.

She searched desperately in the vague hope of seeing him or being able to thank him, but he was nowhere to be found. She recognized the entryway of the inn in front of her. Movement caught her eyes and Clara licked her lips nervously as she moved forward to see more. As she stared at the ground, a blood drop fell from above and splattered against the stone.

Frozen in place, Clara slowly looked up. Someone screamed, and it took her a moment to realize it was her. The man who had saved her from the flock of birds was impaled on the antlers mounted above the inn's entrance.

Chapter 14: Ashlad

—————————————— ϕ ——————————————

*E*lisabeth **paced nervously** as Malthael watched her with his tail flicking back and forth in time to her steps. He was slumped back with his fingers supporting the side of his head and his demon sword across his knees. She had put on a dark blue robe that made her cerulean eyes glow and her golden hair shine. He took in her elegant face and couldn't believe he'd almost lost her. Malthael redirected his anger—unhappy that he'd missed the opportunity to slaughter the assassin at least once.

"Multiple souls?" Elisabeth stopped to ask.

"Enough that Arawn, Lord of the Hunt, wasn't called to handle the matter," Malthael confirmed with a heavy sigh. "As satisfying as it might have been, my sword would have only released a soul."

"That explains why I couldn't pull his soul from his body when I tried," Elisabeth said, still pacing as she spoke. Because he heard the strain in her voice, Malthael didn't point out that she shouldn't have even tried. "However, it doesn't explain why his sword turned to dust."

"Ash," Malthael corrected.

"That's right," Elisabeth agreed, and then stopped to stare at him. "How did you know that?"

"He used a sin-eating sword," Malthael said, letting his hand slide across the flat side of his blade. "When those touch an innocent, they turn to ash because killing innocents is not their function."

"Then why is he hunting me at all?" she asked, pacing again, wearing the rugs down. "What could he possibly gain?"

"I don't know," he responded, shifting in his chair uncomfortably. "But as long as you remain innocent, he cannot hurt you."

"Can't he just use another method?" Elisabeth asked pointedly.

"I don't think so," he said, averting his eyes. "Zod said he was using the Nether to kill sinners. You can't collect souls of sinners unless you have a Sin Eater. He may search for another way to harvest your soul, but the Sin Eater is the only way I know of."

"Zod was here?" Elisabeth asked, clearly upset. "Why didn't you tell me that he was your source of this information?"

"I do not want you entangled with the Det Mor Clan," Malthael responded. "Their assistance always comes at a price."

"What price did you pay?" Elisabeth demanded.

"I saved King Nauberon Det Mor's life. So long as he is king, he shall owe me," Malthael informed her. "All I have asked him for in return is a lifetime of information."

"All my years here, and you still have secrets about your demonic life," she said, looking crestfallen. "What else do you keep from me?"

"I have lived 903 years," Malthael countered, leaning forward. "Secrets are not a necessity. These truths are simply many untold stories of a past life."

Malthael truly was not one to keep secrets from Elisabeth. There was only one truth he had kept from her; the rest he had just not bothered to tell. Nearly a millennium of being an unrepentant demon meant many dark stories he did not wish his daughter to hear. It didn't matter that she was older and had seen the darkness of the world for herself. Malthael would not break his silence now.

Elisabeth gave him a furrowed look. "Why was Zod interested in my assassin?"

"His housing of multiple spirits places the Chaos out of balance. No mortal should be able to live that many lives; he is an anomaly. Before it was of little concern, but now that he is traveling the Nether and killing, the Det Mor Clan will not abide his continued existence. I imagine his actions have thrown our five planets further off kilter, and they will want to fix it before it affects the Netherworld as well," he explained before standing. "I must see to the gate."

"Of course," Elisabeth said as her shoulders relaxed. "How do I know he won't return?"

"Even if he did, his Sin Eater is useless. There is nothing he can do until you take an unwilling soul," Malthael said bluntly. "For now, you should rest and we shall begin again in the morning."

She nodded with her hands on her hips and her face suddenly thin with exhaustion. Her hair was a mess of soft curls, and for a moment he saw her mother. Malthael remembered Serena as though it was yesterday. It had been easier to tell Elisabeth that her mother had died at her father's hands than to explain the whole story.

"Good night," Elisabeth said, pulling the robe closer around her. "I'll see you in the morning."

"Sleep well," he said, heading toward the door with the thick jagged blade over his shoulder.

He walked out into the hallway. As he started to close the door, he paused a moment and looked back at Elisabeth. She was looking toward the window. It was not surprising that Elisabeth found the prospect of someone she couldn't hurt interesting. All her life she'd had to be careful with her emotions, lest she hurt someone by accident. She'd had to keep everyone who wasn't enough of a demon at arm's length.

The door closed, and he walked down the hall. Trotting down the stairs, he turned at the tapestry-filled hallway and walked into the study. It was as always: an eternally burning fire in the hearth, and walls of books interrupted only by occasional vases and stone statues. He pushed aside the tapestry of the fairies of Verten and pulled one of the lamps down, releasing the large stone slab. He pulled on the lamp one more time before walking through the opening to make sure the door closed behind him. The light vanished for a moment before the eerie blue of the mushrooms on the ceiling filled his vision.

He walked down a long hall, his legs taking great strides as he kept the sword over his shoulder. He could have placed it back in with a ritual, but the gate was easier—an advantage of being the gate's guardian. The steps were darker in the great cavern-like basement. The eerie glow of the mushrooms didn't reach this far. When the cavern opened up, the shadows swallowed him.

The gate wasn't like an entrance into a home. There wasn't any wrought metal or squeaky hinges; it was a slab of stone. He turned the dial in the right of the green block. The stone rippled like it was made of liquid, and a mirror appeared. At least it *looked* like a mirror inside a stone exterior. Even Malthael marveled at its size, large enough to pass three people abreast through who were less than ten feet tall. It was a doorway that existed on every planet and allowed entry into the Netherworld.

The reflective substance showed his black-gold skin as he approached. Malthael thought of his home in the Netherworld, where the sword had been hidden in a rock in the garden. A statue held it, and after more than three decades it had never been found, despite being hidden in plain sight. He closed his eyes and concentrated. When the image of it was firm in his mind, he thrust the sword into the gate and it passed though as easily as if he were reaching into a pond. When he pulled his arm free, the sword remained behind in the stone hands of Balor—his former master.

Malthael reached for the starred dial. Only the guardian could see it for what it was; otherwise it was impossible to find. Though most everyone assumed that Malthael had chosen to become the Gate's Guardian, it would have been more accurate to say that the gate had chosen him. He had been drawn to it, and he had gone willingly to the inescapable pull. He had seen the inscription and the dial that opened the gate when others could not.

Every night, Malthael came to turn the dial, as was his duty as a guardian. As of yet, nothing had happened. No message, no guardian waiting, and no requests for passage from the Netherworld. Yet every night he came, and he would continue to do so until his time as the guardian had passed, or he died. He put his hand on the dial and turned from the Nether to Lyreane, and he was not surprised that nobody was there. Beyond their yearly call to council, he rarely saw any of his guardian counterparts.

He turned again, next to Oran, and then to Hystera, and still there was zilch. He turned one last time to Tym Resh and nearly jumped out of his skin when a woman with a heart-shaped face appeared in the gateway's reflection. She looked up, startled. Her dark purple curls shimmered almost black in the reflection, and she looked exactly as she had when he had seen her last—wearing maroon robes and a stern expression.

"Finally, Malthael," she said, relieved.

"Meridith," he said, surprised.

She closed the paper file she'd been writing in. "I have been waiting for another guardian all night."

"Why?" he asked, a little unsettled.

"We had an attack in Tym Resh, in a small village called Loveday," she informed him.

"How does that concern the Gate Guardians?" Malthael asked, though something about her tone worried him.

"It was no ordinary attack." Her face darkened. "They were shrikes."

Malthael fought down a smile. "A bird attack?"

"These were no ordinary shrikes," Meridith retorted harshly. "We found one and identified it. According to our findings, it came from the Netherworld."

Chapter 15: Hystera

— φ —

"Something is wrong here," the man sitting across from Jinq said.

"Why haven't you all left?" Jinq asked, glancing around at their disheartened faces.

They glanced at each other as a common thought seemed to pass between them. Jinq waited, his hand firmly planted on Hibrius's back. He would not risk letting him go for the time being.

"Our spirit animals are gone," a woman finally said.

"What do you mean gone?" he demanded as he studied her taut face.

"Overnight, they just started to vanish," the first man answered with a defeated shrug.

Jinq's hold on his spirit companion tightened, and his fear of breaking the connection grew. Whatever was happening here was worse than he had originally guessed. Jinq looked at their faces and saw only despair. They couldn't leave without dying. Some of them had tried, but every day they stayed seemed to lead them closer to suicide.

"Then the deaths started," the woman whispered. The lines on her old face strained with misery.

"Can you tell me anything about those?" he asked, putting his spare hand on his knee.

"Always families." The answer came from an old man hugging a shaman's staff. "They always go together to their deaths."

"Have you tried anything to deter these events?" Jinq asked

"We tried everything," the man said, sounding almost outraged, the first sign of emotion Jinq had seen beyond depression. "Catching them, locking them in, tying everyone up, and even putting family members in other places. Nothing works. They all end up at that tree, and they all end up dead."

"They always find a way around," the woman said hysterically.

"Calm yourself, Ester," the man commanded. Though his voice was firm, it lacked any confidence. "Your fits are not helpful."

She breathed in and out harshly, her breath catching. Jinq glanced between them, trying to assess the situation before considering their words. These were dark times indeed, and there was more at work in this little village than they knew. Jinq could feel their planet crying out.

"I need to return to my companions and tell them what I have learned here," Jinq said, standing, careful to keep Hibrius in hand.

"Even the Keeper is leaving us," the old man stated as he abruptly stood and ducked out of the large tent.

"I apologize," the man said, glancing after the elder, "Platos has not been the same since this began. He lost his daughter and grandchildren when their family killed themselves."

"It is understandable." Jinq put a hand up. "Do not worry, I will be camped in the plains just beyond your tree line. Tell Platos he is welcome to come to the tree line of Himota and see our tents for himself. We have no intention of leaving here without answers."

"Thank you." He managed a strained smile. He stood as Ester's breathing finally slowed.

Jinq nodded before walking from the tent and into the fading light. He strolled along the path and passed by many dejected faces. Their shoulders were hunched, their heads hung to watch their feet. None of them moved with any sort of confidence or hope. These were a hopeless people, waiting only for their time to die.

He followed the path until he reached the edge of the tree line. He turned south and followed it until he could see Mara. His small party sat watching the tree line with the tent set up behind them at the point where the gloom stopped. He would have them move it back a little further, just in case.

Kerrigan turned and waved when they were closer. He could see an unmistakable relief in her eyes, and he had to admit he felt relieved as well. This place had sapped his strength, and he felt exhausted from such a short visit. Kerrigan seemed on edge as she waited, with Cav asleep on her head and Mara's trunk draped over her shoulder.

"What happened?" Kerrigan asked the moment he was close enough to hear her.

"A family died," Jinq answered. "Something dark is happening here. I need my mirror."

"I'll get it!" she said and took off toward the tent.

Cav screeched and fell backwards off her head. Mara made an unhappy noise before backing away from the village and its gloom. Jinq gave it one last glance before making his way into the tent. When he entered, Mara lay down on her end and seemed to consider herself safe. Yet Jinq worried that none of them were.

Kerrigan carefully unwrapped a large circular mirror with intricate designs and markings on the wide frame. The markings allowed them to talk across long distances. Although mirrors were rare in Hystera, and meant a lifetime of bad luck if broken, they were the best means of communication.

He walked up to the mirror and put his thumb on a blank space. He waited patiently as the runes on the frame began to glow softly, powered by his life force. It wasn't long until the mirror stopped reflecting his face and started reflecting another's.

"Elder Rekis," the young boy on the other side said, "it has been some time."

"It has, Guardian," Jinq agreed. "Though I wish this time was with good news."

"You found something in Himota," the young boy said, leaning forward. "What is it?"

"I need a Seer," Jinq responded without answering his question. "There is something wrong with the land. I can feel it, but I cannot see it."

His face went dark. "Our Seers were killed."

Jinq frowned deeply in utter bafflement that all three of them could be dead. "How did they die?"

"Badly."

Jinq sighed, knowing the Guardian would say no more. "What about in the north?" He was hoping, but he knew the boy was thorough.

"Their two are dead as well," the young gate guardian responded with a frown. "Something is killing them."

"What about the other worlds?" he asked.

The boy nodded as he leaned forward. "The demon's girl, if she has somehow survived this, perhaps can be of use. I shall speak to Malthael at once."

"I need her," Jinq said, glancing over his shoulder toward the village before looking back to Troy. "And I need her soon."

Chapter 16: Ashlad

ϕ

Ki had found the woman with the kind eyes yet had discovered that she was beyond his ability. Perched on her room's inner window ledge, he tried to understand what had happened. His visions had been clear; this woman must die. With the boy safely tucked away, only the woman had been left and he would have completed his mission. Yet her soul was pure, and he could not harm her with his Sin Eater.

He would need to acquire another one; Ra had been clear that it was necessary for him to use a Soulfire weapon to save them. His visions had been clear that sin united the forty-two and that this was how he would fulfill his role as the savior of his people. Yet looking at her now as she peacefully slept, he wondered about—though didn't doubt—his mission. This woman would die by his blade. It was only a matter of time.

His few contacts in the Nether had given him some of the information he needed. She wasn't just a mortal; she was a half-breed. Apparently her father had been a Soul Collector and granted her a tumultuous existence. He could understand what it was like to be alone. He had his elders, yes, but they were not like him. Had their circumstances been different, he would have liked to know who she was and how she seemed unwilling to harm others. He was waiting here until he was sure the hounds were gone. He could do nothing with the girl tonight and she would be difficult to overcome, but he still needed to get that key.

He pushed the already cracked window the rest of the way open and carefully stepped inside. The key had worked wonders to allow him through the gate and beyond the magical wards. He pushed the window back to its original state and then crept along the room, glancing back only when she let out a sigh and rolled over. Her arm flopped back, and a cluster of loose shorter hair got free from her clip.

Instead of stopping, he continued into the house. He closed the door completely and moved down the stairs. He knew somewhere was the gate that led to the other worlds, but it posed little concern to him. Many came here for that, but not Ki. He held up the key Riku had given him and turned it slowly in a circle. When the screaming woman's eyes opened, he started walking. Her eyes opened whenever he was going the right way and closed when he was not. It led him down a hall filled with tapestries that all seemed to be watching him.

He heard someone nearby, so he stepped quickly until the screaming woman's eyes closed. He spun until they opened again on the large wooden door. He opened it and slipped inside. A smoldering fire burned in the fireplace, making the room almost unbearable. It reminded him of the constant heat of the Netherworld. Ki glanced around and then followed the screaming woman on the key to a bookshelf. He waved it around until the eyes opened on a large, leather-bound book.

He put the key in his pocket and lifted the book from its place, setting it on the desk behind him. The thick binding was heavier than he expected. He opened it. Inside was an assortment of skeleton keys. With a cringe, he thought of the picture on the skin parchment Riku had handed him, recalling the spokes and the diamond.

He searched the keys. Surprisingly, it didn't take him long to find the one he wanted. When his fingers wrapped around the key, though, he felt a jolt of electricity run through his body. His body seized up, and he knocked over the book as he collapsed. Keys scattered loudly across the floor as he started to have trouble breathing. His body continued to convulse and his grip on the key tightened. He tried to focus, but a disturbing feeling filled his chest and nothing seemed to work.

Oh no, he thought. He clenched his teeth as he realized what was happening.

For the first time Ki, the undying one, experienced death.

Ki woke with a start. At first his senses were filled with the silence and darkness. When they adjusted, he found himself gazing up at the moon. The chill of evening had set in, and he soon realized he was naked. Standing, Ki surveyed the area and recognized the forest. He was home, in Lyreane, and from the position of the mountains he was not far from where the secret cavern was located.

He started walking toward the mountain. Before long, he began to shiver. Everything seemed to shrivel up as he crossed his arms to conserve heat. The cold on his bare skin was not a pleasant feeling. The ground was unforgiving, and little cuts formed on his feet. Inevitably, the cold made them numb, so he walked faster. The cuts would heal eventually, and he did not wish to die and start over again.

Ki's shivering worsened as the temperature continued to drop, as his breath came out like pale chimney smoke. When he finally made it to the clearing, he found that the people who had been there before were now gone. Very few wanderers stayed long—it was as though they sensed the ugliness that happened there. He stared at the new growth from the summer and wondered if the trees remembered what had happened there—the violence that had befallen his people all those years ago. It would soon be frosted over, and the cycle of regrowth would continue next year. Over the years this clearing, built on blood and bones, would become part of the forest again. The genocide would be forgotten by everyone but him and the Black Council. *They* would be lost to history.

When he finally reached the rocky entrance, he realized belatedly that he didn't have the disk that would allow him entry. Ki tried calling out but no one came. Frowning, he looked up at the mountain's face and knew there was only one way to survive the cold. He would call on his Kemshi. He knelt down and scraped at the ground until he made a pile of loose dirt for the summoning.

On the ground he began marking out the Kemshi's name and a communication spell. Normally having the key, a runic disk the size of a coin, was enough, but the tiger was prideful and did not like being summoned in such a way. Had they been spirit partners, none of this would have been necessary, but the feline had never bonded with him before their village had been destroyed. Without the disk, he would have to appeal to the proud feline. When it was done, he stood and pressed his thumb into the mountain's jagged face, making it well up with blood. When he turned it over, it formed a perfect dome. Without hesitation, he pushed his thumb into the center of his markings and concentrated on the tiger. Through blue lips, he whispered the incantation.

In an instant, he was inside of the Kemshi. The tiger was in the forest hunting. When the connection was made, the tiger stopped for a moment and lifted his head like it was listening for something. Ki called out to it, but the feline's belly rumbled in defiance. Instead, it took off hunting again, and Ki's shaking body could hardly focus on the spell. His thumb was shifting back and forth, and he knew it wouldn't be long before he ruined the markings. Yet the Kemshi still ignored him. Eventually it saw a deer drinking from the stream. Ki saw and felt the tiger begin to prowl along the perimeter. The deer eventually lifted its head, and its long thin ears turned around like the perfectly adapted noise locaters they were. The tiger froze.

The deer returned to the stream and finished sating its thirst. Ki was so enraptured that he momentarily forgot about his own suffering and felt only the Kemshi's hunger deep in his gut as he crouched on the hard ground. Normally this wasn't an issue, but Ki had not considered his weakened state. Ki called to the Kemshi, trying to draw him back as he stalked the deer. The tiger's footfalls were silent and deadly. When the deer finally sensed its impending doom and tried to bolt, it was too late. The feline's massive paw connected with its hindquarter, causing the animal to be swept to the side. Before it could rebound, the tiger bit into the deer's neck, crushing it.

Ki was pulled out of the Kemshi, his shaking fingers having ruined the spell. Half frozen, he curled up into a ball. Breathing was becoming more difficult as his senses dulled. He could feel himself slowly freezing to death. Worse, Ki knew he would just start over again. The prospect was disheartening. He had never died before, so he'd never known how his inability to do so might work. Now he knew he would revive at that tree not far from where their village had been. He knew the story well and easily connected the dots. It was obvious that he'd have to reset every time he died and return to where it all began—where he had become the savior.

Soon Ki felt as though he was floating. He limply rested a hand on the wall. He was so close to salvation and yet so far. His limbs felt distant, and his eyelids began to grow heavy. He could no longer focus, his thoughts straining to form even a single word. The pain of dying last time returned to him as he slowly succumbed. Knowing he would regenerate wasn't much of a comfort.

Heat seared through his limbs. Just as he faded into a blissful sleep, though, something hit the ground above his head. He opened his eyes with a start and struggled to lift his head, but his body protested. The oversized tiger stood nearby over the crippled body of the deer. Blood and organs littered the ground, and parts of the deer were missing. The tiger's hot breath could be seen in the frosty evening. Their eyes met, and the Kemshi watched him with a cold impassivity.

The feline eventually began walking toward him. Too tired and cold to react, Ki curled himself back into a tight ball. The soft fur of the Kemshi pressed up against him, its great mass emitting an abundance of heat. It wasn't long until Ki stopped shaking, and the tiger lay his head down on Ki's shoulder. This was the closest thing to companionship that Ki had ever experienced, and he was loath to say he enjoyed it. The elders had always been around, but they had never been more than teachers.

As Ki fell asleep wrapped in the warmth of the Kemshi, thankful he wouldn't die a second time, he realized he had always been alone.

Chapter 17: Ashlad

—————————— φ ——————————

althael frowned as he discussed the unexpected attack with Meridith. She was a hard woman with a long history of careful planning, and she wouldn't hesitate when it came to protecting her planet. Yet the idea of the Netherworld's shrikes coming into the land of the living worried him. If they could escape, what else could come through? He didn't like to even consider the damage the Weavers could cause with their ability to spit acid.

"Something is disrupting the balance," Malthael responded, remembering what Zod had said.

"The number of unexplained occurrences lately is disturbing," she said, crossing her arms. "Have you had an attack within your house?"

"Yes." Malthael stood up straighter as he answered. "Did you?"

"A murder, actually," Meridith answered grimly. "Our Spiritwalker is dead."

"By a Sin Eater to the heart?" the demon asked with heavy worry.

"Yes," she answered, clearly unsettled. "He was stabbed in the heart. How do you know that?"

Malthael sighed. "Was his heart gone?"

Meridith paled. "Yes." Her voice sounded almost breathless.

"My daughter was attacked, and the assassin tried to kill her with a Sin Eater," Malthael explained. "I thought he was after her because of her abilities. It seems a larger game is afoot."

"Yes," she said with a deeper frown, "but who is pulling the strings?"

Before Malthael could consider forming a response, the gate's surface shimmered. Meridith's image shifted to make room for the face of a young boy. He looked pensive until the image cleared and his features hardened. He was clearly on a mission and did not look thrilled to see them already there. The dots along his hairline marked him for a youth of Hystera, but Malthael knew he was no child.

"What an unexpected pleasure," Troy said with no real enthusiasm. There were tired lines on his face and the edge of stress in his voice. "I

66

take it I am not alone." It wasn't a statement—there was no other reason they would gather.

Meridith asked, "What emergency brings you here, Troy?"

"We are in need of a Seer," Troy answered almost immediately. "One of our planet's Keepers has found a disturbance."

"Something out of balance?" Malthael asked and elicited a surprised look from Troy.

"I have a feeling there is something I am missing," the boy stated pointedly.

"Were the Seers of Hystera killed by a blade to the heart?" Meridith asked, though they both already suspected the answer.

"Yes, or at least where the heart should have been," Troy responded. "How did you know?"

"Sin Eater," Malthael surmised before he started to pace, his tail moving around of its own accord. "Why is this assassin killing those who can see the dead? What is the purpose of the Sin Eater?"

"What is a Sin Eater?" Troy asked, clearly lost.

"It is a blade forged in a volcano in the Netherworld, and its sole purpose is consuming the hearts of sinners," Malthael explained. "The orcs of old made Holy Blades in the Netherworld. The volcano is a mirror of the Ashy Mountains in Oran. Before the orcs were wiped out, they forged swords, the Sin Eaters, to try to destroy what was hunting them. It is the only place they can be made, and to my knowledge only six were forged. Without any living orcs, I do not know how a Sin Eater could be made."

"Who killed the orcs?" Troy interrupted, his demeanor that of an enthralled boy.

"I believe Ashladian texts called him the Black King," Malthael responded as he pondered. "Though he is known by many names, The Final Conqueror and The World Eater."

"We call him The Devouring One," Meridith added.

"The World Eater?" Troy said, his face stricken, "We call him that, but in many of our texts he is referred to as The Destroyer because of what he did."

"An accurate name," the reformed demon conceded. "Only the righteous can get anywhere near that volcano to dip weapons in the ash and create a Sin Eater. These swords were made when the Black King was banished so they would have weapons when they marched him into exile."

"They sound indestructible," Troy said with a worried expression.

"To the sinner, yes," Malthael said, "but a Sin Eater returns to ash when it tries to kill an innocent soul."

"There is one question I have," Meridith interjected. "It was always unclear to me what constitutes a sin."

"It depends," Malthael said with a shrug. "If you have ever purposely caused harm to another person in your life, you have sin. The Sin Eater needs more than a few infractions to work, though. Lying won't do it either. Easiest way, you need to take a life."

"Murder is the only way?" Troy demanded. "My Seer swore to harm nothing, yet this sword worked on him."

"It is an accumulation," he tried to explain, and then looked at Meridith. "What sins did your Spiritwalker commit throughout his life?"

"He was a soldier," Meridith said, clearing her throat. "I am sure there were many."

"This seems ridiculous," Troy finally said. "I am only twelve, but my decisions are sometimes those of life and death. Could this sword kill me?"

"I don't make the rules, Troy," he said with a frown. "Remember this came from the Netherworld, and the Black King was all powerful before his banishment. His magic was used to destroy the orcs, and the wild magic of the Netherworld makes anything forged there unpredictable."

"That still doesn't explain the shrikes," she reminded him, "or how they got here from the Netherworld."

"That I cannot speak to," Malthael responded honestly, "though I can say that the Det Mor Clan sent a representative who informed me that the spirit lines that exist across the worlds are out of balance."

"Is the imbalance caused by the death of the Seers?" the boy inquired.

"They were looking for the assassin. Apparently he has many souls within him, and he is likely your killer," Malthael explained, certain now that the assassin had hunted more before trying to kill Elisabeth. "They claim he is putting the worlds out of balance. So many souls shouldn't exist in one place."

"He is killing those who can see the dead, yet your daughter survived," Meridith said. "She is half Soul Collector like the rest, but the Sin Eater didn't take her. Why?"

"It does not matter what is in her blood. Elisabeth has never taken a life and has devoted her own life to helping others," Malthael responded proudly. "The sword turned to ash."

68

"I and my Keeper are in need of her services," Troy stated abruptly. "I have a feeling this is all connected."

"We need to gather all the Guardians," Meridith declared, raising her head. "Your daughter is the last of our Spiritwalkers that we know of, and we cannot all utilize her at once. She should stay in Ashlad until the meeting. We can present our cases when we are all together. It is unfair to exclude the others from this important decision."

"We do not have time to wait," Troy argued. "We need to know what your daughter sees. Our Keeper feels the planet weakening."

"Enough!" Malthael yelled, cutting his hand through the air. "My daughter is not connected to this at all! She has no obligation to any of you."

"Ask her," Troy responded calmly. "If she is as good as you think she is, I believe she will choose wisely."

"Set the meeting. I can promise nothing else," Malthael growled before pulling the dial out from the wall. The gate returned to stone.

He was fuming as he walked up the stairs and shoved the stone slab open, nearly breaking it off the hinges. Stomping into the study, he pushed the massive door closed himself instead of using the switch just to burn off his excess energy. As he left the study, he realized that something wasn't quite right. Slowly turning back, he saw his book of his keys was open on a side desk with its contents strewn across the floor. Not far from them, gathered in a pool on the ground, was a pile of clothes.

It had not been there before he had gone down to the gate. He bent over and lifted the clothes, startled when things fell out and onto the floor. They clanged and jangled, sounding like more keys, but he realized it was a bunch of knives. With dread, he wondered if there was a man running around his house without his clothes on. He summoned Nathan and Duke to find out.

Chapter 18: Oran

──────────── φ ────────────

Princess Nanette watched the water move around the small pool in the garden. Blue fish that weren't actually blue—just reflecting the light fragmentation of the water—swam around. She watched them with dull interest and waited. She knew all too well what it was like to be a gray fish that everyone believed was a beautiful blue one. It was every girl's dream to become a princess, to attend balls, and marry the handsome prince. Her younger self had thought so, but that dream had soon faded.

She was married to a man who had absolutely no interest in her. It was fair to say she had only been a young, fascinated girl looking wide-eyed at a prince when they first met. She always wondered if it was her good luck or bad that her father had been chosen by the gate to be its Guardian.

Her silk robe was held in place by a thick sash at her waist. The robes were straight lined, the hem at her ankles. It had a high, attached collar and wide sleeves that fell to her knees. Yet it was the complex pattern that was painted onto the outfit that made it beautiful. A score of pink and white blossoms decorated the full length of the dress in a fetching pattern. Every day now felt she was dressed for a celebration. It was royal attire for a Butterfly Princess—the term to describe a commoner who had married a prince.

Watching the fish made her think of her sister Yuna and how fortunate she had been to marry before the gate had chosen. Before her sister had married their new friend, Tidus, Nanette had thought *she* was going to marry him. How foolish she had been, yet she could not hate them, even for her fate of a loveless marriage, because Yuna and Tidus were truly in love.

She glanced around the garden, but the flowers held no appeal. The women at court who were in similarly arranged marriages had told her she would love her children. They would distract her, they said, and her husband would do whatever he wished. The idea did not sit well with her.

Sometimes she dreamed of running away and living her own life. But she had no wealth or money to fund her freedom, so she stayed.

Before her father had become the Gate Guardian, they had been poor merchants, barely making ends meet. Her father had lost most of his money when Nanette was very young, and so she remembered only poverty. Yuna was three years older and she remembered their happy mother and fine dresses.

Their mother had had particular needs, most of which Nanette was too young to remember. When their father couldn't provide them, she'd left. Abandonment had cut Yuna deeper, because she remembered their mother. Nanette was sometimes glad she knew neither their lost wealth nor their selfish mother. Their father had had enough to keep the small print shop going, living on paper and ink, and the generosity of others. He'd liked to think they lived on stories, but she had never endeavored to comfort herself with that level of creativity because all she had felt was hunger.

Now she stood there in the garden as a princess married to the fourth prince of Jord and well secured in her wealth and position. Who would have thought that little starving Ettie would become Princess Nanette of Jord, kingdom of one of the great islands? Certainly not Nanette herself. Though she was grateful to not be starving and to have fine dresses, her happiness had died the day Tidus and Yuna had announced their engagement.

Tidus had been a great warrior, the Great Protector of Jord, who had come to buy a book of maps from their father. Nanette could still remember the way the sun had shone off his straw-colored hair. It had seemed like gold in the sunlight. His smile had warmed her and his words had amused her, but in the end he'd chosen her saccharine sister. The past was what it was.

"Nanette?" Prince Jason asked, his face neutral.

She turned very carefully, making the shoes and clothes appear to be a natural fit for her, though she still felt out of place—like a false princess, even though months had passed since her marriage. To her the clothes were a mask, but one that did little to hid her true face, that of a commoner. A simple gray fish pretending to be blue but who knew its own color.

"Are we ready?" Nanette asked.

"I am," he replied shortly before turning. "I said your name multiple times."

"I apologize. I was lost in thought," Nanette said and took one step away from the pond.

She felt something cold and wet slide around her ankle. Quickly looking down, she was horrified to see a tentacle pulling taunt. She fell straight to the ground, hitting her chin on the cobblestone path. Pain exploded in her face, and she heard the terrible crunch as her teeth broke on themselves. The Prince cried out and backed away, yelling for help but doing nothing to aid her himself.

Her legs went into the water first. She screamed, trying to keep hold of the slick rocks to prevent herself from going under. Despite her efforts, her strength was no match for whatever monster clung to her ankle. Before it pulled her completely under, she took a deep breath. Under the water, she opened her eyes to see a circular silhouette at the bottom with multiple tentacles. It opened its mouth, revealing rows of tiny sharp teeth. She kicked to fight it, but it did not let go.

Despite the blind panic, a thought occurred to her. She reached up into her hair and pulled out one of the two decorative sticks. Nanette gripped the hair adornment in her fist and, at the same time, pulled up on the leg the creature held. When the tentacle was close enough, she stabbed it with all her might. The creature let her go, and the other tentacles retreated to the large mass. Nanette clawed for the surface, her lungs burning for air. She kicked so hard that her silly shoes fell off.

She burst through the surface, taking in a long gasp of sweet air, and then quickly pulled herself over onto the slick rocks. Her heart was pounding and she was terrified that she would feel another slimy tentacle wrap around her ankle. She flung herself up onto the shore and scrambled quickly away, putting as much distance between her and the water as possible. Landing on her stomach several yards away, she tried to catch her breath.

She realized, suddenly, that she was lying on dirt rather than soft grass, and she slowly looked up. The palace that had just been pristine minutes ago was now in ruins.

She knelt, water dripping off of her, and stared in confusion. She couldn't understand what she was seeing. Forcing herself to stand, she rested her shoulder against a rust colored pillar that had once been gold and then turned to the sky. A red light spread across the land in a dull continuous drone. There was no sun, no blue sky.

Nanette swallowed nervously as she looked around at this strange land and feared she knew exactly where she was. Only one place had a red sun illuminating a ruined landscape—the Netherworld.

Chapter 19: Ashlad

φ

*E*lisabeth listened to Malthael explain what had happened, a sense of dread filling her. He had told her stories of the Netherworld and its strange monsters. Some of the most frightening things there were harmless, and some of the sweetest looking things were vicious. Shrikes also existed on the planets and were known as "butcher birds" for a reason. Normally their prey consisted of mice, but it seemed their counterparts in the Netherworld had even larger appetites. Not everything was different in the Netherworld, but when it was, it was rarely better.

"That poor man," Elisabeth said when he finished. "And what of this Keeper? What do you know of him?"

"I do not know Jinq," Malthael admitted, leaning back, "but through Troy I know *of* him."

"Is he a good and honest man?" Elisabeth asked, watching her papa closely. "Is this where we should put our attention?"

"The Det Mor Clan is looking for your assassin," he said, putting a hand on her arm. "I do not want to ask this of you because using your gift makes you susceptible, but Jinq Rekis is known to be a willful but good man."

Elisabeth considered this. She never had viewed her ability as valuable. She was likely the last of her kind, and every decision she made would result in one of the Gate Guardians waiting. She could not deny that part of her was terrified that this was leading to her own doom. Every time she used her curse, she felt it get more and more out of control. Even a simple brush of hands had her demon half wanting to feed, wanting to take the mortal soul. Only her assassin had been immune.

After a moment, she lifted her head and answered, "I would like to meet the rest of the Gate Guardians and hear what they have to say. I have only heard one person's need for a Seer. It would be unwise not to assess other issues among the other planets."

Malthael studied her face a moment before smiling slightly. "I agree. You should meet those who ask for your help. We'll meet tomorrow in the early morning."

They both stood. The study did little to comfort her as he turned toward the hidden entrance. Elisabeth's heart began to pound in anticipation as he stared at the lone tapestry. She was beginning to realize that her cozy life was coming to an end and there was nothing she could do about it. It made her feel small and helpless, like she was being swept along. It didn't matter that she could see spirits and pull souls from the living. What mattered was that she'd never truly been alone. Tiss, Milo, or Malthael were always with her.

"I should like to go out," Elisabeth said.

Her father turned. "Out? To where?"

"If I am to leave home, I want to see a part of a world that I've dreamed of for years," she said almost breathlessly, "and I'd like to go alone."

"You've never mentioned this to me," Malthael said, startled. "Where do you wish to go?"

"We all have our secret wishes, Papa," Elisabeth said and took his arm in her hands. "I've always wanted to see my mother's childhood home."

He straightened, looking stricken. "Your mother isn't from Ashlad."

"I know," she muttered softly before putting her hands out to her sides. "I'll be back before tomorrow morning."

"Take Duke and Nathan," Malthael insisted.

Elisabeth cleared her throat. "And only them?"

Her father seemed to consider it before nodding solemnly. Nathan and Duke were quick to appear. As she sunk into the ground, she imagined what her life would have been like if she had stayed in Lyreane. Malthael had said that those with blond hair were coveted because they were considered to be touched by light. She rarely spoke to Malthael about her mother because it seemed to be one of the few subjects that caused him pain. When she was old enough, he had given her a box of Serena's things. Amongst the belongings Elisabeth had found the deed for a cottage and a portrait of her mother as a young girl.

Traveling along the spirit lines always felt like falling, like she was sinking slowly down a long hole. Using the spirit world as a passage point was not common. Only the dead and Soul Collectors frequented it. She couldn't wander in it herself, but required a guide—which is what Nathan and Duke were for. They were used as guards in the Netherworld and had been Malthael's faithful dogs for ages. Though they had been unwilling to part with him, eventually they'd had become attached to Elisabeth by default. It was the only reason she could summon them.

When she opened her eyes, a snowflake touched her cheek. She raised her head as they materialized outside a small cottage, her boots immediately sinking into the snow. She stood next to the frozen pond and ignored the chill as she looked over at the simple house. It was hard to imagine that her mother had been born in this house—it was unremarkable.

Elisabeth had wanted to come here sooner but had always been too afraid. Now she needed to be brave. As she stared at the neglected cottage, she wasn't sure what she'd expected by coming there. It wasn't this, yet she wasn't disappointed. She took her hands off Nathan and Duke and proceeded to the white fence. The snow crunched under her shoes. A twig snapped nearby, and she froze.

Slowly turning her head, she spotted a deer. Its white spots shone bright against its brown hide and almost seemed to glow in the white light. Beginning to shiver, she stuck her hands into the pockets of her coat, grateful that she had worn such a warm one. Foolishly, she hadn't considered weather when she'd decided to come here. Elisabeth was rarely impulsive, but if she hadn't just come at that moment, she feared she never would have.

Ever since Malthael had given her the deed, she had put off coming here, focusing on her work or anything else. Concentrating on A.J. and making his life better—anything to forget who and what she was. She pushed the gate open, and it protested from lack of use. It opened a foot or so before refusing to open any further, no matter how much she shoved at it.

Frowning, but unwilling to do damage, she slipped around it. Her skirts barely fit, but she managed and walked up to the door. She stopped just short of the porch steps, unsure what to do next. She didn't have the key with her. She had just wanted to see the house, but now the need to know where she had come from drove her further. She put a hand out and Nathan appeared at her side. They passed through the walls together.

It was dimly lit inside, but she could see old rugs on the floor and simple decorations on the walls. The floorboards were worn and covered in a soft layer of dust. She kept her hand on Nathan even though they had rematerialized.

To the left was a small dining area with a door that likely led to the kitchen, and there was a small living room to the right. There were dishes on display above the window and a cabinet that likely had more. In the living room she could see an old loveseat. Bugs had found their way into it, and much of the edges had been frayed. This place had been empty for some time, but not twenty-five years. It made her wonder if she would have met family had she returned sooner. Malthael said she had grandparents, but he had told her it was too dangerous to see them because of what she was. It was safer for them to never know she existed. Elisabeth knew he had been right, but part of her wondered: Would they have loved her and accepted her?

She ignored the hallway in front of her that had two doors, one to the left and one to the right. Instead she walked down the hall to her left that led into the kitchen. It was mostly maintained and was made of good solid wood, but even that wasn't completely intact. She was afraid to touch anything, as she felt sure it would vanish or fall apart. Instead she left it as it was: a tomb of her mother's memories.

When she reached the back door, her arm went out and Nathan appeared beside her again. The back area looked like it had once been a vegetable garden. Berry bushes crowded against the back fence, but most of the yard was snow-covered, empty garden beds. In the middle was a great tree, one likely to produce fruit in the summer. Now, in this frozen season, it just looked barren.

Elisabeth wandered amongst the garden beds with Nathan at her side. When she came to a high gate with a secure lock, she touched Nathan's back so they could pass through it. On the other side she stopped, startled by what she saw. There were seven headstones, all with caps of snow piled an inch high. The one right in front of her bore her mother's name. Beside them were two names she didn't recognize. Likely her mother's parents, but she couldn't be sure.

Elisabeth crouched down and touched her mother's cold headstone. It sat neglected, but enduring, with *Serena* written across in curly scrawl. Studying her hand a moment, she wondered if she had it in her to be courageous like her mother. No last name because she had birthed a child without a husband. In Lyreane, men owned their women, much like on the planet of Oran. If a woman lay with a man and had a child while unmarried, she could not keep her maiden name. Glancing down, she wondered if Malthael had brought her mother's body back here or if they had buried an empty casket. With a sigh, she returned to the frozen garden.

While considering what to do next, she caught a flicker of white out of the corner of her eye and turned back to the window. Her eyes raked over it, but there was nothing there, only her own reflection in the center of a frosted glass. Perhaps it had been a trick of the light. Either that or the eeriness of the hollow place was getting to her.

Blinking back tears, Elisabeth walked around the house without looking back. She slipped through the front gate again and pulled it closed before walking down the lane. Just beyond the cottage road was a main road that would lead her to the small town. As she lifted her arms to summon Nathan and Duke, she looked down and saw the snow moving like a billowing smoke. It took her a moment to realize that a layer of fog was rolling down the lane. Her eyes narrowed as it seemed to grow as tall as her.

She turned and walked down the cottage road, stuffing her hands in her pockets for warmth. Her fisted hands in her pockets began to sweat a little with nervous tension, and her stomach filled with worry. Something was itching at her brain. Somewhere in her mind a memory was trying to surface, a specific detail she was trying to recall. Standing in the road staring at the odd development of thick vapor, she was comforted by Duke and Nathan's presence. She was sure it would not form like this in the middle of the day, in the middle of the road. Soon, though, it was rolling against her knees, obscuring her feet entirely from view. She heard a clicking noise.

Elisabeth stopped breathing and remembered what was bothering her. She took a step back as the something in the fog clicked again. At the edge she could see long spikes, organic but engrained with steel. Suddenly, she heard a thunder of horse's hooves, and the thick mist rose up to her waist. A horse and driverless carriage hurtled toward her, but the horse fell to its knees and gave a strangled cry. A giant spider-like creature jumped clear from the top of the carriage and back into the safety of the fog. Elisabeth's eyes widened and she did the only thing her mind could comprehend. She screamed.

Chapter 20: Hystera

φ

Kerrigan slept fitfully, just as every member of their party had done the last two nights since their talk with Troy. Beside her, Cav dozed softly, breathing in and loudly breathing out. He made soft hooting noises every time he exhaled, which normally gave Kerrigan comfort. Instead, though, she twisted in her covers tonight. The warmth of the day did little to help with the chill of the evening, and their tent didn't seem to be helping as much as it normally did.

Her dreams were nightmares, and her skin was covered with uneasy perspiration as she tried to wake herself. Her blood felt thick, as though it were turning to sap, and yet she still could not wake up. Empty faces were whispering unclear words to her. Her head turned one way and then another until she could finally make them out.

"Kerrigan," the woman's voice said.

Her eyes shot open, and she sat up. Thankfully, Jinq slept through her startled gasp, and she made no further noise. Glancing at Cav, who slept peacefully, she pulled at the blankets to cover herself better. She was about to turn over and return to sleep when she heard her name again. A shadow crossed in front of the door.

She quickly pulled her sheathed knife from under her pillow and crept along the flattened grass before throwing open the tent flap, but there was no one there. Baffled, she stepped out into the sea of pale grass. The light of the large moon winked at her from behind some wispy clouds. It was full, so everything about the plains was clear to see.

"Kerrigan," came on the wind again, and she spun to her right to see a woman reaching for her.

"Mother?" she whispered, shocked, her blood running cold.

"Come," she whispered, her sweet face beckoning as she floated toward the tree line around the village.

This is impossible, Kerrigan thought.

She stood transfixed but decided it couldn't be her mother. Even if it was, Kerrigan shouldn't be able to see her, as she wasn't a Seer. The only explanation that Kerrigan could come up with was that she was still asleep. Trying to will herself awake to no avail, she turned back to see if

Jinq would wake and join her. This time, her mother's voice was urgent. Feeling lightheaded, she let the words sing all worry away. She slowly walked across the grass. Her underlayers were not enough to fight against the cold, yet she barely felt it.

"Mother, where are you going?" Kerrigan asked as the woman turned to face her. Her eyes were serene as they met hers. Her mother moved into the tree line without hesitation.

The wispy shape of her form shone a pale white against the shadowed woods. The trees were tall and thick, but Kerrigan moved around them with ease. Their roots would normally have tripped her, but the full moonlight was enough to keep her from falling. They emerged into a wide field with a single great tree in the middle.

Her mother seemed more solid now, as though she were really there. Her form was kneeling by the tree and humming as she used a broken branch to carve something into the ground. Kerrigan hesitated only a moment before she walked across the open area, curious to see what her mother was doing. As she drew closer, she realized she was drawing letters, but so far it only said 'roat.'

"Will you make the first letter?" she asked, gesturing toward the 'r' as she worried the sticks into the ground.

"I don't know what it is supposed to be," Kerrigan said, shaking her head.

"Silly girl," her mother said. "Let me show you."

Kerrigan knelt across from her mother, who still hummed. Kerrigan leaned forward with one hand on the ground and the knife sheathed in the other. Her mother carved the first letter deep. Kerrigan was mesmerized as the final letter was finished and her mother looked up with a happy expression.

"There we are," she said.

Kerrigan read the word as she heard the stick break. When she looked back, her breath caught in her throat. Her mother's face was hideously deformed, and her entire body seemed to be on fire. Her lips were curled back from her teeth, and her eyes glowed red. Kerrigan screamed, but the scream was cut short when her mother thrust the jagged broken stick ends straight down into Kerrigan's hands and into the ground, pinning them. White hot flashes of pain shot up her arms, and tears welled in her eyes. She tried to pull away, but her mother kept her hands rooted in the dirt.

"Know it, because it knows you," she hissed, her voice filled with anguish. "He is coming."

Kerrigan screamed and woke up back in the tent. She sat up immediately and looked down at her hands. They were shaking badly but otherwise unharmed. Cav suddenly flew into her hair. Kerrigan gave a startled cry and quickly rolled away from him. Her throat felt dry as she disentangled from him. Standing on the floor, he cooed at her, looking worried, as she panted and tears streamed down her face.

"Kerrigan?" Jinq's voice asked her from outside the tent. A moment later he appeared in the entryway.

"I'm sorry," she said, pulling Cav against her chest. "I had a nightmare."

Jinq's eyes narrowed thoughtfully, but he didn't push the issue. Instead, he glanced back toward the village. Kerrigan did everything she could to calm herself, but her breaths kept coming in ragged gasps. Even though she wasn't hurt, her hands stung as though she really did have sticks in them.

"Go back to sleep," Jinq finally said. She barely nodded before she turned over and tried to return to slumber.

Yet sleep did not come to her as she released Cav and let him crawl up onto the pillow to doze against her forehead. His feathers tickled but she ignored it, her body too taxed to care. Instead, her entire being was focused on the dream. She could remember everything as though it had really happened, but the one thing that stuck out the most was the word her mother had carved into the ground. When she closed her eyes, she saw the word carved into her mind: *Croatoan*.

Chapter 21: Lyreane

ϕ

Ki awoke to the Kemshi dragging him. He gave a startled cry when he landed hard on the ground next to his bed. He sat up, and the tiger gave him a pointed stare with the covers still in his mouth. Since the night of his first death, Ki had slept. The elders thought it was because his body was adjusting. He thought it was because he had almost frozen to death again afterward.

Ki glared at the Kemshi, who dropped his bedding. They sat like that, Ki with one arm on his bed and the tiger with the pile of blankets at his feet. Neither moved for a moment as the tiger's ears flicked back and forth. Ki narrowed his eyes thoughtfully, realizing the Kemshi was trying to tell him something.

"What is it?" he asked, standing when he felt a tingling sensation pass over him.

The woman's face, his last target, flashed before his eyes. She looked terrified. The Kemshi turned toward the door. Pulling on some clothes and boots and picking up his weapons, Ki rushed over to the tiger. He jumped on its back and they rocketed out of the room. One of the elders flattened himself against the wall as they barreled by. The elder tried calling after them, but he was ignored by both mount and rider as they continued through the temple.

If the woman died by another means, then his sword would not consume her sins. Without a new sword and without a sin on her soul, he could not save her. Her spirit would not be freed from its demonic burden; he could not release it.

They burst out of the side of the mountain, the tiger moving recklessly along the rocky face. Ki held on and watched as the waterfall drew nearer. The rocks became slick, but his Kemshi was surefooted. When they reached the edge, the Kemshi jumped from the ledge. The waterfall thundered next to them as they plunged into the lake.

The next thing he knew, they were breaking through ice.

The cold settled in, its bitterness only amplified by the water. Ki pushed himself off the tiger and surfaced, resting his elbows on the shore as he glanced around to try to get his bearings. Reaching back, he helped the struggling tiger get its first two paws up onto solid ground as well. Heaving himself out, Ki tried not to dwell on the memories of nearly freezing to death. Once he knew the Kemshi was safely out of the water, Ki saw the fog.

He ran down the road, reaching the edge as a carriage breached and another scream filled the air. Ki watched as a Weaver leapt from the top of the coach. The horse gave a terrible cry. Ignoring everything else, Ki threw himself at her, unsure if he was in time. He heard the carriage crash as he tackled the woman to the ground.

She gave a surprised cry as he collided with her. He glanced down at her and saw she was on her side under him. He could smell her, sweet and feminine, and her almost red lips were slightly parted in shock. Her blue eyes were open wide, and her mouth open even wider.

"Get up," he said, all but hauling her to her feet.

The fog clicked as the horse's carcass was dragged away. When she opened her mouth, he covered it in case she was going to scream. She stopped instantly, quick to catch on. She stood there shaking next to him, but she didn't run even when he removed his hand.

The woman jumped when a shadow appeared but pressed her own hands to her mouth, stifling a gasp. The great tiger stopped when it saw her, and her hands fell away. Some silent conversation seemed to pass between them as her hands went to her sides. After a moment, the two hounds he had seen at the university appeared. He expected her to leave, but instead she turned to him, nodding her gratitude but still looking suspicious.

When the dogs saw him, their tails went up in a defensive position and he expected them to attack. Instead, the woman pointed two fingers in the direction of the Weavers and they turned, their ribbon tails visible as they went into the fog. Ki glanced around as the Kemshi came to his side, but he saw nothing. The silence stretched out, and he could see that she was still shaking slightly. Despite her earlier useless screaming, she'd calmed down enough to be alert and was scanning the fog.

With a sudden screech, a Weaver jumped toward them. Two ribbon tails shot out in unison as the tiger roared. The blades of the hounds sliced across the metal hide of the beast. Most of their blows were deflected, but one managed to strike the Weaver in its soft underbelly. Ki pulled the short dagger from his belt, having been fearful to pull it out earlier lest the polished blade give him away, and stepped forward. He thrust the blade into its eye. Green discharge spewed from the injury. The dying Weaver spat its noxious venom, which Ki deftly dodged.

The acid melted into the dirt, and already the fog was starting to disperse, but it wasn't gone entirely. The Weaver pushed itself up and tried to flee, but the tiger dove and clawed its underbelly, ripping the creature open. Its guts littered the road now, and its only movement was the twitching of its leg.

The woman gave a sigh of relief, and Ki put the dagger back into its holder as the fog fully dissipated. He glanced to the right and yelled as a Weaver screeched and landed loudly in front of him. The woman let out a short scream and fell backward as the Netherhounds lashed out once again, their tails slicing through the air above her head. The dagger left Ki's hand and buried itself in the side of the Weaver's head.

The Kemshi leapt in front of him and started to drag the woman back by her collar. Acid hit the street a second later, right where she had fallen. Sunlight breached the fog and burned the creature's leg. The Weaver screeched before it scurried away.

"Thank you, Ashley," the woman said breathlessly, and put a hand on the Kemshi.

"Who is Ashley?" Ki asked.

The woman looked up at him, both worried and confused. "Your spirit companion." She used the tiger's shoulder to get to her feet.

"But he is a boy," Ki said, looking at the tiger, who peered at him with annoyance.

"Are you telling me you didn't know his name?" she asked.

"No," he said, unabashed.

They stared at each other, and the awkwardness settled in. Ki expected her to run like a scared rabbit. Instead, she straightened her back and looked at him inquisitively. He'd done his duty, keeping her alive so that he might kill her later. So now he should leave. Ki gazed at the tiger. Ashley seemed to be enjoying the woman's affection. His head was turned to the side, bumping her leg, and he made no move to leave her.

"Why did you save me?" she finally asked.

"Your life can end no other way than my blade," he answered honestly. The Kemshi straightened when she stopped petting him.

She gave him a startled look, following by an appraising gaze. "Were it not for your intent, your single mindedness might be impressive." Her words were biting as she moved away from the tiger and back to her Netherhounds. "I will never sin enough that your sword will work. Give up your endeavor."

"I cannot."

The Netherhounds made a rude noise at him as the woman touched their backs. All three vanished. Ki stood watching the spot where she had been and wondered how long it would take her to break. He was going to have to keep a close eye on her so that she didn't get herself killed before he could do it himself.

Chapter 22: Netherworld

φ

*T*his place was getting darker by the minute, and Nanette could feel something watching her. It made her hair stand on end. As she wandered into the wreckage of the building behind her, she heard the wind sing. She had expected it to wail through this place, but instead it sung like an icy lake. It was unnerving to be so afraid and yet have the building whistle almost merrily at her.

She wanted to cry, but knew, even as old streaks of tears covered her cheeks, that more than anything she needed to hide. With every minute that passed, the red light that basked over the land was fading. She had looked for the light source, like a sun, but it just was an endless drone of red. As a child, her father had read her stories about things that came out of the Netherworld to take bad children away. She didn't know exactly what would come for her, but she knew that unless she hid, she wouldn't last the night.

Nanette picked her away across the ruins, tumbled pillars and broken doorways, trying to find a place that could offer her shelter. Oddly, she didn't feel cold despite her wet clothes. She had always imagined the Netherworld, with its heatless light, would be cold. Instead it was strangely arid, and Nanette worried she would need something to drink soon.

She stepped down into what had been the large dining area and ballroom in her world. She had only been in this building once, and that visit had been to this room. Despite the light cast through the fractured ceiling, she recognized the domed shape, which was a similar—but decaying—version of the one she knew. As she watched dust dance in the reddish hue, Nanette wondered if she would ever see the sun again.

Glancing around, she noted that the tall ceiling was held up by four pillars. The other two had fallen over, leaning precariously against another one that had shifted slightly but still remained upright. The entire roof looked ready to collapse. Perhaps instead of hiding, she should get to a high place. It was an alternative if she ran out of time to find a hiding place; she could already tell the light was leaving her.

85

She ambled over more rubble before stepping into a clear part in the room. Kneeling down, she ran a hand over the dust. There, she could see where the perfect decorative flooring remained mostly intact underneath. Moving around the room, she approached a darkened area where the doorway was mostly blocked by a broken stone bookcase. Frowning, she crawled up to see if she could push through. She heard a strange clicking behind her and she moved, startled, closer to the door, her hands resting on the rocks as she tried to peer into the hallway to find sanctuary. She narrowed her eyes but saw nothing readily available. Suddenly, a series of clicks responded to the first in the darkened space in front of her.

Before she could react, something slammed against the rubble, making her screech and fall back. Nanette landed hard, the wind knocked out of her. She gasped a loud painful breath of air and groaned. With barely enough time to comprehend her situation, she heard another thudding noise and a scraping sound of stone on stone. As she quickly rolled onto her side, she saw loose debris start to roll down the pile. Nanette shifted away just as a rock landed right where her foot had been— one that no doubt would have crushed her ankle.

Nanette's eyes widened when a head came through the new opening from inside of the pile. Rows of beady eyes stared at her, and bile rose up in her throat. Its legs frantically dug through the debris that kept it trapped as Nanette struggled to stand. It was some sort of giant metallic spider.

Wobbling, she nearly fell over as she staggered over to the partially fallen pillar. Behind her, more creatures' ticking noises joined the first. The creatures screamed at her, and the whole ruin shook from their struggle to get free. Dust filled the air, making her cough as she pulled herself onto the diagonal column. She tried to keep from crying, but the tears fell anyway. Nanette was halfway up when they burst through the blocked doorway.

Biting back a scream, she scrambled up the column and onto another one that leaned against the wall for support. One of the spiders saw her and clicked away, its metal feet hurrying across the floor. She stifled another shriek as it started up after her. Others below her awaited her fall. The pillar shifted slightly, and she threw her arms around it, trying to keep hold. The spider-like creatures gouged part of the stone with their metal armored legs, but Nanette saw the one behind her was struggling to follow her. One spat at her, but it missed her as she continued up. Solid stone turned into wax where the creature's acid had landed. Nanette sobbed as she struggled to pull herself up along the column, her arms trembling so hard that it was difficult to even hold the stone anymore. Her nails scraped along the column and broke in her desperation.

Nanette glanced back and screamed at how close the creature had gotten. As her hands connected with the top of the column, the creature scraped the back of her calf. She gave a cry as a flash of burning pain shot so deep into her leg that she imagined in horror that her bone was exposed. Blood flowed freely, staining the hem of her dress and the pristine white stone. Suddenly, the creature jumped toward her.

Her grip slipped, and she fell off to the side as the creature slammed into where she had been. The crossed columns gave way under the weight of the spider. She smacked against the ground as another fell. Nanette heard stone scrape again stone in a thunderous crash as the creatures screamed. She coughed and rolled onto her side to try to calm herself down and catch her breath. In the dust, one of the creatures was pulverized by stone as the other half of the ceiling caved in. Hunks of metal and goo flew in every direction, some landing with a sickening splat next to her as she tried to blink the dusty haze from her eyes.

Her breathing shuddered as the light began to fade. Only two columns and the ceiling remained on her side of the room. When the last rock fell, the room filled with silence. Her hair had come completely free and fell in front of her face as she pushed herself into a sitting position. Nanette was about to stand up when something jumped out of the dust and flew over her head.

Nanette screamed as the injured spider-creature collided with the wall behind her. More of the wall gave way, crashing against two destroyed pillars. They had created a cave during the collapse, one the width of the pillar and a little deeper where a chunk of the ceiling had fallen in. With only a second's thought, she began to pull herself toward it. Behind her, the creature began to get to its feet, but two back legs had been pulverized during the collapse, which hindered its movement. When it screeched at her she gasped, but she pulled herself into the hole. She was nearly to the back when the beast jammed its leg after her. The metal tip scraped against her already maimed calf, and her flesh burned where it cut through. She pressed her back against the furthest point as it spat at her.

The room was so dark that she barely noticed the floor next to her fizzle. The acidic smoke it gave off filled her nostrils, making her gag. The creature rammed against the pillar, causing dust to fill her sanctuary. It scraped desperately at the entrance, but it was too large to fit. Nanette curled into a ball with her knees under her chin and started to cry. Her leg burned in both places from the creature's attacks, and she shook from the pain and the terror. It wasn't long before the darkness of the night was absolute and she passed out, listening to the creature try to claw its way to her.

Chapter 23: Ashlad

———————————— φ ————————————

althael watched as face after face appeared in the viscous entrance of the gate: the old man of Oran, the stern Meridith of Tym Resh, the boy Troy with his light Hysteri dots, and the half-blind goddess-like woman of Lyreane. All five of them had never gathered outside of their schedule before; it was strange to see them all now. It made what was happening all that more worrisome. The reformed demon glanced behind him, wondering where his daughter was.

"What did the Seer decide?" Troy asked when the last had arrived.

"She has agreed to meet with you to consider all of your concerns," Malthael said, but he was distracted by the appearance of the Orani gate keeper. "Ruhan, you look exhausted."

"We had an attack." Ruhan's old voice cracked. "My daughter is missing."

The old man turned away, but Malthael could see the sobs rack his shoulders. The other guardians bowed their heads at the news; even Meridith's stern expression showed empathy. A sad silence fell, and Malthael knew words would not comfort a grieving father.

"When?" Elisabeth's voice broke the silence.

Malthael spun around at her voice, ready to scold her for being late, but stopped when he saw the state she was in. Her clothes were dusty, and there was dirt smeared across her cheek. Her hair was wild, and the clip that normally kept it securely in place was gone. He looked at the guardian dogs, Duke and Nathan, and saw they had some sort of strange goop on them.

"Elsa?" he asked in a hushed voice.

She smiled softly at him, her eyes a little dull and worn, but she seemed resolved to have this meeting. He had never remembered her looking so self-assured. Her head was raised, and there was a new sense of assurance in her step as she moved to stand beside him. Nathan and Duke vanished again as all eyes turned to his adopted daughter.

"Two days ago," the Orani Keeper managed.

"What else?" Elisabeth asked, looking from one face to another.

Troy cleared his throat. "In Hystera, our Keeper, the one in tune with our planet, has found a disturbance in the harmony of our world. Our people are killing themselves, and Jinq believes more is to come if you do not see to them."

"We have had attacks," Meridith stated next. "We have lost people to creatures from the Netherworld. Their relatives have come to the church for answers, and they turned to us. We need some way to track these attacks."

Malthael interjected, "I can work on that, Meridith. It may take some time, but I believe I know a way."

"We have had two attacks in Lyreane," Emera said. "A Nightmare brutalized a band of wanderers and killed most of them before they could flee. A second creature took down a ship at sea. Most survived."

Elisabeth nodded before looking to Malthael. "Papa?"

"I sent Gog out to gather information across Ashlad. There has only been one attack here so far. A swarm of butterflies sliced a man with a million cuts and left him there to bleed. It is unlikely that he'll survive his wounds."

Elisabeth took a deep breath. "There is a pattern we cannot see. The Netherworld is bleeding through. I will go to the source of our troubles and try to find your daughter." Elisabeth nodded to Ruhan.

"Many lives are at stake," Troy said, his young face grim. "There are many more tasks that require your attention."

"You demand too much," Emera of Lyreane said, her voice airy. "She is one woman."

"Our need is greater than one lost girl," Troy countered, his eyes narrowing. "Our planet is off balance."

"That lost girl is my daughter!" the Orani Keeper exclaimed in rage.

"You have Shrikes in Tym Resh, suicides in Hystera, and I have just seen Weavers in Lyreane," Elisabeth interrupted. The Guardians gasped at her words. Nothing was more feared in the Netherworld than the Weavers. They were deadly, and if they were ever free of the Netherworld, their hordes would overrun them all.

"Weavers?" Malthael asked; even demons dreaded the Weavers and their numbers.

"Later," Elisabeth said under her breath when Malthael opened his mouth to press for an explanation. "These creatures are coming from the Netherworld, which is likely where your daughter is, so that is where I should go. I shall find your daughter and discover how the creatures of the Netherworld are bleeding through. What is your daughter's name?"

"Nanette," Ruhan said, hope restored to him. "Her name is Nanette."

"Father," she said formally for the benefit of those in attendance. "Since neither you nor the hounds can go into the Netherworld, I need a guide and I need one quickly."

"I must disagree," Troy interjected, his face worried. "If Jinq believes the world is unbalanced, I would ask that you come to Hystera immediately."

"My father has informed me that I am likely the last of my kind," Elisabeth replied pointedly, her jaw set in the same stubborn way her mother's had. "Do you think that you have any right to command me? I will see to this girl and the Det Mor Clan, and I shall do so of my own accord."

Troy sat back and focused his gaze on Malthael. "I believe that means this meeting is adjourned."

When his face disappeared, the others glanced around at each other. One by one they then vanished as well, until only Ruhan remained. He lingered just long enough to thank Elisabeth before he, too, left.

When Elisabeth swayed, Malthael put a hand on her arm to steady her. "Are you all right?" he asked, trying not to think about how she would know Weavers were in Lyreane.

"Tired," Elisabeth said, leaning against his arm. "Today has been a trying day."

"Did Duke and Nathan protect you?"

She huffed as though the words amused her. "My personal assassin saved me."

"The assassin?" Malthael sputtered as he led her up the stairs. "He protected you?"

"I was as shocked as you are," she whispered, looking preoccupied. "Apparently I need to die a very specific way: by his sword."

"So he intends to keep you alive by any means until he can use the Sin Eater on you," the reformed demon stated, his voice contemplative. "Perhaps Troy is right. Perhaps this is all connected."

"That pretentious boy will have to wait," Elisabeth snapped, getting some of her fire back as they entered the study. "Nanette and the Det Mor Clan are my priority."

"I do not cherish the idea of you mingling with the Det Mor Clan," Malthael countered. His expression betrayed his worry. "They are tricksters. Do not eat anything they offer or make any promises."

"You need to find me a guide we can trust," Elisabeth responded, "and you may have kept from telling me about the Netherworld and Morhaven, but you did not keep me out of the library."

"Clever girl," Malthael responded with pride in his voice. "You'll need all your wits in the Netherworld."

"Is it truly like the texts suggest?" she asked. "That nothing is at it seems?"

"It is a place of wonder and of terror. You will be tested at every turn. More so, even, because you will be unable to suppress your demonic half. The Netherworld is your father's home."

He could see the sudden dread on her face, but she made no move to revoke her intent. Instead, she seemed to have an internal debate as she crossed her arms and drummed her fingers, staring absently at the floor. Malthael waited as her mind analyzed the angles, something she had done since she was quite young.

Finally she looked up at him, her hands clasped in front of her. "The King Nauberon will sense where there is a something out of balance in the Netherworld. If not him, perhaps his grandmother, oldest of the Det Morians, will know. They may know where Nanette is and perhaps what is happening. Set up a meeting and find me a guide, Papa. I will be careful when dealing with the Det Mor Clan. I promise."

Malthael watched as she turned and walked away, her hand patting slightly at her leg. She was worried and thinking hard about what was to come. It was good that she wasn't disregarding what was going to be required of her, but he didn't like it. He didn't like that after all these years of their mostly tranquil life, she was going to be thrust into imminent danger. Those that had come for her before had been easily dealt with. The world was going crazy, and his daughter was right at the middle of it. Yet she bore it all like her mother had. Serena may have been mortal, but she had been a force to reckon with.

Malthael had nearly died once at the hand of a Soul Collector, and Serena had stood with a babe in her arms to stop it. She had looked like a warrior mother. When the Soul Collector had taken her deal, with the intent of breaking it, Malthael had broken his horns and driven them into the Soul Collector's shoulders. Though he hadn't been able to do it before Serena had lost her soul, Malthael had been able to spirit the half-breed infant away to safety.

Now the world needed Elisabeth, and this time Serena wasn't around to protect her. She was going to have to protect herself because where she was going, Malthael couldn't follow. He swallowed heavily, his worry as great as hers, but he reveled in one thought—she could not take a soul while in the Nether. Even if she felt the urge to feed on life force, there would be not one mortal around to feed from.

Chapter 24: Hystera

*J*inq helped put the last of the stabilizers up as Mara used her trunk to hold up the top of the tent canvas. After a few nights of strange dreams and Kerrigan's sudden lack of energy, Jinq decided they needed to move further back. Whatever was happening in Himota, it was spreading, expanding out further and further into the surrounding grasslands. He'd been keeping a close eye on the birds. When the sphere of gloom around Himota widened, the fowl steered clear. There had been another suicide the night before.

It had left them all restless and uneasy. Worse still, Troy had not contacted them, which didn't bode well. Every night Jinq was reluctant to sleep for fear of the nightmares that were to follow. Most started out harmless, even dreamlike, but they always ended with one of the people who had died. The words from girl who had killed herself on their first day haunted him, and he could feel the planet weeping.

"A little to the right," Jinq said, stepping back and shielding his eyes from the sun. "That's it." Mara let it down, and the outer skin of the tent dropped perfectly into place. Unwilling to show the village people that they had lost hope, Jinq put it just by the tree line, claiming it was to keep them cooler. Yet he felt these people were already lost, and so far Jinq was unable to find their spirit animals. They couldn't be dead, or all these people would be dead as well.

"Elder Rekis," Kerrigan said, her voice sounding so empty of emotion that he was starting to think he should send her back to the capital, "the Gate Guardian is on your mirror."

"Come and feed Mara," Jinq said, relieved but unwilling to let the girl overhear their conversation.

"All right," she said without much enthusiasm, her owl perching on her shoulder.

He watched the exhausted girl try to put on a smile as she greeted the elephant. Mara's behavior had improved since they'd decided to move the tent back. Setting the encampment up had given them a distraction from the misery behind them. He hoped moving their campsite would do more good than harm, but he worried about what the villagers were likely saying about their relocation.

When Jinq ducked into the tent, the mirror was leaning up against their only table. Jinq walked up to it and saw the hard look on Troy's face. He only had that expression when there was news that greatly displeased him. Jinq recalled that Troy had worn that same look when they'd first heard about the string of suicides.

"What did she say?" he asked before Troy could manage a word.

His young face held the eyes of a wise old man, although the dots on his head showed he was hardly a man. Most guardians were older, and many had children of their own, but Troy was special. He learned quickly, and by the time he was eleven he'd been reading books that even Jinq struggled with. He understood the dynamics of the clans' politics and many of the northern clans' cultures. In the two years since he'd taken on the mantel of Guardian, the now thirteen-year-old boy had proven to be as tenacious as the older Gate Guardians.

"She said our request was secondary," Troy informed him, doing little to hide his anger. "Once she recovers a girl from the Netherworld, she will consider our request."

"Did you tell her about the wrongness?" Jinq asked, having no other word to describe it.

"She disregarded it." Troy's words were biting, but he stopped and added, "Though she is meeting with the Det Mor Clan."

"The Chaos Clan?" His eyebrows rose in surprise. "Why?"

"I haven't the faintest idea," the boy said, his face contemplative. "Although I wonder if it may be because of the attacks across all worlds by creatures in the Netherworld. They would register as unbalance. My temper perhaps clouded my initial judgment."

"What does it mean?" Jinq asked, trying to bring the boy out of his thoughts.

Troy's eyes returned to focus. "It means I judged the Seer hastily. She may be more astute then I thought. I need you to do some reconnaissance in the area, look for any points of entry into the Netherworld. Ask them if they saw any strange creatures or anything that can indicate that the Netherworld is involved. When the Seer returns, I will discover what she has found out and implore her to come here."

Jinq nodded. "I'll look for what I can and report back."

"How is your assistant?" Troy asked, his eyes watching carefully.

"She is competent, but this place is giving her nightmares, and she doesn't appear to be getting much sleep," Jinq replied, glancing over his shoulder. "I have been suffering from similar problems, but meditation has helped. Perhaps this assignment will exhaust us enough to allow us to sleep without dreams."

Troy nodded. "I'll report this to Hipasha. She insists that the girl remains until your mission is complete."

"I will keep her with me, but if I feel she is no longer able to assist, I intend to send her back," he responded, rubbing his chin. "I'll inform you if that becomes necessary."

"Understood," Troy nodded in agreement. "Do everything you can, but your safety is paramount. You are our Keeper and the most connected with the planet. Should Hystera suffer an attack, you must flee to safety."

That was the life of a Keeper. If at all prudent, he must first and foremost remove himself from danger. Keepers should never attack, but if escape was unwise, they could defend. Jinq was the youngest of the Keepers and most able, but because there were not many of them, they could not risk dying before their time. Yet the idea of abandoning even one soul to save his own didn't sit well. It never had.

Despite his reservations, he agreed. "I will do what is best."

"Very well," Troy said, and his image faded.

Jinq set the mirror down and leaned back on his heels. He let his head roll back as he felt the planet cry out. Hystera knew something was wrong. It wanted help, and the Seer had denied them. Which meant it was up to him, and a marked girl of barely fourteen winters. Not good odds.

Chapter 25: Netherworld

φ

Ki stood outside the orc's cottage watching the Night Fairies dance, their wings illuminating the area. Their combined glow acted as a single point of light in an otherwise all-consuming darkness. He stood on the grass listening to them sing their soft song as the gnomes carefully moved around him. Even at night, the gnomes could not rest. The fairies slept during the day on Cyprus trees in Verten and appeared to be ugly little bugs, but at night they blossomed. Swayed by their subtle power, he stood transfixed for a moment before climbing the stairs.

He opened the door, and the heat of the little schoolhouse hit his face. There were many that lived in the Nether's safe havens, but this was the easiest one to pay off. The old orc was still by the fire, cleaning his sword arm, when Ki entered. He glanced up, his eyes dazed, and Ki wondered if he ever left that chair.

He wasn't as sharp this time. Instead, he looked empty, and at first he didn't seem to recognize Ki. Motionless on the threshold of the room, Ki waited, studying the orc. After a moment, he seemed to remember who Ki was, and his shoulders relaxed.

"Have you found him?" he asked, his left arm cleaning his bladed limb absentmindedly.

"No," Ki said, knowing this was a bad day. "I'll tell you if I find anything."

"Good, good," he replied. His mind was half gone as he muttered to himself, "The Black King will pay when he returns."

"As you say," Ki said, as he always did, before turning toward the back of the house.

"The fairies whisper," the orc said, and Ki turned back in surprise. "You should listen."

"What do they say?" he replied politely, but knew the ancient orc was half mad on his bad days. The last time the fairies had whispered, it had been the death of a Gate Guardian.

He looked up, and for a moment his eyes sharpened. "The Golden Demon who tore his horns asunder and became a Mad Dog is looking."

The orc peered down at the sword and seemed to forget Ki was there. Ki's eyes narrowed. "Looking for what?"

He seemed to blink and focus once more on Ki. "Do you have news of the Black King?"

"No," Ki answered slowly, "but I may have news soon."

The orc nodded and returned his attention to his weapon. Ki watched him closely before turning around and going back toward the front. He reached into his pocket, pulled out a single mushroom, and opened the main door.

All the fairies stopped their singing and immediately flew over to him, screeching, "Mine!"

"This food of the living," he said as they flew around him a frenzy, their razor-sharp opalescent wings shimmering, "I offer in exchange for information."

One of them hissed, revealing rows of pointed teeth in her little head before she zipped away. Her two rows of arms and oversized heads were characteristic of the fairies. The first set of arms had hands on the ends, but the second set were pointed and used to attack. Below them, the hideous gnomes took the opportunity to regroup before the fairies noticed. He knew that at least one fairy would not be able to resist the mushroom. It would not be long before he would have his information. Fairies of the Nether were addicted to mushrooms from the planets, which for them were aphrodisiacs.

After a moment, twins flew up and landed on it, laying their heads down lovingly like it was a pillow.

"What is it you wish to know?" one said, petting the mushroom.

"We will tell you," said the other as she, too, lay upon the mushroom's top.

"Betrayer!" some of the other fairies called out, but they were ignored.

"What does the renounced demon, known as Mad Dog of the Nether, want?" Ki asked, remembering his face and his demonic sword.

"A guide," one said.

"For his planet dweller," the other one added as she leaned forward and inhaled deeply, smelling the mushroom.

"A guide to where?" Ki asked, clearly confused, wondering where the woman would need to go.

"Here," one giggled as she sat up and touched the top of the mushroom with reverence.

Ki's eyes went wide while the fairies continued to roll around and rub against the mushroom's top, covering themselves with its scent. They already seemed half gone as they waited for his approval.

"It's yours," Ki said, releasing the fungus. They dug their fists into the sides and absconded with it. The other fairies hissed and cursed at them, but the two seemed to hardly notice as they moved to a dark corner to devour it. He only stayed long enough to see their jaws unhinge.

Turning back inside, Ki again walked past the old orc, who didn't seem to notice him, and went back to the door. The chalk had vanished from the last use, so Ki closed the door behind him and pulled a small piece of chalk from his belt again. He began to write, his hand fast and sure as he marked wood. When it was done, he recited the incantation, which made the runes glow—an old spell his elders had taught him. Pushing the door open, he stepped out into the street.

"Whoa," a voice said.

Ki turned and found a small boy staring at him in wonder. Ki closed the door with a sharp snap, patted the kid's head, and then stepped out onto the stoop. He walked down a few steps before reaching the street. He didn't like moving around in the day because it was harder to keep others from seeing him. This time, however, it was necessary; he couldn't afford to let others offer their services to the demon.

It was strange that they called him the Mad Dog of the Nether. He was by no means a dog, and his old name, the Golden Demon, didn't fit either. His skin was primarily black, though it did have a strange gold hue to it. Many claimed that when he'd had his horns, they had been dipped in gold. Others said that he had been adorned in gold armor and had fought with a golden sword that burned fire itself. Were it not for the fact that Ki had seen the sword, he might have doubted it. That sword had burned like fire, and the hilt had been golden.

Ki walked through the town, drawing some unwanted looks. This was a smaller city in Ashlad, unlike where he had first tried to save the last of his forty-two. The academy was in the heart of Hoziar, one of the largest cities in Ashlad. He hit the outer wall of the demon's estate and continued walking along it. The flat paved sidewalk was strange under Ki's boots, since Lyreane was behind in progress and had only cobblestone in the larger cities. Ashlad was the pinnacle of advancement.

When he reached the gate, he looked down the drive to the house. It stood as a foreboding fortress among the otherwise densely crowded buildings. Glancing around at the sprawling yards, he wondered if anyone knew what lay within those walls. He scanned the sidewalk. Everyone seemed to move about their days, unhindered by wonder and worry about this strange mansion. It took him a short time to realize that no one even looked at the house. From what the elders had told him, the gate kept away demons, but perhaps it also deterred prying eyes and curious mortals.

Crossing his legs under him, Ki sat down in front of the gate and waited, watching the facade of the house. Patience flowed through him as he sat like a statue. If the spirit dogs of the Nether were still guarding this place, it wouldn't take long for him to be found. The sun streaked across the sky over him, soon leaning closer to night than day.

When the lamp lighter came to the gas street lanterns farther down the sidewalk, he gave Ki a strange stare but said nothing as he continued on with his duties. Out of the corner of his eye, Ki caught movement. The bulk of the large man moved toward the gates where Ki lingered, and it wasn't long until a face appeared in lamp light on the road. It was hard not to glance up at the broken horns.

"If you are here when my daughter returns, I will kill you for no other reason than the pleasure of it," he said, glaring.

"I am not here for your daughter," Ki said carefully, not moving a muscle as the two spirit dogs appeared at the edge of the gate with their tails primed.

"Then why are you here?"

Ki uncurled his stiff legs and slowly stood to face the demon. "Your daughter is going into the Netherworld and will need a guide."

"Where did you hear such a thing?" he demanded, giving away little with his static expression.

"Fairies," Ki answered simply. "They are easily bought."

"Only by those who know what to barter," he said, his eyes narrowing. "What exactly are you proposing?"

"To act as her guide," he answered plainly.

The demon laughed, and Ki waited. A moment passed, and the Mad Dog seemed to consider his options. He stood still, his fingers curled around the gate as he watched Ki. Their gazes met, and a small battle occurred there, a silent one, as the spirit dogs waited behind him for a word to strike.

Unexpectedly, the demon pushed the gate open and said gruffly, "You look hungry."

Chapter 26: Ashlad

φ

*E*lisabeth stared out at the rain as it pitter-pattered on the stone and tried to remember how she had gotten here. It was just earlier that week that she had presented her life's work. Now she would be going not to another planet but into the Netherworld to find a lost princess. She held up the strand of string intertwined with the piece of the girl's hair that she would use to find her. Nanette was only seventeen, and it broke Elisabeth's heart to think about what the girl would have to face. It was fortunate that time in the Netherworld moved much slower than their own time.

All that remained was to locate a guide to take her through. She felt part fear and part wonder as she stared out and thought about going. In a way, the Netherworld was half of her heritage. Elisabeth had never wanted to have anything to do with her father, but she did wonder about that half of herself. The part she couldn't get rid of. Even though fear had made her bury it deep inside, it was still there, waiting to get out.

Leaning closer to the window, she looked up at the sky and frowned at the dark clouds. Perhaps on this day the weather was attempting to reflect her dour mood. She worried that her papa would know her inner struggle and convince her to stay well away from the mess. After a long night in the lab with Milo and A.J., she had returned home and gone straight to bed. When she had first seen A.J., his spirit had been sharper and more vivid to her. It concerned her, and she had a feeling there was something happening that was greater than her uneasiness, which is why she was so determined to go. With a heavy sigh, she turned away from the window without dwelling further on her own dark thoughts.

There was a knock on the door. Before she could say anything, Milo pushed his way through the door with a tray of tea.

"How are you today?" Milo asked as he set the tray on the coffee table.

"Tired," Elisabeth admitted as she came around to the loveseat. She had not been sleeping soundly and knew it would only become worse. An assassin hunted her, and she was going into the Netherworld.

Milo poured the tea. "Sugar?"

Elisabeth nodded. "And milk."

There was a pause as he held out a teacup to her. He came around and sat down beside her. He took her free hand, and she could see the worry in his eyes. That she'd expected, but not the guilt.

"What is it?" Elisabeth asked, worried.

"I am sorry I could not protect you." Milo's voice was thick with emotion.

"You were caught unaware," Elisabeth set the teacup down so she could hold his hand in both of hers. "We all were. There was nothing you could have done. I am just happy you are safe."

Milo kissed her forehead affectionately. At first he'd been a mentor to her as a child, but later he'd become more of a sibling, like a caring elder brother. Elisabeth wouldn't have survived her childhood without him. He was family.

"I promise to always be on your side," Milo reassured her, "like I always have been."

Elisabeth blinked her eyes rapidly to keep the tears at bay. "I know."

"Drink your tea before it gets cold. I'd better see to breakfast," Milo said, patting her hand before leaving the room with the tray.

Sipping her tea, she read her book for a while, but her concentration was short lived. Holding the hardcover tightly to her chest, she left the room. She turned toward the dining room, assuming breakfast would have been prepared. She was finally ready to face her papa.

She paused at the door to gather her composure.

Elisabeth opened her mouth to say something and then stopped, frozen in shock. Her assassin was sitting at their breakfast table eating toast. A little pile of grain he had picked off of the bread was off to the side of the plate. He went to take another bite but paused when he saw her. Panic bubbled in her chest as her eyes shifted to Malthael.

"Elsa!" Malthael said with a smile and stood.

"Papa!" She fought down the hysteria rising in her chest, "What is this?"

"I've found you a guide," her papa answered, and she nearly laughed. The only thing that stopped her was the look on his face.

"A word," Elisabeth ground out between her teeth.

"Excuse me," Malthael said as though speaking to an honored guest.

She held the door open, giving one final glance at the assassin as he began to pull grain off another piece of toast. Frowning, she pulled the door closed behind her. The bulk of Malthael turned with a hand up as though to ward away her protest and anger.

"Are you mad?" Elisabeth asked despite his elevated hand.

"He saved your life," Malthael said, glancing around, "and the boy knows the Netherworld. I have been quizzing him all morning since I found him at our gate. Not to mention—"

"He is trying to kill me," Elisabeth cut him off, "and you want me to trust him?"

"He has signed a blood oath," Malthael reassured her. "He cannot harm you so long as he is guiding you through the Netherworld. You know what a blood oath is. You can go into the Nether protected from your assassin and by him. A reprieve of sorts. I thought it prudent."

"Prudent?" Elisabeth jeered. "'Prudent' he says. I want a different guide. One that you didn't invite in for tea after he tried to kill me."

"Elsa." Malthael put his hands on her shoulders to calm her. "The Det Mor Clan is hunting for him. Bring him to Morhaven with you and you can be free of him forever."

Elisabeth stopped as reason took hold. "Oh."

"It is the perfect solution," Malthael explained.

Elisabeth swallowed as she realized her papa was leading her assassin into a trap. If she weren't still angry, she would have acknowledged that Malthael had come up with a clever plan. He waited as she gathered her wits.

Elisabeth's body sagged. "I don't know, Papa. Isn't it too risky?"

"Without a blood oath perhaps, but with one?" Malthael straightened his spine in confidence. "I believe we can take care of two birds with one arrow."

"What if that is what he wants you to think and the Netherworld holds the secret to his success in killing me?" Elisabeth asked in a hushed rage.

"It does not," said a voice suddenly. They both stopped to stare at the assassin, who stood in the slightly open door. She had not heard it open during their discussion. "I will find another way I assure you, but you will be stronger in the Netherworld."

Elisabeth felt her blood run cold. "Stronger?" she asked with a heavy tongue.

"If I need to kill you, the last place I would take you was the Nether," he said. "I am not demon born, so you will be harder to kill. You needn't worry with a blood oath. If I even attack you with the intent to harm you, I die."

"Why help me then?" she demanded, unable to hide her fear.

"If you go into the Nether without me, you will die. Nothing is what is seems. I have spent my life among the ruins and monsters," he responded. Elisabeth nearly remarked he must feel right at home but instead ground her teeth in anger.

"Elisabeth," Malthael said softly, "Nanette is running out of time. He is right—you will be stronger there, and with the oath you are protected." Malthael glared at Ki. "If he tries anything, the pain that will be visited upon him will make death seem easy."

Elisabeth remembered how helpless she had been when she'd nearly died and her assassin had saved her. He was capable, and she could use that. Use it and then lead him to his demise. Frowning, she realized she didn't have much of a choice. If she denied him, he would wait here for her to return. At least if she took him with her, she had a chance to take care of him once and for all.

"Very well," she finally said with a resigned sigh.

Chapter 27: Netherworld

─────────────────────── ф ───────────────────────

anette awoke stiff and sore. She opened her eyes groggily and licked her dry lips. Rolling over slowly, she glanced at the entrance. The spider thing was gone, but there were deep grooves in the stone where it had been clawing its way in to try and reach her. Unwilling to move or do anything, she started to turn herself back toward the darkness of her shelter. Her leg burned where she had been cut, making her hiss in pain.

She pushed herself up just far enough to see the injury before moving to a larger part of her cave where the light came in from the entrance. When she touched her leg, she sucked in another painful breath at how tender it was. But the blood had dried, and a scab was already starting to form. She tried not to think about how disgusting it looked or what that thing might have left in the wound.

Realizing she couldn't stay there, she started to pull herself toward the opening. She didn't want to be there when the spider-creatures came back. She scanned the room. It appeared empty. She reached her fingers out and let the light dance over them. After a moment, she remembered the spiders hadn't attacked until the light had faded.

Did they not like it? she wondered.

She had just started to pull herself out when she heard a clicking noise.

Nanette glanced to her right. There, in the doorway, where darkness pooled together, she saw movement. Moving faster, she stood and did her best to keep most of her weight off her injured leg as she wobbled along the rubble. The clicking intensified as the creature eagerly moved back and forth but didn't dare enter the well-lit room.

She could make out other shapes in other entryways and moved away from them. As long as she stayed in the light, she was safe. Searching the sky, she wasn't sure how much time had passed or how much longer until that inky blackness returned. She needed to find a way out.

Nanette stopped, realizing that she had no idea which direction to go. Glancing back at her safe place, she wondered if she could just go back and sleep. Yet in her heart she knew that if she went back, she would die. If she pushed forward, perhaps she could find a safe haven. There were whispers of them, magical places that were paradises in this red wasteland, places dark creatures couldn't reach.

Continuing through the rubble, she whispered the names of her family to keep her safe. Her father was a Gate Guardian. She knew he would not abandon her. Nanette would not allow herself to think she would not survive. She just needed to survive long enough for her father to come. Somehow, she needed to find a way to contact him. She was nearly out of the ruins when she heard some rocks fall. She whirled around and her bad leg nearly gave way, but she was able to catch herself on a doorframe. Peering into the darkened doorways, she watched the shadows. Nothing moved, but she felt something watching her, hunting her.

Swallowing down her fear, she stepped out into the red light but felt nothing on her skin, not like their sun. This was a cold and unfeeling light. It only seemed to cast a red hue that made everything look dusty and covered in rust. Oh, how she prayed that she would live to feel the sun on her skin again!

She gave the pond area a wide berth, unwilling to meet that creature again, and made her way toward the exit out of the gardens. Moving along the wall, Nanette looked at her almost nonexistent shadow. The light seemed to be cast from every direction, as though the sky itself cast the light. Perhaps there wasn't a single light source, or perhaps there were many. It was difficult to tell in this endless, cloudy red sky.

As she cleared the gate, some sort of flake dropped down slowly from the sky. Nanette thought for a moment it looked like snow. But it was too dark to be snow. Another one fell closer to her, and she put a hand out. When it landed, she rubbed it flat and looked at her fingers. They were covered in ash.

Above her the sky had opened up, and a thousand more gray flecks fell as far as the eye could see. If the ash continued coming down in such heavy sheets, she could be smothered by it. She moved faster, hoping to travel beyond the ash cloud. Her bad leg slowed her down though, and she felt the scab twist and tear with every step. The second wound on her leg was deeper and meaner and almost caused her to fall. When the wound finally tore, she ignored it, unwilling to slow down.

The ash became thicker as it covered her hair and clothes. It clung to her like snow, but it didn't feel fresh or soft. A tear fell down her cheek as she looked at the ruined landscape. It was painful to remember home when the derelict version lay before her. Her legs began to move again despite her exhaustion, and the ash fall slowed. The road was broken in many places, and she had to go around massive holes and sharp inclines. Every once in a while, she saw things moving in the darkness of the buildings, and her fear kept her mobile, even when the pain doubled.

She was nearly to the edge of town when she saw a flash of white light next to her. To her right, a small creature hopped out of one of the buildings. She took a step back, but realized it was only a rabbit. Nanette frowned at the little white ball of fur as it sniffed along the rubble. She was about to leave when a trap snapped up around it.

The creature suddenly flashed its enormous pointed teeth, and its claws, which were as long as her own fingers, began to thrash at the cage. Nanette's breath caught in her throat, and she shuffled on her way. It wasn't long before she could see the city's gate, which was broken and bent back like a giant had stepped on it. She was nearly through when the rabbit screamed. Covering her ears at the piecing sound, she turned in time to see a deep shadow glide across the wall near the rabbit. Nanette's scream joined the creature's before she could stop herself, but she cut it short by slapping a hand over her own mouth. She choked on her own air as the shadow shifted its attention toward her. Nanette spun and half-ran, half-hobbled toward the gate. The injuries in her leg brought tears to her eyes with every step, but she disregarded the pain in her desperation to escape. A broken sob escaped her lips when the rocks shifted under her feet and she fell hard, scraping her knee.

The shadow moved faster than anything she had ever seen as she scrambled up the rubble that blocked the gate. When she reached the top, another shadow fell across her. A figure in black wearing goggles stood above her in a frayed cloak. He was wrapped in tattered clothes with strips of cloth around his mouth. Nanette was paralyzed when she saw him, stuck between him and the horrifying shadow behind her.

The man's wrist moved slightly, and a sword appeared out of nowhere. At the same time, Nanette felt something wrap around her ankle. Quickly looking down, she saw the shadow was no longer flat. It had taken on the form of a great bull-like creature with a fiery horn and tail. She stomped on it repeatedly, her heart pounding in her ears with panic because she couldn't seem to make contact with its incorporeal state. When she pushed at it with her hands, they just passed right through.

The bald man jumped over her and landed on the ground to her right with his sword raised. Nanette threw herself to the ground as it swung toward her. It missed. Moments later, she looked on in astonishment as the goggled man moved faster than Nanette could follow and cleaved the creature's tentacle in two. Somehow, his sword had made contact when she could not.

Shaking off the severed tendril, she scrambled backward away from it. The man pulled his sword free and slowly turned toward her. She stiffened when his eyes rested on her. For the first time, she noticed tattoos covered his bald head. They almost seemed to move as she watched them. He took a step toward her and she twisted away, fearful of the sword in his hand. The man paused and glanced at the sword, and in an instant it vanished. He continued toward her, leaned forward and, astonishingly, put out a hand.

"Please," she whispered, her voice betraying her fear.

He moved his hand insistently. Nanette sat frozen and fearful for a moment. Again the goggled man shook his hand. She hesitantly reached forward and took it. When her trembling hand slipped into his gloved one, he tightened his hold and tugged her to her feet. She cried out from the sudden weight on her injured leg and teetered, but she was able to keep her balance. Once she was able, he turned away and hurried down the rubble toward the trap. He reached in and pulled the rabbit out by the back of its neck. It started to thrash violently but failed to make any sort of contact with him.

After a moment, it slowed its struggle and yawned. It closed its eyes and once more looked like a harmless rabbit. Nanette sighed in relief. He put the rabbit under his arm and snapped its neck.

The last of her strength drained out of her, and she sunk slowly to her knees. The stones dug into her bones as she toppled over, rolling part way down the rubble. Her vision was blurred, and her injured leg burned. She couldn't even try to sit up as the edge of her vision darkened. The man ran toward her hastily and pulled up her tattered skirts. The air was cold on her bare legs.

Nanette tried to protest for the sake of her modesty, but it only came out as a muttered string of incoherent sounds. She gave a weak cry of pain when he probed at the wound with his fingers. He put the rabbit into a brown burlap sack before lifting her up and draped her over his shoulders like a scarf or a prize deer, her stomach against the back of his neck.

"Please," she whispered.

She caught a glance at the pin on his shoulder holding on his tattered cape. It was a pair of intertwined roses, one of them white and the other black. It was her last vision as she began to fade further. Her tongue suddenly felt large as he walked her out of the ruins of the city she had never loved. That was her last thought as she lost consciousness.

Chapter 28: Oran

ϕ

*E*lisabeth tapped her foot in annoyance as she looked at the pond. Her assassin was crouched beside it, writing symbols on the ground. Beside her, the Gate Guardian Ruhan looked on in a fretful state while she watched impatiently. He had been doing this for a good fifteen minutes with no results. She wanted to march them over to Ruhan's home and use the gate. Yet every time she insisted, he refused and said he would figure it out. He was like a determined child who had to have his way.

"What is he doing?" Ruhan asked, having worried the edge of his shirt to deep wrinkles.

"Trying to figure out where in the Netherworld your daughter went," Elisabeth said, softening her tone as best she could.

"It's direct," her assassin said, standing. "We can use the doors inside."

Ki walked past them into the parliamentary building. He picked up the two traveling sacks and threw both over his shoulder. She hurried after him with Ruhan in tow, irritated further by his behavior. He had absolutely no manners.

"Thank you, Spiritwalker," Ruhan said, with tears forming in his eyes, "and thank you… I am sorry, who is he?"

He turned back before she could answer. "I am Ki."

Elisabeth realized then that she hadn't even known his name. Her cheeks burned from embarrassment. She was entrusting her life—at least on the surface—to a man whose name she hadn't thought to ask. It was likely that he didn't know hers either.

He set the packs down and started to draw on a door in the hallway. Why did that door matter, anyway? As he pulled out chalk, she marched up to him and thrust her hand out. "I'm Elisabeth."

He glanced back, clearly startled. "I know."

"I am trying to introduce myself properly," she pointed out, shaking her hand a little. "It is proper for you to shake my hand in accord."

"You don't seem to like when I touch you," he said, sounding confused. Her cheeks burned worse.

"I am entrusting my life to you," she said, pushing down her worry. If she was going to trick him into entering Morhaven, she needed to make him believe she was on board. "The least I can do is extend my hand to you."

He considered this a moment, studying her face and then her hand, but in the end he took it. His fingers were surprisingly gentle, and she tried to ignore their warmth and the fact that he was a person. They shook once before he retracted his hand, but continued to stare at her.

Finally, she swallowed and asked, "What is it?"

"No one has shaken my hand before," he said before turning back to his work. He used the chalk to make strange symbols on the door.

What kind of life had this man led? She studied him and his clothes, seeing that they were old but carefully maintained. The stitching and patchwork were simple, without embellishments. The only companion he seemed to have was the spirit tiger that he couldn't communicate with. Yet during their brief encounter, Ashley had expressed a quiet affection for Ki.

She was about to inquire into his life when he stopped writing and put his hand on the door. As he whispered, the markings began to glow. When it was done, he reached down and picked up both packs before holding one out to her. "It is time."

Elisabeth nodded and took the rucksack before turning back to Ruhan. "If she is alive, we will find her."

"I pray that you do," he said, and although his old eyes held hope, his entire body was saturated in grief. Even his clothes drooped with it, as if he had just stepped out of a lake.

Elisabeth couldn't blame him. Nanette would have had to survive a night in the Netherworld, and even Elisabeth worried they were too late. Yet even if the girl was dead, Elisabeth would at least bring Ruhan closure and then get answers from the Det Mor Clan. Not all would be in vain.

Ki opened the door. When she stepped past him into the Netherworld, she felt a sharp tug against the inside of her ribcage. She gasped as Ki stepped in behind her, and time slowed. She could feel her breath in her lungs fill and empty, and every fiber of her body was suddenly aware of the world around her. Her very bones sensed this breezeless place as it swayed out of time. Part of her recognized it and reveled in it—a part of herself that terrified her.

She felt his hand on her arm and started to turn. Every fiber of her being was alive. Suddenly, she began to fall. She was lightheaded, and the world was slowly spinning. Ki caught her arm. Even in slow motion, he moved quickly. Elisabeth rested a hand on his shoulder. Her entire body seemed foreign to her. She couldn't breathe.

His lips moved, but everything seemed lost to a hurricane of sound within her own mind. His expression was concerned, and he repeated the question with exaggerated enunciation. As Elisabeth listened, her entire world seemed both overwhelmingly bright and completely black.

"Have you fed?" he asked, holding her up.

"I ate," she whispered, but she instinctively knew that wasn't what he was talking about. A hunger rose within her that she had always suppressed, a more powerful urge than she'd ever felt before. It brought her to her knees.

Ki started to pull her toward him while she tried fighting him off, but she was no match for him in her weakened state. He turned his head and suddenly pressed his lips to hers. His eyes remained open and so did hers, and instinct kicked in. She opened her mouth and a dead lump of coal within her burst to life as she pressed her palms to his cheeks and began to draw his life force out of him. She could feel it leave his body and fill her, sating the unusual hunger. It flooded her veins, filling her with energy as it ignited a fire in her belly. When she was full, she hit his shoulder and he turned away, breaking the connection. They were left kneeling on the ground, gasping. Elisabeth looked at him, stunned.

"Soul Collectors need life force to survive," Ki explained as she backed away from him. "Without it, they turn into catatonic statues."

"They eat souls? I thought they just collected them." Elisabeth was suddenly disgusted with herself. She put a hand to her throat.

"When they harvest a soul, they keep part of it. Nothing a soul can't do without," he said. "It sustains them."

"It has always been there," Elisabeth whispered more to herself, "but never like that."

Elisabeth wanted to throw up, yet her body felt exhilarated. She felt more alive than she ever had without the life force coursing through her veins. Looking around in wonder, she could see the spirit lines, the highway to how spirits traveled as they ran throughout the five planets. She had used them before, but she'd never seen them.

Swallowing her worry and undeniable excitement, she swayed on her feet again. He caught her arm once more as she blinked once to try and clear the haze. Her mind was clouded with light, and she wondered how anyone could call the Netherworld red.

"Be careful," Ki said, and she tipped her head to look at him. "Your system isn't used to it."

Around him spirits danced in a circular motion. His hair and eyes were black, but a light also seemed to shine off him. She could see his wings, white feathers intertwined with black shadowy wings. For a moment he was the most beautiful thing she had ever seen.

Elisabeth was suddenly self-conscious as the memory of their lips meeting rushed back to her mind. She pushed herself off him and turned away, touching her fingers to her lips. Resolved to forget it, she dropped her hand and hardened her emotions.

"Why do they say the Netherworld is red?" Elisabeth asked, changing the subject.

"It is red," Ki twisted around. As he answered, the spirits that twirled round him hugged tighter against his body. "What do you see?"

"It's almost like moonlight," Elisabeth said, looking around. "But a pale purple."

"Interesting," he said before reaching into his pack and pulling out an amulet. "Hold this."

She took it hesitantly, but the moment her fingers touched it, the room they were in turned into rubble and the pale purple hue faded out for a dull red. It was as though the sky was lit by burning embers. The ruins she stood in were exactly like the hallway she had left, only most of the roof was gone and the pale stone walls had cracks running throughout them.

"The sky is burning," Elisabeth said in a forlorn voice.

"I use the amulet when I want to see the Nether somewhat the way you described," Ki explained. Elisabeth refocused her attention on him and noticed he looked the same as when they left Oran. "It seems touching it has the opposite effect on you. I always wondered how beings of the Netherworld saw their home."

She stared at him a moment longer, until his eyebrows furrowed and he looked ready to ask her a question, so she looked down at the amulet. It was mostly an unimpressive piece of rock, with two metal strips connecting along its face. It looked like a chunk of stone, nothing more than coal, but it seemed to shine. The metal was designed in strange fashion—when she looked at the face, it reflected her, but with black eyes.

She nearly dropped it. Unwilling to dwell on what it meant, she asked, "What is it?"

"Volcanic gem," he answered cryptically. "It makes you see things through everyone else's eyes."

"That doesn't make any sense." She looked up at him in disbelief. "It could be anyone's eyes."

"It is a Netherworld Gem. All the rules don't apply. You can't rely on logic, not down here," he replied before picking up his pack again and slinging it over his shoulder as he started walking. "It is time to get going."

When she put the chain over her head, the rock fell against her chest. "Where are we going?"

"Following this," Ki said. He held up the charm that Elisabeth had given him with Nanette's hair intertwined in it.

She glanced back when she heard a clicking noise she recognized—thankful for the red light as it chattered at her. Frowning, Elisabeth turned again, unwilling to meet another Weaver, and followed Ki as they strolled further into the Netherworld.

Chapter 29: Hystera

⟡

Kerrigan stared across the desert. They had been walking all day, and the further she went from the village, the better she felt. Whatever was happening in Himota was affecting her more every day. Out here in the hot plains, she took her first relaxed breath in a week.

Beside her, Jinq sat cross-legged on the ground right on the edge of the grass, facing the desert, with his eyes closed. They had come here to try to determine where the darkness originated. Apparently Jinq believed that if he sat between the desert and the village he could access the planet and find out what was happening. According to Jinq, the desert had very little life and was an easy place for a Keeper to commune with Hystera.

Kerrigan wasn't sure what he was looking for, but Jinq seemed to be serene in everything he did, as he was now. Only when the villagers had denied them entry had he shown any level of frustration. When the villagers had found out that the Seer was not coming, they'd said the Keeper was no longer welcome in Himota.

"Do you feel it?" Jinq asked without opening his eyes.

Kerrigan jumped slightly at his words. She'd thought he might have fallen asleep. Right before she'd spoken, she had been half-tempted to lean forward and wave her hand in front of his face to see if it did anything. Pushing that thought aside, she glanced at Hibrius, but his eyes were closed, too, as he lay curled around the elder.

"Feel what?" Kerrigan asked, looking around as though she expected to see something.

"Sit down," he said.

After a moment she did. "Now what?" she asked, her legs crossed, as she shifted uncomfortably. The ground was hard on her bottom and the sand was uncomfortable.

"Use your connection with Cav to feel Hystera," Jinq said quietly, with an irritating level of calm.

Pursing her lips, she shot him an annoyed expression before settling in and closing her eyes. She focused on Cav as he slept on her shoulder, trying to use her connection to him to connect to the rest of the world. Nothing happened at first. All she felt was the grass brushing her arms and cheeks. And then she felt the air, with its growing heat, and the soft cooing of Cav as he slept.

"Relax," Jinq said. Kerrigan fought the urge to growl at him.

After a moment, though, the tension left her, as if the grass itself was gently coaxing it out of her. The dark gloom of the village faded away, and she made another attempt, focusing on the connection with Cav. It wasn't long before she felt the ground vanish and she was left floating. She could feel the soft caresses of the whole planet against her skin. Like she was in a dream, she could make out Cav as he glowed in front of her. In her mind's eye, she could see everything. It startled her at first, which almost broke the connection, but she held it by permitting herself to unwind. Never before had anyone told her how to connect to their planet, and now that she was linked with it, she could see its beauty. Its exquisiteness wasn't a sight to behold but a feeling deep within her soul. A soft smile touched her lips as she felt its warmth and harmony.

"It's beautiful," she whispered softly.

"You can see it? Good," Jinq said, his voice as clear as day. "Your spirit is strong."

"It is so warm here," Kerrigan replied softly.

"That is Hystera's spirit lines that run throughout the planet. You've connected to just one of many. Try to move along it." Jinq instructed.

She tried. In her mind she tried running, jumping, and walking from where she was, but she stayed rooted in the same spot. It was like the night sky was swirling around her in a dark purple but she was caught in a steam of glowing lavender. The warmth of the planet remained around her, but she couldn't seem to move. Her face scrunched up in concentration as she tried to fight the planet's hold.

"How?" she whispered, struggling to keep the connection amidst her frustration. She had to remind herself to relax.

"They are like rivers. You have to let yourself go and let them take you," he said. His voice gave her the confidence she needed.

Kerrigan tried to imagine herself falling and swimming, yet the planet kept her rooted in place. Every inch of her will fought to free itself from the gravity. Just when she was about to give up, she was pulled free, and the spirit line pulled her along like a river current. Her senses filled with the rest of the planet as she floated by. She felt the life of the grass and the animals. Further away, a soft rain soaked the earth—she would have to remember to mention that when her senses weren't overwhelmed.

Cav was awake, floating along with her in a sea of perfect melody, beaming. They were together on this journey.

"Are you on the river?" Jinq asked.

"Yes," she said and felt like a child, free from her worries.

"Come back," Jinq told her. "Swim up the river."

Kerrigan felt herself turn and try to swim, but the river was too strong. She fought it, but the pressure was immense. It was as though something was fighting her, pushing on her body to keep her going down the river. She tried again to return to her original location, but a wave of discord crashed over her, which left her gasping. Startled by the sudden force, she started to slip downstream again. It was though something *in* the spirit line was working against her. The waves were growing more persistent, and panic set in. Something was dragging her to Himota.

"I can't," she cried, her voice shaking.

"Don't fight the waves. Float over them," he said, but it was too late.

Her panic overcame her reason, and she felt something dark touch her. Her hands tightened into fists as she started being dragged to the center of the village. It wasn't the calm gentle floating she first experienced, but instead an insistent jerk.

When it slowed, she gasped. A burning planet was before her eyes. It was superheated from the inside to the outer core, and fire burned everywhere. A dark figure suddenly reached for her, and on his hands were bloody red letters carved into his skin. She gasped because it was the same word her mother had written under the suicide tree—Croatoan.

Just as the letters were about to touch her, she screamed. A hand made of blinding light covered her wrist. She couldn't even see what it was as it wrapped its arms around her and brought her to safety.

Her eyes snapped open, and she scrambled away until her strength gave out and she fell on her back in the grass. Cav made a screeching noise of concern and circled above her as she lay panting. Tears were streaming down her face, and her nose ran.

"What did you see?" Jinq asked, casting her in his shadow.

"Death," Kerrigan answered, her adrenaline making it difficult to catch her breath. "I saw death."

Chapter 30: Ashlad

— φ —

althael stared at the glass of whiskey and wondered what it was like to get drunk. Getting intoxicated was extremely difficult for the eternal. It was probably possible, now that Malthael had lost his horns and most of his powers, but he figured it would still take a lot. He needed to drink away his sorrows, a planet dweller's ideal.

Regardless, his sorrows remained. Instead, he was three bottles into his strongest brew and brooding in his chair, listening to the emptiness of his house. Not even Nathan or Duke could bring him out of his melancholy state. When had quiet houses led to drinking?

When his daughter had gone to the Netherworld with her assassin in order to face the Det Mor Clan and save the universe. That was when. The thought made Malthael down the last of the glass in one gulp.

Ki, the would-be assassin, had been an unexpected factor. Malthael's normally reliable gut told him that Elisabeth didn't really need a guide. Her biological father was more connected to Morhaven and the Netherworld than most Soul Collectors were. He had been an elite member of the Divine Court before his punishment. Malthael was pretty sure that the moment Elisabeth stepped foot in the Netherworld, her demonic half would drive her to Morhaven.

Hopefully their ploy would end in Ki being taken care of by King Nauberon. He'd sent word to Zod that the abomination was heading straight for Morhaven. Ki was deadly, to be sure, but he wouldn't stand up to King Nauberon or his court, particularly if the King sent the Lord of the Hunt, Arawn. What stuck out as strange was how well-versed the boy was regarding the Netherworld. The only topic Ki had avoided when questioning him were the elders that raised him. Some sort of strange cult, Malthael imagined. It was the only thing that explained his guileless behavior. It has seemed odd that a man with mortal sins on his soul had been content to pick the grain off his toast. He had killed greater sinners than himself but it still bore a cost. It would take many deaths before Ki would face his final one, however, so there was still time for redemption.

118

"Now that is old magic," Malthael grumbled, pouring the last of the third bottle into a glass.

He held it in his fist, trying to remember where that phrase had been used before. It had been many, many years since he had heard of such a spell—a lifetime at least. Hundreds of years, and since the beginning of his mostly mortal existence and his breaking his horns, his memory had become worse. He didn't know how these planet dwellers did it, living nearly a hundred years with such limited mental capacity.

He grumbled some more and took another sip. Nathan raised his head in question, hoping for something to do, no doubt, but when Malthael said nothing else, he settled it back down. They had both been taking turns keeping an eye on him since Elisabeth had left. The last time she'd been gone, when she'd left to finish her dissertation project, he had sulked around the house for weeks. Nathan and Duke had taken turns watching him then, too—meddlesome dogs. Yet a part of him appreciated the company. Although he couldn't communicate with them anymore like Elisabeth did, he still felt them. They had been his in the Netherworld and continued to be his, although he was no longer bound to them. The price of tearing off his horns had not only been his immortality.

He did not like the idea of his daughter out in the Netherworld with her assassin, and the hope of getting drunk was the only solace he had. Blood oath or not, what Elisabeth was doing was still a risk. Yet Ki was the least of Malthael's worries. He knew King Nauberon would try to entrap Elisabeth.

"She won't find out," Malthael whispered, taking a hearty swallow and finally feeling the lightheadedness of intoxication. Serena had died trying to keep Elisabeth alive.

"You remember her, don't you, Nathan?" Malthael asked.

They were called hounds, but they really looked more like boars with wolves' heads. Looking at Nathan's narrow face, Malthael revised his assessment to foxlike. They were cunning for sure, and their deadly tails reminded him multiple fox tails. Nathan lay back down with a harrumph.

"She sure knew how to pick a fight," he chuckled. "You nearly took her head off when she showed up on my doorstep." Malthael sighed. "Luckily, she had bought my favor from a member of the Divine Court. She asked only that I keep her daughter safe. It wasn't until she mentioned the baby that I noticed it in a pack on her back." His face contorted with confusion. "Who'd ever heard of a mortal buying demonic favors?"

Nathan just stared contentedly "No one!" Malthael cried.

He chuckled again and took a drink of his whiskey. Perhaps if he had another he would feel the full effects of being drunk. Then he could forget that Elisabeth would one day know the truth about how her mother had died. He downed the last of the glass, pushed himself up from the chair, and lumbered over to the liquor cabinet. Squinting over his spectacles, he frowned deeper when he realized there wasn't any left.

"Well, that's disappointing," he said before going back across the room and collapsing in the chair.

He watched the fire silently. It was always so cold in this place compared to the Netherworld. The Netherworld never knew cold of night. He laid his head against the side of the leathery chair and acknowledged that he'd pay for his indulgences in the morning. But for now, he wanted only to sleep. He wondered, as he drifted, what his daughter was experiencing. What strange wonders and horrors would she stumble across as she traversed the landscape? Malthael hoped he had made all the right choices. If not, he intended to cash in his favor with the Det Morian King and see to it that Elisabeth was released from the Nether. It would cost him his life, but his life meant nothing without her. With that sobering thought, he passed out.

Chapter 31: Netherworld

——————————— φ ———————————

*H*er dreams were that of nightmares, every single one. Nanette grew restless in her sleep until finally she could not rest a moment longer. Opening her eyes slowly, she saw dark stone. Her ribs protested as she made herself sit up, letting out a little groan of pain as she did.

Blinking away some grogginess, she realized she was in some sort of little cave, one hardly large enough for the bed she was in, a dresser next to it, and a little chamber pot. Pushing the blankets away, she pulled her skirt up and looked at her leg. She was pleased to see it so well dressed. The bandages were pristine and had been wrapped to stay in place, but not so tight that they hurt. Blushing, she remembered the way he had exposed her leg. She felt a rush of gratitude for his concern and care.

Nanette glanced around. The rock face had been scratched with many intricate designs she didn't recognize. Slowly getting to her feet, Nanette hobbled over to the wall and rested her hand on it. Moving carefully along it, her fingers tracing the designs, she realized it would have taken years of carving to do this. It made her a little sad but also impressed. It took dedication to do this. When she felt the bald man come up beside her, she stepped back and nearly jumped out of her skin.

"I'm sorry," she immediately said on instinct, feeling as though she had violated something precious.

He reached up and slowly pulled off his goggles and mask. She could see the markings on his head. They were tattoos, but they seemed alive and twisted in the light. His green eyes almost glowed as he stood there watching her. Nanette swallowed down the fear that the intensity of his gaze and his imposing posture brought out in her. If he were going to hurt her, he would have already done it. When she didn't react, he moved into the cave, ducking to get through the smaller door, and dropped the sack on the ground before setting his mask and goggles down on top of the dresser.

Even with his lack of hair, he was handsome, in an alien sort of way. His arms rippled with muscle as he crouched down and rifled through the pack. It was twice her size, and it was hard not to stare at his glistening tan skin. Nanette couldn't pinpoint his age, but he couldn't be more than a decade her senior. She watched him set something on the dresser by his pack, her injured leg growing tired from her weight on it. She glanced toward the exit but didn't have any idea where to go.

When she turned back, he was standing so close to her that she nearly fell backwards. He reached out and caught her arm with one hand, doing it so quickly that she almost didn't even see the movement. Nanette stared into his eyes, entranced, and felt her cheeks warm up. "Thank you," she whispered.

He nodded his head to the side, gesturing for her to sit. Nanette wobbled a little, and he put his arm around her waist. She felt her face grow warmer. Never had a man except for her father and Prince Jason touched her. And even *he* had never touched her as gently as this stranger did. She dared not look at him. Instead she concentrated on getting back down onto the mattress.

When she was sitting, he knelt by her leg and started to pull up her skirt. Instinctively, she put her hand down to stop him. He looked up at her, his eyebrows raised in surprise as her hand rested on his. She quickly curled her fingers around the hem of her dress and bowed her head in embarrassment, focusing on her bandaged leg. She saw his hands hesitate a tick before checking the dressing. He was careful, likely making sure she hadn't ruined it in her sleep. When he was done, he looked up at her, and she became acutely aware of his closeness. They stared at each other, frozen. Her breath caught in her throat as she wondered what he was going to do next.

He stood up abruptly and went back to his pack. Exhaling, she nervously pushed a loose batch of hair behind her ear. She tried to look away, but curiosity won out, despite her awkwardness. Not exactly sure what he was or why he wasn't trying to kill her, she tried to assess his intent. He pulled out something out of the pack wrapped in cloth before turning back to her.

He held it out to her and waited. Whatever was in the cloth was no bigger than her fist. Nervous, she took the bundle. He watched her eagerly as she unfolded the contents. She was shocked to find a persimmon on her lap. She inspected it closely as her belly rumbled in anticipation, but instantly felt terrible.

"I can't," Nanette said, setting it back down. "I'm not of the Netherworld." She didn't want to be trapped in this place.

He pointed up and nodded his head. Her eyebrows furrowed as she watched him try to tell her something in gestures. She attempted to put the pieces together, but nothing made sense. Shaking her head caused him to stop.

"I don't understand," she admitted.

He frowned before taking a seat next to her. He held out his hand and nodded toward her arm, indicating he wanted to hold it. She lifted it, and he took hold of her wrist and started to trace something on her forearm with his other finger.

Nanette giggled, "That tickles!" He instantly stopped and gave her a reproachful stare. She gasped at his silent censure, worried that he might toss her out into the Netherworld. "I'm sorry, I'll pay attention."

He tried again, and she realized he was writing letters on her arm. She ignored how badly it tickled, or at least she tried to. She understood that this was a serious matter, but she was having trouble keeping a straight face. She was very susceptible to being tickled—her sister used to torture her when they were children.

"Oh, 'planet!' You got this from one of the planets." She cried when the letters came together.

He nodded and she smiled at the persimmon. Nanette picked it up and was about to take a bite but faltered. He went back to whatever he was doing with his pack. Looking down at the fruit, she wondered if there was any reason he would trick her. Since she had come here, everything had tried to kill her, from bunnies to shadows.

Nanette peered at him and then back at the soft outer skin of the fruit that she had always loved as a child. It was orange and inviting, and she was starving. Its temptation was too great, so she took a bite. She figured she would have been dead without him anyway, so he had no reason to kill her. The honeyed flavor filled her mouth. She chewed slowly, stuck between devouring it quickly and enjoying it.

Her savior set items out on the floor next to his pack before he began put them back in their places throughout the room. She wondered what his story was and why he wouldn't speak. Instead of asking right away, she observed him. He moved like a dancer, fluid and confident, which fascinated her. It reminded her of the performances at home; the dancers had been flawless. His jawline was strong and his skin was perfect besides the tattoos. She wondered what they meant. How did they slither over his skin like that?

After a moment, he came over and held out a teardrop-shaped sack. Nanette hesitated. He uncorked the top and she realized it was a water canteen. She took it, but glanced up at him and made a circle with her fingers before pointing up, making sure the water was from the planets.

He nodded before returning to his work. She took a sip, figuring that if he was lying about the persimmon, what did she have to lose by drinking water? When nothing happened after a while, she took a full drink. It felt good running against her dry throat, but she was careful not to drink all of it. She rested her head back against the wall of the cave. This little bit of excitement had exhausted her.

She watched him through tired eyes as he came over once again. He uncurled her fingers to take the water and the cloth stained with the persimmon's juice. She curled her fingers around his wrist before he could walk away.

"Thank you," she whispered, wanting him to understand how much it meant, "for your kindness."

Chapter 32: Netherworld

———————————— φ ————————————

Ki glanced over his shoulder and saw that Elisabeth was keeping up with him. She didn't seem at all fazed by their trek. In fact, he was sure that he was more tired than she. Since he had given her some of his life force, she had seemed energized, even after hours of walking.

He couldn't believe she had never taken another's life force, but it did explain how she'd remained innocent. She had looked so startled by everything that was happening, but when it was done, she had stabilized. Elisabeth was lucky he had known what was happening, or she might have lashed out and hurt someone.

He nearly stopped short at the thought. That was exactly what he wanted her to do. He wanted her to commit a large enough mortal sin that his sword would work. Though he had not yet acquired a new one—the elders were busy with that—he still needed her to lash out at an innocent. Elisabeth's soul needed to be ready for harvesting when another sword was found. He could still do that, he thought, glancing at her.

"You don't need to keep checking on me. I am keeping up just fine."

He continued pushing forward, smiling at her stubbornness. Wiping his amusement from his lips, he reminded himself he needed to refocus. She was stronger here. Yet she was making it difficult to do so. She had a penchant for surprising him. He could still remember the way her hand had gripped his without hesitation.

When they came over the next ridge, he stopped and surveyed the valley behind him. They had decided to keep as far from the roads as possible. It was unwise to be caught unaware by the monsters that lived in this place. The dull red light was starting to fade, and a sense of disquiet gripped him.

"Night is coming," Ki informed her as she came up to stand beside him.

"Should we take cover?" she asked, looking back as well.

"You will need to take the amulet off so the darkness will not affect you. You will see the spirit lines and their light despite the overpowering inky blackness that is this place. Only I will be affected by the dark, but thankfully I have the amulet." Ki held out his hand.

He watched as she hesitated a moment before pulling the amulet off and handing it over to him. When it touched his skin, the fading red light vanished, and he saw the spirits. He preferred the many shades of purple that made up the spirit world. They moved along the lines, swirling and dancing like fish in a slow moving stream. He put the amulet on and turned to continue, but Elisabeth's hand wrapped around his wrist, stopping him.

"What is that?" she whispered.

Ki looked at it where she was pointing and saw ahead a small door cut into the face of the mountain that rose above them. The facade looked like an inn entrance, but with a burning red door. Ki stiffened in surprise. He knew exactly what that meant.

"Demon," Ki whispered as he moved them toward the other mountain to the right.

"That's a demon's home?" Elisabeth said, staring at it. "Why does it make me sad?"

"Trapped souls," he answered plainly. "Your other half must sense it."

"How?" she asked, her fingers digging into his wrist.

"Sometimes places in the Nether bleed into their corresponding location on the planets and lure people into them. It looks like a regular inn and people just wander in," he told her as her eyebrows furrowed. "Their souls are trapped, and the demon slowly feeds off them."

"That's terrible." She let his wrist go as she started up toward the foreboding door.

"What are you doing?" he called after her, but she didn't seem to hear.

What a fool! he thought as he hurried after her. He reached out to grab her, and they stopped just short of the door. Ki had to hold her in place to keep her rooted. She turned to him, and it wasn't Elisabeth that was looking at him anymore. Her other half had come alive. The amulet aided his eyes in revealing her skull on the left half of her face.

"A demon that feeds on souls is just a mortal who died by terrible means," Elisabeth whispered, and he realized her other half was acting on instinct.

"That isn't true," Ki commented before he could stop himself. He had never heard of such a thing. "Only the Divine Court can make demons."

126

"Not all demons. These are the mortals that fester in their emotions and die by terrible means. They are reborn to wreak havoc upon those that destroyed them," Elisabeth said before facing the door. "We must simply release them from their hatred."

She spoke like that was as easy as getting dressed or buttoning a shirt. Releasing a demon was unheard of, with the exception of what Malthael had done, of course, but he'd done that to himself. Elisabeth pushed her way through the double doors and went down the room-wide steps that greeted them. Ki stepped in to find a bustling inn before him. The entry area was circular, with tables and benches filling the center. Pillars with the circumferences of tree trunks supported the ceiling, and an enormous hearth filled the room with heat. He followed her toward the center of the room, amongst the inn's customers.

"Welcome to the Green Dragon Inn," a woman said. She wore Orani clothes and bowed when they approached. "A room for two?"

When Elisabeth continued to look around and didn't answer, Ki said, "No, we are just stopping to rest our feet."

"Perhaps some food then?" she asked.

Ki studied Elisabeth, but she still wasn't paying attention. "We're fine."

Elisabeth finally looked at the woman and touched her. "Be free."

The woman's body disintegrated, and Ki watched a sliver of light hover in front of him for a moment before it disappeared. The only thing that remained was a pile of dust on the floor and the dangerous silence behind him. He touched the amulet and realized that it wasn't strong enough here, meaning he was seeing what any mortal would see instead of what Elisabeth was seeing. Whatever this demon was, it was stronger than Ki had anticipated. Many of the patrons began to stand.

"What do you see?" Ki asked Elisabeth.

"They're all dead," she said, glancing back at him. "You were talking to a trapped spirit. Half her soul had been consumed, and her body was covered in marks."

"What kind of marks?" Ki asked as the patrons started to move toward them.

"The kind that looks like long thin blades grouped together."

"Like claws?" he asked, subtly pulling out his daggers.

Elisabeth surveyed the room. "Like a pitchfork used by farmers." Ki brought his daggers up when the patrons rushed forward, but Elisabeth called loudly, "I demand the master of these puppets show himself."

The dead patrons paused. They stood, bodies swaying, as they waited. Ki looked around, trying to figure out who she was speaking to, but apparently Elisabeth could see something he couldn't. This part of her was something he would have to deal with later to avoid additional trouble. A man dressed in Orani-style women's clothing stepped out of the shadows. He wore a gold robe with a thick black belt and moved gracefully for a man of his bulk. He giggled, but it sounded like a woman's laugh as he slowly moved along the edge of the room, always in profile. Ki watched him closely, preparing to strike, but Elisabeth stepped forward.

"What do you want, mortal?" the demon asked in a deep voice.

"I accept you for what you are," Elisabeth said plainly.

The demon froze and turned his head. A different, feminine voice said, "I do not understand what you mean."

"When you were rejected and cast out because of what you were, your heart broke," Elisabeth said. The demon still looked confused. "Remember your life. You liked pretty things and loved men. You didn't fit in your body."

The demon twisted around, and for the first time, Ki saw the other half of his face. It was that of a woman. How strange it looked to see two halves of a person stuck together. Ki cringed internally.

"They hated me," he said. "Despised me."

"You felt trapped," Elisabeth said, the compassion in her voice making Ki almost forget there was a very powerful demon before him. "Like you didn't know what you are, or who you were supposed to be. You felt as though you were a woman trapped in a man's body."

"I am a woman," he cried, and the walls shook with his anguish. "Why wasn't I born that way?"

"We cannot choose what we are born, only how we live," Elisabeth said, taking a step forward. Ki wanted to reach out and grab her, but he had a feeling that would be a bad idea and would break the spell. His gaze rolled over the swaying patrons. For now, they remained benign.

"When they killed me," he hissed, his voice feminine again, "they didn't regret what they did! They were happy I was gone."

"They were wrong," Elisabeth said, reaching out her hand. The dead patrons parted before her. "I accept you for who you are."

What was happening? Ki wondered, as the demon seemed intent on taking her hand. He seemed as though he was going to let his hatred go, but Ki didn't trust him for a second. Increased awareness and being able to see to the heart of the Netherworld didn't mean she was powerful enough to see through a trap. Just as their hands were about to touch, Ki caught a malevolent glimmer in the demon's eye. He snatched Elizabeth back by her shirt, and the demon roared.

The patrons suddenly surged forward, and Ki's daggers were instantly slashing through the air. Elisabeth said something to him, but he was already burying his weapons into the closest patron's chest. Sand spilled out of the holes the made, and the creature tried to cover them to stop the bleeding. Ki jumped off the first one and lunged for a second Ducking under an arm, he buried his daggers in a third. Seeing from of the corner of his eye that Elisabeth was running to the double doors through which the demon had fled, Ki began to fight his way toward her.

Chapter 33: Netherworld

φ

*E*lisabeth nearly screamed in frustration when Ki took hold of her arm, stopping her as the demon fled. Ki couldn't hold her long, though, as he was forced to turn back to the attacking patrons.

She turned only to see him move with killer speed. His daggers dug into the chest of one before he struck another and buried them up to the hilt in a third. Before the demon could get too far, she pushed her way through the first group of trapped souls, who turned to dust at her touch. The rest were quick to move out of the way before they could meet the same fate. Only she could see the spirits of the ones she managed to touch being released. Finally, after so many years of captivity, they were free of their prisons.

Elisabeth shouldered her way through the slightly ajar doors and hurried down a hallway full of gloomy framed paintings and smashed mirrors. Many of figures in the paintings had their eyes scratched out. The demon couldn't stand to be what he was; he didn't want anyone to see him. He couldn't accept it.

Something was driving her, some instinct she had never felt before leading her here. Her blood felt alive with energy as Elisabeth pushed a curtain out of the way at the end of the hall to find the demon kneeling before an altar on which rested a picture of a man, his face harsh but pleasant. The room was square and reminded her of a step-down pool, except the bottom was covered in fine rugs. Elisabeth let the curtain fall as she stepped into the room. The demon turned, his male half looking at her, and sneered.

"You don't belong here," he snarled, but she made no move to leave.

"That is who you loved?" she asked.

His face softened as he turned back and touched the picture tenderly. "No. It is my brother. He died protecting me when the others threw stones."

"He loved you, didn't he?" Elisabeth said, stopping behind him. "He knew and accepted you for what you are."

"He did," the woman in him said, her voice full of love.

Elisabeth understood what it was like to be different. She had always been afraid for anyone to see that part of her. Her demonic half had nearly cost her everything as a child when it had awoken. As an adult, she knew it isolated her because she was either feared or ridiculed. The only comforts she had were Malthael, Milo, and Tiss, but even they were enough. She needed to accept herself, which was easier to think than do.

"I know what that is like," she said. In that light, the female half looked almost beautiful before she shifted away. "To be rejected from the world because you are different."

"How are you different?" he snapped, his male face showing again. "You are beautiful and confident."

"And half demon," she pointed out.

The feminine face became demure as she asked, "Do you believe what you said earlier?"

"Yes," Elisabeth said, coming forward. "I accept you."

"Then you may go," she said, looking away toward the altar with the picture. "I will let you leave."

"I won't leave until you accept yourself," Elisabeth said softly, and the demon finally faced her fully to let her see both faces.

She didn't even flinch. Perhaps it was because she had grown up around demons that she wasn't surprised. Her upbringing had given her a steadfast belief that the surface of a being did nothing to reveal what he or she was like inside. Malthael was full demon and terrifying to look at, but he was gentle and loved her. Not to mention Milo and Tiss.

The demon looked startled when its face didn't scare her. Both halves seemed conflicted as Elisabeth stepped forward and the demon let her put her hands on both sides of his face. The woman half looked hopeful, while the man was suspicious.

"Thank you for revealing yourself to me," she said softly. "Can't you see how beautiful you are?"

"I am ugly," the demon spat, trying to pull away, but she refused to let them go.

"If you believe that, then that is what you will be," Elisabeth insisted. "If you want to be beautiful, accept yourself as such."

Years of self-hatred and rejection had created this demon. Only acceptance would free him from his current state. More than outside acceptance, the demon needed to accept itself. When he fell to his knees in defeat, tears streaming down his faces, she went with him. Kneeling, she wrapped her arms around him.

"You are exactly what you were supposed to be," she said softly as the demon sobbed.

"Thank you," he said. "Thank you for your kindness."

Elisabeth leaned back on her heels and watched as the demon turned back into a spirit, a ghostly version of pale purple light. The specter began to rise slowly. The heavy burdens weighing him down were lifted, allowing him to leave. She hoped he would be born again, hopefully this time as the beautiful girl he was on the inside. Perhaps they would meet again in her lifetime and she would see what The Fates had decided.

She lifted her hand as he ascended to wherever the dead went. She watched the soft blue of a peaceful spirit rising and, soon, leaving her alone. She could feel Ki's strange existence as he stepped into the room, as the last of the demon faded. The urge to cry was strong, but her heart was too happy to allow it. Instead, she let her hands fall back in her lap.

"He is free," she said as Ki came down the steps.

Suddenly, the ground started to shake. Ki hurried down the last few steps and held his hand out for her. "That's our cue to leave!"

She couldn't help but to smile as she took his hand. She gave a startled cry a moment later, though, when she was yanked up two steps. "Wait!"

"Hurry!" Ki called.

Elisabeth ran, picking up the picture of the demon's brother before following Ki. He took her hand again, and they fled through the rumbling inn. Dust swirled around the room. At first, Ki tried to go around the swirling vortex of spirits, but there wasn't time. The wind swept her hair across her face. She pushed her hair away so she could see the spirits. Her hand clamped down on Ki's. She could sense that the souls just wanted to leave. She knew they wouldn't hurt them. Pulling Ki though the center of the inn, she focused on the large double doors of the exit.

The building started to collapse as the gale forced the doors open. Ki and Elisabeth dashed through the opening. Dirt and debris shot out behind them, and Elisabeth covered her face, coughing. They watched as the whole building flattened out and the spirits escaped their prison. A part of her felt at peace as she watched, knowing that a portion of the demon was staying with her. She could feel his energy coursing through her veins.

"What will happen to them?" Ki asked, staring at the ruins.

"They will pass on to whatever comes next. I hope the demon will be reborn to try to redeem his soul for the lives he took." She looked at him. "Thank you for trying to protect me."

132

"It is my duty," he said. "I swore an oath."

She tried to keep the annoyance off her face at this response. "Ah, yes, your oath," she said, releasing his hand as she started to pick her way across the mountainside. It was a moment before he joined her.

Night was coming. Elisabeth could feel it. The droning red hadn't started to fade, but it soon would. She thought about the pendant and wondered what it would be like to see nothing—for the entire world to go dark. She assumed it was basically like being blind, a thought that terrified her. She glanced back at Ki as the amulet bobbed against his chest with every step. He studied her, but she ignored him. Soon, the soft purple was intersected by the blue of the spirit lines as the inky blackness of the Netherworld consumed them. It was clear and bright enough to see the mountain's rocky base, though, so she continued on. Monsters moved in the dark, but she wasn't afraid. She was part of the Netherworld.

Chapter 34: Hystera

ϕ

*J*inq **picked up the** pocked fruit and rolled it in his hand as he watched the small band of people gather around. Kerrigan had stayed back at their little camp to sleep. She had been pulled toward the darkness in this place like she had been caught in a flood. She had seen more than he had, and Jinq wanted to know why.

Unwilling to put her at risk again, as she was far too young and untrained, he decided to go to the source. Though Hipasha wanted her niece to be trained, if there were any more mishaps, he would send Kerrigan back to the safety of the capital. Hibrius had his head in Jinq's lap, equally unwilling to break their connection. His hand was on the panther's head as he reassured himself that Kerrigan would be safe with Mara and Cav. Between the two of them, she would sleep peacefully while Jinq handled the villagers. It had taken some convincing, but they allowed him back in with an escort.

They watched him with suspicion and desperation. The last time he'd come to them, all he'd found out was that their spirit animals were gone. Without them, it was impossible to figure out what had happened here.

What had happened to make them go from a normal village to the village of death? Jinq frowned and petted Hibrius as the last villagers gathered in the meeting hall. He'd already tried to get the information once, but no one had seemed to know anything about what happened. One moment they'd been whole, and the next their spirit animals had been lost. But maybe now that the Seer was eventually coming, he could press them for more information.

"Any news?" one of the men asked.

"We are petitioning to have a Seer come and look around the area," Jinq informed them, which sounded better than *We think the demon's daughter might be coming.* "I need to know all the details in order to have a successful petition when she returns. I need you to tell me everything that happened the night your spirit animals went missing, no matter how insignificant or minor it might seem."

"Where is she?" they asked. Jinq had to walk a fine line here.

These people might not know about the gates, but everyone knew about the Netherworld. It was impossible to hide the Soul Collectors. They went where they were summoned, called by a duty and to the dead. They brought order to chaos, all for some strange belief the Det Mor Clan had, which was enforced by the Morhaven King.

"She is in the Netherworld," Jinq answered honestly. He would have to be careful to conceal her when she did come; they could not know other worlds existed beyond the Netherworld, and her appearance would give her away.

Murmurs ran among them, filled with worry and heartache. They could not understand why she'd had left them to enter such a dangerous place. Many knew about the Soul Collectors and their owners, but that was it. Only the elders on the council, the Keepers, and the Gate Guardian knew the whole truth. Even Kerrigan didn't know, but that would change, as he would need her help to hide the Seer.

"Will you tell me how it started?" Jinq asked, talking just barely over their whispers. "Tell me everything."

"We went to bed one night, and our animals vanished," a woman said and shuddered. "I woke up from a nightmare, and he was gone."

"It wasn't just Rina. We all had nightmares the night that our spirit animals vanished." The man's voice was filled with despair.

If their spirit animals were dead, every person in that room should have died with them, unless something dark was at work keeping them alive. A shiver crawled up his spine at the possibility.

"What were the nightmares about?" Jinq asked.

They all glanced at one another. Jinq could see their eyes asking each other if they should say any more—if they should keep the details of their dreams to themselves or share them. He was beginning to believe they were hiding something from him. It must be a terrible secret to withhold, though, in such dire times. He suppressed the clench of worry in his gut as he wondered what was more terrifying than death.

"The plains around our village were on fire," one woman finally said. When someone tried to hush her, she pulled her arm free. "I remember feeling trapped."

"I remember blood," another said, her hands shaking as she looked at them. "It was all over my hands."

"That was in my dream, too," one of the men agreed, his voice filled with agony at the memory.

"There were men in robes in mine," another man said.

"They were chanting in my dream," a woman with dark hair said, her face drawn and pinched.

Jinq listened as they recounted their shared dreams. Some remembered that the men were chanting; others said they were silent. Many remembered seeing other spirit animals, but not their own. Jinq sat listening, letting their words wash over him as he took in the themes of chanting men, fire, and blood.

"What does it mean?" one of the women said.

"Shared dreams are nothing good," Jinq admitted. "Give me leave to explore this area."

"Our council did not agree," said their elected temporary leader, whose name had escaped Jinq's memory. "But I will ask again."

Jinq nodded before rising and moving toward the exit. He glanced back at the people around the room watching him with deadened expressions. Their hopelessness was like a plague. He kept his hand firmly against Hibrius's back before leaving. His walk through town was much the same as it had been the first time, but he felt something darker, and he remembered Kerrigan's words. She had seen death in this place—darkness so powerful that it had dragged her in there like a vortex.

She had been rattled by what she saw, a burning planet. Jinq had been blocked from it. He had seen nothing, and that worried him more. Kerrigan was more susceptible to whatever was happening here and would continue to be if the toxic gloom of this place continued to spread. When he reached the edge of town, an idea struck him. He stuck close to the edge of the forest and began searching. It wasn't long until he came across a small seared rock that had been licked by flames not a fortnight ago. He lifted it up to the sun and knew things in Himota were not as they seemed.

Chapter 35: Netherworld

— φ —

*n*anette tossed and turned in her sleep as she listened to the scratching. The spider creature was trying to get at her, and it wouldn't stop. The darkness of that night—an unrelenting pitch black—had spread around her, but the sound had been there, a scraping noise. Were it not for her complete exhaustion, she imagined sleep would never have come. The grating sound continued, and she wanted to scream.

She could smell its strange metallic blood and saw the gouges in the stone. She heard it clicking, listened to its call for food, hunger seemingly overcoming any pain of its crumpled hind legs. The noises made her feel half insane. It was there now, trying to get at her in the darkness. She tried not to move or breathe, but it was coming.

Nanette awoke in complete darkness. Fear gripped her as she immediately tried to push herself out of bed. She screamed on instinct, her eyes seeking out any light they could. Her skin broke out in a cold sweat as she listened for the clicking, but she couldn't hear it. Her breathing was hard and sharp as a light glared to life. She immediately shielded her eyes as her savior came close. She reached out for him instinctively, her fear of the dark making her sob uncontrollably.

He set the light down and pressed down on her arms. At first she was so frantic to take hold of him that she fought his grip on her. After a moment, she realized he was trying to calm her down. She felt her breathing start to slow as his face came into focus. His hands were still on her arms, so she locked her hands onto his elbows. She inhaled and exhaled in a measured way, trying to reign in her wild heart.

"I'm sorry," she said, glancing around as she tried to see further into the darkness and failed. "I don't like the dark."

She couldn't keep herself from shaking as she slowly let her arms fall. He released her shoulders as she pulled her legs up against her body. It was difficult not to act like a child when she was so afraid. She wrapped her arms around her legs and brought them to her chest. Putting her head on her knees, she squeezed her eyes shut and let the tears fall against the blanket.

After a moment, she opened her eyes and glanced up. Her savior was holding fire next to a small cylinder. She watched as the fire came to life and specks of light fell across the bed and walls. He pushed it and it started to spin, and she realized they were horses running across the wall. She pushed the sheet flat so she could watch it run.

"Thank you," she said, looking up again, but discovered he was gone.

Rising, Nanette went to the edge of the room and peered down the hall. She stood, pensive, as she tried to decide what to do. Glancing back at the dancing horses, she put an arm out into the darkness. It was strange that the light didn't seem to penetrate it. The darkness ended where this room began.

When she pulled her arm back, it was unchanged. It had been lost to the darkness for an instant as though an obscuring fog had descended upon the Netherworld rather than simply night. That first night, she had been so exhausted and hurt that she'd assumed her little sanctuary had made it so dark. Now she realized it had been much more than that.

"Where are you?" she asked the empty air as her hand touched the barrier.

Frowning, Nanette turned around, unwilling to brave the darkness unless she had to. As of yet she hadn't left the sanctuary and did not know where the long dark corridor led. She walked over to the lamp that still cast horse-shaped shadows, but they no longer ran. Twirling it, she laid her head on her arms as it spun and contemplated how her savior had created such a thing. She was just about to return to the bed when she heard someone grunt and the sound of the something hitting the ground.

Nanette froze, her eyes scanning the darkness as she breathed softly, wishing to make herself small and invisible. Her eyes went wide when she realized he could be hurt. Picking up the light, she lifted a long thin blade he had left on the wall and stepped up to the darkness. Taking a deep breath, she stepped into it, and instantly the bright light dulled to a soft glow. Her ring and pinky fingers ran along the rough stone as she followed the hallway, the blade gripped in the other fingers.

As she lifted the dimmed lantern, she realized she must be crazy to be risking herself. On the other hand, though, if something happened to him, she would be lost. In a few more steps she saw a soft light. She moved toward it and nearly tripped over him. He lay on his stomach and a dull red light burned in his lamp. She put the back of her hand on her nose at the smell. Whatever it was he had put in the lamp to ward away his

138

attacker had worked, and she could smell why. It reminded her of singed hairs and sour milk.

Nanette put down her lamp and slowly rolled him over, careful not to cut him with the blade. When he was on his back, she patted his shoulder and whispered, "It's all right."

She put the knife down across his chest so that it lay there as she lifted him up by his armpits. Pushing the light back with her foot, she heard it scrape against the ground. She dragged him toward the safety of the cave but nearly dropped him when her leg protested. It welled with pain at his added weight, but she tried to ignore it, though tears were burning her eyes.

When she tried to reposition the lamp, her foot slipped, and she fell. Her body was jolted as she fell half into the room with a groan. Getting her feet under her, she pulled him along the floor and into the chamber. By the end, she was mostly rolling him across the floor until he was safely inside the cave. Sighing, she patted him on the head.

"You're as solid as a rock and as unmoving as a boulder," she said, pushing him off her leg, which had somehow gotten trapped underneath him, and further into the sanctuary. The room was dark except for the soft glow from the overturned lantern that lay between the room and the darkened corridor.

Standing, Nanette hobbled over and plunged her hand into the darkness. As her fingers wrapped around the handle, something touched her wrist. She gasped in surprise and tried to pull her hand back, but whatever was coiled around her wrist refused to budge. When the lantern bounced off the ground, she realized she'd dropped it. As Nanette sucked in a breath to scream, whatever was holding onto her wrist pulled her into darkness.

Chapter 36: Netherworld

φ

K **i's eyes followed** Elisabeth as she ambled along the base of a cliff. The charm in her hand seemed to glow brightest whenever she stood under its opening. He could see the entrance to a cave that was up on the face of the mountain. It would be quite a climb, and he would have to do it alone without Elisabeth's special sight to assist him. He could see light, and he could see some of the lesser demons, but Elisabeth could see everything.

"She is up there," Elisabeth said, pointing up.

Just as quickly as the light burned bright, it began to fade. Ki frowned. "She was."

There was movement as the mouth of the cave, and Ki could see a bald man at the edge. The man didn't notice them at first as his gaze searched the horizon. Elisabeth took a step back, which drew his attention, and he looked startled to see them there. His face contorted in anger as he jumped from the opening. Elisabeth stumbled back. The edges of his tattered clothes flapped around him as he fell, and he landed in a crouch where she had been. Ki shifted to the space between Elisabeth and this strange man, his hands wrapped around the hilt of his daggers.

"Where is she?" Elisabeth demanded.

The bald man stopped, glaring at them both. He frowned as Ki stared at him with an even expression. When the man took a step toward Elisabeth, she pulled back from him, but when Ki took a step forward, she held a hand up to stop him. The man leaned forward and inhaled, taking in her scent, and Ki knew, without knowing why, that he should heed Elisabeth's wishes. .

Elisabeth looked at him, confused and clearly uncomfortable, but it didn't seem like she felt she was in danger. Ki kept his hands on his daggers nevertheless. He didn't like the feel of the bald man with bandages over the lower half of his face. Ki pulled his steel half out as a warning, but he paused when Elisabeth gasped.

"You're a…" she began, but he put a hand up to stop her.

He put a finger to his lips, and Elisabeth nodded. He pulled his hand back and started to make signals. She nodded again. He bowed to her slightly before he pointed up and then dashed away. As Ki walked up to stand next to her, Elisabeth seemed dazed. She stared at where the man had been, and something inside of Ki was displeased with her expression of awe.

"What is he?" he asked, disrupting her thoughts.

"I can't say. Names have meaning here," Elisabeth answered vaguely before looking at him. "He is going to take us to her."

"It could be a trap." Ki's mood had soured, and it was reflected in the sharpness of his voice.

Elisabeth shook her head. "He thought we took her," Elisabeth said, and Ki glanced at her, befuddled.

"How can you know that?" Ki asked as the bald man appeared again and made his way down.

"His face." Elisabeth's voice was airy. "She has only been here two days, and already she has charmed him. I want to know this woman who can survive the Netherworld and charm"—she glanced at him before adding—"his kind."

The bald man put a pack over his head, and when he turned, Ki saw the markings on the man. His eyebrows rose, and he instantly understood. Those were runes, markings of great power, the kind used by the Chaos Clan. The kind that were reserved for those who had done terrible things and deserved their punishment—it was a powerful prison. Yet something about these marks struck him as different.

"Is it wise to follow this stranger?" he said, taking her wrist.

Her startled gaze rested where he held her firm, but her voice was mostly even. "He will not betray us to them, and he knows who took Nanette."

He let go of her wrist and she visibly relaxed. Elisabeth was worlds away from falling victim to his Sin Eater. In the days he had spent with her, she had been a shining example of goodness and virtue. Part of him hoped she would never fall victim to it, but that part was so small within him that he endeavored to ignore it.

Ki fell silent as Elisabeth trailed behind the bald man. He had no choice but to follow as well. There were few things in the Nether that he could see for what they were, like Elisabeth did. If those markings were any indication, the bald man was powerful, or had been. He didn't know exactly what the runes were or why they seemed to shift about on the man's skin every once in a while. He would have to ask the elders after they returned to the planets.

They traveled through the night. Normally they would have been in danger, but whatever the man burned in his lantern kept the monsters at bay. Ki could see it burning a strange off-red and could smell the pungent scent. Between that and the power emanating from Elisabeth, the creatures of the Netherworld stayed at a safe distance. He could feel them in the darkness, though, and every once in a while he heard clicking. Weavers could not hurt a Soul Collector, and they would dare not try, yet they could still hunger for one. Ki had never known a Weaver to be picky.

Hours passed as they continued their walk, never resting as they picked their way across the countryside of the Nether. It was littered with ruins and barren fields. He admired the strange beauty of this derelict place. Eventually Morhaven came into view, its bright summery light penetrating the darkness. It was as though an artist had splashed green against a red canvas. Ki could see the barrier of Morhaven repel the night of the Netherworld, marked only by the change of rust to a field of green.

"Amazing," Elisabeth breathed, her voice full of awe.

The man didn't wait for Elisabeth to overcome her wonderment. Ki made sure that Elisabeth was safely through before following her. When he glanced up, he beheld the strange weeping willow. Lights danced in the soft wind and stirred with the leaves. Ki was entranced as he strolled toward it. The bright red flowers seemed to dance in the wind, beckoning to him. He was lulled into a state of calm. A rough hand caught his arm and hauled him back. He struggled against it as Elisabeth's face appeared in front of him. She was trying to say something but he ignored it, trying to shove around her.

Then, suddenly, he was back in the Netherworld. He panted and gazed longingly toward the lush green. Elisabeth was still on the other side of the barrier. The soft breeze rifled her hair, brushing it across her shoulders, as though she were a mirage. When she stepped across the threshold, her hair settled. Once Ki stilled, the bald man stepped back.

"What happened?" he asked, still dazed.

"You were called in by the Poppy Tree," she said, crouching down beside him. "It seems you are more of a planet-dweller than you let on."

The bald man stood went to the grass before turning back and saying in a bizarrely deep voice, "We must leave him here."

"He spoke," Ki said, shocked and still feeling dazed. He pointed at the bald man and looked toward Elisabeth for an answer.

"The runes suppress my voice until I return home," he replied, and Ki slowly started to stand. "I shall only be free when I am in Morhaven."

"You're…" he started before glancing at Elisabeth. "I cannot trust you with them."

Elisabeth hesitated and glanced at the bald man before sighing heavily as though conflicted. "I cannot trust you to come through here. The poppies of Morhaven are deadly," she said, standing. "Stay here. I'll be careful."

"I will take care of her," the bald man said.

Ki began to protest, but Elisabeth stopped him. "Ki," she said, her voice a whisper, "you can't come."

He remembered how cautious she'd been earlier. He leaned forward and whispered, "Take some of my life force."

She tried to pull back, but he caught her arm.

"No," she said, her voice tight.

"That demon only gave you some, and you need everything you can get," he said, pulling her closer.

Her eyes were full of fear. Ki disregarded her protest as well as the baseless pang of disappointment that he dismissed as an after-effect of the Poppy Tree. He pressed his lips to hers before she could protest, and he felt her mouth open as she put her hands on each side of his face. Elisabeth might deny him, but her instincts would kick in. Soul Collectors couldn't take life force from the living, but she was half-living and half-Soul Collector. The rules did not apply to her. After a moment he turned his head, breaking the connection.

When he met her gaze, there was revulsion in her eyes, and tears welled. He turned his head away as she stood. He knew he had done the right thing. She needed it, but that didn't make him any less guilty. She had been unwilling, and it had not been necessary as it had been when she had first stepped through.

"Stay here," she whispered before turning and fleeing through the barrier.

He watched them go. Standing, he studied the tree, still remembering his mindless need. She was entering a world of trouble. The Nether had its monsters, but the worst of them were the Det Mor Clan. They would be her greatest challenge, and he had no choice but to let her go. Sitting back down with crossed legs, Ki put his elbow on his knee and leaned against his fist, thinking that she had better not get herself killed.

Chapter 37: The Divine Court

———————— φ ————————

"**H**er hair is so plain," a high pitched voice said, rousing Nanette from sleep.

"It does feel like silk though," another voice answered. She opened her eyes slowly when she felt something brush through her hair.

"Oh, she stirs," a voice said with a giggle.

Two sets of large golden eyes gazed at her, filled with curiosity and wonder.

"Where am I?" Nanette asked.

"Morhaven," one of the girls popped up and said. "More specifically the Divine Court, home to the Det Morian King."

"What are the Det Morian?" Nanette asked, sitting up although her ribs protested.

The girls exchanged glances. The peppy one who thought her hair plain had vibrant green hair with flowers braided into it and a poppy-shaped adornment over one ear. Two marks started at the top of her forehead in a single curl and then fell down on each side of her nose before fading toward her pointed ears and ending in a single dot. The other, who had thought her hair silky, had short, spiked red hair. A black mask covered her eyes and went into her hair. The long streaks of lines of black going through her fiery red hair reminded Nanette of dying embers in a fire.

"They are the great clan, the Chaos Clan and the Balance Keepers," the green haired one said with an aloof air. "Led by King Nauberon."

"Long be his reign," the other one said, as though by instinct. "What was he like?"

"Who?" Nanette asked, her mind still a little foggy.

The flower girl glanced over her shoulder before leaning forward and whispering, "The banished prince."

"Who?" Nanette said, as her memories came back to her.

"The cursed one," she responded, glancing down at her companion. "The wordless one."

"My savior," she whispered. Nanette was suddenly fully awake. "I have to go."

Her memories came back sharp as an arrow, and she immediately tried to stand. The girls, who only came up to her collarbone, put up their arms and tried to stop her. She pushed them aside and walked toward the door. She had to get back to him. He was hurt.

"Stop, mortal!" the fiery one said, her arms wrapped around Nanette's waist.

"I have to find him," she said as she pushed the doors open.

What she saw behind them made her gasp. The room in which she had awoken had been much like her home in Oran. Paper doors, simple but intricate designs. But when she walked through the doors, she was in a place of trees. Glancing up, she saw that the trees were holding up the ceiling.

White petals seemed to be falling to the ground in an internal cycle. She put a hand out, and one of the petals glanced off her hand. One of the girls pulled her arm down and started to turn her. In awe, she let the girls take hold of both her arms and turn her around and back toward the room.

"You are not to leave!" the green haired one said.

Nanette took a few steps toward the room before stopping in her tracks and turning back again. The girls called after her, but she ignored them. Her ankle hurt, and she had to put her arm across her waist as she walked. Petals brushed against her face as she made her way into the tree room.

"Stop!" they called behind her, but their cries only made her move faster.

She went to the end of the hall and pushed open two great double doors. Behind them was another room, this one full of purple trees that looked like fluff. Opalescent flowers twined around the base of the trees in long massive strips and seemed to move in the wind. Nanette gawked around her in wonder as she kept staggering, the girls running to keep up. They couldn't be much younger than her, yet they were so small. They looked like teenagers yet were the size of pre-pubescent children.

When she pushed into the next room, the doors to the previous room closed behind her and a lumbering tree-like beast moved by. Nanette stumbled out of way in shock as something spilled out and sloshed at the floor by her feet. The creature made a soft trumpeting noise as its steps shook the floor. Moss and small plants spread out across the floor from the spilled liquid.

The foliage stopped just before her feet, and the girls caught up to take hold of her arms. "What is it?" Nanette asked.

"An elemental," the flower girl said. "We are their caretakers."

"You?" she asked in astonishment, glancing down before looking back up as the leafy creature made its way down the hall, "You take care of that?"

"They are instinctual," the same girl answered. "We must keep them safe when they venture into the Dusky Woods beyond the safety of the Divine Court."

"I see," Nanette asked, glancing down what seemed like an endless hall. "How big is this place?"

"It holds all of the beauty of the worlds here," she answered, turning her around. "The Dusky Woods, Morhaven, the Endless Well, the Det River, and the Poppy Fields. It is the home of the king of Morhaven and guardian of the Netherworld."

"You forgot the ruins of Old Haven," the girl of fire said.

"I didn't forget. I don't like that place," she answered, sticking her nose in the air. "Not even a caretaker will go there."

"So many places," she said as they led her away. "Why is the prince cursed?" she asked.

Again they exchanged glances. Finally, the flower girl answered, "His brother cursed him."

"Why did his brother curse him?" Nanette asked absentmindedly while she let herself be steered back.

"Fanta! These matters are not to be discussed," the fire girl snapped before the other could speak.

"We can't have her face the King without information," Fanta replied.

"The Fates will decide what becomes of her, not the King," she insisted, putting her hands on her hips.

They stopped walking as Fanta leaned forward. "You're so stubborn, Tohru!"

"I don't want to be reprimanded because you couldn't hold your tongue!" Tohru snapped, her hair shimmering suddenly and seeming to burn like fire.

"Who are The Fates?" Nanette interrupted, and both girls stopped to look at her.

"The trinity of life, the past, present, and future," Fanta answered before Tohru could shush her.

"That sounds worrisome," Nanette said as they passed into the white petal room. She noticed a waterfall at the far end.

"Melody is very wise because of all her knowledge of the past, Serenity is the conduit between the future and the past, and Destiny is so full of hope that she represents our future," Fanta answered excitedly as Tohru grumbled.

"We should not be telling a planet-dweller this," Tohru muttered under her breath as she sulked.

As Nanette they entered the original room, her mind was working. How could this woman Destiny be able to see the future? Wouldn't the future be known then and their destiny always predetermined? The idea did not sit easy with Nanette, and she rubbed her forehead, trying to drive away her headache. This idea of peering into the future didn't sit well, and it was giving her brain an overload of thoughts.

"Let's get you ready!" Fanta said, clapping her hands together in excitement. "And then we shall make you look like you belong here."

Nanette nodded and let herself be washed and changed. Her mind was on her savior. Strange that he should be an exiled prince and she a butterfly princess. Perhaps *fate* was pre-destined. This set of circumstances only supported the assertion. She tried not to sigh as she wondered if he was safe and, for that matter, if *she* was safe. It wasn't until Fanta and Tohru were ushering her out the door that she realized she still didn't know his name.

Chapter 38: Hystera

_____ φ _____

*J*inq was roused awake by Cav's squawking. In his hurry to get to his feet, he nearly hit his head on their little makeshift table. It took a moment for the haze of sleep to be blinked from his eyes and for him to be able to see their small tent. Behind him, Hibrius was instantly on alert as well.

Jinq's eyes fixed on the bird as it went wild against the tent. At first Jinq didn't know why, but then he saw that the bed was empty. His blood ran cold as he forgot the bird and hurried out into the grass. He didn't even take a moment to put on his shoes. Hibrius bound beside him.

"Mara, keep him here!" he called. There was a short trumpeting noise followed by some crashing clamors as the elephant attempted to catch the little bird.

He tried not to cringe as he bound across the plains. The grass brushed up against his arms as he ran, his old body protested at every jarring step. When he reached the edge of the wood, he put his hand on Hibrius and felt the burden of gloom lessen. His heart quickened as they entered Himota, approaching the tree of death.

He nearly yelled out when he saw the people gathered around and realized there was a figure in the tree. She still had Cav, he reassured himself. It wasn't her. He kept his steps careful as he walked toward the crowd, and relief filled him when he saw it was the woman from days earlier who had spoken of the dream. She was ambling along one of the branches like it was a tightrope.

"Please come down," one woman cried, but her plea was halfhearted. Her pain was real enough, deep and stanched. It was on all of their faces, but as he scanned the crowd he didn't see the one face he wanted to.

He pushed his way through the crowd yelling, "Who is the man you are flying away from?"

They parted for him in a slow, staggering fashion, and he continued to skim the faces around him. The woman in the tree stopped and glanced down, and the crowd gasped softly. Her head tilted to the side as she put her hand to her throat.

"I cannot see, but he burns," she said, her voice filled with ecstasy. "He burns!"

Jinq swallowed as she danced across the branch, swaying in sweet delight. He could hear her humming. Suddenly, she stopped and glanced down, her gaze seeming distant. Jinq narrowed his eyes to try to see her better.

She pointed behind her and whispered so softly that Jinq barely hear her. "He'll be here soon."

With that, she leaned forward and plummeted to her death. Jinq didn't turn away as she fell, her face twisted in pleasure. He heard the sickening crunch as her neck snapped. She lay mangled in a pool of her own blood. He'd wanted to save her but knew it would have been only temporary; they always found a way to die. This was an easier death than most had been. He could still remember the charred remains of the family who'd set their home on fire. The villagers had told him they'd heard the family singing as they burned to death. This was the seventh death he had seen since coming, though she had been the first to die alone.

"May the spirits take you," he whispered, no longer denying the suicides a prayer.

Whatever was happening here was dark and out of these people's control. He had a feeling that they were being manipulated. The villagers glanced at him, some wandering off like lost souls. He stood, rooted, his eyes watching the broken woman. They didn't even bother to cover the dead anymore. Someone would come later and move her away so another sorry soul could die without other bodies in the way.

"Kerrigan!" he yelled suddenly, craning his neck.

Worried that she would become like this woman, he felt this desperate need to find her. The crowd was dispersing, yet she was nowhere to be found. He glanced in the direction in which the woman had pointed and then turned back to camp. The men and women of the village watched him closely as he left, their eyes glittered dark in the moonlight.

He felt his sleeping socks scuff on the ground. They would be ruined soon, but Jinq hardly spared them a thought. After he and Hibrius entered the tree line, he continued a few paces before turning left. He followed the edge of the tree line toward where she had pointed. Moving carefully with the silent panther by his side, he considered his options. Jinq's eyes were alert and piercing, his hand was steady on Hibrius's back.

It didn't take long until he heard the soft chanting of many voices in a chorus as one. Curiosity and a drive to know the truth pushed him forward. He came to a small opening between tightly woven bamboo trees. They made a distinct clacking noise when the wind pushed them. They rose up in tight succession without much give. Jinq leaned forward, gazing through a break in the wall.

Men in black robes stood around a slab of stone. They had their arms raised, and their voices were turned to the moon. They did not shout, the power of their voices soft and steady. Jinq listened to them, sure that whatever was happening in Himota was caused by them. He took a step back, and a branch snapped under his weight.

One stopped chanting and turned in his direction. Panicked that they would find him, he considered running or fighting. Hibrius responded first by moving around in front of him and shape-shifting. The area hummed with the power they had raised, but without that other voice, it was falling flat. He heard voices stop one by one.

"What is it?" he heard one ask as leaves rustled.

Eyes glazed out across the darkness and peered at where Jinq had been standing. He was crouched down now, perfectly hidden by a boulder. Hibrius had shapeshifted to hide him perfectly, but if they went too much further, they would round the illusionary boulder.

"Nothing," he said, and his voice faded as he returned to the protected clearing. "I thought I heard something."

"Let us raise our voices," another said, and once more a hum filled the air as they became one voice.

Hibrius waited minutes before changing back to his panther form, and Jinq relied on his good eyesight to lead them away. Every step he took moved him further from their discovery, but he was no fool. Those men had power and lots of it. He could not say what the slab of gray, featureless stone was for. Darker workings were at play, and Jinq needed that Seer. He needed her to see what he could not.

When he reached the tree line, they found Kerrigan pacing in front of the tent. She looked worried until she saw him. When she ran toward him and threw her arms around his chest, he nearly lost hold of Hibrius and tumbled backward. He just managed to keep his footing and keep his fingers touching the panther.

"I was so worried," she said, her voice shaking. "I awoke from a terrible dream and walked along the plains, and when I came back, you were gone. I thought something had happened to you."

"I'm fine," Jinq said to reassure her, patting her on the back.

She untangled herself and quickly stepped back, her face etched in worry. "Someone else die?"

"Yes," Jinq said, glancing away for a moment, "but she gave us a clue before she did."

"Like the other woman?" Kerrigan asked, hopeful.

"Much like the other woman, but I cannot understand why," Jinq responded, deciding not to mention the strange men. "I need the Seer."

Chapter 39: Morhaven

φ

*T*he poppy fields were alive with trees and fields of red flowers. Elizabeth had seen other colors of poppies in her life besides red such as yellow and orange, but none existed here. The ones here reminded her of blood, as though the forest was bleeding. She didn't glance back as she walked away from Ki. She had tried to push down the feeling of disgust at her need to consume life force. She frowned, her face pressed low by the memory. She loathed this part of herself, the part that had to feed. She hated what the Nether had forced her to confront, and she didn't like dwelling on it.

"What should I call you?" Elisabeth asked, wishing to distract herself from these thoughts.

He glanced at her, his worn clothes and bald head doing little to hide that he was from here. His fine features and muscular figure only made her certain he was a Det Morian, but it was the eyes that sealed the deal. Her demonic half had sensed he was a member of the Divine Court, but she'd read about the Det Morians and their brilliant green orbs. Problem was, she had no idea who exactly he was.

"I have many names," he said quietly, as though considering how best to answer. "All of which would be difficult for you to pronounce and difficult for me to impart in such a way that you would understand."

"What would you have told Nanette?" Elisabeth asked pointedly, knowing full well there was power in a name here.

Elisabeth saw the barest of smiles at her name before he answered without hesitation. "Ethandirill."

"I am Elisabeth," she told him but did not offer her hand as she would with anyone else.

She brought her hand up and brushed the back of her hand against his cheek, and he did the same with hers. It was strange custom that the Det Mor Clan upheld with fervor. It was supposed to show kindness, an intimacy even, at a first meeting.

"We are known," she said, and his voice married hers.

152

"You know the custom," he said with a pleased smile that could have melted a mortal woman into piles of sensual goo. "Who taught you this?"

She cleared her throat as her mortal half tried to melt. Instead, she managed, "My adoptive father."

He nodded before turning. "The Mad Dog."

"I have heard him called that," Elisabeth said, hurrying after him. "Why was he given this moniker?"

"He was a fighter, a very strong one, but he decided to bite his master's hand and hold his own leash," he said, glancing at her. "It was because of a mortal that he tore his immortality from his head and condemned himself to a limited lifetime. Only a mad dog would do this."

Part of her was saddened that her papa would do something as brash as condemn himself to a mortal life. Yet without his having made that decision, she would not have survived. A life for an immortal life, it seemed. She could not imagine Malthael now as anything but what he was.

Soon they left the poppy fields and entered the edge of the forest that ran between the poppy fields and the fortress of the Divine Court. The trees were tall, and the leaves were purple, faded in places and blotched with yellow and a deeper purple in others. The deep brownish green of the roots matched the purple almost perfectly. To her left she could see where the more sinister version of the Dusky Woods existed. Unlike the rest of the Nether, these woods seemed to be lit by natural sunlight. Elisabeth knew magic when she saw it, though, and she couldn't feel the warmth on her skin.

A thundering came from the distance.

"We need to hide," Ethandirill said, moving back before ducking behind a large shimmery rock.

"Oh my," Elisabeth said as beings galloped by.

Their coats shimmered and their tails were impossibly long. Single horns stuck out from their heads and the opalescent scales on their back caught the light. She was half over the rock in wonderment when the prince of the Det Mor Clan dragged her down.

"Unicorns," he said with his back pressed up against the rock. "Beautiful but vicious."

"I thought they were pure white," she whispered, remembering the stories. "And kind."

"Foolish planet-dweller," he scoffed, but his lips betrayed his amusement. "So full of hope. You see them for what they are—wild, shimmering with color, and selfish."

She listened as they stampeded by, and she knew this memory would remain with her. When all fell silent, Ethandirill looked over the top of the rock. He surveyed the area before darting across the clearing. Elisabeth hurried behind him, her leg brushing up against a strange red plant as she went.

"How much further?" Elisabeth asked and then stumbled a little.

She looked down at her leg and saw that it was smeared with red. Her eyes opened wide as she reached down and pulled out a single barb. Her hands shook as she hastily threw it. She tried to say something, but her tongue was swollen.

"Not much further," he said. She fell forward, and he turned back in surprise, "Elisabeth?"

She moaned, and he hurried to turn her over. Her entire body went numb. He must have seen the marking on her leg, as he frowned. Elisabeth was trying hard not to panic, but it was become more and more difficult. Her breath was coming in short bursts, each one harder and harder to take

"The lilies here are deadly," he said. He set her down and strode over to pluck the flower from which the barb had come. "You need to drink."

He knelt down and lifted her head. He opened her mouth as he pried the closed bloom open. Bitter liquid poured into her throat, which she tried to swallow but couldn't. Seeing him press a hand over her nose and mouth, she tried to scream. She couldn't feel anything except for the movement of her throat as he forced her to swallow. When he moved away his hand, she gasped for air.

"It will be over soon," he said.

Elisabeth's fingers began to work first, and after a moment she could lift her arm. She tried to move her legs, which were slower to respond, as she wiggled her tongue around in her mouth. He helped her sit up. She turned her head as she wrinkled her nose at the revolting after taste.

"Don't say it will be over soon. That sounds so ominous," she choked out, half glaring.

Ethandirill raised his eyebrows in mocking surprise. "Any Netherworlder knows to avoid the flowers. All of them have their own way to kill."

"Ki would have known," she grumbled.

154

"Ah yes, your pet," Ethandirill said, offering her an arm.

All parts of her but the leg that had been stung were now completely fine. Apparently the poison took as long to spread through her system as it did to wear off. She wobbled a little, but he kept her steady as he glanced around. She thought for a moment before she made a decision to be honest.

"He's my assassin," she corrected him plainly.

He turned his head back to her in surprise. With a little chuckle he asked, "Who do you need to kill?"

She all but rolled her eyes as she took a measured step forward. She nearly stumbled, and he caught her arm. "You misunderstand. He is my assassin. He intends to kill me," she replied.

He squinted at her as though he thought she was joking. It was a long moment before he finally turned back to her. Frowning, he studied her face, his sharp green eyes seeming to glow.

"If you keep staring at me like that, your face will get stuck," she muttered as she took a few steps on her own.

"Why do you let him follow you?" he asked finally.

"He can't let me die until he can be the one to kill me." She sighed heavily as she continued to walk, her leg gaining strength with every step. "Until then, he is like a guardian."

"He both protects you and promises to kill you?" Ethandirill asked, coming around to walk at her side.

"Basically," Elisabeth conceded with a sheepish grin. "My life seems to be too complicated lately. I much preferred when I tried to determine the stranger things in life. Fringe sciences and ectoplasmic research now seem so normal."

Ethandirill began to slow, and Elisabeth could see the towers of the Divine Court. They could only be so many paces away. The architectural details of the complex building caressed the skyline. The elegant steeples were arching and ethereal. The greyish stone was almost white in some areas, and she wondered if time had changed its color.

"I can go no further," he responded as she saw the edge of the woods. "This is where I leave you."

"Thank you," she said, adjusting her pack.

She turned to leave, but he caught her arm and said softly, "Tell Nanette my name. I want to her know it."

Before Elisabeth could respond, he swiftly moved into the shadows that the forest provided. His gaze was sharp as it watched something. Elisabeth's eyes opened wide as she followed the direction of this stare. A man nearly twice as tall as her stood between them and the Divine Court. She walked slowly forward toward the edge of the hedgerow and saw that great antlers crowned his head.

"Daughter of life and death," he said, his voice so deep that she felt it shake the very ground she walked on. "I am here to escort you to King Nauberon. Long be his reign."

She stepped from the tree line to see all of him. He was muscular and wore finely made embroidered leather. On his black chest were thick long claw-like red markings. His pitch-black skin was marked with golden tattoos, much like the ones on Ethandirill's head, and he stared with dark eyes. He carried a great bow on his back, carved with intricate details.

"Arawn," she said. She knew who he was from pictures in books, but the static images did not capture his intensity.

He seemed pleased that she knew his name. She gawked, trying hard not to fear him, but he was the King of the Hunt. No one could match him, and if he'd been sent to fetch her, she could only imagine what King Nauberon thought of her. Was it meant to intimidate or show respect? When he turned to leave, she followed, sparing only a single glance back in Ethandirill's direction. The further she got from the Dusky Woods, the more she realized she was very much alone.

φ

"**T**here has been no** word," Milo said with a frown. His body was fully recovered, and he stood before Malthael with a face of displeasure.

"She should be in Morhaven by now," Malthael said, pacing in his study, "or already to the Divine Court."

"You should not have let her go," Milo said harshly, finally voicing the irritation that had been on his face all morning.

"She is her own woman," Malthael countered, but his words sounded hollow even to himself.

"She adores you. She would do anything you asked," the lesser demon countered.

"I wanted her to stay, but the worlds need her," he all but yelled, his temper snapping at the edges. "A need greater than the wants of one father."

"She is your daughter," he said, his young face contorted in discontent. "You should have sent her to Hystera. It is not as dangerous as the Nether. You should not have sent her where we cannot see or help her!"

"I wanted her to go to Troy, but I could not stop her when she chose the Nether!" he bellowed before stalking out of the room and toward the kitchen.

He stomped all the way there. His temper didn't dissipate with every slammed door and every stomp but instead grew and swirled with his worry. Elisabeth was all that mattered now. She was all that ever had mattered, but he couldn't control her. He swore that she would make her own choices, and now he would have to live with it. All of the consequences were not borne by her alone, though; he felt them just as keenly.

When he burst into the kitchen, Tiss gasped in astonishment. The snake demon turned her beautiful face, which was already made up, as her serpentine body coiled around the kitchen. He hunkered down at the small table used by the staff and grumbled to himself.

After a moment he said, "Coffee, black."

She was already pouring the cup and set it down in front of him without adding milk. "To match your mood."

"I have no need for your wit this morning," he said, snatching the cup from her fingers.

"How about my reason?" Tiss asked as she went around the table and sat down.

He barely kept from grumbling as he muttered, "What logic of yours could possibly improve my mood?"

"That she has seen worse things in this house; she has grown up amongst demons. That she is as much a part of this world as she is of the Netherworld. That the Det Mor Clan has more to gain by keeping her alive because without her the balance would be thrown off. At least one half-breed must exist."

"Thank you," Malthael managed, his voice hushed. She'd thrown logic at him, making him realize that he was letting emotion cloud his reason.

"Now go," she said, pushing herself up and moving around to the kitchen counter where she had been cutting. "Go and do something useful."

He swallowed the coffee and ignored that it scalded his mouth and throat. The pain would fade in a moment, and he needed the extra boast, though coffee was about as ineffective as alcohol on him—which is why he bought the highly concentrated kind of both. He went around the counter and kissed her softly on the cheek.

"Your wisdom, though not your face, show your age," he said, patting her on the shoulder.

"Your compliments aren't needed," Tiss said, but he could see her swell with pride.

Snake demons were extremely vain, and she was no different. It has been some time since he had taken a moment to appreciate her. He was glad he could take a moment now and give her the compliment she needed. Elisabeth was much better at filling that role, and with each passing day Malthael was coming to realize more and more ways that Elisabeth had taken care of him. She had run this household when she was here and had made sure Malthael knew what to do when she was gone. This time had been different.

He walked with purpose as he returned to the study. Milo was gone, so he would have to apologize for his behavior later. Milo was right, yet he was also wrong. He was right to worry, but he was wrong that Elisabeth couldn't handle herself. She was his daughter, and Malthael had not spared any expense on her thorough education. Only the Netherworld had been kept from her.

When he clicked open the passage and the slab of rock turned away, Nathan and Duke appeared at his side. They followed him down, their great hooves clicking on the marble. He went down into the underbelly and to the gate. He pulled the dial back, and it instantly clicked through the different areas. They had been keeping meetings lately, but Malthael had another objective.

When Troy's face appeared and Meridith's as well, they turned to him in surprise. Troy sat up and asked immediately, "Has the Seer returned?"

"No," Malthael replied, "but I need to know where Elisabeth should go when she returns."

"It is out in the plains," Troy said and then disappeared, though his voice could be heard. "A small village called Himota."

"What is it, Malthael?" Meridith asked, her face worried.

"If Nathan and Duke know where to take her, she can go to your elder faster," Malthael said, and saw the surprise on Troy's face.

"That makes sense," he replied in an even tone as he held a rolled parchment in his hand.

"It does, the map," Malthael said, gesturing toward it.

Nathan and Duke crowded around him as Troy cleared his throat and unrolled the map. He pointed and said, "Here is Himota."

"Is that enough?" Malthael asked, looking down at the two dogs.

They sniffed the gate before Nathan sneezed. They both looked up at him with their sharp fur and their tongues rolled out of their mouths. They most certainly knew what they were doing. Malthael petted their head for good measure. Though they looked more like boars, their demeanors were that of domesticated dogs.

"When Elizabeth returns, I shall direct her there the moment she is ready," Malthael declared, reaching out to turn the gate closed.

"Malthael," Troy said, putting a hand up to stop him, "send her my regards."

It was as near to an apology as Troy would manage. The light marks on his head reminded the demon of truly how young Hystera's Gate Guardian was. Malthael tilted his head but nodded without adding a verbal chide. Troy was young, and he would learn that apologies did not cost as much as he thought.

"Of course," he said before clicking the dial back in place and returning the gate to stone.

Chapter 41: The Divine Court

*n*anette was ushered toward a short door. She couldn't help but glance at the beings guarding it. They were large and wore strange masks—long triangles that very much reminded her of crows. The masks had frowning mouths, and the swords they carried were meant to bite and kill. She stared at them and the blades exposed on their backs, her mind imagining what they could do.

They wore long robes of red and grey, belted at their waists, and tall boots. The details of every stitch of their clothing were amazing. She studied it as they escorted her. Her attention waivered when they entered certain rooms, as some bore great gardens, and in the hallway they had turned down were rows and rows of uniquely ornate doors. It was overwhelming, but she focused on one that was a soft crystal because it reminded her of Yuna.

It had been hard to think of home, but as she made her way to meet The Fates, she could not keep it from her thoughts. Her mild-mannered sister came to mind and her kindness. Would they never share sweets again? She reminisced about her father and wondered if he had lost weight because of all his worrying. She couldn't help but to wonder if Tidus would miss her. Even now she mooned for a married man; what a fool she was.

Suddenly, the guards stopped in front of a set of blue doors. They opened them and waited. Nanette took a hesitant step into the room. It was something of a fairytale—one of the nice ones. There in the middle was a brightly painted house the color of cerulean. It had a white door and seemed to glow as it lit the otherwise dark room. It sat on a little island surrounded by a small river.

One of her guards pointed, and she stepped toward the bridge that connected the rest of the shrubbery-sized forest with the perfectly nestled cottage. When she strode on the bridge, she glimpsed over the side at the water and saw that golden strings danced in it—not sinking or floating, just drifting. They shimmered softly when the light from the house caught them. They reminded her of golden reeds.

160

When she stepped off the bridge, the door opened. Nanette hesitated only a moment before stepping into the tiny cottage; she nearly had to duck to get inside. Her mouth dropped open once she crossed the threshold at the intricately painted ceiling rising high above her. An old woman wrapped in robes sauntered over, smiling as she did. Nanette swallowed hard as the woman closed the door. Her face had no eyes. Where sockets and eyes should have been, there was only flesh.

"It's bigger on the inside," Nanette managed as the woman gently moved her further into the room.

"Why of course, everything of any importance always is," she responded, her voice lithe and pleasant. "I am Melody."

"I am Nanette," she replied politely.

"And these are Serenity and Destiny," Melody said, waving her arm toward the only other two people in the room. "Forgive them. Serenity cannot speak, and Destiny hardly ever stops."

"Sister!" Destiny scolded before holding up a bowl, "Pomegranate? A delicacy in your world."

Nanette remembered the stories of eating food from the Netherworld, and how it was bad. Yet she took a few seeds from the top and put them in her pocket. "For later," she said politely.

Serenity turned and lifted the veil from her head to reveal that her mouth was only a flat surface of flesh. She glanced at Destiny and found a smiling woman who matched Melody, as she had no eyes. Yet despite their lack of eyes, Nanette had the peculiar feeling that they could all see better than anyone else she had ever met; she took an instinctive step back from them.

"Don't worry about the glass." Destiny spoke softly, but Nanette could make out every word.

"What glass?" Nanette asked in my middle of another step backward.

Her elbow caught the top of the pot and it shattered on the ground before she could catch it. "Oops," she said instinctively.

"I said not to worry about it," Destiny said, rising, "It has been a long time since we have had a planet-dweller here."

"Have you been to my world?" Nanette asked, hopeful, as she stepped away from the shattered glass.

"All the time," Destiny responded, taking her arm. "Whenever something important happens, I am there."

"Amazing," she responded as she was led to the back of the cottage. The cottage's interior was far too vast for what she had seen, and it still overwhelmed her. She felt caught between shock and awe. The Divine Court had so many secrets within its walls. No wonder they kept nearly everything from the planet dwellers.

They stepped into a circular room in the back. A single shaft of light came in. It took a moment for Nanette to realize it reminded her of moonlight. A large fountain ran at the other end, and she could see the same glittering reeds, but here they danced like excited fish. Serenity shifted around her and pulled the length of her robes back to reach into the water.

"Every golden thread of fate dances in here, brushing against the other ones on their journey." Destiny informed her as Melody came to stand on Nanette's other side.

"They come from the Lake of Eternity in the Moonvale," Melody said as Serenity drew out a single thread. "A good walk from The Divine Court."

"Ah," Destiny said, leaning forward and pointing. "There is yours."

"Mine?" Nanette breathed in, her lungs suddenly feeling tight.

"How else are we supposed to know your fate?" Melody asked, and in unison they took hold of the thread.

Past and future took each end of the thread, with Serenity in the middle. Nanette realized suddenly that she did not want to know her fate. Knowing exactly where she was going would ruin the journey. She didn't want to know if she would live a long time or if she eventually would have children. She didn't want to know if Jason would be the only man she would know, if Yuna and Tidus would always be happy and have beautiful babies, and if she would fade into memory.

"Stop," she whispered, and they turned to her. She said more forcefully, "Don't!"

"Don't worry," Destiny smiled, her face so full of hope. "Your future is like a labyrinth. Every choice you make leads you down another path. Only your choices can make your future. We can only determine the possibilities ourselves."

Their heads went back and their mouths moved as the golden string began to glow. She saw an eye form on Destiny's left hand and Melody's right and nearly screamed. Instead, she clapped a hand over her mouth as they raised their arms. She squeezed her eyes closed, not wanting to see what came next. She could hear them muttering. Nanette did not want to know her fate.

"Daughter of the planets," Destiny said, her sweet voice bringing Nanette's eyes open, "you shall live on this day and be returned to Oran. Someone is here for you."

Nanette's eyes popped open. "My father?"

"No," Melody replied. "Are you not curious, mortal?"

"No," she said, wanting badly to leave. "I don't want to know any of my possible futures. I'd rather find them out as I live them."

"Wise." To Nanette's surprise, Destiny's voice was full of admiration. "I give you warning though: One wrong choice and you shall see disaster, but one right choice and you shall have eternal happiness. Remember that your choices make your fate. Remind *her* as well."

Nanette glanced among the three fates. "Who?"

"She meets the King," Melody said with a smile. "The living dead."

Chapter 42: Morhaven

φ

*E*lisabeth was no warrior, and the likes of Arawn terrified her, but she kept her face carefully neutral. They passed though the outer courtyards, where she carefully avoided the flowers. When she returned home, she fully intended to cut a few roses in Ashlad and put them in a vase to remind her; perhaps she wanted to a little out of spite as well.

The great doors opened, and she realized two guards were parting them. Their strange triangular helmets hid their faces, but they stood taller than her. On their backs, long blades with ornate designs winked at her amid their black armor; they reminded her of raven heads. She wanted to frown as she entered the Divine Court, but the rows of blossoming trees raining petals made her glance around in awe.

They escorted her through the first set, and a single path made of stones led them into the next room with no doorways but large decorated archways. The final room, where rows of people rose in their seats, was ornate. Many were advisors like Zod, who came to Malthael from time to time, though she knew he, specifically, would not be here, as he spent most of his time in Ashlad and used the gate to return when he was needed.

She hesitated, but Arawn did not. He continued down the great walkway that led to an ornate throne in the middle of the room. A man in fine robes stood, his face set as his court settled around him in a horseshoe arrangement of seats around the raised platform. Creatures of every color of a painter's palette surrounded her. There were creatures as tall as trees, and some as small as bumblebees. She turned her attention back to a single platform at the head of the room. She could not see steps leading up to the dais, but he stood upon it all the same. Leaves rained down from above in a constant pattern, but she saw no trees that could produce such a number. The ceiling was decorated with a single rush of creatures from the Netherworld; she recognized it as the Wild Hunt.

"Daughter of two worlds," he said. He wore a half crown of branches crafted around his skull and resting on his ears.

164

She could make out red, white, and black berries decorating it, and pearls dripped from the edge by his face. His tan face was beautiful, more beautiful than anything she had ever seen, and yet it was emotionless. Pale blond hair framed his face and was bound by metal clips on each side. The rest flowed over his muscular shoulders. This was Ethandirill's elder brother, and yet they looked so dissimilar. The only thing they had in common was their height—both were impressively tall. She wondered if anything lay beyond those cold eyes and unforgiving features. His voice filled the room with ease, and it was as unfeeling as his face.

"King Nauberon," Elisabeth said with a polite bow. "I come for Nanette."

"So pointed," he said, and although his face didn't change, she felt his emotions. "This is your homecoming, Elsariel."

Elisabeth froze at the mention of her other name. Just as she had two parts within her, she had two names. Elsariel was the name that had been given to her by the Det Mor Clan, and Elisabeth the name her mother had given her. Malthael called her Elsa, a shortening of her demon half, to show her that he accepted every part of her and to remind her of what she was. It was important, he said, so that she might never falter or forget, for it could be fatal to another if she did.

"This is not my home," Elisabeth responded. Some of the court murmured at her affront, but the king did not flinch or move a muscle. "And my name is Elisabeth."

"Perhaps in Ashlad, but here you are Elsariel," the king responded, his face not matching the force of his words. "Do you reject my welcome?"

"Do you reject my request?" Elisabeth countered, raising her head in defiance.

Arawn began to laugh, and she glanced at him in surprise. "She is as her father was. All cheek and wit. I have missed Darienith all these years, and wait for his return," the hunter said.

"Return?" Elisabeth said, betraying herself before she could catch her tongue.

"Yes, child," Arawn responded. "He rests in the Garden of Defilers. Until he receives the part of himself that he gave up making you, he is but stone."

"Arawn, get the planet-dweller," King Nauberon commanded, not seeming all that surprised or annoyed by Arawn's interjection.

"As my king commands," Arawn responded before turning and leaving.

King Nauberon stepped off the platform, and vines rose to the ground to meet his feet. He walked down them until he was standing before her, his face unchanged the entire time. An irrational part of her wanted to hit him just to see if it would break his endless emotionlessness.

"Will you walk with me, Elsariel?" the king asked, but he did not offer his hand.

According to the books Malthael had in their library, it was considered impolite to touch the king. He would rarely invite it except from those who had his complete confidence or had influence over him. It was said that only the queen could touch a king, and the leader of the Det Mor Clan was always one or the other. Ethandirill was only a prince, so it was right to touch his cheek in greeting, but a king was known by everyone and needed no introduction.

"I shall," Elisabeth responded, and the king swept by with his long robes.

She walked beside him, but a step back, just enough to show deference. No one was to surpass the king in all of Morhaven and the Netherworld. He led wherever he walked with anyone, and only the queen might walk beside him. He glanced back at her, his fine cloak dragging behind him.

"You know your protocol, Elsariel," he acknowledged, and he seemed pleased.

"Enough," she responded, finding that her quick pace naturally matched his own. "I've read a few books on the subject."

"Your better half is calling to its true home," he answered and she nearly laughed at his pompousness.

"I believe it was more a matter of curiosity and a love of reading," she managed to keep the bite out of her words. "I am only here as a matter of urgency."

"Ah yes," King Nauberon responded as he started up a set of stairs. "There are matters to discuss beyond your misplaced planet-dweller."

"Yes," Elisabeth agreed as they moved toward a door halfway up the wall. "There is the manner in which she got here." He seemed unmoved by her words.

A door was opened for them, and they stepped out into an elevated courtyard. Instantly, she froze as she looked across it and realized exactly where he was bringing her. Multiple statues stood in the garden, each draped in thick robes that had turned to stone with them.

Elisabeth took a hesitant step into the garden as she scanned the statues. One of them must be her father, but she wondered why their souls hadn't returned. The door closed behind her, and she was left alone with King Nauberon. She felt him watch her every movement as she weaved through them, and she was careful to keep her emotions off her face.

Turning, she looked at one. She couldn't see anything, as they wore thick concealing cloaks, but he had a sword in his hand. She moved amongst them until she found him. At his feet, draped over by his cloak, were two horns. They had to be Malthael's. When the man who was her blood had turned to stone, they had been cemented with him. The stone from which he was made was black, and there were veins running through it. She realized he was marble, a smooth outer shell to hide the deadliness within.

"All souls like yours were released and should have returned to their rightful owners. Their missing half should have been returned when their offspring died, which would make them whole, and yet," King Nauberon said, sweeping his arm to indicate them, "they remain as they were."

"How many were there before this started?" Elisabeth asked as she glanced at the other statuettes.

"There are forty-two souls like yours, and with every death that should have freed them, the barrier between the Netherworld and the planets just grew thinner. Something is keeping these souls, something beyond even my sight. The abomination that travels with you must be killed before he can murder the last of the forty-two."

"Ki?" Elisabeth asked, and then a realization dawned on her. "He's been with me, and I don't think he is behind this."

"Those that created him are," the king said, and for the first time, his expression was contemplative. "The shadows on the wall I cannot see."

"Where are they?" Elisabeth asked.

"Hystera," he responded, his eyes narrowing slightly. "You are brave to face these shadows alone."

"I won't be alone," Elisabeth replied, her face impassive as she thought of her papa.

He regarded her for a moment before offering her a hand, and she stared at it as though it were covered in spiders. "A gift," he said as though offering her a drink, but Elisabeth knew it wouldn't be that benign.

Her eyes met his, and she wondered what he was thinking behind that icy stare. She heard him say something under his breath in a language she didn't recognize. Elisabeth hesitantly took his hand, and a wave of light exploded off their hands when they touched. The force of King

Nauberon's power faded quickly as her hair settled back around her shoulders. She stood in awe. He held her hand a moment longer before releasing it. She looked down at her hand and saw a strange shimmering symbol.

"Should you ever need assistance, say, 'By the grace of King Nauberon, I summon thee,' and Arawn will come to you," he said. She instantly put her hand as far away from her face as she could.

"You gave me the ability to call him?" she all but snapped, holding her hand away from herself. Her response was more impulsive than normal. Elisabeth curled her lips between her teeth.

"You seem upset," he said, his eyebrows rising for the barest of moments. "It is only once, and then it will be done. Do you reject this gift?"

"No. What do I owe you for such a generous gift?" she said, looking at her hand with mild distrust.

"Only what you would do already," King Nauberon said, walking back toward the doors. "Destroy these shadows, and prevent whatever they are planning with the souls of the forty-two."

"That is it?" Elisabeth clarified.

"It involves more peril then you think," the king said as the doors opened. "Here is your girl returned to you. I shall see you again, Elsariel."

Elisabeth's head came up as a petite young woman stood just beyond the door. Her eyes grew wide when she saw the King, and she moved back carefully when he swept by. She was short, with jet black hair and eyes that were tipped at the corners more than was normal for Orani citizens. She looked nothing like Ruhan and had the wisdom to bow as the king moved by.

"Nanette," Elisabeth said, coming forward, ignoring the thing that was her father, "I am here to take you home."

"My father sent you?" she said hopefully.

"Yes, to return you to Oran," Elisabeth said and saw her face fall.

"Of course," she muttered. "To Oran."

"You have been careful not to eat the food?" she asked as they stood close to each other.

"Yes," she said, nodding her head vigorously. "I remember the stories. My savior brought me food from the planet, but nothing more."

"You must be hungry, but my packs are back with Ki," Elisabeth said without sparing more than a momentary glance back at the statue that was her birth father. "Your savior?"

"The man who saved me, a bald man," she said as they walked down the stairs. She turned toward Elisabeth. "Fanta called him the banished prince and the wordless one."

"Ah," Elisabeth responded, glancing around. "Let's leave first."

"What do you mean?" Nanette asked as they hurried out of the palace.

When they were safely beyond the courtyards of the Divine Court, Elisabeth whispered, "He is a banished Det Morian prince, brother to the king. His name is Ethandirill."

"That is a beautiful name," Nanette responded, and Elisabeth saw her expression soften as they entered the tree line. "I do hope I can thank him."

"Your acknowledgments aren't needed," Ethandirill said from behind the same tree. "It was a pleasure to have company after such solitude. It is I who am in your debt."

Nanette came to a halt and looked startled. That quickly faded away as she looked excited and happy to see him. She took a step forward before stopping and pointing at him. "You can talk!" she exclaimed.

Chapter 43: Netherworld

—————————————— φ ——————————————

Ki stood at the edge of the Netherworld and paced. His reason was slowly leaving him. Elisabeth should have returned by now; they were taking too long. He looked the sky as it filled with light. The red of the day would last for a few more hours. Worst of all, he could not forget the look in her eyes as he had touched her—the deep disgust.

He could not blame her, nor could he understand why it bothered him. Perhaps he felt a kinship with her because they were alike. Like him, she was different and had been both that way. The elders had told him he'd been chosen because when everyone else died, he had survived. His mother had given birth to him right before she had been killed, and no man, no matter how determined, would kill an infant. Soul Collectors came for baby killers, after all, and carted them down into the Nether. So most children had been left for dead. Something else would—and did—eat them anyway. But not Ki. He had survived because he was the savior.

He heard a crackle behind him. When he turned, Riku walked over to him. Ki took a step back, his hands instantly on his daggers as the demon slinked over. It was not a good sign that Riku would come now when he had neither key to give him. Ki's plan was to get them when Elisabeth returned to Ashlad.

"Hello," Riku said, sauntering around him.

Ki turned to keep the demon in front of him. "What do you want?"

"You know what I want," he responded, tipping his head. "Yet you haven't brought them to me."

"I had them both, but you failed to mention that one was booby trapped," Ki responded, turning as the demon circled him. "I died."

"Fortunately for us, you have many lives," the demon said, throwing a hand up. "All of which," he added in a sweet voice, "I could extract with exacting measure if you failed me."

"I haven't forgotten our bargain, demon," Ki spat. "Malthael will give me that key, and I shall return them both to you."

Riku clicked his tongue, the leather of his pants pulling tight as he moved. "Malthael cannot know he parted with the key."

"That wasn't part of the agreement," Ki replied as the demon stopped.

With a flick of his wrist, the contract rolled out. He pointed. "Right here. You cannot tell the owner of the key about the key."

Ki leaned forward and read exactly the line that Riku was indicating to. Frowning, he continued to read some of the other requirements. He stopped on the last one and glanced at the demon before straightening. He slid the daggers back into their sheaths.

"So long as we are contracted, I cannot hurt you," Ki said with no small amount of disappointment.

"Among other things," Riku said, rolling the contract back up. "You should read contracts more thoroughly before you sign them."

"A lesson for the future," Ki grumbled as the scroll vanished. "If there is nothing else…"

"Nothing, except I do wonder at the half-breed," the demon said, turning his head. "What is her story?"

"She has nothing to do with our bargain." Ki bared his teeth a little as his fingers instinctively wrapped around his blades' hilts.

Riku put his arms up as he replied, "I was only asking. No harm done to your little sweetheart."

The demon turned and whistled as he walked away. It was a slow tune, and one that made Ki's hair stand on end. Ki continued to watch him until he vanished in a little puff of black smoke. He let go of the daggers as he considered Riku's words. The Keymaster had been clever with his contract, and Ki had been foolhardy in his haste.

He turned toward the Poppy Fields and saw two people coming toward him. The Det Morian prince was carrying a limp body as Elisabeth picked her way across the field. Poppies made everyone want to sleep; they lulled people into an eternal rest and then consumed them by pulling them into the bark, the roots, and even the branches. Only those of Morhaven could walk the fields unhampered.

Elisabeth was the reason he had been so hasty; he had wanted to finish the last of his forty-two. Though the boy was still hidden, he thought these would be enough; she would be enough. Yet she was proving to be difficult, her soul more innocent than the boy's. The Sin Eater knew what it could and could not take; the boy he could have taken, yet Ki knew the boy could repent and live a life that made up for the mortal sin on his soul. Though the others didn't have time to correct their wrongs, the boy did.

When she saw him, she waved as though greeting an old friend. She even smiled a little, and his apprehension over their last encounter dissolved. She was becoming something of a friend to him, the closest he had ever had, yet in the end she would disappoint him and he would have to kill her. Her stained soul would complete his mission, and she would become a memory. A bittersweet memory.

When she stepped through the barrier, Ki could see the limp body was a woman and that the prince carried her with reverence. He showed careful concern as he laid her on the ground. She had hair as black as the night sky and a sweet face. The prince moved a single piece of hair away from her mouth, careful not to touch her skin.

"I worried that you wouldn't wait," Elisabeth admitted with a heavy sigh.

"Nanette, I assume," Ki responded, nodding toward the girl.

"Yes, we had to knock her out to get her through the Poppy Fields," she responded, and he could see that she was distracted. Something was weighing heavy on her mind as she knelt by the girl. "Nanette." She patted her cheek lightly, and the woman was roused.

Nanette opened her eyes slowly, as though coming out of a dream. Smiling at the prince, she put her hand on his hand. There was a dreamy look on her face until she glanced around him, and then her eyes widened. She began to look around frantically as she sat up.

"Whoa," Elisabeth said, shooting a glance at the prince as she pushed Nanette back and tried to reassure her. "It's okay. I'll keep you safe."

"We're back." Her voice was full of terror as she spoke.

Little did she know that the place from which she had just come was far more dangerous than where they were. The Det Mor ruled from the Divine Court, and they were old and powerful. Unlike those from the planets, the creatures and beings of the Nether lived quite a long time. Many thought them immortal, but that wasn't accurate. They aged very slowly, but they still died and they could be killed.

"I'm taking you to Oran." Elisabeth spoke slowly and carefully. "Remember? I'm taking you home."

"Oh," she said, and her eyes shot over to the prince. "That's right. Home."

She didn't seem excited as Elisabeth helped her to her feet. Nanette dusted herself off for much longer than was necessary. The prince watched her closely, his eyes bright and swirled with emotions. Elisabeth glanced between them before she picked up her pack.

172

"Anything exciting while we were gone?" Elisabeth asked as she put the strap across her chest.

"Nothing," Ki answered instantly, the first lie he had told her. "Not even a shadow."

"Good," Elisabeth replied absentmindedly. She scratched at her palm before she added, "We'd better go. Ethandirill explained a shortcut to me, but we'll end up back in Ashlad."

"Who are you?" Nanette asked as she stared at him.

"Ki," he said simply strolling away from them.

"Don't worry, he's always like that," Elisabeth commented, but she seemed more amused than angry.

Ki paused on the ridge. Nanette nodded before turning to walk beside Elisabeth. She glanced forward once at Ethandirill, the apparent Det Morian prince of Morhaven, who took up the lead. They picked their way across the landscape as Nanette and Elisabeth talked in front of him. He listened, although he pretended not to care.

"Thank you, Elsariel," Nanette said, and Ki's eyebrows rose at the name.

"Call me Elisabeth, Elsariel is"—Elisabeth paused before finishing—"my other name."

"Oh, Elisabeth, a much simpler name!" Nanette exclaimed, and Ethandirill glanced back. "You are from Ashlad?"

"I wasn't born there," Elisabeth answered. Ki hadn't known that. "My mother was from Lyreane, and I was born there. I lived there for a short time until, well, things happened, and I ended up with my adoptive father, Malthael."

"How exotic," Nanette replied as Elisabeth helped her up unstable rocks.

He'd had no idea that she was of his home. He glanced at her blond hair and remembered the girl in the tower, the prisoner. He wondered if that could have been Elisabeth if she had been born to someone other than a Soul Collector. If it could have been her hair that he would have cut and used to complete his first mission leading up to the ritual.

"Your father told me you were a Butterfly Princess. That seems far more glamorous," Elisabeth countered, and for the first time since she returned, he saw a genuine smile on her face.

"What it really equates to is an arranged marriage," Nanette said with a heavy sigh. "My husband is an idiot."

"He did seem selfish and self-absorbed." Elisabeth laughed but then seemed to try to stifle it. "I am sorry you have such a husband."

"My choice," Nanette said as they went down the other side of the hill of rubble. "I cannot take it back now."

Ki listened to them chat. Nanette talked about her family, her sister and her sister's husband. They discussed what it was like growing up without a mother. Ki blushed slightly when they talked about what it was like to bleed for the first time and have no women to talk with. Even though their voices were hushed, he could still hear them. He felt his ears burning as he turned away and seemed to take in the landscape.

The one topic that Elisabeth seemed intent on avoiding was herself, specifically her demonic half—the spirit of death. Nanette must have sensed this as well because she did not press Elisabeth on the subject. Time seemed to go by more quickly as he listened to their discussions. He discovered things about Elisabeth that he hadn't known: that she didn't really have any friends because she was afraid to get close to anyone and that she had been as alone as him. Nanette related to that, as she'd felt like a fraud since her marriage. It was interesting to watch them bond so quickly.

Ethandirill Det Mor stopped and pointed. Down below was a small ruined village. They came to stand beside him as he directed their attention. There, at the bottom, was a ring of shadows. Ki's eyes narrowed as one of them moved. Nanette tried to take a step back, but Ethandirill caught her arm before she fell.

"Thank you," she said, but she still seemed like she wanted to get away.

"Why aren't they attacking?" Ki asked, glancing along the shadowed ridge as they rippled.

"Us," Elisabeth said before glancing toward him. "Ethandirill and I can kill them. They won't be any trouble."

Elisabeth began her descent, leaving Ethandirill to help Nanette down the hill. Ki quickly followed after Elisabeth, as he still had to keep her from getting herself killed. He was surprised that she had come away so easily from her meeting with King Nauberon. He was very old and very clever. Perhaps being nearly the last of her kind made her special to him.

They hiked down between the gates. The shadows swirled, but she was right that they didn't attack. Ki walked a little faster as they entered the ruined town. One building remained standing and pristine, and Ki immediately knew why. Like the orc's house, this was an oasis in the barren landscape. Something cackled from the inside of a partially caved-in house, but Elisabeth no more than glanced at it.

Nanette was talking to Ethandirill, who nodded or shook his head when appropriate. His face was softer when she talked. As they passed by, Ki glanced back toward the house, narrowing his gaze. He took a step closer and saw instantly what lay within. He took an immediate step back as one of the birds ruffled its feathers and opened its eyes.

A sudden screech sounded, and Ki didn't hesitate to turn and run. "Get into the house!" he yelled

Elisabeth, who was in front, looked back at him as he ran. An army of shrikes bulleted out of the house as the shadows moved away from them. Ki's chest was tight as they sprinted toward safety, a little paradise in the wasteland. He watched in horror as Nanette fell and Elisabeth turned to face the army of wings and beaks. One moment she was Elisabeth, the woman he was hunting, and the next she became someone else entirely. It was the sudden impulsiveness that had him the most suspicious that something was happening within Elisabeth.

Ethandirill hauled Nanette up, and Ki caught up with them as the three of them ran toward the house. Yet Elisabeth remained, her eyes becoming as dark as black ink. An unknown wind picked up at her clothes as she moved toward the swarm. One bird out front dove and struck Ki's shoulder. He cried out in pain but hardly staggered.

Elisabeth took a step forward, and the dust on the ground moved away from her as light started to swirl around her. Something crackled like muted thunder, and Nanette gasped as a flash of Elisabeth's skull under her skin became visible. This was her darker half; this was Elsariel. Those of Morhaven and the areas beyond had little dominion over those in the rest of the Nether. They could kill and maim, but they didn't have control over them since they were creatures half dead. They couldn't quell creatures that were made by the planet-dwellers or monsters that were born from their actions.

Ki feared the Weavers because they were born from war. Each soul lost in battle that fought not for honor or country but just to kill became a Weaver. They were killers, ruthless and ugly, forever bound to the darker side for their deeds. The shrikes were something worse because they were born of innocent blood. In the Nether, the blood formed into handfuls of these vengeful birds. They were literally born of blood and made from the blood, and all they wanted was more of it to keep themselves whole. Children went somewhere else; Ki didn't know where.

Emotions, violent terrible emotions, in the planets were always reflected here. Great kindness or sacrifice made a sanctuary, but too many times the ugliness resulted in something vile. Ki stopped in front of Elisabeth as she continued to walk forward. She stopped when he got in the way and the birds started to sweep down.

She lifted an arm and they were flung off as he yelled, "We need to go."

"You do," she said. The birds cackled at her angrily, but they didn't sweep down again. "Go."

Above them, the birds circled in one massive angry black cloud. Ki's hair was on end; he was right in their line of attack, but Elisabeth needed to be brought to reason. Her demonic half would fight even when there was no way to win. He needed her mortal half to comprehend the risk.

"I will not leave you to face them," he yelled above the rising gale. "Don't be foolish. You do not know your own limits. I do not intend to die because I broke the blood oath."

"Perhaps we should find out," Elisabeth answered, but her voice wasn't right.

Nanette yanked her toward safety. As Elisabeth fought her slightly, Nanette told her, "You are not Elsariel. You are Elisabeth,"

Elisabeth blinked, and the raging wind fell as they stepped across the threshold. She muttered as though coming out of a dream. "I am."

Like the orc's house, this was another safe haven, a healer's hut. Ki clicked the gate closed as Elisabeth blinked a few times and glanced between them, clearly confused. Something had brought her demonic side out—it explained her recent impulsiveness.

When her eyes rested on Nanette, she asked, "Why?"

"You saved me, came all the way through this." Nanette waved at the Netherworld in general to make her point. "I couldn't leave you out there acting so unlike yourself."

"Thank you," Elisabeth said, pulling Nanette into a fierce hug. "That must have been scary."

"No worse than when I am hungry." Nanette laughed, hugging her back. "I become a completely unreasonable person!"

"We need to go," Ki said tentatively, watching as Elisabeth turned away and seemed to wipe away a tear.

"Yes, of course," Elisabeth resounded with only a slight twinge of red in her eyes. "To get you home."

"Home," Nanette parroted, but her voice held no excitement.

Ki saw her reach into her pocket as Elisabeth and Ethandirill turned toward the house. Ethandirill knocked on the door, and an old woman answered. She looked much like any old woman one might see on the planets, with one exception. She was about half the size of a planet-dweller, the size of a small child.

"Det Morian," she said, holding up her hand. "Payment."

Ethandirill reached into his pocket and pulled out a strip of paper. The old woman squealed with excitement as she took it and consumed it in a few short bites. Ki gave her a strange look, his eyebrows furrowing together as he wondered what the paper was. He glanced back over his shoulder as Nanette put something into her mouth.

Chapter 44: Netherworld

─────────────── φ ───────────────

*E*lisabeth reacted slowly as she turned and saw Ki and Ethandirill rush toward Nanette. The Orani was on her knees with her hands at her throat. She was choking as she fell forward, and after a moment she spat six little seeds onto the ground before slumping over. Elisabeth looked between the seeds and Nanette and knew what Nanette had done.

Ethandirill put an arm around Nanette's shoulders as she gasped for breath. As Elisabeth's shadow fell across her, she looked up without a shred of guilt as she put a hand on Ethandirill's arm.

"What do you think you were doing?" Elisabeth all but yelled as Ki picked up one of the seeds to examine it.

"I won't go back," Nanette whispered. "Not after what I've seen, and survived."

"So you decide instead to trap yourself here?" she roared, snatching the pomegranate seed from Ki's hand before shaking it at Nanette. "There is no coming back from this."

"I don't belong there," she replied. "I've had more kindness from you and Ethandirill in these last hours than I've had in this long year since I've married Jason. I cannot return to such an existence. I shall be a Butterfly Princess no longer."

"So you choose here?" Elisabeth asked, kneeling down. "I would have taken you to Ashlad if you'd asked."

Nanette blinked in surprise as she whispered, "Really?"

"I've never had a friend before," she replied, and her heart hurt at the admission. "Not a normal one anyway."

Ethandirill helped Nanette to her feet, and she blushed. Elisabeth stood and glanced at Ethandirill, who seemed to be slow in realizing what had just happened. Or perhaps he was just hiding behind a mask of thought. Nanette didn't look at him as she reached out and took Elisabeth's hand.

"Friends," Nanette said with a smile.

The woman in the doorway pointed at Nanette and yelled, "She is touched."

The door closed with a sharp snap as Elisabeth looked down at the seeds before she took Nanette's hand and turned it over. There was nothing on her palm, so she took the other one in her hand. There was also nothing there. She held both palms in her hands, waiting for a mark to appear. Beings of the planets could be drawn into the Netherworld if they ate anything of that world. If they did, a black mark would appear on their hand, condemning them.

Elisabeth looked up desperately before demanding, "How many did you swallow?!"

"I don't know," Nanette responded hysterically, and Ethandirill shifted in front of the gate as something dark floated toward them.

Elisabeth froze as a Soul Collector hovered in front of the gate. Its partially translucent black robes floated around its body like a thing of nightmares. She propelled Nanette back as Ki moved to her side. If she insisted on protecting Nanette, Elisabeth knew Ki would do everything to protect her. He needed her still and was unlikely to stop now. His resolution had not wavered before this moment, which was what she was counting on.

"She has taken a fruit within her," the Soul Collector said, pointing a long bony white finger at Nanette.

Nanette made a terrified sound as the creature flicked its wrist and her hand came up. Her palm bore a soft black mark that was almost grey in its faintness. Ethandirill held his hand up in protest, and the Soul Collector turned to him with nary a care.

"You have no power, wordless one," it crowed before turning its hand over and curling its fingers one by one, beckoning Nanette forward.

She took a step forward but was restrained by Elisabeth's grip. Elisabeth narrowed her eyes and watched Nanette struggle to pull her hand back. And still, strangely, the pale black didn't darken. She had never heard of such a thing—a pale mark of the Nether was not in any of her books.

"Wait!" Elisabeth called, putting her hand up, "What is her punishment?"

"A month of every year she must spend here in the Netherworld," he stated, to her surprise. Elisabeth had expected a harsher punishment for consuming Netherworld food.

Elisabeth drummed her fingers in the empty air as she calculated what the best counteroffer would be. A month in the Netherworld was actually two on the planets. After a moment, she glanced at Ethandirill, who gave her an intent stare. She realized instantly that neither Morhaven nor the Divine Court had claimed Nanette, so Elisabeth could claim her.

Putting hand across to bar Nanette's movements, she declared, "I, Elsariel daughter of Darienith, claim her for myself, and Ethandirill, prince of Morhaven of the house Det Mor, shall be her keeper in my stead for her time in the Netherworld."

"You are only half," he replied, but his tone wasn't as sure as his words. The Soul Collector dropped his hand. "You cannot claim her."

"She is only partially of the living and the Nether, as am I," Elisabeth countered, feeling as though she was gaining ground.

The Soul Collector seemed to consider this. Elisabeth whispered out of the corner of her mouth, "Evoke your right."

"What?" Nanette asked, and Elisabeth made wide eyes as she nodded toward the Soul Collector. It took Nanette a moment to catch on, but when she did, she yelled, "My rights! What are my rights?"

"Your voice carries more power," he answered. Soul Collectors could decline to answer, but they could not lie. "Your right is to declare your master, surrendering yourself to his or her will during his or her lifetime."

"Master?" Nanette repeated, dumbfounded, before she swallowed heavily. "I surrender myself to Elisabeth," she managed through tight lips.

"It has been said," the Soul Collector boomed, "and so it shall be."

Nanette let out a cry and bent over her hand as she gripped her own wrist with her other hand. Elisabeth put her hand on her back as she turned to him and demanded, "What are you doing to her?"

"Transferring her ownership," the Soul Collector said before he sunk back into the ground from whence he came.

When Nanette held up her hand, it bore a very different mark. It was pale grey with a single point of black in the middle. Nanette looked up at her, confused, and Elisabeth glanced at Ki and Ethandirill. She had no idea what it meant, but what mattered was Nanette was safe.

"I'll return her for her one month when this is over," Elisabeth told Ethandirill before walking around Nanette and knocking on the door.

The lady opened the door just a little before Elisabeth put her hand on the door and said, "I've claimed her, you've been paid, now let me in."

"You reek of planet," the woman snapped, but she opened the door. Elisabeth held open the door for everyone to enter.

"It's time to go, Ki," Elisabeth said pointedly, watching him closely and wondering if he suspected anything. "Malthael must be beside himself with worry."

180

She averted her eyes as Ki went into the house, pulling out his special chalk as he went. She doubted he knew the reason she had reacted to the shrikes was just as much about him as it was about Nanette and Ethandirill. Nanette and she had become friends, and yet she felt this strange understanding of Ki. The more she found out about her demon side, the more he didn't seem to mind. It was as though he were just as accepting of her as Malthael was—a strange thought to have about one's future murderer.

She watched as Nanette and Ethandirill parted, and she wondered what that was like. It was clear their hearts ran in tandem. Nanette put a strand of hair behind her ear and thanked him. He touched the side of her face and she looked up, her eyes both scared and hopeful. Elisabeth dropped her gaze when he kissed her forehead, a soft promise that he would wait for her return and what would come when she did.

"Goodbye," Nanette whispered so softly that Elisabeth could barely hear it an instant before she hurried into the house.

Elisabeth looked up at Ethandirill, searching his eyes as he watched her go. No one could feign that look of affection, so deep an attachment in such a short time. He turned to her and nodded, a gesture that spoke volumes. His place was there, he was leaving Nanette in her care, and he was grateful to her—but he fully expected her to be timely with her return of Nanette to him.

He turned and left, the gate squeaking slightly when it closed, and he didn't turn back. She studied his back as he went into the Netherworld, a dark dot amongst the red. She switched her vision and stared at the world as her other half saw it. Purple suddenly swept in, and instead of being dark he shone bright. He was so bright that she couldn't bear to look at him, and she had to squint before switching back.

With a final look into the red of the Nether, she took a step back and closed the door. She hadn't told anyone that she was beginning to sense her own abilities. When she had first entered the Netherworld, they had been difficult to use, but now they were coming to her slowly. She could feel the dark seed of burning power growing, and part of her was terrified. By coming here, she had let Elsariel out; she had let her other half free, and it was more powerful.

"Elisabeth," Ki called out. "The door is open."

Elisabeth turned as she quieted the power within her, sparing only a glance at the old owner of the house. The woman flinched and shied away, but neither Ki nor Nanette could see what the woman did. Elisabeth was changed, but she fought the growing need within her as she raised her head. She saw Nanette step through the makeshift gate. An ordinary door bent to Ki's will by some markings with chalk to fill the opening with a watery substance. Elisabeth stared at her reflection, which rippled.

As she went to step through, Ki took hold of her arm and stopped her. She turned to him, confused, as he snapped a bracelet around her wrist. She gasped, her mind trying to process what was happening, and her powers flared out. Bands of metal coiled around her, tightening her arms against her sides. The more she fought them, the tighter they became. The only thing that kept her standing was his hands gripping her arms.

"What have you done?!" Elisabeth hissed, sure he was nothing but a liar and a cheat.

"I'm protecting you from yourself," he said before pushing her unceremoniously through the door.

Chapter 45: Ashlad

φ

Malthael tapped his black nails across the wood of the chair. He listened to the thud of his ring finger as the thicker nail hit the wood on his right hand. All demons had Weaver venom under their ring finger, and Malthael was no exception. It was potent enough to eat a man from the inside out with exacting cruelty. With the kind of mood he was in, he very much wanted to use it on the next person who walked through the door. With the exception of Elsa, of course—the one person he wanted to see.

That girl was going to be the death of him. It was entirely irrational to become so emotionally attached to another individual. Yet here he was sulking again, and this time the door was locked and the twins forbidden entry. Malthael had at least some influence left over this household, more so than over his own sensibilities. Truly, she would be the end of him.

He raised his head when he heard something open and saw the once-locked door yawn open. Viscous liquid filled the frame. It slowly started to form into a strangely lit room. Malthael stood and watched as figures started to form. A girl stepped through and looked up, startled, as surprised to see him as he was to see her.

He had temporarily lifted the protection spell on the house that normally kept out unwanted visitors just long enough for Elisabeth to make her way home. If this girl had come from the Nether, she was likely with Elisabeth.

Her weariness and slight fear suddenly dissolved as she pointed at him and exclaimed, "You must be Malthael."

"That is correct," the demon answered before adding. "Nanette? Ruhan's daughter."

"Yes, that's me. Elisabeth did say you were a bit scary, but she said you're harmless to friends," Nanette replied. She was about to say more when a body was hurled through the portal, knocking them both to the ground.

He looked down in surprise as Nanette sprawled across the floor with Elisabeth wrapped up in a strange metal. She hit the ground with a thud when she rolled off Nanette. As he took a step forward, she yelled, "I will kill you!"

Malthael stopped instantly at the menace in her voice. Ki stepped through and replied, "You'll thank me later. I should have caught on sooner that Elsariel was free and just waiting to return before revealing herself."

"I am going to drain every last drop from your miserable body and then hunt you down again and drain you until you have nothing left!" she yelled as Nanette slowly got to her feet.

"When you're back to yourself, I'll expect an apology as well as a thank you," Ki replied calmly and closed the door.

She strained against the metal. Something quivered before another string appeared, and she let out a frustrated noise. Elisabeth had murder in her eye as she turned back to him. "I will never say thank you to a murderer!"

"What," Malthael boomed over them, "is going on here?"

Ki turned back as the door clicked closed "Father! Help me," Elisabeth yelled.

Her voice wasn't right. Something had happened to her—and because she had been in the Nether, *anything* could have happened. Not to mention that she rarely called him "father." He looked up at Ki, who met his gaze with a level stare. Nanette glanced between them but made no move, although she looked like she very much wanted to help his daughter.

"She took some of my life force to survive the Netherworld," Ki explained, looking down at her. "We'll need to wait until she releases it all into the metal bracelet I have wrapped around her or it runs out. Why didn't you tell me she'd split herself in half? I'd assumed she just had control over her demonic half. But somehow she'd quite literally split herself in two and had buried Elsariel so deep that only when she entered the Netherworld could her other half escape."

Malthael raised his eyebrows as he looked at his daughter. Squirming against her bindings, she gave him a moment's glance that confirmed what Ki was saying. Elsariel was staring at him now as much as Elisabeth. Elisabeth was no longer dominating; they had become equal parts within her, vying for control. Malthael had always thought his daughter strong enough to keep Elsariel at bay, but he should have considered the effect the Netherworld could have on her.

"How long?" Malthael asked, and Elisabeth hissed.

"Soon," Ki replied as Nanette fell to her knees.

"Oh Elisabeth," she said as she pushed his daughter's hair back from her face. "Please don't struggle so."

"I command that you release me," Elisabeth snapped, and Nanette reached out.

Ki yelled, but it was too late. Nanette reached down and pulled on the metal bands. At her touch, many of the strips gave free. Ki all but hauled her away as Nanette struggled against him. Elisabeth hissed, fighting further against the remaining bands.

Malthael came around the room toward her. "You're weak. Fight the thing within you," he boomed and Elisabeth went very still.

"You tore your horns off," Elisabeth snapped as she glared. "You are mortal. You're the one that is weak." Malthael recoiled like he had been slapped.

"Serena would be disappointed in you as a daughter. She is all that is Elisabeth. Do not give into your father," Malthael responded.

She looked stunned and stopped struggling, stopped moving entirely. Then she closed her eyes, and he saw the chain glow blue before falling off of her. The bracelet circled on the hardwood floor before settling beside her. When she opened her eyes, they were filled with tears.

"I'm sorry," she sobbed, rolling onto her side. "I'm so sorry."

Malthael gathered his daughter up in his arms and felt her cry softly against him. He understood what it was like to realize one had a darker person inside of her. Her dark passenger, hovering at the edge of her consciousness, longed for a moment to be free. Malthael tightened his hold as he realized that only Elisabeth could overcome it. She would need to come to terms with who she was or risk losing herself. Elisabeth had always kept her other half buried deep. Now that Elsariel had come out to play, Malthael feared she wouldn't be satisfied any longer with second place.

Chapter 46: Ashlad

───────────────────────── φ ─────────────────────────

*n*anette opened her eyes slowly as she tried to remember where she was. For a moment fear filled her. Was she still in that cave in the ruined palace that was a mirror of Oran? Was the spider-like creature still clawing at the stone trying to get to her? Her panic rose, but then, as her eyes focused on the decorated ceiling, she sighed.

The events of the previous day came flooding back to her, and she turned to her other side. Instead of a sleeping Elisabeth, though, she found that the bed was empty. Startled, Nanette sat up and quickly scanned the room around her. She saw a movement by the window and Elisabeth turned to look at her. Elisabeth appeared worn and ashamed. Relief filled Nanette—Elisabeth made her feel safe. Without her nearby, Nanette was afraid she'd never sleep again.

"It's freezing!" Nanette said, pulling the covers up around her. "Aren't you cold out there?"

She shrugged and replied, "A little."

"Well, get over here," Nanette called, and saw the surprise on Elisabeth's face.

"Aren't you afraid of me?" Elisabeth demanded as she uncurled herself from the windowsill, "I *ordered* you to do something against your will."

"No, Elsariel did," Nanette replied, although she was a little hazy on the subject.

"She is within me," Elisabeth reminded her as she pressed her hand against her chest.

"But *you* would never have done that," Nanette replied with a frown, "and your toes look cold."

Elisabeth glanced down and looked at her toes. She looked back up at her in bemusement and laughed. It was the kind of laugh that came out at a funeral, where one cannot help but to feel overwhelmed and then a humorous moment breaks the intensity. Nanette smiled as Elisabeth hurried across the room and slipped into the blankets beside her, leaving a good space between them on the spacious bed.

"You should be afraid of me," Elisabeth whispered before turning her head and looking at Nanette. "I am capable of terrible things."

"Yet you still haven't done any of them," Nanette reminded her, moving closer to get some of Elisabeth's warmth in the cold room.

"I feel as though it is only a matter of time," she replied, and Nanette wasn't sure how to comfort her.

Nanette admired Elisabeth for her strength and her resilience. Yet she knew that inside of her friend was a darkness she would have to fight daily. Nanette sat in the silence of the room, admiring the tapestries as she tried to think of what to say. The tassels and frills in a dark purple color were charming. She could tell it was Elisabeth's room.

"I promise that if you ever do anything that you shouldn't, I'll tell you," Nanette replied finally and looked at her friend.

Elisabeth blinked as she looked at her, astonished, before smiling and turning forward. She bumped her shoulder against Nanette's and responded, "Thank you. It is nice to have a friend."

"I agree." Nanette sighed, remembering the other women she had been fond of but never felt comfortable with.

In a way, Nanette owed everything to Elisabeth. Her life, and the second chance she was given. She even owed her for reuniting her with Ethandirill. A blush rose to her cheeks whenever she thought of him, so she pushed him from her mind. She would see him for her month soon enough. Whatever Elisabeth was, she seemed so alone. The only other people she ever seemed to talk about were Malthael and the other demons in the house.

Nanette had nearly fainted when they had taken her to the kitchen for food and met Tiss. She seemed to Nanette the most beautiful woman she had ever seen—until she saw her tail. Well, except for some of the people she had seen at Morhaven within the Divine Court. King Nauberon had redefined what beauty meant. Malthael had explained to her that Tiss was also a demon and their house's cook. Ki hadn't seemed fazed, but Nanette almost couldn't keep herself from staring.

By then Elisabeth had gone to bed, and Nanette had decided to join her, partially because she was afraid of Tiss and partially because she didn't want her friend to wake up alone. She used to sleep next to her sister before Yuna was married.

"Your father will be there later today," Elisabeth said softly. "He wanted to let you rest."

Nanette immediately averted her eyes. "Oh."

Elisabeth's fingers brushed against Nanette's arm. "Is something wrong?"

When Nanette looked at the open concern on Elisabeth's face, the words came tumbling out. "We don't exactly get along. We have fought often since I married Jason."

"Why?" Elisabeth asked softly.

Sighing heavily, Nanette realized how much she'd blamed on her father. "When he became the Gate Guardian, our life changed in so many ways. I blamed him for my choices. But just like the seeds, it was my decision."

"It was very silly what you did," Elisabeth replied, staring at nothing, "but I know why you did it."

Nanette felt her cheeks burn as she said, "It was foolish."

"A choice of passion, I believe," she replied with a sideways glance.

"Fine!" she cried, throwing her arms to her side and her head back. "I am half in love with a demon."

"He isn't a demon," Elisabeth replied with a little laugh. "He is a Det Morian Prince. They are completely different. He is a son of the elements with powers to evoke things by using words."

Nanette felt her mouth form a circle as she realized her mistake. She scrunched up her face in thought before she asked, "Then why is he 'wordless'?"

"Those that are within the Divine Court are all blessed, but the Det Mor Clan has always held power because of their ability to conjure things with words," Elisabeth explained. "From the books I read, it sounds like about fifty years ago in our time Ethandirill attempted to defy his father's command. I'm not clear on the details, but it was some sort of purge of a specific sect on one of the planets. When he refused to help, they fought, and Ethandirill spoke words that led to his father's death. His brother, the present king, cast him out. Only when he is within the boundaries of Morhaven can he have the power of his voice, which can only be used in the service of his king. After seeing the tattoos myself, I know at least that that part is true—he can only speak in Morhaven."

"That's terrible!" Nanette cried.

"It is," Elisabeth agreed, "but they will live for hundreds of years while we live but one."

"I suddenly feel very small," she replied and gathered her legs to her chest.

188

"I do, too," Elisabeth admitted, "and I will not live much longer than a regular mortal, so I cannot comprehend the idea of living for so many lifetimes."

"Perhaps I made more of a mistake than I thought," Nanette replied, resting her head on her knees. "Ethandirill seems far too old to be interested in a mere planet-dweller who will exist for so short a time. I won't stay young for that much longer! How can he possibly care?"

"But he does," she countered with an amused smile. "He is interested in you."

"I hope so," Nanette admitted before she glanced at Elisabeth. "Since I'm being honest, you should, too."

"About what?" Elisabeth asked, looking confused.

"About Ki," she responded with pride. "You like him."

Elisabeth opened her mouth and then closed it. She drummed her fingers against her arm as she stared forward. Nanette waited patiently with her chin resting on her knees as she watched her. There was something soft in Elisabeth's eyes, and Nanette wondered if that was what *she* looked like when she thought about Ethandirill.

"I do," Elisabeth whispered as though she was afraid to admit it aloud. "I've never meet anyone like me, and I'm inexplicably drawn to him. It is utter madness."

"I think he likes you, too," Nanette replied with a happy bob of her head. "Why else would he have stopped Elsariel?"

"I don't know," she admitted, and she sounded distracted. "I wondered the same myself, particularly because he is supposed to be trying to kill me, has tried to kill me."

"What?" Nanette gasped, her head coming up with a snap.

"Indeed," she countered with a laugh. "I fancy a man who swears he intends to kill me."

"What a pair we make," Nanette laughed as she leaned against Elisabeth's shoulder. "A married woman in love with a hundreds-of-years-old Prince, and a half demon who is love with her assassin. Those sound like they would make terrible romance novels."

"You read romance novels?" Elisabeth asked, and Nanette could feel her turn to look at her.

"Can you honestly say you never have?" she countered. After an extended silence she added, "Thought so."

"It was only one or two," Elisabeth finally said in defense, and Nanette lifted her head to look at her.

"I like the ones that have happy endings after terrible things happen," Nanette admitted.

"You're right," Elisabeth said, throwing the blankets back as she got out of bed. "If I can't help my happy ending, I can sure help others."

"Where are you going?" Nanette asked as she pulled the covers closer around her.

"To Hystera," Elisabeth said as she started to tug the nightgown over her head. "To see an old man about missing animals."

"Taking Ki?" Nanette said coyly.

Elisabeth pursed her lips as she pulled a dress from her wardrobe. "I may be attracted to him, but I don't trust him. This is something I'll do alone."

"At least take those killer dogs," Nanette pleaded.

Elisabeth chuckled. "Netherhounds. And I plan to." Elisabeth touched Nanette's arm. "If nothing else, promise me you will give your father a chance when he visits this evening."

Nanette contemplated her answer before she realized she wanted to reconcile with her father. "I promise."

Chapter 47: Hystera

*J*inq looked out across the plains as Hibrius slept across his feet. He had stayed close to camp, watching the village but unwilling to enter it. Ever since that night he had seen the men and their chanting, he had stayed on high alert. Kerrigan wasn't allowed to leave, and Jinq had created trip wires in the grass around their tent.

Yet despite his worry, Hipasha had insisted Kerrigan stay and see this through. Troy had agreed grudgingly since Malthael assured them the Seer would be there any day. Yet another day passed and there was still no sign of her. He crossed his arms as Kerrigan dozed in the tent behind him. She rarely slept at night now; it was dark and full of terrors.

Instead, she slept during the day while he kept watch. Cav and Mara didn't stray far, but Cav seemed to have been as affected as Kerrigan was. If the Seer didn't arrive soon, he wouldn't heed what Troy and Hipasha said any longer—he was sending them home. Kerrigan was far too young to be dealing with whatever evil lay in Himota.

Suddenly, he saw a woman appear with two strange creatures to his right. He glanced toward the village and then back at the tree line, wondering where she had come from. Her blond hair was pulled up in a stylish bun, and she was gazing at the village. After a moment, she turned, waving when she saw him.

His eyes narrowed as he waved back very slowly, sure she had not been there before. He expected her to walk toward Himota, but instead she turned and walked toward him. He realized it was the Seer, though this woman seemed too petite and not that much bigger or older than Kerrigan. She wore a fine dress. It was a very odd sight in Hystera, but he knew that long dresses and high collars were common in Ashlad.

He turned his attention to the two creatures with her. They had ram horns, with long doglike or foxlike faces and bodies similar to that of a boar. The most unique thing was their tails, which were elevated and seemed to be made up of sharp dagger-like spikes. He narrowed his gaze and was sure he felt something similar to spirit animals within them.

Hibrius raised his head, smelling the air before standing. He stayed close, but Jinq could feel that he was on edge. The creatures she had with

191

her were very powerful. The panther moved with Jinq when he started walking toward the girl, careful to step over the trip wires.

"Elder Rekis," she said, in a very pleasant voice, "I'm Elisabeth."

"Please," he replied, offering his hand, "call me Jinq."

"What a unique name," she said as she took his hand. "I believe you need me for something."

"I do," he said, putting his other hand over hers. "We have been waiting for you."

"I was in the Netherworld gathering information, only to discover that this was where I was meant to be," Elisabeth informed him. Her features were serious but pleasant. "Shall we go to the village?"

Jinq glanced behind him toward Kerrigan's tent and decided she needed to come with them. He turned back to the Seer and said, "I need to wake my companion."

"Of course," she replied, waving her arm forward to indicate he could go.

He moved back over the trip wires with Hibrius at his side. He pushed the tent flap aside and found Kerrigan still fast asleep. She was curled up and seemed to actually be resting. Jinq hesitated to wake her, yet she needed to see this as much as he did, and he didn't want to let her out of his sight.

He moved forward and bent down before shaking her shoulder. "Kerrigan," he called softly.

Her eyes shot open. "What's wrong?" she said, wide-eyed.

"The Seer is here," he said, and she sat up suddenly.

"Here?" Kerrigan asked, pushing the covers back.

"Yes," he said and kept the smile from his lips.

"For how long?" she demanded as she jumped into her boots, tugging them on one leg at a time while she hopped on the other leg.

Mara lifted her head, but Jinq patted her shoulder and she settled back down. There was no need to make all of them go to that gloomy place. The elephant would scare anyone away who tried to come to their tent, enough to deter the villagers, he hoped.

"Moments," he answered as she pulled her wild hair back. "She wants to go straight to the village."

"Good," Kerrigan said, slipping a satchel on before reaching over and picking up Cav.

The owl made a noise of protest and tucked his head. She set him on top of the pack, and he quickly fell back asleep as they left the tent together. The Seer turned to them as they emerged, and Kerrigan hesitated. She glanced at Jinq, obviously also surprised by the Seer's appearance.

"Kerrigan," Jinq said, stepping past their outer defenses. "This is Elisabeth, the Seer."

"Kerrigan," the Seer said with a gentle smile. "What a beautiful name."

There was something oddly serene about the Seer. It was as though she had seen ugliness and beauty and decided that was the way the world was. She seemed to have an inner peace, which Jinq had to admit was admirable. Yet something was still off about her—something below the surface she wasn't showing them. Although her smiles were genuine, they were a little sad.

"Thank you," the young girl said with a soft blush.

As they moved toward the village together, Elisabeth asked, "What can you tell me?"

"There are many things I do not understand," Jinq admitted. There was no point in lies now. "We have a number of suicides, missing spirit animals, and a group of mysterious men in black."

"Aren't suicides against the beliefs of your culture?" she asked, glancing at him.

"Indeed," Jinq replied, impressed that she knew something about Hystera. "Suicide is considered the greatest sin, even beyond taking the life of another."

They entered the tree line, and she moved with relative grace among the thick trees. Bamboo could grow thick, and there were patches they had to go around. Yet this far into the plains, it was great for making homes and roofs from. Given how quickly it grew, there was no end of its supply as long as they were careful to plant more each year.

"A unique notion," Elisabeth commented before she glanced over. "Hibrius is very loyal to you."

Jinq nearly tripped as they made their way to the clearing. He glanced down at his panther, who was looking in Elisabeth's direction. She glanced down at him again and smiled, and he nearly choked. He knew Seers could talk to spirit animals, but it was startling to see firsthand.

"Can you talk with all spirit animals?" Kerrigan asked before he could do the same.

She turned to the girl with a friendly smile as she replied, "Why, yes. Although they sense your emotions and extreme thoughts, just as you can theirs, I can understand them just as I understand you."

"Is it like a voice in your head?" Kerrigan inquired further, her curiosity evident on her face.

"It is more complicated than that," the Seer said, her face furrowed in concentration. "It isn't so much words as impressions. Although I do get their names as clear as words in my mind. It is almost…" Her voice trailed off as they stepped out into the clearing.

The tree stood in front of them, and she took a hesitant step toward it. "What is it?" Jinq asked.

Elisabeth gasped as she fell to her knees, leaning back on her heels as she covered her mouth. Jinq came to stand by her as tears filled her eyes. He glanced around, expecting to see something, yet all that lay before him was the clearing and the tree. As far as he could see, there was nothing else.

"What do you see?" Jinq asked, glancing back at a startled Kerrigan.

Her lip quivered as a tear fell down her cheek. "They are all here."

"Who is here?" he asked, glancing around again but still not seeing anything.

"The animals," she whispered, her eyes sweeping back and forth, "and men alike."

"They're here?" he asked, glancing around, "All of them?"

She swallowed before nodding and answering, "They are trapped. I can hear them muttering something."

He was about to ask more when Kerrigan stepped forward and gasped. Elisabeth glanced back as Kerrigan turned and ran, leaving them alone as she retched in the woods. Jinq could hear her throwing up the little she had eaten that morning. He walked around the Seer. Elisabeth had drawn something in the sand. Letter by letter, it became clearer.

"What is 'Croatoan?'" Jinq asked, looking at the Seer.

She glanced up at him, her eyes sharp as she answered in one word. "Blackness."

Chapter 48: Ashlad

--------------------------------- ϕ ---------------------------------

Ki **watched as a** lesser demon that looked like a plant-dweller conversed with Malthael. His eyes narrowed as Malthael seemed to start yelling, but Ki couldn't hear him. Glancing at the ceiling, Ki moved along the banister before sliding down a level. He squatted as he looked down at them.

"You were supposed to be watching her!" Malthael snapped, pointing toward Elisabeth's room.

"She can literally disappear through the floor!" the lesser demon replied.

Ki frowned as he realized they were fighting over who was to blame for Elisabeth's sudden disappearance. The woman was as slippery as an eel and had been acting as though nothing had happened. A sense of serenity that Ki had never known seemed to have descended upon Elisabeth. There was something beautiful and haunting about her now that Ki had never seen before, and it moved him.

The look in her eye that morning had captured his soul and held it hostage. Whatever Elisabeth had been before she went into the Nether, she had come back as something more. It sung to Ki's spirit and passed beyond simple mortal flesh. No words had been said, but an understanding had passed between them. His mission no longer seemed worthy in comparison to her.

Yet here he stood, hiding in the shadows as she continued to fight whatever evil existed in the world. He looked down at Malthael as he stalked away, likely in search of something to locate her with. The other demon punched the wall, and the stone was smeared with blood before he left. This household rallied behind her, yet Ki felt her disappearance more deeply. She didn't need him anymore; he had guided her in and out of the Nether. His job was done.

Stepping back off the thick railing, he glanced up at the gargoyles. It was strange to have them within the house. Yet nothing about this place made much sense. He moved toward the study now that he was assured Malthael had gone in that direction. He needed to retrieve at least one of the keys to give to the Keymaster and buy himself time.

He walked down the hall of tapestries, his footfalls nearly silent in the still passageway. Malthael couldn't know about the second key that Riku wanted, but he already knew about the first. Ki hadn't told him and therefore hadn't broken the terms of the contract, but he could demand the return of what was his. When Ki had died, his clothes, belongings, and the key had all been left behind.

He nearly opened the door and walked in, but instead he paused and knocked. After a moment, he heard Malthael growl, "What?" Ki opened the door and Malthael blinked in surprise, "What do you want?

"You have something of mine," Ki replied, stepping all the way into the room. "Our agreement."

"Oh right." Malthael stood and pushed off of the wall where the passage led down to the gate. "And you want it now, I imagine."

"Yes," Ki responded and saw thinly veiled anger pass over Malthael's face.

He pulled out the book of keys and tossed it roughly on the table behind him. He heard the keys rattle inside and cringed, but Malthael hardly noticed. Clicking it open, Malthael rifled the book open to the box of keys, then spun it around and thrust it toward him.

"Take your blasted key," he grumbled and walked away.

He reached in and wrapped his fingers around the key, the one with the screaming woman, as he asked, "Where did she go?"

"I don't know," Malthael replied, heaving a heavy sigh, "but I am planning to find out."

"She is stronger than you think," Ki said, putting the first key in his pocket. "She could have let Elsariel out for destructive purposes in the Nether, but she used it only once to defend."

"Of course she is strong!" Malthael snapped. "But how long do you think she can be strong before it breaks her?"

"With you by her side?" Ki asked rhetorically, before adding in all seriousness, "A lot longer than you think."

Malthael stopped at that, and his eyes narrowed. Ki met his gaze without flinching as the demon seemed to consider his words. Malthael had not lived that long without being astute. The demon had to be as quick as a whip to have survived.

"Do you still intend to kill her?" he finally asked.

Ki already knew the answer. He realized he'd always known. "Not if it isn't necessary." The words filled him with a sense of peace.

"Hmm," Malthael said, pulling the door open. "Charmed you, didn't she?"

"Impressed me," he replied, "more than anything, and I do not think the Sin Eater will be able to take her soul in this lifetime."

"You're leaving then?" Malthael asked, clearly sensing Ki's decision.

"Yes," Ki answered honestly, "to find another way."

The reformed demon nodded. "She'll miss you. Even if she won't admit it, I know she will."

"It has been an honor meeting someone who is more determined than me," Ki admitted.

He had been outdone by her persistence, and in the end he had not allowed her to undo herself. Ki would accept this failure because it felt right. Before it would have never occurred to him to go against the wishes of the Council, but this he could not do. The Black Council would have to find another way to accomplish their mission—this woman did not need to be saved.

"Use the gate," Malthael gestured with a nod of his head. "It's faster."

When he emerged on the other side of the gate, Emera was waiting. She was a beautiful young woman with hair that was silvery blond. Her willowy frame was dressed in a fine robe of white with silver embroidery. She was the picture of elegance and beauty, despite her single milky eye.

"Friend of the Gate Guardians," she said, gesturing behind her, "welcome home."

When the gate had been taken, stolen from the Shadow Clan, it had been moved to the opposite side of the continent. They had moved it along the spiritual lines that connected directly with the Netherworld, but it could not leave the continent of Artium. It was bound within a finite space. Why was a mystery even to Ki, but that was the way it was.

He stepped down the steps into a room of pure white. A meandering steam of water ran through the room as though it had cut its way through. There were worn decorative tiles on the floor. The dark, green marble of Ashlad was more haunting, while this place was elegance and nature.

"Thank you," he managed as she led him through the labyrinth of tunnels.

They said nothing as she guided him, each footfall landing as though she knew exactly where to step, though everything around him looked the same—tall walls and a dark grey ceiling embedded with little lights that twinkled like stars. He followed closely, worried he would be lost in this great place. It wasn't long before they stepped out into an antechamber.

Great white pillars rose up to the ceiling, imparting a refined opulence. She stepped down a flight of steps, her gown sweeping behind her as Ki descended as well. The floor was interwoven with metal vines that swept along the floor in their own intricate fashion. They walked down another set of stairs through a narrow passageway into a smaller chamber.

"This is where we part," she said, her hands still tucked within the sleeves of her robes.

Ki nodded before turning and stepping toward the doors. He reached out to push them open, but the great stone doors, as thick as the length of daggers, parted on their own. He glanced back at Emera, who stood with a straight face, making no effort to explain.

"Thank you," he muttered. With a bold step, he crossed the threshold, emerging on the other side. Suddenly, the barrier behind him started to hum, and he heard the stony-faced Emera gasp. The doors started to close, rushing toward him, and he had to roll down the entrance steps to get out of the way.

He glanced over his shoulder. Emera was coming toward him, pointing at him as she yelled, "Enemy of The Gate!"

The doors slammed closed violently. Ki quickly oriented himself. They were at the base of a mountain; he had been inside a great mountain. He pushed himself up from the snowy ground and into a run. He was not willing to find out exactly what Emera meant or what she intended to do about it. Instead, he scurried away as fast as he could and kept at a jogging pace until night fell. He climbed into a tree, finally, and slept soundly until the first light of dawn.

Jumping down from the tree, he heard horses and men in the distance. He had managed to go far and fast, but they had horses. Instead of continuing on foot, he reached into his pack and summoned the Kemshi. He smiled as he remembered his name was Ashley. All these years, and the woman he intended to kill had given him the name of his only friend. And in the end, she had given him even more than that.

When he finished the markings on the ground, they glowed softly. The sound of horses grew louder, and now he could hear their riders calling. His eyes opened in Ashley's as the tiger hurried to a water source. Ki had retrieved many things from Malthael's house. The last had been the keys, but he had also recovered the disk along with his clothes. Pulling the necklace out from his clothing, he held the disk. Standing, he kicked at the dirt in haste to remove the markings. He took off in the direction the glowing designs on the disk pointed—likely in the direction of the closest water. The horses had quieted and were replaced momentarily with the voices of men and barking. They had found where he had rested for the night and were almost upon him. As he broke the tree line, Ashley heaved his bulk from the water.

The tiger shook his body and wore a look of annoyance on his face. He knew the Kemshi would forgive him, though, once he heard the dogs. Sure enough, it did not take but a moment for the tiger's ears to twitch and his head to look first in Ki's direction and then towards his pursuers. Still looking annoyed, he turned and sat down, waiting for Ki to get to him.

"Let's go!" he yelled as he grasped the tiger, and the tiger nearly snapped off his arm as he plunged them into the water.

He came out of the water sputtering as the tiger swam away from him. Apparently, he had no intention of helping Ki get out of the lake. With a sigh, Ki started swimming and the tiger pulled himself onto the shore, shaking water from its fur. They were back under the waterfall in southern Lyreane on the largest continent of Artium. It was an easy walk to the hidden home of the Black Council.

When Ki went to pull himself from the water next to the Kemshi, the tiger put a paw on his head.

"Hey now," Ki protested.

The tiger—Ki had to remind himself again that his name was Ashley—made a disgruntled sound but didn't let up on the pressure of his paw. Ki slipped back into the water and glared at the tiger. It was bloody freezing; he could see his breath in the air. He glared at the tiger, who licked his paw as though nothing was happening.

When Ki tried to pull himself up once more, the tiger put a paw back down and stopped him.

"I'm sorry I summoned you," Ki yelled.

Ashley moved his paw and walked toward their home. With an exasperated sigh, Ki pulled himself onto the shore. As he started toward the door, he started to shiver. Soon his teeth were chattering and his entire body was shivering violently. His feet crunched on the cold ground, and he knew there would be snow soon. There were clear disadvantages to traveling via Kemshi in the middle of winter. He started running, his stiff arms and legs protesting until they got into a rhythm. When he passed the tiger, it made no move to pass him back.

When he reached the entrance to his home, his hands were shaking so badly that it took him both hands and three tries to get the key in. Ashley half ran him over trying to get inside first before Ki removed the key and slipped inside. The cold of their mountain home did nothing to warm him, and the trembling continued. The Kemshi had likely abandoned him for food or warmth, and Ki followed, seeking both.

Even though he had been gone such a short while, it felt as though everything was different. It took him a moment to realize, as he shivered up the stairs, that it wasn't the place that had changed but him. Had this place always been so gloomy?

He scratched his face and felt the barest hint of facial hair forming. He stepped into their main temple area, the sun blinking at him through the hole carved in the ceiling of the room but giving off little heat. The normally warmed hearths and blazers were cold, which made him gather it had been some time since the elders had been there. It felt abandoned.

He started a fire and he began to feel his fingers again. He pulled out some worn blankets and sat cross-legged by the fire, planning his next steps. He needed to speak with the council. After he was warm, he intended to tell them exactly what he had done. Elisabeth had saved his life, and he had saved hers. Their bond went beyond a mission, and there had to be another way. And if that were so, maybe the little boy hidden in the Nether would also have an alternative to death.

Despite the rightness of it, he didn't like going against his family. They had been his everything, shaping him into the man he became. If the elders ordered him, he didn't think he could kill her. It was creating a conflict within him, turning his insides into knots. He didn't know what would be worse—going against his family or being unable to help Elisabeth.

200

Chapter 49: Hystera

φ

Kerrigan wiped the bile from her mouth as she turned back toward the clearing. Elisabeth had written the name that had haunted her dreams. Before now, Kerrigan had been able to delude herself into believing the visions of her mother had all been a dream, that it had no bearing on the real world.

She panted as the taste of vomit sat heavy on her lips. She hadn't told Jinq about the word, afraid that saying it aloud would give it life. So she had buried it deep, ignoring and denying its very existence. She was about to turn back and call out when she saw a movement out of the corner of her eye. Her head snapped around, and she scanned the trees.

Kerrigan searched the woods with her eyes and then turned frantically back toward the Seer and Jinq. The Seer was still on her knees, and Elder Rekis was staring at the tree in the middle of the clearing. Her fingers reached out for Cav instinctively, but they seemed to almost be frozen.

As Kerrigan opened her mouth to call out to the Seer and Jinq, she heard movement behind her. She could hear the woods whispering, but not *what* they were whispering. She narrowed her gaze as she saw a shadow in the tree line. Black water dripped on the ground around the figure like thick tar, and her dress was doused with water. The dress hugged every inch of her. Her head was tipped forward, and her hair covered her face.

The whispers grew, and now Kerrigan could make out the words being chanted over and over again at a speed that made them almost unrecognizable: *He is coming.* Unwilling to find out who exactly "he" was, Kerrigan turned to leave. Standing directly in front of her was her mother.

"Run," she whispered.

Kerrigan screamed as she fell back hard onto the ground. Cav finally awoke—it had seemed as though he and everything else had been frozen until now except for her—taking flight as he screeched. Kerrigan scanned her surroundings for her mother, but she was gone.

"Kerrigan?" Jinq called as Kerrigan scrambled to her feet and fled toward their campsite. All this time she'd thought her mother had been haunting her. Her insane ramblings hadn't made sense half of the time in the dreams, and Kerrigan hadn't wanted to believe that they had been anything *but* dreams. But when Elisabeth had written "Croatoan" in the dirt, Kerrigan had realized that all of the dreams, including her mother, had been real.

"Kerrigan!" Jinq yelled, his voice bouncing around the trees behind her, but she was not stopping now.

The brush slapped against her arms and legs as she ran. She pushed the branches aside, speed her entire focus. She jumped over a log and dashed around a particularly thick patch of trees. She wanted to leave this place for good.

Her arm went up and she heard Cav's wings behind her. The baby owl, her faithful friend, would follow her. His wing span cast shadows on the ground as he flew just a little ahead of her, his form moving in and out of the trees. She could see the light getting brighter as she neared the edge of the tree line.

Hope filled her as she imagined gathering her things and returning to her aunt. Hipasha would understand what these dreams were. Kerrigan would be able to go back to her training and forget this awful nightmare.

As she was about to step out onto the plains, a black figure blocked her path. He was fully robed in black, and Kerrigan worried he was a Soul Collector. The aura around him was sinister. She stopped short and struggled to keep her balance. She heard Cav give a cry and looked to her left, where he was caught in a small net. She reached out to him as she fell on the ground.

"Cav!" she screamed, her own voice filling the eerie void of silence in the forest.

Scrambling to her feet, she moved toward him, but a hand clamped over her shoulder. She reacted without thought as she twisted his hand around and her foot connected with his stomach. The man stumbled back. These were men, not monsters. They could be defeated. Kerrigan immediately went into a defensive pose as she fought to get to Cav. She had to save him!

When the next man came at her, she blocked his attempt to grab her by forcing his hand away, and the palm of her hand struck his shoulder. The two men that held the net containing Cav struggled to pull the screeching bird out. Something grabbed her foot. The hand belonged to the first man that she had kicked in the stomach. Swinging around, she brought her other foot down across his face, knocking him out. As she ran towards the two men, the thinner one came to meet her. She ducked under his arms, her right hand wrapped around his arm as she kicked her left leg up to the front of his neck. Her right leg came up behind his head before locking his neck between her knees as she propelled her arms and twisted them both to the ground. She reached back and delivered a powerful punch to the side of his head causing his eyes to roll back in his head.

Kerrigan pulled her legs free as looked up at the last man, who held Cav firmly in his hand. Kerrigan charged towards him, giving a war cry with the intent to attack. Instead, she watched in horror as the man broke Cav's little neck. All fight went out of her as she stared at the owl's broken body.

"No!" she screamed and waited for death.

Instead, a rough hand covered her face, silencing her. There was something in his hand, and the chemical burned her nostrils. She looked up at the hard eyes of her attacker, her vision became blurry, and then she knew no more.

Chapter 50: Hystera

——————————————— φ ———————————————

"**T here are so many** souls," Elisabeth whispered as she tried to keep herself from crying.

Never had she seen this many souls wandering so aimlessly. It was as though they didn't realize where they were, so all they knew to do was drift. Scanning the ground, she quickly deduced that they were trapped within the confines of the clearing. These poor souls probably didn't even realize they were deceased. Narrowing her eyes, she prepared to get to her feet.

She heard a scream and turned toward the sound, as did Jinq. Kerrigan, who Elisabeth thought was just behind them, had completely vanished from sight. Elisabeth could feel her heart beating hard.

"Kerrigan?" Jinq called.

Abruptly, Kerrigan appeared again and immediately started running from them. After a moment, she was lost to the thicket.

Jinq kept yelling her name. Elisabeth turned her abilities up and expanded them out. Her eyes searched for any sign as she let every sense go. A darkness—like when she had discovered the word—spread in and through her. Whatever it was, it was close. It was disturbing, and yet a strange calm overtook her. It was somehow familiar.

"Something's here," Elisabeth whispered and put an arm in his path before he could move. Just because it was familiar didn't make it any less dangerous.

"What?" Jinq demanded, and Elisabeth took a measured step forward, gazing deep into the bowels of the forest.

Straightening her spine as Jinq took two steps away from her, she summoned Duke and Nathan to her side. They arrived with pointed tails and low set heads. Clearly, they had come prepared for a fight—furthering Elisabeth's belief that danger was close by. Elisabeth had sent them back into the spirit stream to keep from scaring the villagers, but now she didn't think that was a problem.

"Nothing good," Elisabeth said in response to Jinq's question. It was giving her goose bumps in the sweltering heat of summer, despite even her having her abilities to comfort her.

She took a step back as the animals stopped meandering. They moved around her with purpose towards the tree. The border of the clearing had nothing as she slowly picked her way across the open space. Jinq followed her but kept his distance from the demon hounds.

Elisabeth touched the tree, and she gasped as she saw a burning planet. A dark figure turned to her. She knew him as well as she knew herself. He whispered one word, and she stepped back from the tree. On the ground, burned letters appeared along with old markings. Markings she had seen in one of Malthael's books. A chill went up her spine.

"It is the word again," Jinq whispered, clearly feeling the menace in the air. "What does it mean?"

"Not a *what*," Elisabeth answered as she felt Elsariel rise within her. "A *where*."

They heard another scream, a word that they couldn't make out. "Kerrigan," Jinq whispered.

A shadow appeared at the edge of the woods. Living villagers stepped from the shadows to line the edge of the clearing. Elisabeth studied them as they created a barrier, closing off any escape. Duke and Nathan grew restless but waited for Elisabeth's command. Reaching deep within herself, Elisabeth tried to see the villagers for what they were. After a moment, she realized they were puppets. They reminded her of the patrons at the inn with the demon—trapped souls.

A man in a long thick cloak stepped from the edge of the trees to her right. Elisabeth turned to face him, as did Jinq. She couldn't see his face, and he had his hands tucked into his sleeves. As she had done with the villagers, she opened herself, but when she tried to see him for what he was, she found only a void. Whatever he was, he was hidden from her. All she could see was his hatred.

"Come willingly, or we kill the girl and old man." His voice made her skin crawl—not because it was dark or deep or evil, but because it was so normal.

Elisabeth narrowed her eyes as she considered what to do. Her fingers strummed against her arm, and Nathan and Duke growled. As far as she knew, she was the last of her kind and likely the only one keeping whoever these people were from completing their plan. A part of her realized that Ki was somehow wrapped up in all this, and she was glad she had left without speaking to him.

"Who are you?" Elisabeth demanded. She deserved at least that much. "What have you done with Kerrigan?"

Silence followed, and she could feel Jinq shifting behind her. Duke and Nathan were watching closely, their razor sharp tails primed for attack. The people around the edge remained unmoving. The man didn't answer. As the silence continued, she crossed her arms.

"What are you doing with these people?" Jinq demanded behind her. "What have you done with Kerrigan?"

The villagers' swaying back and forth along the threshold was distracting, but he was dangerous. He was the type of being that would light the world on fire just to see it burn. Whatever he had planned, she refused to be a part of it.

"He tried," Elisabeth called out, breaking the second stretch of silence. "Ki tried to kill me, but I have no sins on my soul."

"You cannot deny your instincts forever," he called out as though he fully intended to wait her out, but he glanced over his shoulder. Something told her he was not being entirely honest. Whatever plan he had, she wasn't going to wait around for it to happen. She reached back and wrapped her fingers around Jinq's wrist as she touched Duke's back.

When she normally would have phased them out into their spirit forms, the Keeper remained. Ripping her fingers off him as though he were a hot coal, she gasped at her burned hand. She let go of Duke as she gripped her wrist and saw the seared red skin.

Then the reality sunk in. "I can't take you," she whispered.

"Stop her!" the man in black yelled.

"Go." Jinq nodded.

With tears in her eyes, she whispered, "I have not abandoned you."

Elisabeth touched the backs of the Netherhounds an instant before she felt herself drift into the spirit realm. More men in dark robes appeared as the villagers charged. Twelve men joined the first with robes of black and hearts as dark as death. As she sank into the spirit lines, she focused on Jinq, who faced the mob.

Could he not see their evil? she wondered as the darkness of the place washed over her. Although she intended to return, she still had to leave Jinq there while she fled. She closed her eyes, unwilling to see what became of him.

Chapter 51: Ashlad

φ

*M*althael threw the book across the room and watched as it rattled the bookcase. He nearly howled from frustration and considered burning the entire collection simply to satisfy himself. These were dark thoughts, old thoughts. He had not been so ruthless or hateful in some time. Yet here he stood, about ready to burn everything.

The door to the gate slid open, and Milo poked his head in. "What?" Malthael growled.

"It is the Lady Emera," Milo replied with worry on his face. "She has pressing news and requests you urgently."

That made Malthael pause. Emera was never one for urgency. The woman was as stiff as a corpse; he had never even caught a whiff of agitation in her voice. In the decade he had worked with her, he had observed little range of emotion in her beyond compliancy. The fact that she had stressed the urgency of the matter made Malthael push his anger aside.

He started toward the door, and Milo held it open. The lesser demon waited for Malthael to pass before pulling the door closed behind him. They hurried down the stairs into the great green marbled room. The open gate revealed a pacing Emera on the other side in Lyreane.

Malthael raised his eyebrows as he stepped off the bottom step and into the main room. Emera had never been one to pace. The fact that she was doing so now made the bottom of his stomach squirm with worry. When she saw him, Emera stopped marching across the gate's opening. She had a look of fury on her face of which he hadn't thought her capable.

"Do you realize what you have done?" she asked, her words biting. Her hands were animated. He half expected her to walk through the gate and slap him.

"Emera," he replied patiently, "you need to explain."

"He was of the Forbidden!" she replied, and for the first time he saw the fear under her anger.

"Who?" Malthael asked, still confused.

"The man you sent through," she replied, pointing at him. "When he crossed the barrier, the temple sealed itself and a skull appeared on the door."

"A black skull?" Malthael asked, feeling his stomach fall to his toes.

"Yes," Emera confirmed. "It is them, Malthael."

"They were killed off," Malthael reminded her. "King Nauberon took care of that and ensured that they would never rise again. I was there. I saw them fall to the Wild Hunt."

"I saw the mark upon the wall with my own eyes," she countered. "They have had fifty years while we were unaware. You know exactly what they would try to do. Who they will try to bring back."

"The boy is not fifty years old," he reminded her. "King Nauberon checked with The Fates. No daughters or mothers remained alive."

"We know he had thousands of souls of his people within him," Emera countered as Milo shifted his feet. "He could have aged slowly."

"Just as Elsa does," he said absentmindedly. She might look only twenty or so, but Elisabeth was nearly thirty in plant-dweller years. Between the proximity to the gate and the fact that she had Soul Collector blood in her veins, her life would likely be extended. Perhaps Ki had gotten his life prolonged even further; it was not outside the realm of possibility.

"We have to find them," Emera replied, and he heard the steel in her voice. "The Shadow Clan cannot be allowed to continue. They must be destroyed before they figure out how to bring *him* back."

Malthael didn't even want to think the name and could understand Emera's resistance to speaking it aloud. His mind began to work out all the angles. Ki was killing with a Sin Eater, gathering the souls of sinners. Malthael realized, however, that they were specific sinners—demonic half-breeds, to be exact. Half-breeds of Soul Collectors specifically that had been damned all those years ago by King Nauberon. Most didn't know what Soul Collectors were, but Malthael did, and it filled him with fear.

"By the Nether!" he whispered, his voice filling with emotion as he looked up at her. "It is already happening."

"What do you mean?" she demanded before she gave a startled cry.

Pain filled him as the edge of a blade entered his back and pierced his spine. He fell forward, the blade still in his back. He gasped as he turned his head to see Milo standing above him with an expression of hatred. The lesser demon cast off his mortal face, and beneath the green of his skin betrayed what he was.

"Malthael!" Emera said and stepped toward the portal.

"Close"—Malthael gasped the words as the blade burned—"the gate."

As Milo looked up and hissed, Emera did as he asked with one final regretful look. The gate went solid and the lesser demon's fists hit the stone. He beat against them once before turning back to Malthael. Malthael could feel that it was no normal blade in his back. This one was meant to hurt demons specifically.

"All this time?" he asked as Milo walked over, giving him a look of pity. Malthael wanted to strangle him, but he needed information.

"No," Milo replied before kneeling down just out of reach. Not that it mattered. Malthael couldn't move, and with every breath the blade went deeper.

"When?" he demanded.

"Our Elisabeth was meant for greater things than hiding," he replied, and Malthael could see the love on his face. "She should rule the planets and the Netherworld."

"Rule?" Malthael demanded and remembered the look in his daughter's eye when she'd returned, remembered Elsariel.

"Yes," Milo responded as though he were superior. "Though I doubt your puny mind can understand her potential. She has Darienith the Betrayer's blood, the strongest of the Soul Collectors. He tried all those years ago to kill his offspring for fear of this day. Now it has come, and she is everything they hoped she would be. Soon she will have everything she deserves."

"Why now?" Malthael asked as the corners of his vision turned black.

"They have everything they need now." Milo leaned forward and whispered, "They found the sixth gate."

Malthael's eyes went wide as Milo stood and strolled away, clearly done with him. He grunted and tried to reach for the blade, but his arms refused to cooperate. He lay there like a fish out of water. His useless limbs failed to respond as Milo ascended the stairs. He knew Milo wouldn't hurt her at least—Elisabeth mattered more to the lesser demon than anything else. Although his loyalty was twisted, Elisabeth would not be stabbed in the back.

Malthael knew exactly what was stuck in his back. It was an old cursed blade for immobilizing demons. Thrust into the spine, it kept the demon from healing or moving. It had been made by the Black Council, a group of elders who had once served the Black King. When he fell, all the creatures of Morhaven had fallen upon the world of men in order to finish the Shadow Clan and their ties to the World Eater. A Wild Hunt to end a war.

Air struggled to fill his lungs as he tried to blink the blackness from the edges of his vision. He knew the blade wasn't supposed to kill him, but he was no longer a full-fledged demon. Without his horns, he was at a severe disadvantage, and the blade affected him in worse ways. If the blade was removed, he might be able to heal, but with every passing second, his chances faded.

With a heavy sigh, he flung his arm down, feeling it slap against his hip. With every fiber of his being, he summoned the strength to reach into his pocket. His fingers protested, not wanting to work properly, as he struggled to get his hand inside it. He struggled not to lose consciousness. He needed to reach the talisman and warn Elsa. His daughter might not have to worry about Milo, but if they brought back the Black King, no one would be safe. He very much doubted Elisabeth would consent to be his Queen, and then he would kill her. Malthael needed to hurry.

He glanced down as his hand, no longer obeying his commands, slumped to the ground. He looked at his other hand, but it, too, refused to respond. He fought to stay awake. He thought he heard Elisabeth's voice, but an instant later his eyelids slipped closed and he relaxed into a blissful nothingness.

Chapter 52: Lyreane

φ

Ki sat cross-legged on the floor of the abandoned sanctuary. He could tell the elders had not been there since he had gone with Elisabeth into the Netherworld. Although it had been only two days in the Nether, it had been nearly thrice that time on the planets. Yet the ash in the hearths was as cold as winter, and the food was beginning to rot from neglect.

Frowning, he poked at the fire and tried to decide on his next move. Ashley sat behind him curled up around his back, the tiger taking in the warmth of the fire as well. He had devoured a slightly old and cured bit of ham and seemed sated. Apparently, he had been here wandering around hunting on his own since the elders had left. Shifting the blanket around his shoulders, Ki let his thoughts wander.

The person who had started this journey was not the same person who sat in the cold temple. Part of this transformation was owed to him being away from the influence of the council, and the other part had been Elisabeth. It was impossible for him to deny that she had a hand in it. Malthael had also influenced him in opening up his eyes to making his own choices. Ki was starting to do just that.

He couldn't and wouldn't kill Elisabeth, not after what she had become to him. At first he had thought he admired her. But then he'd seen Ethandirill and Nanette together and had recognized a deeper, more intimate, bond growing between them. Now when he looked at Elisabeth he could see nothing but what they had in common. Yet remembering the look of disgust when he touched her, he knew that these feelings were obviously his alone.

Whatever she was to him, he could not expect her to return these strange new emotions, yet he struggled with the idea that he could just let her go. He still wanted to protect her and preserve her innocence against the evil of the world. But he was as much the evil in the world as anything else. He did not know what he would do if he had to choose between Elisabeth and the twelve men who had raised him.

Love was a weakness to the elders, and it had not been permitted. When he had fallen and scraped his knee, it had not been seen to with tenderness; it had been a tool for training himself against pain. When he was sick they made him work thrice as hard to make his body stronger. He had not recognized that the love and loyalty he felt was one sided. They had sheltered him, taught him, and been his companions since birth. He'd known no other life, and yet as he sat there in the cold, damp place, he didn't feel at home—not like he would have months ago. Now, this place felt hollow. He had seen the world, seen the way Malthael had rocked his crying daughter, and he knew that something was missing from his life.

He nearly jumped out of his skin when he heard hushed voices. He stood, and the blanket fell away from him. He wore little beneath it but his pants, and the chill of the temple swept in against his bare skin. His Kemshi lifted its massive head and his little ears became alert. Ki bent over and pulled his undershirt over his head as he walked barefoot across the cool stone.

The voices grew louder as he walked toward their archive. He had never been one for books, but he could remember listening to Elder Ha talk about their past—the wrongs of the people who had fought against the Shadow Clan and what the Black Council would have to gain by getting their revenge.

"It is over here," he heard Elder Ha say as he pressed his back against the wall.

"I don't see it," Elder Il replied, clearly not amused.

Ki peered around the corner at the two men. They had their backs to him, which was why their voices seemed muffled. They were looking through one of the bookshelves of scrolls, and he could see some of the scrolls scattered by their feet. He had never known Elder Ha to disregard a scroll like that; he cherished them and had cared for them as long as Ki could remember.

"It must be here," Elder Ha replied as he unrolled another one before dropping it by his feet.

Elder Il unfurled one before looking up at his fellow council member. Ki could see the annoyance before he heard it. "We need it to extract the final shard."

"Ki could still come through," Elder Ha replied hopefully, his wrinkles deep around his eyes. Ki was about to say something to them when he stopped. Something about that statement made him pause, and he continued to listen intently.

"You heard what she said," Elder Il snapped. "He couldn't use the Sin Eater. She has denied her other side, and now we must extract it by another means."

"That isn't his fault," he countered, his voice pitched high.

"There are two pieces missing," Elder Il said as he dropped another scroll on the ground. "Where is the second one?"

"I don't know where the boy is," Elder Ha admitted, and Ki's eyebrows knitted. "He was probably similar to the woman and couldn't be killed by the sword."

How could Elder Ha know about Ki's vision of the boy? He hadn't told any of them, and they hadn't asked. He thought he alone knew of the forty-two, and yet Elder Ha knew about the boy. He pressed his back against the wall and closed his eyes a moment. What else were they keeping from him?

"Ra believes we only need one more now that we have the vessel," Elder Il responded, sounding excited. "I believe he may move forward with only the forty we have."

"Would it still work?" Elder Ha asked, sounding surprised.

"We have waited long enough," Elder Il said, seeming to dodge the question. "If we can find this scroll, we can locate the last one and strengthen his chances."

Ki heard another scroll hit the floor. "What if we have to draw it out?" Elder Ha asked.

"We summon him into the vessel and have him draw it out," Elder Il snapped, clearly losing patience.

"And the woman?" Elder Ha asked, which made Ki stop breathing.

"If she returns, we have him do the same," Elder Il replied with a sigh.

The two Elders had always been at odds because of Elder Il's short temper. Of the Elders, Il had always been Ki's least favorite. The man was as loving as a coiled cobra, while at least Elder Ha used to slip him fruit on his birthday.

"Aha!" Elder Ha yelled, and Ki stiffened at the sudden sound. "Found it!"

"About time," the other old man grumbled. "We should locate Ki while we are at it."

Ki slinked back toward the fire and the tiger. The tiger raised his head again, giving him a quizzical look as Ki tugged on his boots. They had always trained him to sleep with his boots on. He secured his knives in the boots and then quickly messed up his hair as though he had been sleeping and rumpled his clothing.

"Who's there?" Ki called and heard the two men still.

"Ki?" Elder Ha said, and a moment later his face appeared in the doorway. "Ki!"

"Ha!" Ki exclaimed with a smile, and when Il's face appeared he added, "Il!"

"Boy," Elder Il replied soberly as Ki drew closer to them. "How long have you been here?"

Ki smoothed his mused hair. "Less than a day," Ki responded as Elder Ha patted him on the arm. "Where have you all been?"

They exchanged glances before Elder Ha answered, "I believe it is about time we showed you."

"Showed me?" Ki asked, tilting his head to side as though he were confused, though everything was becoming clear to him. "Show me what?"

"You'll know when we show it to you," Elder Il retorted as he turned and walked toward the back of the archives.

Elder Ha gestured, and Ki followed them to a door in the back. It was engraved with specific markings that would take them to the same place over and over again without fading. Elder Il opened the door and didn't hesitate to step through. Ki paused and glanced at the much shorter Elder Ha. He smiled and urged Ki forward, so Ki felt he needed to.

When he stepped through the door, the heat of the day hit his face first. He took another step forward as he turned in a circle. Elder Ha stepped through as well and closed the door behind him. There was a door in the middle of the woods, one they had constructed a door. It stood like a short fat tree amongst the tall narrow trees.

"We are in Hystera." Ki gaped as he glanced around.

"Yes," Elder Ha confirmed as Elder Il left them behind, "and that isn't the most amazing thing."

He almost didn't reply but then remembered that normally he would. After a moment, he stopped looking around in amazement and said, "It isn't?"

"Come," Elder Ha said and led him through the trees.

The trees were grouped more tightly together the more they walked until they emerged in the clearing. A warm wind pushed against his skin as the bamboo trees clattered. An unconscious girl was chained to a great stone slab that had been positioned in front of the only tree in the clearing. An old man was bound and being guarded by two people Ki didn't recognize. Most of the elders were gathered around the other side of the slab, between it and the tree. They were scratching something into the ground with long decorative sticks.

214

"You can't do this," the old man yelled, but his cries were ignored.

Elder Ra looked up when they approached and looked pleased when he spotted Ki. He stepped away from the group, and they all turned their heads toward them. The youngest of the elders stood tall among scooped necks. His spine was made of steel.

"Ki!" he called and held his arms out as though he wished to embrace him. "Finally, you join us."

"I have returned in shame," Ki managed, trying to keep up his ignorant mask. "I failed to save the woman."

"We shall fix that later," Elder Ra responded, putting hands on both sides of Ki's shoulders. "Now you shall know why you are our savior. You have given us the means to return the Shadow Clan to its former glory."

"What is this? Who is she?" Ki asked, glancing around.

"So much to tell you." Elder Ra all but sang his reply. "Where should I start?"

"With her," Ki said before he could help himself.

"Good idea!" Elder Ra boomed. "She is the offspring of our fallen king. He came into this world with the help of a powerful elemental called forth by another follower. He impregnated a woman, and she bore this child. This beautiful child shall be his vessel into this world."

"She is only a child!" the old man yelled.

Elder Il turned. "You keep yelling and I'll remove your tongue," he hissed.

The old man leaned back, clearly startled. Ki didn't even glance back for more than a moment; he knew Elder Il would follow through on this threat. Whoever the old man was, he was not long for this world.

"Who is he?" Ki asked, finally sparing a glance back to take in the dots on the old man's face.

"The Keeper," Elder Ra answered, hardly glimpsing back himself. "I want him to witness this and return to tell others what happened on this day. Not only that, but he is leverage if the woman you couldn't save returns."

"It is time," Elder Lo called. "He believes forty are enough."

"Then we shall proceed," Ra replied and looked at Ki. "You have made this possible."

"Who is *he*?" Ki asked, genuinely confused this time.

"Our King, the Black King of Croatoan," Ra explained with pride. "The World Eater."

Chapter 53: Ashlad

———————————— φ ————————————

*E*lisabeth **rematerialized in** her father's study and was surprised to find that he wasn't there. Nathan and Duke looked around the study as well, seeming confused. She was about to send them to find him when the tapestry shifted and the stone door opened. She took a step forward, expecting Malthael, but instead Milo stepped out.

"Milo!" Elisabeth cried out, relieved.

"Elisabeth?" he replied, seeming startled. The stone door sealed off the passageway.

Elisabeth rushed over and threw her arms around him, hardly noticing his green skin. Milo had been with her since she was a child, and it was a relief to see him healed. She was near tears, and hugging a lifelong friend made her sniffle from the sudden rush of emotion. She suppressed them, but she was suddenly relieved.

"Where is Malthael?" Elisabeth asked as she put a determined smile on her face.

"Looking for you," Milo responded, clearly relieved as well. "We were all so worried when you left without saying anything."

"I felt like I needed to go alone," she admitted before patting Duke's head as Nathan went over and lay down by the fire. "With the exception of Duke and Nathan, of course."

"What has you so upset?" Milo asked, drawing her over to her father's overstuffed chair.

"I went to Hystera," Elisabeth replied, thinking about the twelve men and the fact that she'd had to abandon Jinq. "I think I found Ki's family, and they are planning something. I fled so I could come back and get Malthael. He would know what to do."

"Before he went to find you, Malthael spoke with Emera of Lyreane," Milo replied, putting a hand on hers. Elisabeth braced for the pain from her burn but it never came. "They spoke of a Shadow Clan. They were worried that the clan planned to use you."

She glanced down at her fingers that had been seared earlier and found only pink and tender skin, benefits of her demonic half no doubt.

Elisabeth cupped their hands together, relieved to have someone she loved with her.

"I think the Shadow Clan had a plan for me as well," Elisabeth admitted. "Although I don't know what for. I haven't taken a life, and I don't have a mortal sin my soul, so they cannot take anything from me. I have to go back." The realization hit her, and she knew she could no longer fight the inevitable.

"Not if your life is in danger," Milo insisted, and she looked up at him with a smile.

"Don't worry, Milo. I have a backup plan," she said, glancing down at the swirling mark on her palm.

"Well, I won't let you go alone," he insisted, standing. "We can send Duke or Nathan to find Malthael, and then you and I can go back to Hystera."

"I do worry that the longer I wait, the more likely that Kerrigan and Jinq will suffer," Elisabeth admitted, concerned that it was already too late.

"Then we should go right away," Milo replied and held out a hand.

She took it and stood. "It's fortunate that you are a demon and can travel with me through the spirit lines."

"It is fortunate," he responded with a crooked smile.

"It's good to have you back," Elisabeth replied, looking closely at one of the people who helped raise her. "I missed you, and though Malthael wouldn't admit it, he did, too."

"I have missed you as well," Milo responded, squeezing her hand as she held her other hand out.

"Nathan, go and find Malthael," she commanded.

Nathan stood and shook his great head before fading into his spirit form. She held her hand out and Duke came to her. It suddenly felt wonderful to be doing something, but more so to be doing it with someone she trusted. All through her time at the university, he had been there to help her. She had gotten her doctorate in Fringe Sciences because of her abilities. She'd wanted to understand herself and the world better, and throughout that adventure Milo had been her support.

They sunk into the floor and she closed her eyes, readying herself for the fight ahead. When she opened them, they were in a darkening world, the last remnants of the sun falling away and dusk settling in. Leaves fell around her as she took a step, aware that she was not very far from the clearing. She didn't see or sense anyone there as she walked slowly forward.

"We will have to distract them," Elisabeth whispered without turning back. "Perhaps then we could…"

She paused as the clouds started swirl above her head. They turned black and stormy. As they continued to spin, she moved a little to the left so she could see it better. It was as though something was controlling the storm, the wind picking up and leaves rustling across the forest floor. She was running out of time.

Elisabeth heard a yelp like that of an injured animal. She turned back and saw Milo bent over Duke. She nearly screamed his name but then remembered where she was. She didn't want to alert anyone to her reappearance. The rock next to Duke's head was covered in black blood and for a moment she thought the wind had somehow picked up the rock. But then she considered its size.

When Milo looked up at her, her breath caught in her throat. There was no shame or regret or worry; there was only pride. Elisabeth felt her ribcage expand as she fought to keep herself calm. She shook her head, not believing what she was seeing. A knife of betrayal was stuck deep within her gut, and she felt it twist. She couldn't run from this or the truth.

She felt all the blood rush out of her face and into the pit of her stomach as a thought occurred to her. "What happened to Malthael?" Elisabeth shouted over the storm as she took a step back.

"I had to delay him," he replied, and she felt the treachery of his actions cut deeper. "He should live long enough to see what you were meant to become."

Fear touched her fingertips and traveled up to her brain. She felt it start to take hold of her as he took a step forward and over the unconscious Duke. She felt sick to her stomach as she turned and ran. Without Duke, she was trapped here, but she could still call Nathan. He would be looking for Malthael, though, and she dared not pull him away yet.

She looked over her shoulder. Milo was following her, but he wasn't running. She veered toward the clearing, the center of the storm making her hair slap wildly around her face. The bun she had clipped her hair back in came loose. She slowed when she reached the edge of the clearing.

Every villager had their hands above their heads and their palms touching. It looked like the stained glass at the cathedral, but she knew they were not praying to some divine god. She approached them and saw that their eyes were completely white. They were all muttering the same thing, a language she didn't recognize.

Let me out, a voice whispered, but she ignored it.

Out in the clearing were a group of twelve men with their hands raised to the sky. The wind whipped their cloaks around wildly. She could see many of their shadowed faces and pale bony fingers. Her eyes darted to the old man who was held in a kneeling position. Jinq looked on with terror, and beside him stood a younger man who was half turned away but seemed familiar. They were both looking at the same place—the slab of stone. She glanced over her shoulder and saw Milo growing closer.

She ducked between two of the people on the clearing's threshold, going under their elevated hands and into the clearing. Behind her, she heard Milo shout something as the girl seemed to wake up and start screaming. Kerrigan fought against the chains that bound her wrists and ankles. Her screams were mostly lost to the storm as the stone behind her started to ripple.

Elisabeth heard someone shout as she darted toward the ring of men. She saw a hand come out from the other side of the gate. The stone behind Kerrigan was no longer stone. A dark shadow appeared behind the girl, and her eyes grew wide with fear as she stopped struggling. She looked over her shoulder, and her face portrayed true terror.

"No!" Kerrigan screamed, and then the shadow passed into her.

Elisabeth shouldered her way between two men. She felt her powers rise, and she glowed from the sudden release. She might have lost the boost from life energy, but she hadn't lost her natural abilities. Kerrigan was mortal, and her soul could be saved. Elisabeth's hand was outstretched and her fingers reaching. She was steps away when an arm wrapped around her waist. She felt her fingers move through Kerrigan's wispy hair as she was pulled aside.

"Let me go!" she shouted as the sound of the storm began to lessen.

"Stop," she heard Ki say. "You cannot do this."

"I have to," Elisabeth said, reaching out for Kerrigan.

"It's too late," Ki said, and she felt his warmth around her against the storm.

She fell between his arms, and he let her down gently to her knees. A tear fell down her cheek and splatted against the dead soil. She felt sick from betrayal and worry as she gazed upon the innocent girl. All stilled as the storm stopped and silence fell.

After a moment, the girl seemed to stir. A strained moment passed. It was as though no one dare to breathe for fear that time would leave them upon the next inhale. The girl lifted her head back and drank in a deep breath. When she leveled her head and opened her eyes, they were red.

Chapter 54: Ashlad

—————————————— ϕ ——————————————

*N*anette had been reading a book about the Netherworld when the dog burst into the room. She was only in a nightgown, having changed some time before. She stiffened and drew the blankets up around her in a futile attempt to protect herself. When the dog turned, she realized it was just one of the guard dogs Elisabeth had told her about.

It wasn't what she would call a dog exactly. Its tails chimed together as it held them aloft. She wondered if the spikes on the tails were as deadly as they looked. She looked back at its face.

"Yes?" she asked tentatively as the dog's full attention was on her.

It ran back out of the room, and she relaxed back against the headboard. She was about to return to the book when the dog dashed back in again. It bounced up and down before sprinting back out of the room and then returning with an expectant look on its face. She gave it a strange look, wondering if the poor thing had gone insane.

Then it looked out of the door and whined. Nanette's eyes went wide and she asked, "You want me to follow you?"

Its tongue rolled out of its mouth as it looked happy again. She didn't know how, but this guard dog, with all its terrifying features, actually looked adorable. Perhaps she was becoming accustomed to these strange things. With a sigh, she stood up and set the book on the bedside table. Luckily, she had borrowed one of Elisabeth's full-length nightgowns and only had to step into a pair of her shoes. Elisabeth was a little bit chestier and taller, but her older clothes fit. Not sure exactly how to put on Elisabeth's strange clothes by herself, Nanette decided to follow the dog right out in the nightgown. She paused by the door to pull on a long gray coat, though, to fight the chill of the house.

The dog led her down the hallway and down the massive staircase. She was happy she'd decided to put a pair of the indoor shoes on, and she buttoned the coat. The shoes scuffed softly against the cold stone as the dog waited patiently for her at the bottom of the stairs. Metal chimed as its tail swung back and forth.

Nanette smiled at him. Once she reached the bottom, he led her down another hallway. She followed. When they turned down the hall with the tapestries, she knew where they were—by the study where she had first entered the house. The dog ran toward the closed door and vanished, but to Nanette's surprise she could just make out its hue a second after it did so. It wasn't clear, but it looked like the light didn't bend around it right.

Elisabeth had warned her that with time she would see a little more of the hidden world around them. She would never see like Elisabeth saw, but she would experience more. She had taken the spirit world inside of her, accepted a small part of it, and now she was bound to it. However, knowing and seeing were two different things, and she paused a moment.

Waiting patiently, she went to the door and turned the knob. It turned without hesitation and she pushed it open. The demon dog waited on the other side. When she saw him and hurried over, he pawed at one of the large tapestries. She closed the door behind her before going to the tapestry. She pushed it aside and saw a great stone wall. It looked completely blank. When she touched her hand to it, she immediately sensed that everything wasn't what it appeared to be and that something lay beyond it.

She looked down at the dog and asked, "How do I open it?"

The dog whined, and its tail shot out. It pointed like a glittering deadly arrow at a light fixture. She had to go up on her tippy toes to reach it, but when she touched it, nothing happened. Frowning, she looked down at the dog. He bobbed his tail and his head at the side time. She looked back up at the light and put her hand against the stone as she went up on her toes again. Her fingers wrapped around the metal, and she pulled down.

With a click, it gave way, and the door popped open. Nanette had to jump back to avoid it and nearly tripped over the demon hound. He hurried around her and down the stairs. She slipped through the doorway and hurried after him. She couldn't see much at first, but her eyes soon adjusted.

Around her the richest green color she had ever seen met her every glance. The dark marble was constructed and carved to cover every inch of the floor. The railing matched the pillars, which were inlayed with intricate gold designs. The splendor of it was beyond anything Nanette had ever seen—and she was a princess!

When she neared the bottom, she saw the dog whining over a limp body. She lifted up the slightly too long dress further and hurried down the last of the steps. Recognizing his skin immediately, she hurried over to

Malthael's side. She knelt down by him and saw the strange black blood spread around his back.

Then she saw the blade and the outline of a hilt buried in his back. If she shifted too much, its golden handle vanished. She touched Malthael's shoulder and shook it slightly. "Malthael?" Her voice echoed softly in the room, and it gave her the chills.

The demon didn't respond, and she bit her lip slightly. She didn't know what to do exactly, but she had to do *something*. When she looked up at the demon dog, he whined and licked Malthael's outstretched hand. Frowning but determined, she reached out and wrapped her hand around the handle.

When she tried to yank it out, Malthael gave a startled cry and his eyes opened wide. She immediately let go, leaned back on her heels. Her hand smeared in his blood as she cried, "I'm sorry."

He blinked a few times and squinted before whispering, "You can't pull it out."

"Why not?" Nanette asked, putting her hands on her folded knees.

"Cursed," he whispered, clearly fading in and out.

"What should I do?" she asked, trying to keep the fear and worry out of her voice.

"Elisabeth," Malthael whispered his eyes pleading. "Find Elisabeth."

Nanette glanced around as though she expected to see a way to find her. She shook her head. "How?"

"The gate," he said almost breathlessly, looking up toward a green stone slab. "Use the gate. Nathan will lead you."

Standing, she took careful steps toward the gate, but it didn't seem to move. Nathan hurried beside her, and one spike on his tail tapped against a dial. She glanced back at Malthael, but his eyes were closed and his breathing was labored. She fought to turn the dial, but it wouldn't budge. Nathan made a jerking motion with his tail. Wrapping her bloody fingers around the dial, she pulled it back, and instantly the gate started to glow. She gasped, and her mouth opened slightly in awe. It was beautiful, like looking up at the sun while swimming underwater.

She put a hand out and prepared to walk through when the demon dog shouldered her leg. She looked down at him, and he tapped his tail against a specific spike on the dial. She turned it once, and the light color shifted to blue. She turned it again, and it shifted to black. She was about to shift it to the red, the one he had indicated, when she heard Elisabeth's voice.

Her eyebrows rose in surprise, and she looked down at Nathan. His ears were perked up as well, and he looked equally as surprised. She hesitated a moment and glanced back at the demon. He had fallen unconscious again. She could tell by his steady breathing and slumped posture. She pressed her lips together before she put a hand out and stepped through the gate.

Chapter 55: Hystera

— φ —

Ki studied the faces of the twelve elders who had raised him. They were all looking at him in surprise as Elisabeth knelt at his feet in a state of distress. When he looked up, he saw a girl he didn't know stir, and a moment later she lifted her head. Red eyes stared back at him, and a cruel smile touched her lips. Her head went back slightly as she took in a deep breath of air.

"Hystera," she said, but it didn't sound like the girl's voice. It sounded overlaid with a second voice behind it that was distinctly male.

"The place of your banishment," Elder Ra called, and the girl shifted her eyes toward him.

"Beautiful," she said, and with a jerk the chains shattered and she was on her feet. "It is good to take in fresh air again."

All twelve men fell to their knees one by one in a deep bow and cried out, "My king."

"Yes," she said, holding up her hand. "Apparently I fathered a girl. Interesting."

Her hands ran over her body a moment as the cuffs around her wrists sat like bracelets. The broken chain hung from her wrist and ankles as she took in the scene around her. They called her king—he might have the look of a girl, but the Black King reigned within her body. It was he who spoke to them now.

The Black King took in a deep breath and then looked down at Elisabeth. "I smell myself."

Elisabeth stared at the girl. Ki couldn't see the look on Elisabeth's face, but instinctively he moved forward. The Black King paused and looked up at Ki instead. His red eyes gave Ki a measured stare before assessing him.

"So many souls," the Black King said in that same eerie voice. "So many lives."

"He collected your souls," Elder Ra declared from his place on the ground, lifting his head slightly.

"By my count," he said, holding up his hand with two small fingers extended, "I am still missing two. Although it seems you have brought one to me already."

Ki shifted until he was standing completely over Elisabeth. The Black King started laughing. "You mean to protect her? Against me?"

Even though it was the girl who raised an arm, Ki felt a great force slam against his body. He was thrown backwards and barely managed to twist himself so he landed on his side instead of his back. He felt his shoulder take the brunt of it and felt it pop from its socket. He shook his head as he sat up. Ki was back by the farthest point of the circle. Elisabeth was looking over her shoulder at him, and he saw her worry, which raised his spirits.

"Nothing will stop me now," the Black King sang. Suddenly, he heard a soft chanting.

The Black King froze, and the feminine face turned dark. Ki saw a flash of loathing. The King bent his legs and pressed off the ground, propelling the girl's body through the air and out of the circle. Ki was suddenly aware that this Black King was far worse than anything in the Netherworld or Morhaven.

"Keeper!" the melded voices screamed before landing in front of the old man, who was on his knees praying.

"By soil and wind," Ki heard the old man say before the Black King put a hand around his throat and cut off his words.

"You and your kind banished me. Now you will be the first to see my revenge," the Black King cried, the girl's voice almost completely overrun by the masculine voice.

"The planets will defend themselves," the old man gasped in defiance as the girl hoisted him up with one hand. The chains on the shackles swung back and forth as the Black King tightened his hold.

"No!" Elisabeth screamed suddenly, as though coming to her senses, and Ki slowly rose to his feet.

He heard the sickening sound of a fist punching through the old man's body. Blood splattered on the dead soil, and the old man gasped. The Black King pulled back a bloody arm before discarding him on the ground. Then he turned around and smiled with the girl's sweet face at Elisabeth as he ran the girl's bloody fingers down her face. She skipped toward the circle, her face filled with such merriment. The Black Council studied her as she passed by but stayed bowed down.

"Women have such light bodies!" the Black King declared, lifting the girl's arms, "Don't you think?"

Elisabeth glared at her, and the girl's arms dropped. Her lips curled into a pout as though it really bothered her and she strolled up to the sitting Elisabeth. "You liked him?" she called, sounding more like a girl again. "You shouldn't, since you have part of me in you. Which part are you?"

She crouched in front of Elisabeth with her elbows on her knees. The girl looked at her from side to side, but Elisabeth kept her gaze straight. It was defiant and angry. Ki took his wrist between his knees and used his other hand to throw his shoulder back into place. He tightened his jaw and gritted his teeth against the pain but didn't make a single sound. Normally, it would have taken minutes for him to fix it properly, but he didn't have minutes.

"I am Elisabeth," she yelled boldly, "and you cannot have my soul."

"Darienith," the girl hissed, and then her voice went deep. "My betrayer and my favorite piece."

Ki wanted to move toward them, but he could feel their powers mounting. Elisabeth responded, and her voice could have drawn blood. "You are incomplete, and in that body you can do nothing."

"The smartest piece, too, it seems," the girl said, biting her lip as though she felt pleasure. "I want it back."

The girl plunged a hand into Elisabeth's chest. Ki took a step forward at Elisabeth's cry but stopped when Elisabeth's raised her head. Her eyes were glowing blue as she opened her mouth. All of the Black Council's heads came up at once as she drew their life forces from their bodies. Ki realized she was extracting just from the council and no one else. That showed control that he hadn't thought she had—and it worried him.

When she stopped, she thrust her own arm into the girl's chest. Ki glanced down and saw that the council was still alive. "I want her soul," Elisabeth demanded.

"Fine!" The girl's lips moved, but it was a man's voice that shouted the words.

They both fell back from one another, and a shockwave came off them. Ki put his arms up in defense at the sudden rush of power. In front of him, the Black Council fell back. When he lowered his arms, Elisabeth was lying back and the girl was on her side. Ki hurried over to Elisabeth and touched her head.

She turned over to him. In her arms was a bright blue soul shaped like a sleeping girl. She smiled sheepishly at Ki and reached out for him.

He nearly cried out. Elisabeth had taken a soul. Yet her serene face forced him to say nothing as he took Elisabeth's hand and helped her up while she cradled the soul with her other arm.

"To the old man," she whispered. Her voice was hoarse, as though she had spent hours screaming.

Ki half carried her toward the old man. He lay there his eyes open, staring at the world with dull lifeless eyes. Blood pooled around his body. Far too much of it had been lost. Elisabeth fell to her knees beside him. She took the soul and pressed it into the old man's body. The hole in the old man's chest slowly became skin again, but he didn't stir.

Ki helped Elisabeth back to her feet and started moving them away from the Black Council as they began to stand. When she swayed, he lifted her up into his arms but paused when she touched his face. When he looked over at her, she pressed her lips to his. His eyes were wide open, but hers were closed. For a moment, he thought she was going to draw his life force out, but when she didn't he closed his eyes and kissed her back. His heart stirred.

When they parted, she smiled at him and whispered, "Thank you."

"I want it all!" Ki heard the girl yell. "You give it to me!"

Ki was about to turn and leave when Elisabeth moved out of his hold. Instantly, he felt the change in her. She wasn't Elisabeth any more. He let her legs down, and when he stood back up she kissed him square on the mouth with a loud smacking sound. Her lips were curled into an impish grin.

"She did it for you," Elsariel whispered a breath from his lips. "You should run while you still can."

"Stop," he whispered, but she patted him on the face and walked around him.

"Don't shout, you big baby," Elsariel yelled at the Black King, putting a finger in her ear as though to block out the sound.

The girl that housed the Black King's soul stopped and looked at her. Her eyes narrowed and she asked, "Who are you?"

"Her demonic half," Elsariel answered with a smirk. "And trust me, I'm a lot more fun."

The girl's eyes narrowed, but he saw desire. The girl licked her lips as Ki glanced between them and the forest's edge. There was obvious lust in her eyes as Elsariel stepped over the unconscious old man. Elsariel pushed one of the Black Council members out of her way as she sauntered toward the Black King.

"How so?" he asked.

"Loose moral judgment, a penchant for power, and"—Elsariel took the girl's face in her hands and kissed her square on her mouth—"I swing all sorts of ways."

The girl was stunned for a moment as Elsariel wandered past her and toward the gate. Her hips swayed from side to side seductively, and Ki felt torn. He couldn't bring himself to leave her, no matter what she desired. Ki had no idea what would happen with Elsariel in charge, especially since somewhere inside Elisabeth still resided.

Ki turned and walked toward them as he called out, "Elisabeth."

"Not here, sweetie," Elsariel called out with a little laugh.

"I won't leave you," Ki called, stepping past the circle of men partially drained of their life force.

"She left you," she replied with a hand on her hip. "She is hiding in here"—she tapped the side of her head with her finger—"because she can't bear what's happening to her."

"I won't ever leave you," Ki said, ignoring Elsariel's comments.

Before he could say more, the Black King stepped in front of him. The girl's fist collided with Ki's chest, knocking him backwards. He lay on his back, the wind having gone out of him, gasping for air. He rolled over and tried to stand despite the pain. The Black King walked up to Elsariel, a strange sight in his current body.

"I want to see it," Elsariel said, patting the side of the stone slab, and nodded her head toward the slab. "I want to see Croatoan." He regarded her suspiciously before asking, "Explain to me what you are. Demon halves are a part of the whole. You cannot be separate from her."

"I can if she rejects half of herself," Elsariel replied. "I am everything she has ever suppressed in the last fifteen years, her demonic urges being the bulk of it. She denied me for so long that she gave me life. Now I get to come out and play."

"She fractured her personality?" the Black King replied, but he wasn't actually asking a question, "Fascinating."

Ki's eyes watered as he lay on his stomach in the dirt. Elsariel seemed about ready to respond when a movement by the gate caught Ki's eye. A black hand appeared at the gate a moment later. Nanette stepped from the gate with one of the Netherhounds by her side. Everyone froze as all eyes turned to the girl and the hound. She looked startled by what she saw.

"Um," Nanette said, her eyes taking them all in.

The Black King took a step forward and put an arm out, but Elsariel called out, "Nanette, my little servant."

"Elisabeth?" Nanette asked, turning to her. Then her voice was pitched low. "Elsariel."

"Miss me?" Elsariel asked, pushing off the slab.

The Black King's eyes admired Elsariel warily. "She is yours?"

"Willingly, too," Elsariel said as the hound whimpered.

"You are more like me than I thought." The Black King sounded impressed.

"Where does the gate lead?" Elsariel asked, tipping her head to the side while she stood in front of Nanette.

"Into my fortress on Croatoan," the girl responded, but with every passing breath the girl's voice faded and became more like a man's.

"Good," Elsariel replied and pushed Nanette backwards.

Nanette gasped, but any other noise was lost as she fell back into gate. Ki's mouth dropped open in shock as Elsariel put her hands up in surrender and turned around. She had a face set in mischief as she said, "Now I am going to have to go to Croatoan to retrieve my servant."

The Black King seemed taken aback. Ki stood, his chest still in pain, and moved towards Elisabeth. The Black King glared at him, an expression that quickly turned to manic and promised to lead nowhere good.

"Very well," he said to Elisabeth. Then the girl pointed at Ki as he spoke to Elder Ra. "Find me the last soul. The boy knows. Get it out of him."

Elsariel and the girl housing the Black King's essence strode into the glowing red gate. Ki pushed himself into a standing position as the twelve elders of the Black Council held their arms out. They were weakened, but there were twelve of them and one of him. As they made a perfect circle around him, he resolved with gritted teeth to find a way to Croatoan and get Elisabeth back by whatever means necessary.

Chapter 56: Croatoan

——————————————— ϕ ———————————————

*n*anette landed hard on her backside, and she let out an unhappy noise for good measure. With a groan, she got her legs folded under her as she sat up. When she saw the red in the reflection of the gate, she stopped rubbing her side. She had expected she would be back in the green cavern with Malthael, but when she turned around all she saw was black.

It was as though the entire world was scorched black. A great fire burned in a large circular hearth. It reminded her of a fountain, but instead of water this was a constant blaze. Standing, she looked around at the open sky. Nothing dampened the endless twinkling of stars.

She heard rustling and saw Elisabeth step through with a girl by her side. The girl rolled her shoulders and shadows engulfed her body. Her frame twisted in the growing shadows. Nanette glanced at Elisabeth, but it was Elsariel who stared back. She looked excited, not worried, by what was happening.

When the shadows started to dissipate, a tall thin man in long sweeping robes stepped forward. On his head he wore entwined dark metal that looked like a crown with spikes. They looked as pointed and deadly as his sharp features. His nearly black hair swept back from his crown with slight curls at the end. It reminded her of the crown she had seen on the Det Morian King, but it was less elegant.

How did he do that? Nanette thought as she averted her eyes in fear.

"Well, that's better," Elisabeth purred, breaking the silence. "More like a Black King."

Nanette gave her questioning look. Elsariel was absolutely insane!

He smiled at her then. His grin was crooked, and it gave Nanette the creeps. Although the Weavers terrified her, something told her she should be even more afraid of him. She glanced between Elisabeth and the Black King and wondered about how she always seemed to get herself into these situations.

"You are shameless," he said, but his words held an underlying desire. "You don't quiver in fear or bow to me."

"I am just like you. I even have a part of you within me," Elisabeth replied. Nanette was having a hard time keeping up. "It would be like you bowing to yourself."

Elisabeth started down the stairs, and Nanette realized she shouldn't be thinking of her *as* Elisabeth. Elisabeth wasn't running the show. It might be Elisabeth's face she was looking at, but they were Elsariel's words she was hearing. Yet Nanette couldn't bring herself to call her that either. Elisabeth was Elisabeth, and even her demonic half belonged to her friend.

"Good point," the Black King said, striding down the stairs as well.

Nanette hesitated for a moment, but once she glanced back and realized that the gate was open, she took a step toward freedom. "Nanette, you won't go through that gate without my permission," Elisabeth ordered.

Her legs fought to move. She tried to will them to do so, but they refused. With a defeated sigh, Nanette turned around and started down the stairs. There were pillars and platforms and fires burning everywhere, but little else. Elisabeth got to the bottom step and glanced around.

"What do you eat?" Elisabeth asked, her voice curious as she stared at the firelike fountain. "I'm famished."

"This planet is my will," he replied with a turned hand. "What do you desire? What will sate your hunger?"

Elisabeth seemed to be considering it as her fingers traced along the stone fountain. She paused and then glanced back at Nanette, who was standing at the bottom of the stairs. With a wicked smile, she turned back to the Black King and said, "A pomegranate."

With a flick of his wrist, a pomegranate appeared in his hand. Nanette felt her jaw drop open a little and her eyes grow big. She had never seen any magic like that before. Elisabeth didn't seem all that moved. She held out her hands and caught it when he tossed it to her.

"Can I do that?" Elisabeth asked as she brought the fruit close to her face and smelled it.

She peered over the red fruit as she waited for his response. He seemed to be considering her question as he moved around the edge of the fountain. The fire cast shadows on his face, and his dark eyes watched her. Elisabeth didn't seem at all affected by his imposing gaze. She returned it with equal intensity.

"Perhaps," he finally replied, stopping to stare at her across the flames. "Imagine something simple in your mind and will it into being."

"As simple as that?" Elisabeth asked, setting the fruit down on the edge of the fountain.

"Nothing is simple about it," the Black King responded, and Nanette felt as though she was watching something that she could see only half of, as though more was being said and more was actually happening. She tried to stay as still as possible as not to attract any attention to herself.

Elisabeth cupped her hands, held them up, and closed her eyes. He watched her intently as a look of concentration came over her face. Nanette took shallow breaths. Elisabeth's face relaxed, and then suddenly a white bowl appeared in her hands. She opened her eyes with a smile and looked up at the Black King in triumph.

"Excellent," the Black King said, and raised his arms. "Shall we celebrate?"

He didn't wait for a reply, and the barren area was suddenly filled like a grand party. Glass shards strung from pillar to pillar twinkled as the firelight reflected against them. People in mirror masks suddenly appeared around them, and Nanette took a startled step back as they danced in a circle around the fountain. Nanette looked down. She was no longer in her nightgown and jacket but instead wore a simple black dress.

When Nanette looked up, she realized that Elisabeth wore a finer version of that dress, one that was silver and shone bright. The man was dressed in fine black attire that seemed to have a gleam to it, and when he reached for Elisabeth's hand, Nanette saw that his hands were gloved. Elisabeth took his offered hand. Her own were gloved in a soft silver color to match her dress.

Her dress had long sleeves, and sequins made it shine. No words were spoken as music filled the air and the dancers changed from a flowing movement to a twirling one. They all wore red and black. Elisabeth and the man joined the line of dancers, and he spun her around and around. He still wore his crown, and now Elisabeth wore one, too, made of mirrors and pearls and silver wire. It all glistened against her blond hair and the dark sky.

When the song was done, Elisabeth stepped from his hold and out past the circle. She wandered past the ring of decorations and out into the cold barren landscape of the world. She stood out on a balcony, gazing up to the sky. The Black King followed her there and stood back admiring her. Nanette followed them, fearful for what Elsariel might do in Elisabeth's body.

"I cannot tell if my admiration for you is because you have a part of me or because you are like me," he said, breaking the silence.

"A bit of both, I imagine," Elisabeth said, turning around. Her gown spun with her. "The sliver of your essence is still within me. I'm surprised you don't want it back."

The Black King shifted his posture. "I had never thought to rule with another," the Black King said, changing the subject, and Nanette's breath caught in her throat. "To have a queen by my side."

"The Black Queen," Elisabeth replied, as though considering it. "It does have a haunting ring to it."

"Let me show you what we could make of the worlds," he said, his voice full of desire and ambition. "We could make the planets our playground."

"Why leave this place?" she asked with a wave of her hand. "You are a god here."

"One world is not enough," he replied, as though confused by her question. "I made Croatoan this way. I want them all to follow my will."

Elisabeth pouted as she glanced over her shoulder. "That seems boring."

Nanette couldn't look away. It was like watching a battle occur, but instead of swords they were using words. Nanette didn't know what to make of their clashing. The Black King seemed to give in to his baser needs, but Nanette knew there was more going on. He reminded her of Jason, always planning even when he was charming. Elisabeth was the one that Nanette couldn't figure out.

"Boring?" He seemed offended. Nanette tightened her fingers in the fabric of her dress.

"You're alone here," she replied. "I've been alone all my life. It is underrated."

"What would you suggest?" he asked, clearly unimpressed.

"What use is the title of king unless there are subjects to rule over?"

He unfolded his arms at that and regarded her with a frown, one that seemed more contemplative than negative. After a moment, he countered her question with another question. "You want to rule the planets?"

"I want to rule over everything," Elisabeth said, coming toward him, "and everyone."

Nanette felt ill. It seemed that Elsariel stood for the opposite of everything that Elisabeth did.

"People are useless," he countered, but he seemed to be giving credence to her words.

234

"They are the thing of life," she said, passing him by, and he watched as she reached her hands out for Nanette. "She taught me that. Being alone is not nearly as fun as sharing it with someone else."

Nanette took a hesitant step toward her and then another. Hope blossomed in her chest as her eyes swept back and forth between the Black King and Elisabeth, who took her outstretched hands. The gloves felt soft against Nanette's skin as Elisabeth clasped her fingers. Nanette swallowed; even her demon half seemed determined to protect her.

"She is nothing," he countered and lifted his hand.

"If you harm her," Elisabeth said without turning around, her eyes sharp with intent, "I will deny you with every breath. You will never get that final shard and never be whole."

His hand hesitated to carry out whatever terrible act he'd imagined; apparently Elisabeth had made a large impression in a short time. She dropped one hand and pulled Nanette behind her as she turned and faced him. He lowered his arm, and Nanette looked up at Elisabeth. She grinned as though she hadn't threatened the most powerful being in all the known planets.

"Very well," he replied, and his cold eyes regarded Nanette fully for the first time. She tried not to squirm under his gaze, but it was difficult. His eyes seemed dead somehow, which frightened her.

"Are you going to ask me to dance again?" Elisabeth asked, holding out a hand.

With a raised eyebrow, he moved toward them. Nanette saw her chance and whispered, "Malthael is injured. He needs you."

Elisabeth looked down at her, and when their eyes met she saw her friend. Elsariel and Elisabeth had few things they seemed to agree on. But one that bound them together was Malthael. In a flicker, Elisabeth was gone, and her demonic half returned as the Black King took her hand. She smiled and allowed herself to be led back into the ring of dancers.

Nanette went to the edge of the balcony, where she stood partially hidden by a pillar. Whatever Elsariel had planned, Elisabeth was still in there. Malthael had seemed desperately in need of help. She looked up as they danced, and she wondered how long Malthael could survive without it.

Chapter 57: Hystera

φ

"**I**t was all a lie," Ki managed as he looked around at the faces of the men who had raised him.

"The deception was necessary to make you believe," Elder Ra replied. "Although it is true on this day that you are our savior. You have bought us back."

"Where is the boy?" Elder Il asked, and Ki gritted his teeth.

He didn't have any weapons except for the knives in his boots, and twelve powerful men surrounded him. Ki was about to keep talking when he heard a growl. The old men cried out as the demon dog barreled through the edge of the ring. Elder Ra lifted his arm, but Ki leaped for him, his fist connecting with Elder Ra's throat before he could start chanting.

The man choked on his words as he stared at Ki, startled. Others started up their chant, but two suddenly stopped, silver cutting through their backs. The second demon dog threw two of the men over his head like discarded rag dolls. Ki ran toward the sudden opening as the two dogs coordinated their attack.

The twelve men were immune to most deaths, but they could not stop things of the Nether. The demon dogs would make short work of them. He ran for the tree line but came to a stumbling halt as villagers poured into the clearing. They moved as though possessed. Their targets were the dogs.

He remembered what Elisabeth had called them and yelled, "Duke. Nathan. Run!"

Their heads came up in unison as Ki turned back to face the rushing men. His fist collided with the head of the first one, and the man fell to his knees. Ki's knee connected with his face as he put a hand on the shoulder of a second man and thrust his fist against his ear. The man stumbled back as Ki leaped over the body of the first fallen man.

He made a continued run for the edge of the clearing as the dogs plowed through the line of men and followed him. He was running toward the door but was only vaguely aware of what was happening. He couldn't remember for sure where it was, but he knew it was in the general direction in which he was sprinting.

There was blood smeared all over both Duke and Nathan, but Duke, the one with the chip in his horn, had demon blood on him. The dark, almost black, blood gleamed red, but it was as black as the night. A demon had recently fallen victim to those blades. Ki glanced back so long that he nearly tripped over a fallen log. He stumbled to keep his feet under him as the horde of possessed people followed.

He nearly missed the door and had to rebound of the tree to keep himself straight. When he corrected his direction, he ran full out toward the door he'd first come through. All he needed to do was get through to Lyreane and then get Ashley to take him to wherever Elisabeth was. There had to be a body of water somewhere.

The demon dogs were suddenly running by his side. He thought of a new plan. Perhaps he could go to Malthael and get more information on the Black King. The dogs were protecting him, and he was sure Malthael would forgive his involvement. All he wanted to do was get Elisabeth back, something they could agree on and work toward.

He reached the door, slamming into it before turning the knob. He stepped through, and the dogs nearly trampled him to follow. Half stepping and half falling over them, Ki slammed the door closed behind him. Then he hastily removed the markings with the sleeve of his shirt to keep anyone from following them. Once a member of the Black Council reached the door, he would make the markings to allow passage, but Ki planned to be long gone before then. He braced his hand against the door as he panted.

Swallowing his exhaustion, he straightened and called, "Ashley?"

There was no response, so he moved toward the fire. The click-clack of the hounds' hooves followed him into the next room. It was nothing but low burning embers and ash now, and there was no tiger in sight. Frowning, he crossed his arms and looked around. Without hesitation, he crossed the room and collected his weapons and clothes. He was tying his overshirt when one of the dogs stopped and growled.

The second one started doing so, too, as the tiger stepped from the shadows. Ki put his hand out. "Calm down!"

He didn't have time for a bunch of dogs to chase around a very large cat. They all looked at him, the two excited dogs and one unperturbed tiger. The Kemshi didn't seemed all that moved by the two large dogs or their dangerous tails. He sat down, his tail moving back and forth, and just stared at them. It was as though he intended to stare them to death.

"We need to get to Malthael," Ki said, but at the mention of his name Nathan whined. Pitiful eyes looked up at Ki, which made him realize something was wrong. Nathan licked a wound on Duke's side as the tiger looked on with the same bland expression.

"We must go to Malthael," Ki said, securing his blades on his hips.

He finished securing his weapons and clothes, glancing around at his home. It was like saying goodbye to a part of him. He was leaving everything in the past and starting anew. The men who had raised him had used him and lied to him. He'd thought he was saving people, and instead he had been killing them. Elisabeth might have been among them, and he might have never known her. The thought chilled him to his marrow.

He felt a tongue on his hand and was startled from his thoughts. Ashley was staring up at him with his bright yellow eyes. Nodding, his head Ki agreed, "This is no time for getting lost in thought."

Ki mounted the tiger as the dogs pressed in close enough for Ki to touch them. They all vanished, and Ki felt the spirits pass over him. His hands gripped fur. Almost as soon as it began, it was over, and they were standing on the courtyard by Malthael's sprawling gardens. It was raining. The tiger slowly trotted forward as the demon dogs hurried inside.

Ki shook the water from his hair and got off the tiger. He moved toward the house and was greeted at the door by one of the dogs. The tiger followed at its own sauntering pace, as though it was bored. With a shrug, Ki followed one of the demon dogs, likely Duke from the cut on its side and the mark on his horn. The dog led him through the house and into the study. The tiger stretched out in front of the fire before laying his great mass down.

Sparing only a glance and realizing the tiger had no intention of following, he pulled on the handle of the lantern the way Malthael had and moved back when the slab swung open. Holding the tapestry aside, he watched Duke hurry past him and then followed. He was halfway down the stairs when he saw Nathan lying beside a fallen body. It took Ki a moment to realize it was Malthael. He hurried the rest of the way down the stairs. Nathan whined, but Malthael didn't stir. Ki walked up to the reformed demon and saw that he had a pool of black blood around him.

"Malthael," Ki asked, crouching beside him, "what happened?"

When he didn't answer, Ki shook his shoulder slightly and said loudly, "Malthael!"

238

The demon blinked his eyes open slowly as though by great effort. He squinted up at him before asking, "Elisabeth?"

Ki's felt crestfallen as he responded, "With the Black King on Croatoan."

Malthael looked terrified. "She must remove the knife," he whispered.

"What knife?" Ki asked, leaning forward.

"You can't see," he managed before licking his lips.

"Why?" Ki asked, peering at the strange, almost translucent, handle over his back.

"Only half breeds and those of the Netherworld can see," he managed, though his voice was hoarse. "Only a half breed can remove it."

"You need Elisabeth," Ki said, and then his eyes opened in realization. "Or someone like her."

Chapter 58: Hystera

───────────────── φ ─────────────────

*J*inq **opened his** eyes to chaos. There were people yelling, and it took him a moment to understand what was happening. He slowly sat up, and as he did he felt constant warmth in his chest. He touched his neck and remembered the pain. He'd thought the Black King, the World Eater, had ended his life. In fact, he remembered the feeling of a great pressure on his chest followed by intense agony.

With a gasp, he looked down at the hole in his clothes and remembered Kerrigan putting her hand through his chest. With a rush his memories returned, but none of them explained why he was sitting there now. He had been floating away, being sucked into a void of darkness, when the planet had reached out for him.

She put me in you. Kerrigan's voice was in his head, and he choked on the saliva in his mouth.

What? he thought. He coughed as he tried to catch his breath.

No need to yell. Kerrigan sounded tired. *Elisabeth put me in you to save us from the darkness that resides in this place. It would have consumed your soul, and I would have been a passenger to the Black King.*

Suddenly he saw the boy that Elisabeth had known run across the clearing. He had Elisabeth's strange creatures with her, and a mass of the villagers was chasing him. They moved in quick jerking movements, as though being commanded. The two creatures were covered in blood, which glistened in the moonlight. That was when he noticed the crumpled bodies dressed in black.

Where is Elisabeth? he managed.

She went into the gate. Kerrigan's voice was fearful

He turned his head to look at it. The gate was empty now and had returned to solid stone. There were still chains hanging down it. He felt Kerrigan's fear. Nothing good would come of Elisabeth going anywhere with the Black King. He knew what it had taken to trap the Black King all those years ago.

We need to leave, Kerrigan urged.

His eyes opened wide as thoughts ran through his head. Then he asked her in his head, *Where are Hibrius and Cav?*

His question was met with silence, and he forced himself into a standing position. Most of the people in the clearing had run into the woods after the young man and the two creatures. He turned and stumbled toward the tree line.

They killed him, Kerrigan finally managed, and it sounded like her voice was breaking. *They killed Cav. I don't know where Hibrius is.*

He likely died, Jinq thought, just barely keeping his emotions in control as he swallowed, *when I did.*

His words were met with silence again and he thought he felt her great distress. Jinq stumbled through the woods and toward Mara. He only hoped she had been spared because she had been so far beyond the village. His legs carried him as his mind reeled at what had happened. He nearly tripped over Hibrius's unmoving body.

Falling to his knees, he gently touched the panther's head. He nearly choked on his sob, but he could not give into his emotions. He bowed his head and swallowed his pain. When Kerrigan was taken care of and he transferred the Keeper mantle, Jinq would ask that Elisabeth take his soul as well. A life such as this was would not be worth living.

Jinq, Kerrigan whispered. *Jinq, you need to keep—*

"I know," he muttered.

Mara, Kerrigan whispered in his mind, and it sounded like she was struggling with her emotions. *Mara can take us back. We can warn the Guardian.*

"What good will that do?" Jinq said out loud to himself. It was strange not to be able to think without having another mind listening. Despite his deep feelings of hopelessness, he forced himself to stand and not look back. He would come back and bury his friend later.

I am not a mind, Kerrigan corrected him. *I am a soul. Once balance returns, Elisabeth will remove my soul, and I shall be free. The darkness will not take me. When we reach the Gate Guardian, we shall warn him about Hipasha and the coming darkness.*

It is rising, Jinq confirmed, glancing over his shoulder as he walked through the woods. *I can feel the world darkening.*

Kerrigan fell silent as he walked through the woods and out into the tall grass of the plains. The tent was flattened, and there were no signs of Mara. His heart fell as he approached it. He began pulling the tent apart to find the mirror. To his surprise, he found two bodies, one with a broken neck and the other one trampled. He crouched down next to them and looked at their lifeless glossy eyes. He pushed one of the bodies to the side a little bit and saw the shattered mirror. He rubbed his head with his palm before standing up.

"Mara?" he called and then stood as he moved toward the other forest. "Mara!"

A sad little trumpeting sound came in response. Relief and worry flooded into him, and he wasn't sure if they were his own emotions or Kerrigan's or both. He picked up a few things, throwing them into a pack that he slung over his shoulder. He moved toward the sound, seeking out grey with his eyes. He caught the movement first as he turned.

She seemed apprehensive as he approached, so he put out a hand and said softly, "Mara, it is me."

By the stars! She isn't dead, Kerrigan whispered in his mind as a second wave of relief flooded through him and he recognized the emotions were not his own. She had held back her relief until Mara had been found. He realized Kerrigan had suffered under a heavy burden all her life and so expected the worst.

Mara's trunk wrapped around his outstretched hand. He half expected her to start crying as she got up. He saw her struggle to stand and walked around her, inspecting her legs. Her back leg had a knife buried in it. He pulled it out, and she gave little trumpet of protest. He patted her side as blood leaked out but quickly settled his pack on the ground and rummaged through it for a medical kit.

Jinq undid the salve that worked on cuts and worked it into the wound. Mara put her trunk on him and watched out of the corner of her eye. When he was done, he wiped his hands in the grass as he considered what to do next. The numbing agent would reduce Mara's pain, but he wasn't sure she could carry him.

Before he could respond, Mara backed and bowed, waiting for him to get on. The exhaustion of the day's events hit him all at once, and he sagged as the adrenaline left him. He hesitated but then realized that while he had two souls, he had only one body. It was little weight for Mara to carry back home. He mounted her and rubbed behind her ears. She moved carefully and deliberately but showed no signs of stopping or signs of pain. Apparently, he wasn't the only one ready to leave this place.

He smiled down at the elephant as he said, "Let's go home."

Chapter 59: Netherworld

——————————— φ ———————————

Ki stood in front of the young Seer as he floated in perpetual sleep. With focused effort, Ki pulled the body of the boy out of the strange substance of the mountain. It moved like gelatin and glittered like gems. When the last of his forty-two was free, he lay on the ground without moving, but for the subtle rise and fall of his chest.

Duke and Nathan had apparently never returned to the Nether. When he told them what needed to happen, they refused at first. They growled and were threatening with their tails, but finally they whimpered until they relented. Ki couldn't risk the council being able to find him or the boy. With them, the Black King would have everything he needed to take over the worlds. He would be whole again.

Ki glanced back, worried the twin demon dogs had become lost. He shifted from one leg to another as he waited and swung his dagger around his fingers. Shoving the blade back in his hip sheath, he felt the urge to pace but resisted it. When they appeared, Malthael was still unconscious between them. Soon after telling Ki about the knife, the demon had become comatose. Nothing could rouse him, which made Ki worry.

"You know what to do," he said to the demon dogs.

They moved back into the shadows of the cave. They continued back until he couldn't see them anymore and he was satisfied no one could. Then he turned back and knelt by the boy's body. He continued to sleep peacefully as the effects of the mountain wore off. There was a reason it was called the Dreamer's Range. It made dreams a reality, and it took some time to wake up from.

He reached out and shook the boy. "Time to get up."

The boy didn't move, so Ki shook him harder. Finally, his eyes opened and he sat up. "Where am I?"

"I'm hiding you," Ki replied calmly, trying to keep the urgency from his voice.

"Who are you?" the boy asked wearily as Ki helped him up.

"I need you to pull the knife out of his back," he replied without answering the boy's question. "If you do that, this nightmare will be over and you can go back to dreaming."

He seemed dazed. "I have been enjoying nice dreams."

"Good," Ki replied, propelling him forward. "Pull out the knife."

The boy looked down at Malthael and froze. When his legs stopped moving, Ki nearly knocked him over. His eyes went wide as he pointed and demanded, "What is that?"

"Part of the nightmare," Ki insisted before pointing. "Can you see the knife?"

"Yes?" the boy replied as he started to look around as though coming out of a fog. "Where are we?"

"This is nightmare," Ki replied, pushing the boy forward. "What do you fear more than anything?"

"The Netherworld," the boy whispered. He visibly paled when Duke and Nathan growled.

"I can return you to your dreams," Ki insisted, taking advantage of his confusion. "Just remove the knife."

Ki saw him swallow hard before bending down. In one easy yank, the knife that Ki hadn't been able to see suddenly appeared in the boy's hand. He looked at the knife and whispered, "This feels so real."

Ki felt cold steel penetrate his back. He gasped, and so did the boy, who dropped the knife. Ki felt a hand around his throat. When he glanced back, Riku smiled wickedly.

"What have we here?" Riku asked, clicking his tongue.

"What do you want, Riku?" Ki demanded as he felt the knife twist in his back. He gritted his teeth against the pain.

"My keys, but this seems much more entertaining," Riku replied, looking down at the crumpled body of Malthael, "Who would have thought I wouldn't need the key to kill Malthael?"

Ki tried to elbow him in the face, but the demon moved out of the path of his swing. The boy tried to run, but Riku shoved him up against one of the hard rock faces that existed within the mountain's interior. The boy collapsed on the ground, and Ki realized he was running out of time.

Ki saw Duke and Nathan out of the corner of his eye. "I have your keys," Ki told Riku, reaching into his waistband and tossing a small sack at his feet. "Our deal is done."

Riku waved his hand and the two keys flew out of the sack and into the air. He smiled and took them in his hand. A noise came from the end of the cavern.

244

"Well, apparently Malthael is just a bonus," Riku replied. He stepped toward the body before calling out, "Your missing soul is here, too."

Elder Ra stepped into the light. The man looked tired but alive. His eyes shone with a brightness Ki had never seen. They stared at one another without moving or saying anything. Ki watched him with cold clarity; he now knew what they were.

"Repent," Elder Ra finally said, breaking the silence. "I shall return you to our fold."

"I would never return," Ki retorted, squaring his body as he bent down toward the boy.

"You cannot win here," Elder Ra replied.

"You're right," Ki said between his teeth. He pushed the pain down before calling, "Duke! Nathan!"

The demon dogs leapt from the shadows as Ki picked up the knife. In two quick steps, he buried the knife in Riku's side. The demon hissed as he crumbled to the ground. He tried to grab the knife, but it was stuck. Ki couldn't see it anymore, and the demon couldn't pull it free. The demon shook his head as Duke and Nathan hurried over to Malthael.

Ki kicked Riku over and declared, "You are nothing."

When Ki turned around, Ra and the boy were gone. Without hesitating, he called to the demon dogs. "Get him out of here!"

He ran through the interior of the mountain, his pulse wild as blood splashed behind him. Pushing away the pain, he sprinted with both daggers primed. When he saw a shadow moving, he called out, "Stop!"

The figure paused and looked back. Elder Ra had the young Seer over his shoulder as though he weighed nothing. Elder Ra was illuminated by the glimmer in the cave, but Ki could see his determination. Ki could see where the cave diverged into two tunnels and Ra stood at their juncture.

"You won't stop us," Elder Ra insisted. "Others have tried and failed."

Ki felt the blood drip down his leg and into his boot. His foot was slick. He was losing blood quickly, but he couldn't let Elder Ra get away. He kept his breathing carefully even and gripped his weapons tightly.

"I will," Ki said as he began moving forward.

He felt a sudden and sharp pain his back. His back bowed as he stumbled forward a few steps before another part of his back exploded with pain. He tried to continue to move forward, but when the third blow struck, he fell to his knees. He could see the shafts of the arrows protruding from his back. Tears streamed down Elder Ha's face as he held up a quiver stocked with arrows for Elder Il to shoot.

Elder Ra stepped up close to Ki and whispered, "I forgive you."

Then in one violent jerk, Elder Ra slit his throat.

Chapter 60: Croatoan

———————————— ϕ ————————————

a **great feast was** laid out, and Nanette sat beside Elisabeth as she ate a small pastry. It was white with a red teardrop on it. Her eyes were closed as she savored it and the Black King watched her. His fingers gripped the top of a crystal glass. His eyes were dark and thoughtful as she ate.

Nanette very much doubted Elisabeth would approve of what she was wearing. The ball gown had been exchanged for dinner attire. The black capped sleeves and plunging neckline of this dress left little to the imagination. The matching black bodice was tight, and the dress fell in a heavy layer to her feet. It was lace that overlaid a simple black fabric. The result was stunning and matched the silver circlet encircling her head. It shimmered like starlight, and the large black gem twinkled blue in the firelight.

When Elisabeth opened her eyes, she turned to him and asked plainly, "Still don't trust me?"

"Not a wit," he replied, but his face betrayed his lust.

Elisabeth laughed softly as she reached for her glass. "I wouldn't either. You never know who you are dealing with, me or her. At least until you decide what to do, I'm providing you with entertainment."

Nanette had this peculiar feeling that they moving around each other in a battle of wits. At first Nanette hadn't been able to decipher their discussions, but now she was catching on. Elisabeth was trying talk the Black King into ruling the planets instead of remaking them.

"Now that we agree on," he responded with a curl of his lips.

The Black King hadn't tried to harm Nanette again, but his every glance that was spared in her direction and every word directed at her still put her on edge. He rarely spoke to her directly, and when he did she wanted to make herself as small as possible. Despite everything, she tried to remain strong for Elisabeth. Her friend would need her help.

There was a soft hum, and Nanette lifted her head to look in the direction from which it had come. The gate shimmered a moment before two men in robes stepped through. Nanette tried to stand. Her instinct was to run, but Elisabeth's hand grasped hers, keeping her from rising all the way. They had with them a boy that they carried in their arms. Nanette swallowed on instinct. She knew something bad was going to happen.

"We found him," said the younger one, who had two patches of grey at his temples.

The Black King rose and he looked pleased. "Bring him here."

They came down the stairs and set the boy on one of the stone tables. The fire from the fountain flickered as they walked past as though it was reaching for them. Nanette turned to Elisabeth, who continued to stare without blinking. Her face remained emotionless.

"The Savior tried to stop us," the man told the Black King as they stepped back from the table and the boy.

"You raised him wrong," the Black King responded, glancing in his direction. "The behavior of the child should dictate punishment to the parent."

The Black King's hand struck the side of the man's face. His neck snapped back. Nanette put her hands over her mouth to keep from screaming. He had struck him, an ally, without hesitation. She glanced at Elisabeth, who shook her head, and Nanette kept silent.

"I punished him," the man responded, but he didn't seem bitter about being struck.

"His usefulness had ended," the Black King responded.

Elisabeth popped a grape in her mouth. "I beg to differ," Elisabeth called and stood slowly.

"Of course you do," the Black King responded.

"People need to have a hero to get behind," Elisabeth explained, her hand trailing on the stone table as she walked toward him. "That way when you crush him, you crush their hope."

"You want me to kill him after he has established himself as a hero?" he asked, his eyes narrowing in suspicion.

"When you go back to the planets, word of your return will spread," Elisabeth explained as she reached the end of the table. "They will look to a hero, like the Keepers of old, to send you back here and seal you in again. When that happens, Ki will be among them, and he is special. When you kill him and word of his defeat spreads, you will also defeat hope. Without hope, people will turn into cattle and you will rule as the Black King."

"Clever," he commented, "but you don't have the entire picture. Isn't that right, Ra?"

"That's right," Ra replied diligently.

Elisabeth put her hands up in the air. "It was just an idea. Just enjoying the idea of being the Black Queen and thought I'd give it a try."

The one called Ra looked over at Elisabeth in surprise, and Nanette realized that Elisabeth had said that on purpose. She was trying to do something as she gazed at the Black King. A moment passed as they stared into each other's eyes, as though trying to peer into each other's very souls.

"Once I've harvested this soul, I believe we should go on a walk through southern Lyreane," the Black King declared with a smile. "To go and see your old friend."

"Ki is hardly a friend," Elisabeth said with a laugh, and Nanette tucked her head down to keep from betraying what she knew. "The man was sent to kill me. Let's just say I'm happy to join you on your walk."

"We shall see," the Black King responded before turning back to the boy.

Nanette looked up at Elisabeth, who watched as the Black King reached into the boy's body for the last of his missing soul shards. The boy began to struggle. He looked so young and helpless that Nanette had to look away as he begged for mercy. She didn't understand how Elisabeth could watch such cruelty and do nothing. Perhaps this wasn't Elisabeth anymore; perhaps this was Elsariel. That would not bode well for Nanette's fate.

She forced herself to look when the boy went silent, bile rising in her throat. His head was turned toward them, a lifeless arm was extended in a desperate plea for help, and his glossy dead eyes betrayed that it was too late. Nanette's lip quivered as she fought down the tears. The Black King held a shimmering purple shape in his hands that he drew into himself. He was wrapped in a soft red glow for a moment before it faded and a red gem appeared on the center of the primary spike on his crown.

"Ah," the Black King said, lifting his hand, which swirled with black shadows, "at last, all my pieces but one insignificant shard. My power is whole." He turned back and held out his hand to Elisabeth. "Shall we go for that walk?" he asked.

Elisabeth took his offered hand and replied, "I thought you'd never ask."

Chapter 61: Ashlad

 φ

Malthael came to, and for a moment he thought he was dead. Something was covering his face and was blocking out all light. Blinking, he moved a little and the curtain was lifted. A soft light assaulted his eyes, and he groaned as one of the demon dogs licked his face. With a grunt, he pushed the dog back and realized that curtain had been fur.

Duke lifted his head from where he sat on the floor and leveled it at Malthael. Nathan had been laying his head across Malthael's. The dogs leapt up, tongues hanging out in excitement as they all but hopped around. Malthael pushed on Duke's head as he got to his feet. Everything in his memory was a blur, and his back hurt.

His legs wobbled slightly as he remembered and whispered, "Milo."

Duke barked and waved his tail around. Malthael drew his hand back and saw flakes of brown on his dark palm. It was then that he realized the dogs were covered in the same brown substance. He leaned closer. It was blood, and the black flecks were demon blood. Apparently his demon dogs had fought to protect Elisabeth. Her name, and what Milo had planned for her, came back suddenly.

"Where is she?" Malthael demanded.

Nathan and Duke whined as their tails drooped. They looked up at him with misery in their eyes. He fell back onto the couch and put his head in his hands. He needed to remember everything that had happened, but his back throbbed as he tried to focus. He closed his eyes and concentrated, remembering what had happened after Milo.

He recalled falling on the ground and Milo leaving. He heard Elisabeth's voice and then another female voice. His eyes shot open as he remembered Nanette. She had been there and had seen the knife. She had gone to get Elisabeth, but it didn't seem that she'd returned. He reached back and touched the wound. His fingers were smeared with blood, but he'd heal. Everything after that was darkness. He looked at the dogs as they sat before him with their ears pulled back.

"What happened?" Malthael asked, completely lost.

The demon dogs glanced at each other before Nathan whined. Duke looked annoyed and shouldered into Nathan. They glared at each other for a moment before Nathan seemed to sigh. Malthael glanced between them, his gaze narrowing as he waited for something to happen. Duke barked at Nathan and they glared at each other a moment.

"Just tell me!" Malthael bellowed, standing up over them, ignoring the throbbing pain in his back.

The light dimmed in the room from his growing anger as the shadows of his rage spread. The demon dogs whined again, and Nathan's tail shot against the rug and cut two letters into it. Malthael's eyes widened when he realized it spelled "Ki." When he looked up, Nathan looked embarrassed and Duke looked triumphant. Demon dogs didn't like to do things that were considered mortal. Learning to read and write were considered planet-dwellers' proclivities—likely Elsa's doing. His girl was always trying to get them to do things they didn't like to do.

"Take me to him," Malthael demanded, standing again.

They glanced at each other and were clearly hesitating. Malthael was like a half-demon; he couldn't transverse the spirit lines without help and could only use the gate. Furthermore, he was injured. Worse, he had enemies that were just waiting for him to make a mistake or travel the lines. Yet he knew in his bones there was more at stake than his daughter's life if the Black King was allowed entry into their world.

In the end, they could not deny his command. The moment his hands settled on their backs, he felt the spirit line wash over him. It had been so long since he had last traveled along the passages that he felt himself gasp internally. When traveling among the spirits, none of the normal senses worked beyond the feeling that he was floating.

Demons didn't have souls. They were made, not born. When he'd torn his horns, he had forsaken his immortality, but he had gained a soul, or at least a partial one. It was why he needed help moving through the spirit lines. He could not completely undo the fact that he had been a demon, but he now had part of a soul. Elisabeth was half mortal and had a soul, but her father was a Soul Collector, and his demonic blood put her in tune with the spirit realm. They were different but the same, trapped between two worlds.

When he opened his eyes, he was standing in a forest. It was early morning and the colors of the world streaked across the sky. For a moment he wasn't sure where he was, but at his feet a very naked Ki slept against a tree. Malthael blinked and then glanced at Duke and Nathan. They stared ahead unabashed; apparently they felt no shame in his nakedness.

251

"Well, that's disturbing," Malthael whispered as he remembered the pile of clothes he had found in his house.

At his voice, Ki was roused. His head came up slowly and he opened his eyes as though coming out of a deep sleep. It took a moment for him to lift his head and look up at Malthael. When he did, he smiled before his head slumped back down.

"Time to get up," Malthael said and tapped Ki's foot softly with his boot.

"Resting," Ki slurred as though he were drunk.

Malthael crouched down and asked, "Where is Elisabeth?"

"Croatoan," he whispered and tried to lift his head.

Malthael suddenly understood the seriousness of the situation. It was like a punch in the gut. Croatoan had been cut off from the other five planets. Its gate had been destroyed, leaving only five and a useless sixth dial. Malthael used to turn to it to remind himself of why he had been made and what for. He was to be a servant of the darkness, serving Balor and the Divine Court, but he had chosen the light. More like chosen the grey, to be accurate, but it was better than black. That was where Elisabeth was—facing true evil.

Malthael had faced the Black King and seen him for what he was. If Elisabeth had even one hair on her head out of place, he'd rip Aryan the Black limb from limb. Malthael was about to ask more when Duke suddenly shifted and looked to the west. Standing, he heard voices as men approached. Duke and Nathan moved together to form a small line, but Malthael didn't want to fight. The longer he spent fighting people, the longer he wasn't helping his Elsa. She needed him!

"We need to go," Malthael told Ki.

Ki's head swiveled around and he looked to his right. "Clothes." He tried to point with his chin.

"By the stars!" Malthael declared before walking over to root around in a bush. "Why didn't you say so earlier?"

He pulled out a pack of clothes and a blanket. He threw the blanket on Ki before helping him get to his feet. His feet mostly just flopped, and Malthael had to carry the boy over to the dogs. With one hand holding his arm around his neck and the other on the boy's waist, he stood in between the dogs. Still holding his arm, he reached out and touched Nathan's back.

"Stay here," Malthael whispered, and they vanished into spirit form. Duke pressed up against his leg to join them.

A moment later, men in black approached. Malthael's eyes widened as he recognized the man in front. He was younger than the rest, but he was older than Malthael remembered him being. His master, Balor, had been looking for the Black Council, but they had not been found. Their souls had been gone, or hidden, and even now Malthael could not sense them. With a little tug on Nathan's back, they sunk into the spirit line, but Malthael was shaken to his core. Emera had been right; the Shadow Clan had survived all these years and was behind what was happening. The Black Council, elders of the Shadow Clan, lived.

Chapter 62: Hystera

———————————————— φ ————————————————

*W*hen they stepped through the gate and out into the clearing, Nanette didn't know what to expect. She gagged when she saw the crumpled bodies. Some of the hooded men had twisted bodies covered in gore. It was unnatural that they could still be alive but she could see their eyes moving and she had to turn away. She stared at the back of Elisabeth's head. She wore a fine gown and a matching black circlet embellished with pale grey pearls. Apparently the Black King could create things in Croatoan that could continue to exist on the other planets. That kind of power terrified her.

She had half expected the Black King to return to his earlier female form, but instead he remained the same. His sharp features and dark presence intensified in the soft glow of an evening sun. In Croatoan he had belonged, but here among the green, his dark contrast was severe. Even Elisabeth's blond hair couldn't lighten all the black he wore.

"What happened here?" Elisabeth asked, glancing around.

"Two Netherhounds helped our savior escape," the one named Ra answered dutifully, but he seemed wary of Elisabeth. He glanced to the Black King and added with a bow. "We punished him. Some of our members should be returning with him for your pleasure, my King."

"How many lives does he have?" the Black King asked and Nanette suddenly wondered if he had a name.

It was hard for her to imagine that he had ever been anything but what he was. Yet he had to have been born and have lived a lifetime ago. He had been a child once, and had had a mother who'd bore him into this world. The idea struck her as odd as she inspected his features. He had been someone before he had become what he was, before he had become the Black King.

"Hundreds," Ra answered. His voice betrayed no emotion. Nanette wasn't sure if he was an expert at hiding his emotions or if he simply didn't have any.

"Hmm," the Black King considered, glancing at Elisabeth. "You shall have the first death."

"He shall die slowly," Elisabeth said, and Nanette's blood ran cold at the venom in her voice. "And he will not enjoy it."

"Elisabeth," Nanette whispered before she could stop herself.

"I am not Elisabeth," she snapped, turning back. She took Nanette's chin in her fingers roughly and forced her head up. Her eyes were dull and filled with a darkness Nanette didn't recognize. "Call me by my name."

Nanette felt tears threatening as she whispered, "Elisabeth."

The back of Elisabeth's hand struck the side of Nanette's face before she could react. Nanette stumbled and fell to the dusty ground. She put a hand to her cheek and looked up at Elisabeth in shock. Rage filled Elisabeth's eyes.

"Say. My. Name!" Elisabeth enunciated each word. She could have commanded it, but still she held back.

"You are Elisabeth," Nanette told her defiantly as she looked up at her. She lifted her hand to strike again as Nanette added, "There isn't any Elsariel. All of you is Elisabeth. You have to accept that."

Elisabeth hesitated a moment as though surprised. Nanette saw something flash in her eyes—and Nanette swore she saw Elisabeth's softness. Then it vanished. She smiled wickedly and said as sweet as poison, "You're wrong. I'm Elsariel. There is no Elisabeth anymore. I don't need you anymore. Go back to Ashlad and wait for me. I'll call you when I want you again."

Nanette stood and walked back toward the gate before she knew what to do. When she went through the gate, she half expected to end up back in Croatoan, but an order was an order. She stood blinking at the green walls of the under sanctuary.

Perhaps Elisabeth wasn't lost! Nanette was elated at that thought.

When she looked back, she was surprised to see solid stone. As eerie as that was, Nanette hurried up the stairs. It took a few tries to get the slab to swing open, and when she rushed into the room she stopped cold. Nanette nearly fell back when she saw Malthael holding up a cane. She raised her arms to block him. Her eyes immediately darted to a very naked Ki as he drooped against the center table. The blanket he had on did little to cover anything.

"Oh!" Nanette gasped before averting her eyes. Compared to Jason, Ki was all toned muscle and an impressive set of man parts. She felt the blood rush to her cheeks as she purposely looked everywhere but at him. She'd have to remember to tell Elisabeth later.

"You!" Malthael called, lowering the cane. Then he demanded, "How did you get here?"

"Elisabeth ordered me back here." Nanette couldn't keep the astonishment from her voice. "And somehow that worked."

"You saw her?" Malthael demanded, his expression desperate.

"I just left her," Nanette said, glancing over her shoulder.

The demon took a step forward, but Ki called in a hoarse voice, "Malthael."

He turned back with a desperate look on his face as he yelled, "We know where she is! She is back in Hystera with the Black King. I will not leave her to her fate and the whim of Aryan the Black."

Aryan? she thought. That seemed like such a nice name, but there was nothing nice about him. His soul was as black as tar, and he seemed as cruel winter—unforgiving and harsh. He was toxic, and his toxicity was infecting Elisabeth.

"If we rush in, we will be no good." Much to Nanette's relief, Ki managed to pull the blanket further around him.

"He is right!" Nanette called instantly, remembering her reaction. "Elisabeth needs you alive. You are the only one who can bring her back. Elisabeth surfaced when she heard you were in trouble."

Malthael hesitated. He clearly wanted to rush into things, but his common sense was kicking in. Nanette turned back and pushed the slab closed. She had to put nearly all of her weight behind it. When she turned back, Malthael seemed resolved to their reason.

"Elisabeth isn't our only concern," Malthael admitted.

"The Black King," Ki agreed. "Now that he is whole, nothing will stop him."

"If you are part of the Shadow Clan, you can," Malthael told him as Ki sunk into a chair.

"How?" Ki demanded, leaning forward, and Nanette made herself look at only his face.

"I don't know, but only the Shadow Clan can bring him back and send him away," Malthael said. Suddenly, Nanette remembered something Elisabeth had said.

"He isn't whole," Nanette whispered. "He isn't whole!"

"What?" Malthael demanded. "Ki just told me before you got here that the last half-breed was taken and that the Black King took Elisabeth's shard."

"A sliver of it remains within her," Nanette declared.

"You're sure?" Ki asked, looking hopeful.

"Positive," she replied and felt very confident about her answer.

Chapter 63: Hystera

———————— φ ————————

*E*lisabeth curled up tightly in the endless field of light and snow. She had frozen herself in her mind, unwilling to leave her prison. She had taken a life, pulled a soul from a body before its time, and damned herself. Milo had betrayed her, and Malthael had lied about her father's existence. She was somewhat aware of what was happening, but it was like a far-off, dull ache. She ignored it all as she tried to sleep in her world of snow and ice.

The snow crunched, and she opened her eyes. A panther stared at her as she lay on her side; his breath came out in crystalized fog. She recognized him immediately. He was Jinq's panther. Pushing herself up, Elisabeth stared deep into his dark eyes.

"What do you want?" she demanded, unhappy about having her sleep interrupted.

He said nothing but continued to stare at her. She quickly grew impatient under his gaze and lay back down. She closed her eyes and pulled her legs further to her chest, trying to cover her feet with the edge of her pale blue and white dress. The world needed to leave her alone; she no longer wished to be a part of it now that Elsariel had sent Nanette back to safety.

The snow crunched again, and when she opened her eyes the panther's face was mere inches from hers. Unmoved by his sudden closeness, she glared and whispered, "Go away."

Before she could react, an owl screeched and landed on her hip. She knew he was Kerrigan's owl and refused to look at him. The panther lifted his head as the owl turned toward Elisabeth. The bird made his way up her side, his talons digging in just enough to remind her that he was there. When he reached her shoulder, he bobbed his head to see her better.

Glaring at him as well, she whispered, "Why won't you leave me alone?"

The bird cocked his head to the side at an impossible angle. It clicked at her before jumping off and flying over her shoulder. The panther turned and followed its feathered friend. With a heavy sigh, Elisabeth tried to close her eyes again. Then she heard Malthael's voice.

She pushed herself up and looked around the endless field of white. At the base of a mountain, the panther and owl waited. Without hesitation, she stood and ran after them. Her bare feet hardly felt the cold as she ran. Mountains lined the horizon as she followed them through a snowy pass. Her arms and legs moved in tandem as she ran toward Malthael's voice.

"Elsa," she heard more clearly as she followed the animals out of the mountains.

She paused at the edge of the snow. The fields of white turned to fields of green. If she reentered them, she would have to face herself. Glancing back, Elisabeth longed to return to the ice, snow, and solitude. If she was alone, no one could ever hurt her again. She could be safe within her own mind.

"Elsa!" Malthael's voice was more urgent this time.

Turning forward, she realized she had hidden long enough. This time her feet hit the ankle-tall grass without hesitation as she ran into the fields. The panther and owl were out ahead, leading her. Her dress flowed out behind her in ribbons of blue and white. They ran for what seemed like hours until she came to a field of white. Flowers of snow white bobbed in a friendly summer breeze.

In the center, a woman played a strange instrument and sat completely still. She wore deep blue robes that were similar to Elisabeth's. Her hair was long and as pale as black as night. When Elisabeth stepped into the ring of purple flowers, the woman plucked at a string and hummed softly. Elisabeth came around her and found that she was looking at Nanette.

"Elisabeth," Nanette said with a smile, "you need to accept who you are."

"Where is Malthael?" Elisabeth asked.

"Do you know why he calls you Elsa?" Nanette asked, plucking at the instrument.

"Because he loves me no matter what I am," Elisabeth declared without hesitation. She knew exactly what Malthael felt, as he had told her many times throughout her life.

"Why can't you do the same?" Nanette asked as her fingers struck a soft melody. "Why can't you accept every part of you?"

"Elsariel is not a part of me!" Elisabeth yelled before turning around and running from the circle.

"You can't run away from the truth," Nanette called, still plucking at the instrument.

Elisabeth didn't return to the mountains. Instead she ran further away from them, hoping that she might find her papa. She wanted to ask him why he'd lied and then forgive him. None of it mattered as long as he was alive. She had seen too much death.

"Elsa! Where are you, my girl?" Malthael called, and he sounded blissfully close.

The owl screeched as it flew overhead, gliding almost silently on the air. Glancing back at the panther as he sat inside the ring of flowers with Nanette, his tail flicking, the owl watched her. Unwilling to return and listen to what Nanette was saying, she ran from the soft green grass into an area filled with trees raining red leaves. It reminded her of the Netherworld, specifically the trees in Morhaven, but it was no place she had ever seen.

She stopped running when she saw Ki sitting on a rock by a lake. She hesitantly walked up to him, happy to see him despite herself. He was meditating with his legs crossed and sat completely still. When she reached the rock, she leaned forward toward him, her right hand slowly reaching toward him.

The moment her left hand touched the rock, he turned back to her and said, "I've always accepted you as you are."

"I know," Elisabeth replied, pulling her fingers back. "As I've accepted you."

"You need to accept yourself," Ki told her, waving toward the water. "Kerrigan and Jinq were saved because of you. You must accept what has happened."

"It's too hard," she replied, her voice pitched low as she looked down. "So much has happened, and I don't want to deal with anything else."

"You have to," Ki said, touching her under her chin to make her raise her head.

Elisabeth took a step back and Ki stopped moving. Cav, the owl, landed on his shoulder, and Ki turned around to return to meditating. Elisabeth spared him one final glance before she turned and continued through the forest. Without owls or panthers to guide her, she followed her instinct.

"Elsa," Malthael called, his voice sounding airy, "come here."

Elisabeth stopped when she saw the door in the middle of the woods. It was carved with the image of poppies around a sliver of a moon. She touched the door, her fingers running over the image as she reached for the knob with her other hand. The door handle turned, and she pushed it open as white light washed over her.

She sat on the floor in Malthael's study as he smoked a small pipe. The room was filled with the smell as the fire burned. She glanced up and saw that it was winter outside, with frost obscuring the windows. He was reading a book but paused when Elisabeth continued to stare at him.

"There you are, my girl," he said softly, taking the pipe from his mouth. "Where has my little Elsa been?"

"Lost," Elisabeth managed, feeling like a little girl again.

"Have you found yourself?" Malthael asked with an all-knowing smile.

"Why did you lie?" she asked, ignoring his question, "All my life you've never lied even when you should have, but you did now. Why?"

"You know why," Malthael said before puffing on the pipe. Rings circled up from the opening.

"You wanted to protect me," Elisabeth replied without hesitation. Her protection had driven him to do mad things, including becoming Malthael, the Mad Dog. He had foregone an eternal life to guarantee her continued existence. He had become her surrogate family after her mother had died.

"He accepted us, but you don't."

Elisabeth stood and turned to face herself. Unlike Elisabeth, who kept her hair up, Elsariel left her blond hair loose, and her face was set in a mischievous grin. It was eerie staring at herself; it made her hair stand on end.

"I almost killed a boy the last time you made an appearance," Elisabeth said.

"He deserved it," Elsariel replied. "You were just afraid."

Elisabeth swallowed the sudden excess of saliva in her mouth. She wanted to run back to the frozen wasteland and hide. Elisabeth's breathing increased, and it felt like her chest was being crushed. She fought for air.

"Coward," Elisariel mocked.

Pushing down the tears, Elisabeth felt a sudden fire in her belly. "You have no right to call me that. If I'd let you have your way—your impulsive, wild way—we'd be dead. Ki's blade would have worked."

Elsariel put her hands on her hips. "You don't know that."

"I do. All of my counterparts on the other planets are dead because they let their other halves out. I wanted nothing to do with you." Elisabeth pointed her finger accusingly.

"You wanted nothing to do with our father," Elsariel corrected her. "His hatred made you push me away."

"You wanted to push the rules, break them even. Malthael made those rules for a reason." She was yelling now and couldn't seem to get control. The words were pouring out of her unchecked.

Elsariel stepped right up to her. "That is what I am. In pushing me away, you buried your gifts. They are bare illusions of what you could do. The Black King is right. We could rule this place. Our father may have taken our mother, but he left us with his power." Elsariel tapped a finger against Elisabeth's chest. "Combined with that shard and the sudden fluctuation in the balance because we are the last of our kind, we are as powerful as if we were a full Soul Collector. Only better because we can pull life force from the living."

"That is all you care about." Elisabeth pushed her back to break their connection. "Power!"

"How else are we to protect them?" Elsariel shouted back.

That made Elisabeth pause. She blinked in surprise. "Protect who?"

"You may have buried me, but I've always been there." Elsariel shook her head. "Malthael is our father, adopted or otherwise. He is everything to us. He accepted me even when you wouldn't."

Elisabeth looked back at the frozen Malthael. Tears welled in her eyes. She wanted nothing to do with what her father was, but Elsariel was right. Malthael *was* their father. Her papa. Elisabeth felt a hand on top of hers, and she looked over at a mirror of herself as a child. The child version of herself looked hopeful as she smiled. Elisabeth realized this was the part of her she had rejected as a child. This was what Elsariel had started out from and now only wanted to become whole.

"I'm the reason he calls you Elsa," the girl whispered, her eyes full of hope and longing.

"I'm sorry," Elisabeth said, drawing the girl into her arms. "I should never have abandoned you."

Her little arms wrapped around Elisabeth as she whispered, "I know, I understand."

"Can you ever forgive me?" Elisabeth asked as tears welled in her eyes and she closed them.

"I already have," the younger version of herself replied.

She took in a breath and opened her eyes. She was standing in a field in Hystera. In front of her the Black King was talking to Ra. She had all of Elsariel's memories because now they were her memories. Better

262

yet, she felt twice as in control and twice as powerful as before. She couldn't help but to feel her lips curl up in anticipation as she glanced down at the palm of her hand. It was high time she set everything right.

Chapter 64: Hystera

— ϕ —

K **i and Malthael crept** through the woods with Nanette close behind. She had stubbornly refused to be left behind with Elisabeth in danger. If it weren't so perilous, Ki might have admired her determination. Yet when they reached the woods it didn't seem like a lot was happening beyond the Black King and Elisabeth talking. The two demon dogs were in their spirit form out ahead ready to warn them if any danger was ahead.

"Should we distract him?" Nanette whispered.

Ki was about to respond when Malthael stopped dead. Ki nearly ran into him and was about to say something when he saw the seriousness of his expression. His hand was up, and he was looking out into the field. He saw Elisabeth crossing the field with a look he had never seen on her.

"She's whole," Malthael whispered softly. "I can feel her power."

The Black King looked up as the wind started to swirl. It caught speed as he lifted his hands and Elisabeth put a hand up to stop his attack. Suddenly, Ki felt something tickle his stomach. He opened his mouth as part of his life force was drawn out of him. The same happened to Malthael and Nanette, lines of blue leaving them. Every villager and Black Council had their life force drawn out of them as well, and it was all placed into Elisabeth.

"You betray me so easily, Elsariel," the Black King called to her, his face shadowed with contempt.

"My name is Elisabeth," she called back as the wind swirled tighter just behind her, "and it is high time you returned to Croatoan."

"You can't defeat me," he laughed. "I am the Black King."

"I can't defeat you alone," Elisabeth called as the wind stopped and the swirl of air settled. "But I expect *we* can."

Arawn stepped out of the circle as it settled. His black elk-like antlers and the bow across his chest made him imposing sight as he stood tall behind Elisabeth. Her heavy black dress whipped around as she faced the Black King. Ki swallowed hard despite himself. Arawn was the most feared member of King Nauberon's court. No one dare challenge the Lord of the Hunt.

264

"Aryan the Black," Arawn said, pulling a double-headed axe from his waist. It was nearly as tall as Elisabeth. "You're still as ugly as I remember."

"Arawn," the Black King retorted as he bared his teeth. "The Flower King's pet." He sneered.

"King Nauberon suspected you might be involved, and it is in his honor that I now fight you," Arawn responded, pointing the end of the axe at Aryan the Black. "I relish our coming battle."

"I shall relish mounting your head above my fire," Aryan the Black replied before he lifted his hand and brought it down.

Elisabeth lifted her arms and crossed them in front of her face. She was shoved back slightly as a red shining force shaped like a comet hit her glowing barrier. It rippled with the same blue energy she had drawn out of them. Arawn didn't hesitate to jump over her barrier and move toward the Black King. With a single movement, the Black King blocked his downward strike and moved to the side.

"What are they fighting with?" Nanette whispered behind him.

"Their life force, which is why Elisabeth needed as much as she could get," Malthael whispered. "We need to figure out a way to get the gate open. It is the only place that can trap the Black King."

The Black King and Arawn continued to dance while Elisabeth attacked from another direction when she could. Yet her attacks did little to slow him down. He side-stepped each attack with ease and deflected the ones he couldn't move out of the way of. Arawn was giving him more trouble, his blades moving with a power that was almost difficult to watch.

Arawn put his axe back on his hip before drawing his bow in one fluid motion. It was arrowless until he drew the bowstring back. Then an arrow of light appeared. It whistled through the air before striking Aryan's shield. It threw him back, and he landed hard in the dirt. When the Black King stood, his clothes were covered in dirt, which matched the scowl on his face.

"The Black Council can open it," Ki whispered, glancing toward Ra and the other men.

"They would rather die," Malthael whispered back, glancing over his shoulder, "and we know they cannot die as long as their souls reside within you."

Ki touched his chest and was suddenly sick at the thought of their dark souls within him. They were liars who only wanted to further their agenda. Ki glanced toward Ha and he steeled himself against the possibilities. He couldn't pick and choose; he had to reject them all.

Arawn crashed against the tree line as Elisabeth moved in between the hunter and the Black King. She unleashed a wave of blue light that struck Aryan's barrier. It thinned at her attack, giving Arawn the time he needed to recover. Running towards the Black King, the hunter leapt over Elisabeth as he pulled his axe free. He brought it down on Aryan. It drove the barrier into the ground, creating a crater in the dirt. Suddenly, Aryan had a long blade made of light in his hand.

"I am of their blood," Ki admitted, though it burned deep in his belly. "I can open the gate."

"I'll distract the Black Council," Malthael said and his arm went out. A blade that burned red as though it had been heated appeared in his grip. Nanette gasped but said little else as Malthael stood. Ki stood as well, but Nanette took hold of his pant leg to stop him.

"What will I do?" Nanette asked, clearly unhappy to be left behind.

Ki glanced down at her and saw her determination to help. The Netherhounds moved to Malthael's side, and they all vanished. Elisabeth was brought to her knees by an attack as the Lord of the Hunt and the Black King fought axe against energy blade. Once she was on her feet, Elisabeth attacked again before blocking a return assault. Arawn shifted and brought the blade down, leaving a menacing hole in the ground where the Black King had been.

"When we open the gate," Ki told her as he focused on Elisabeth, "call to Elisabeth."

"What? Why?" Nanette asked, and he turned back to her.

"Call to her so she isn't close to the gate," Ki said, realizing what he was going to have to do. "If you call for help, she'll come to you."

"Ki, wait," Nanette called as she tugged on his pant leg. "Why do I have a bad feeling?"

"Just call to her," Ki said and pulled free from her grip to join the fray.

Malthael appeared by Ra and drove the sword deep into his belly. Ki knew they could not be killed, but they needed time to heal. The Black King hardly took notice of them as Ki moved around the edge of the clearing. The villagers huddled together, their eyes barely recognizing anything. They seemed to be alive but in sort of a dream state, and they did nothing to hinder his movements.

Ki knelt down and waited as Malthael and the two demon dogs wreaked havoc. The Black Council banded together quickly and attacked where they could. Ki ran out into the clearing as Malthael drew the Black Council away from the gate. One of the fallen council members reached for Ki as he sprinted and he jumped over the man's body. When he reached the gate, he touched it and started to chant the words he had heard the Black Council use. He had an excellent memory but had missed some of it to the sound of the wind. Whatever it took to save Elisabeth, he was willing to try.

Normally, many people were needed to recite the words, but he was one man with many souls. The souls of his people were in him and every soul of the Black Council. It had to be enough. He didn't let worry or doubt distract him from his task. He looked to the sky as he chanted, and the clouds started to darken and churn. He heard shouting but ignored it as he continued the mantra. The wind began to swirl, and so he continued. Just as the gate was starting to open and Ki could see the red of Croatoan forming, something conked him on the back of the head.

Chapter 65: Hystera

φ

*E*lisabeth nearly cried out when she saw Malthael appear amid the Black Council. She very narrowly blocked the oncoming attack that would have cut her in half. The blue of her shield glowed bright and sure as it hummed with power. Her arms came down as Ki shot across the clearing toward the gate. Her eyes went wide as she realized what was happening—they had a plan.

Turning toward the Black King and Arawn as they continued to exchange blows, she hurried across the clearing to move behind them. She needed to push them toward the gate so that the Black King could be driven back to Croatoan. She put up an arm when the Black King threw a backhanded attack at her. Her blue shield hummed again, reinforced by the life force she had stolen. Their presence explained the added power in her belly.

Focusing a targeted attack, the Black King threw up two shields to defend himself, one for her and one for Arawn. His shield also glowed blue, but it sparked black. She didn't know what that meant, but she knew they were different. They both might be half breeds, but he was something more. Somehow, he must have changed himself. Above her, the sky started to swirl and black clouds gathered. Elisabeth centered another energy attack at Arawn's side as he doubled his efforts. She had been right to save the Lord of the Hunt for that moment. Elsariel had not done everything for herself; some of what she did was for Malthael, Nanette, and even Elisabeth. She could feel her in her thoughts and in every attack.

The Black King finally noticed the swirling charcoal clouds and turned his head toward the gate. When he lifted his arm, Arawn forced his attention and Elisabeth attacked from behind. He formed a full shield but dropped to his knee. For a moment, Elisabeth thought he had been weakened, and then the barrier expanded and threw Arawn back. The hunter landed on his feet, but he had been thrown back a good distance. Elisabeth raised her shield but was forced back slightly across the ground by another of the Black King's assaults. The distance of her slide was evident by the trail her heavy dress left across the parched ground. Her shield pressed thin, but it held.

When she looked up, the Black King was raising his arm and Elisabeth felt herself yelling, "Ki!"

The wind had picked up and her dress was pulled to the side as she took a step forward with her arm out. The force of the Black King's attack glanced off Ki. He fell forward and bounced off the stone before it shimmered and the gate opened.

"No!" Elisabeth yelled, and the ground cracked around her.

Her vision became hazy as she took a step forward. Elisabeth lifted her arms over her head and brought them down. The Black King blocked her attack. Arawn stood ready to go on the offense, but at her second attack he hesitated. Her entire body glowed — she could feel it prickle her skin — as she faced The Black King.

She didn't lift her arms but instead let her will work. It crashed toward him like a wave, hurtling with increasing force. He raised his shield, but it crashed all around him and threw him back. He knelt to keep himself from falling and raised his head.

"That is your true power," the Black King called. "Finally."

Aryan lifted his arms, but she jerked her head. The energy slammed into him, tossing him to the right. He skidded across the ground toward the gate. He quickly got to his feet but he wavered. Elisabeth could see the doubt forming on his face. Arawn continued to hold, waiting.

He should be afraid, Elisabeth thought.

"I will tear you limb from limb," Elisabeth seethed and knew not the depths of her own rage.

"You are my equal!" he called, lifting his arm, and she deflected his attack with ease.

"I am your superior," she called to him as she lifted her hand.

"Elisabeth!" Nanette called out, and she hesitated.

Before she could react, arms wrapped around the Black King and Elisabeth saw Ki's face. He smiled sadly at her for a split second, and she realized what he was going to do. She reached out for him, trying to call his name as she ran forward. Before she could stop him, Ki pulled the Black King through the gate. They vanished into the void as Arawn lifted his axe. It cut through the stone as Elisabeth tried to stop him. His axe skittered across the ground—the damage was done. She fell in front of the halved stone and touched it, trying to make something reappear even though she knew it wouldn't.

"No, no, no," Elisabeth whispered over and over again as tears filled her eyes. Malthael touched her shoulder, but she pushed it away. "You shouldn't have let him!" she cried.

"He saved us all," Malthael said to her as Elisabeth started to cry. Tears streamed down her face as her mind struggled to understand.

"He shouldn't have," Elisabeth whispered, her head bowed low as she leaned against the cold stone. "He should have stayed with me."

"Elisabeth," Nanette's voice broke her grief.

"You!" Elisabeth said pointing at her and standing, "Why did you call my name?"

"He told me to," Nanette said and sniffled. Her eyes clogged with tears begged for forgiveness as she repeated, "He told me to."

Malthael touched Elisabeth's shoulder, and she looked up at Arawn. The hunter put the axe away, and she saw that his eyes betrayed no regret. Elisabeth considered lashing out at him but saw no benefit to it beyond easing the pain in her heart. Before she could do anything, laughter broke through the clearing.

Ra lay on the ground as laughter shook his broken body. Disgust filled Elisabeth's every sense as she walked over to him. Nanette and Malthael followed closely with Duke and Nathan close behind. Arawn turned slightly but showed little interest.

"What is so funny?" Elisabeth demanded as she looked down at his crumpled body.

"He did the wrong chant," Ra said, blood coming out of his mouth and dripping down the side of his cheek.

"What does that mean?" Elisabeth asked as something like dread filled her gut.

"They aren't in Croatoan." Ra laughed as he coughed blood. "He muddled the incantation and sent them somewhere else."

In one fluid motion, Malthael severed Ra's head form his body. He kicked the head so it rolled away, his face still fixed in a wicked smile. He spit on the body and cursed, "Recover from that."

"So they're still on one of the planets?" Elisabeth whispered, relief and hope flooding her senses.

"No," Arawn interjected. "I do not sense Ki and his strange monstrous state on any of the planets."

Elisabeth's chest hurt and she pushed her against her heart to ease the ache. "Then where are they?" Elisabeth demanded angrily, tired of getting her hopes up.

"One of the places we cannot go," Arawn replied.

Her knees gave out, and she sunk down. Nanette gave a cry as she rushed forward and wrapped her arms around Elisabeth. She put a hand on her friend's arm as Elisabeth stared into nothing. She hardly noticed when

Arawn vanished and Malthael came to stand beside her. She closed her eyes and leaned back into her friend as hopelessness took hold. She rode the wave of grief as it consumed her.

Chapter 66: Ashlad

———————————— φ ————————————

*T*here was something about the way that Elisabeth moved that told Malthael she had plans. She walked past him again and into the kitchen, her head buried in a book. She was better, though, than she had been when they'd first returned. She had moved listlessly around the house and seemed lost in her thoughts. Curious, Malthael followed her into the kitchen.

Nanette was chatting with Tiss, who looked startled when Elisabeth strode in. Malthael followed quietly as Elisabeth looked up from her book. She set a list down on the countertop and set the book down with her thumb, holding her spot.

"I need everything on this list," Elisabeth said, pushing it across the counter toward Tiss. "As soon as possible."

Then she buried her head back in her book, picked up a piece of toast, and put it into her mouth before she left. Malthael held the door open, and she muttered a thank you without looking up. Malthael glanced back at Nanette, who looked stunned before she got up and hurried out after Elisabeth.

"What is she doing?" Malthael asked.

Nanette shrugged. "Until yesterday, she barely responded to anything I said."

"What happened yesterday?" Malthael asked.

"She woke up before me, and I had to search all over the house for her," Nanette replied as they followed Elisabeth at her breakneck speed.

"Where did you find her?" Malthael asked as they followed her, hurrying down hall after hall.

"The library," Nanette said as Elisabeth turned and walked through the library's great double doors. "She's practically living in there."

"She was reading a very old book." Malthael could tell from the pages.

"Elisabeth?" Nanette called as she crept into the room.

"Yes?" Elisabeth asked as she leaned back from the edge of one of the bookshelves. Just as quickly as she appeared, she disappeared.

"What are you doing?" Nanette asked, glancing at Malthael before rushing toward where Elisabeth had been.

"Researching," Elisabeth muttered as she read over a book. "I came in here to find a way to take Kerrigan's soul out of Jinq without killing them both, but I stumbled across something else."

"What?" Malthael asked, stepping up to peer at the piles of books.

"Books on the Netherworld"—Elisabeth pointed at a rough map—"that discuss gates to places that aren't one of the five planets." She paused. "Six planets."

"What does that have to do with Kerrigan and Jinq?" Malthael asked, turning the page of one of the books absentmindedly.

"It doesn't," Elisabeth replied, putting her hands on her hips and facing them. "It has to do with Ki."

"Elsa," Malthael began, but she put up a hand to stop him.

"He isn't gone. He is just lost," Elisabeth told him, and he saw all the emotions on her face. "And I am going to find him."

Notes from the Author

Do not worry! Even though this book is over with, the adventures with Elisabeth are not. Elisabeth and all the characters of *The Sixth Gate* will return in 2019 in *The Nowhere Gate*. If you enjoyed this book, please leave a review with your favorite retailer.

To give you some background, I wrote this book for Harmony, a friend who is more like a sister. I hope you recognized that this book was about Elisabeth accepting who she was. Harmony has always accepted me for who I am—flaws and all—and to repay her for a lifetime of friendship I've dedicated this book and entire series to her. Thank you, Harmony.

In the meantime, happy reading,

K.T. Munson

Other Titles by K.T. Munson
1001 Islands

The sliver of moonlight cast eerie shadows across the deck of The Dark Revenge. The Silence at the helm stood embracing the obscurity. His foreboding presence matched the anticipation aboard the ship, and no one spoke for fear they would break the stillness that encompassed them.
Tonight, everything changed.
The Dark Revenge gained on the Regatta. The raiders said nothing but he could hear the shuffle of taut female clothing and the tension in the air. It hadn't sensed their existence, and drifted like heedless prey. Princess Roxana slept, unsuspecting of what was hunting her in the inky blackness of the night.

Twitter: http://twitter.com/ktmunson
Facebook: https://www.facebook.com/K.T.Munson
Subscribe to my blog: http://creatingworldswithwords.wordpress.com